Scarlet Sunrise

Leigh Bristol

WARNER BOOKS

A Warner Communications Company

WARNER BOOKS EDITION

Copyright © 1987 by Donna Ball, Inc. and Shannon Harper
All rights reserved.

Cover art by Elaine Duillo

Warner Books, Inc.
666 Fifth Avenue
New York, N.Y. 10103

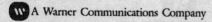 A Warner Communications Company

Printed in the United States of America

First Printing: January, 1987

10 9 8 7 6 5 4 3 2 1

She was trembling all over...

She was naked beneath the eyes of a man, beneath the touch of a man, and it was wrong and she was frightened...but it was Jed. When his warm weight descended to cover her, she could do nothing but raise her arms to welcome him and let his kisses draw her again into that sweet and helpless rush of mindless pleasure.

Never had Jed wanted like this. It was madness, it was weakness. But he knew nothing but the burning need to be with her, to bury himself deep within her and never let her go. "Elizabeth," he whispered thickly, and, feeling her small fingers on his face, in his hair, he tasted her skin and the texture of her neck. And all he could do was whisper again, "Elizabeth..."

He felt her nakedness beneath him, smooth white limbs and gentle feminine flesh. He kissed her and she lifted herself to him, and he knew he should stop...and knew he could not.

*   *   *

Scarlet Sunrise

ALSO BY LEIGH BRISTOL

AMBER SKIES

Forthcoming from
WARNER BOOKS

To all the Elizabeths of the world

CHAPTER
One

May 1839
Near Mobile, Alabama

Elizabeth Coleman was more than a little frightened. She paused at the edge of a dusky clearing, her eyes moving warily over her unfamiliar surroundings. Her horse, its muscles quivering with Elizabeth's communicated anxiety and its own innate restlessness, shifted and tossed its head. Elizabeth's hand tightened on the bridle and the stallion snorted, disliking his female rider's temperamental traits.

The slaves said these woods were haunted. They gossiped about mysterious lights and sounds in the dead of night. Elizabeth did not believe a word of it, of course, but when an overhanging branch snagged her riding bonnet, she gave a small cry.

She had never intended to come this far. She should never have left the plantation grounds without a groom and never, ever should have taken this high-spirited stallion who was unaccustomed to the sidesaddle. But her groom had been ill and the other slaves were busy with the house party, which had been going on for three days. She hadn't wanted to cause anyone any trouble. All she wanted was to be alone with her thoughts. She had never intended to be disobedient or impulsive. It had all started out so innocently. But then, so had most of the misadventures in Elizabeth's short life.

The wooded enclosure was oppressively heavy and still with cool, dark humidity and the dank scent of dead and rotting things. Thick, gnarled tree trunks stood around her like ancient soldiers, their branches draped with Spanish moss, their gnomelike faces glaring in the shadows. Scant light filtered through the close canopy of foliage, turning the cheerful mid-morning into a dusky twilight. Elizabeth strained her ears for some sound, but beyond the restless breathing of her horse and the crackle of twigs and leaves beneath his hooves, there was nothing. Not even a bee droned. It was like being at the edge of the world, and Elizabeth's throat was tight. She wanted to go home, but she didn't know where home was.

She should never have invited that stupid dog, Caesar, to come with her. She didn't even like the animal. But he was William Bledsoe's prize hound, and when she looked down and saw him bounding along beside her, what could she do? Still, all might have come to rights had not the dog picked up the scent of some small animal and dashed between her mount's legs, causing her horse to rear and bolt. By the time Elizabeth had brought the horse under control again, the dog had disappeared, and that was when she first began to realize the improvidence of not planning for the unexpected.

Mr. Bledsoe might forgive the use of his stallion, for he was in most respects a tolerant man, but he would never forgive the loss of his prize hound. And it would be all laid at her door. She would have no choice but to confess how her illicit morning ride, which she had hoped to keep secret, had led to the loss of the dog.

But she did not dread Mr. Bledsoe's wrath half as much as she did the gentle remonstrations of Miss Nancy Lea, who was the mother of Elizabeth's best friend, Margaret. Miss Nancy had been Elizabeth's chaperone and moral guardian since her own mother's death two years before. The thought of that sorrowful, disappointed look in Miss Nancy's eyes as she lectured her once again on the proper deportment of a well-bred young lady was enough to outweigh even Elizabeth's fear of the haunted woods, even her fatigue at wrestling the recalcitrant stallion, even her very good sense, which told her to give her horse its head and let its fondness of the feed bag lead them both back to the safety of the Spring Hill stables.

The house party at Spring Hill marked the eighteen-year-old Elizabeth's emergence from a two-year mourning period after her mother's death; it was her very debut into society. If Miss Nancy found out what she had done, she would be confined to her room for the duration. She would be disgraced in front of all present, treated like a schoolgirl upon her very first opportunity to act the young lady. She simply *couldn't* allow that to happen.

She lifted up in the saddle and called out, "Caesar!" But no answering bark replied. The air itself seemed to swallow up the sound of her voice and give back nothing but heavy silence.

Elizabeth was sticky with perspiration but chilled with uneasiness. Her heart beat heavily in her chest, and she wanted nothing more than to be away from this eerie place and back at the gentle festivity and peaceful civility of the lawns of Spring Hill. But her courage failed her at the thought of returning to Mr. Bledsoe and Miss Nancy without the hound. She had no choice. She must push on.

She swallowed on a dry throat and cast one last uneasy

glance around her. Then, gathering up her courage as she gathered up the reins, she clucked to her horse and nudged him onward, deeper and deeper into the shadows.

Jed Fielding was not a superstitious man, but after years of living alone with nothing but his own good sense to guide him, he had developed a sort of sixth sense. He did not believe in gifts of the supernatural, but twenty-five years of living had taught him that there was danger in ignoring what one could not explain. He had seen a horse's nostrils flare long before his rider smelled the smoke, and rabbits hurry to their burrows an hour before the storm clouds gathered. He knew for a fact that his own life had been saved more than once by that indefinable prickle of awareness, an uneasy hunch of trouble ahead.

He was far from the mountains of Colorado or the wilds of Texas, and there wasn't a bear or an Indian for miles around. But his instincts were still working, and he couldn't shake that uneasy feeling of expectancy. He studied his surroundings, searching for the cause of his wariness. Had this tenseness just come to him that morning? Now that he thought of it, he wondered if it had been with him, in one form or another, since the moment he had stepped back on Alabama soil.

Or maybe it was just sentiment, although Jed would not have been quick to accuse himself of that, either. He had a lot of memories associated with this place, and returning home for the first time in ten years brought them all flooding back. He could hear his mother's voice, soft and low as she said grace over the supper table; he could see his father's face, stern in the candlelight; he could feel the way the wind came through the chinks in the logs in the winter. He had no love for this place, but he had his memories. And they weren't all bad.

Maybe it was best, he thought. Maybe every man owed it to himself, once in his life, to take good stock of where he had come from, just to get his sights fixed firm on where he was going. He had always expected, someday, to come back here. But he had never expected it to be like this.

Jed had been staying in the cabin for the past week while he finalized the sale of the farm, and he hadn't done much to fix it up. He had closed the sale the day before, and the cabin still looked much as it had when he arrived. The walls were sagging and the sod foundation was mostly washed away; the interior was strung with cobwebs and littered with dust and assorted debris that recent storms had blown in through the broken windows. A family of pack rats had made its nest in the corner, but Jed had shared quarters with worse. It just made him sad to think that his pa had worked his whole life, and this was all he had to leave his only son—a rotting log cabin and a few acres of tangled, unrepentant soil that the wilderness had already begun to reclaim.

A small fire burned in the hearth, and a spring breeze stirred the dust on the scarred oak tabletop. Shaking himself out of the reverie, Jed moved across the room to pick up his saddlebags, his moccasined feet making little sound on the littered floor. This was a melancholy place, and he was suddenly anxious to be away.

There wasn't much he wanted to save. His father's tools were rusty and his mother's dishes were cracked. He picked up the family Bible from the mantelpiece and looked at it for a moment, then wiped the dust on his jacket front and placed it in his saddlebag. He bent down to douse the fire.

The soft whinny of his horse alerted him even before he heard the crackle of a twig. In less than an instant his rifle was in his hand. It was loaded and ready, as always. Where he came from, a man who forgot to reload was a man with a short life expectancy.

He faded back against the wall, moving silently toward

the window. Then, in a single fluid movement, he swung the rifle into position and peered out, his finger on the trigger.

When the stallion's ears pricked and then flattened slightly, Elizabeth impatiently urged him on, thinking such jumpy behavior was not unusal for the indomitable beast. Thorns tugged at the skirt of her riding habit, and she ducked only a moment too late to prevent her hat from being knocked askew by a branch. The horse was increasingly restive, and Elizabeth had a faint, wild hope that he might have gotten scent of the dog. She let the horse have his head.

The tangled undergrowth was giving way to high grass, and the dark woods were clearing into something that might almost have been a trail. Elizabeth breathed a cautious sigh of relief. Still no sign of the wretched hound, but at least, if there was a trail, she must not be completely lost. . . .

They broke out of the woods into a stubbly, rock-strewn clearing and in the distance Elizabeth thought she faintly heard the bay of a hound. She drew up sharply, and her horse tossed its head in protest. Eagerly she turned in the saddle, looking around, opening her mouth to call the dog—and then she saw what it was her mount had sensed long ago.

Wood smoke. Just ahead, not thirty yards off, the faint wisp of wood smoke drifted from a broken rock chimney, the shack to which it was attached almost completely obscured by vines and scrubby brush. She had almost ridden upon it without even seeing it, without even realizing that the tangled ground under her feet was actually part of a neglected yard. Her first reaction was one of enormous relief, for she realized the fire meant there was someone to help her . . . and then everything inside her went still.

Haunted, the slaves had said. But not haunted . . . her heart began to beat with new force. She had no idea where she was, but she did know the kind of blackguards who might inhabit a deserted shack in the middle of the woods. Escaped prisoners, highwaymen, runaway slaves, any one of which would like nothing better than to come upon a lone woman in this remote place.

She began to breathe more rapidly, and every nerve in her body quickened with alarm. Quickly, quietly, she must go back the way she had come. Oh, how right Miss Nancy had been. How foolish she was to ride alone....

The sun filtered through the trees and fell warm and heavy on her shoulders. Something moved against a nearby blackberry bush and set a branch to bobbing. Elizabeth's throat grew tighter. She could almost feel eyes upon her.

"Come on, boy," she whispered, and her mouth was so dry, she could hardly form the words. She pulled the reins gently. "Let's go."

The horse turned and then stopped, throwing back his head with an angry, alarmed whinny. Elizabeth jerked the reins, her heart leaping to her throat, and with a furious scream the horse pawed the air. It happened so quickly, all Elizabeth knew was the terror, the urgent struggle to maintain her perilous seat, and the certainty that if she slackened her hold on the reins, she would most certainly be killed.

The horse fought the bit, pawing earth and rearing. The animal had gone mad and was trying to bolt, and if he did, she surely would be dashed against the trees or trampled underfoot. The leather straps bit into her gloves, bruising her hands; she tried not to sob and fought desperately on, all the while wondering what horror her horse had seen that she had not, what even now was lying in wait for her....

She caught a glimpse of movement from the shack ahead, perhaps even the flash of sun on a metal barrel, and she knew, in that instant, that she was going to die. The horse reared again, she cried out, she heard the sound of the shot, and then she knew nothing more.

CHAPTER
Two

Consciousness returned in weak, swimming circles of bilious green and yellow. At first she knew only an awful aching in her head and a desperate suspicion that she was going to be sick. With a tiny sob that sounded like the mew of a kitten, she fought back the nausea, and then her eyes began to focus and abject terror replaced everything else.

Above her was the blur of a man—a huge man with dark, stern features, shaggy blond hair, and fringed buckskins. Heavy hands were pulling at the buttons of her blouse, exposing her flesh to the touch of his rough fingers, and she wanted to scream, but fear had closed its icy fingers around her throat. She did not know the word *rape*, but she had heard whispers of the abominations performed upon hapless females by men of evil intent, and she had heard it said it was preferable to die. For the first time in her life her wits deserted her, and all she could do was lie there, paralyzed, and wait for the worst.

And then his voice came, soft and surprisingly matter-of-fact. "No, I didn't shoot you." He pushed the stiff white material of her bodice away from her throat, baring a portion of her chest and collarbone but little else. "I didn't shoot your horse, either, though I probably should have. He could've killed you."

He moved away, and Elizabeth closed her eyes against the sudden glare of the sun. Her chest was rising and falling with excruciating slowness. She couldn't move; she couldn't scream. Oh, please, why couldn't she scream?

His shadow fell over her again, and in the same moment she felt something cold against the base of her throat. Her eyes flew open, but she saw he was only bathing her with a damp cloth. As he did so, he spoke casually. "It was a snake that spooked your horse—a cottonmouth. I had to shoot it. Most horses will try to kill a snake with their hooves, and I figured yours would get around to it sooner or later. But it looked like that devil of yours had a mind to get you on the ground with the snake and take care of you both at the same time." He removed the cloth and sat back, watching her. "I don't think you're hurt; just had the wind knocked out of you. Just lie still for a minute. You'll be all right."

It began to occur to her, slowly and from a great, fuzzy distance, that perhaps he did not mean her any harm at all. She stared at him, still unable to move, and like a child learning to read, she tried to digest what he had said. But she was too weak, and the world wouldn't stop spinning. When she tried to think, the aching in her head increased. She wanted to cry but was afraid even to do that.

Jed knelt beside her on the grass, holding the spring-dampened cloth in his hand as he stared at her, moved by twin emotions of wonder and pity. In the far-reaching lands of the West, where the only women a man saw for months at a time were the ones he conjured in his head, hungry imagination would likely have invented something exactly like this. But not even grandiose daydreams could have done her justice.

She was a lady, obviously, and what she was doing way out here riding a half-broken stallion Jed could not begin to guess, nor did he particularly care. In other circumstances Jed would have felt tongue-tied and clumsy with such as she, for even in her disheveled state she was a striking young girl and obviously wealthy. But now all he could see was her fragile, supine figure, the rapid rise and fall of her small chest, her huge green eyes, stark with terror in a white face. Her dark, glossy hair was disarranged and her bonnet hung by a ribbon around her neck; her chalky cheeks were smudged with the dust of her fall and her white blouse was grass-stained. Her skirt was tossed up to show several inches of frothy petticoats and, yes—the feminine curve of a white-stockinged calf.

Noticing that, Jed was embarrassed and knew she would be even more so if she discovered it. She was frightened enough as it was, and the last thing he needed was to be accused of accosting a lady. Moving quickly and casually so that she wouldn't notice, he rearranged her skirt to cover her boots . . . but not before registering that glimpse of forbidden femininity with a pleasurable warmth in his chest and a tightening in his throat. There weren't too many things in this world that could set a man's blood to racing quicker than a glimpse of hidden female attributes, and the fact that she was a lady didn't stop him from being male.

She noticed. He saw her eyes go wide with alarm and the skin tauten across her cheekbones. Annoyed with himself for upsetting her, he let his hand fall quickly.

Looking at him with wide eyes, she whispered, hoarsely, "Please—sir . . . what are you going to do with me?"

She was taut, expecting the worst. Jed thought that if he told her he was going to cut off her fingers one by one and feed them to the animals, she wouldn't have been surprised. He had to hand it to her—she might be terrified, but she was doing her best not to let it show.

But he did not like being the one who was scaring her half out of her wits, and irritation with the fact gruffened his voice as he got to his feet. "Right now I'm going to feed you some tea. Lie still."

For a moment Elizabeth was helpless to do anything else. Tea . . . snakes . . . the rifle shot . . . He was trying to help her. He might have, in fact, saved her life. She was in no danger, and that was the first thing she needed to realize and accept.

And then she remembered his hands unbuttoning her garment. His eyes had glimpsed her petticoats and that part of her anatomy no male had seen since old Doc Simons had put a poultice on her sprained ankle at age seven. If she had not been so relieved by the mere fact of being alive, mortification would have finished her on the spot. Miss Nancy would never recover if she found out. A good, obedient young lady would never find herself lying in the grass in the middle of an isolated wood, her head cushioned on her folded riding jacket and her blouse open, a strange man gazing at her. . . .

Moving as quickly as she dared, Elizabeth pushed herself to a sitting position, swallowing hard several times as patches of blue sky narrowed to pinpricks of light. And then, holding her face gingerly between her hands, as though by doing so she could hold the world steady, she closed her eyes and took several deep breaths.

When she opened her eyes again, the man in buckskins

was kneeling beside her, offering her a tin cup of some steaming liquid. When she hesitated, his lips turned down at the corners in rueful encouragement.

"It won't poison you," he assured her. "I went to too much trouble to catch your horse to do away with you now. He's tied up out back," he added, pressing the cup into her hands, "thinking on his manners."

Elizabeth took the cup, and the faintest hint of a smile pulled at her lips. "Th-thank you," she said. She held the cup tightly in both hands to keep it steady, but suddenly she was no longer frightened. No, looking at him now, what she felt was something entirely different altogether.

He was the most incredible man she had ever seen, and only her panic and disorientation had caused her to mistake his strikingly unusual looks for something to fear. He was large but leanly built with wide shoulders, a strong chest, and big hands. His skin was taut and bronze but weathered by sun and wind and etched with tiny little lines around his eyes and mouth. He possessed a magnificent mane of golden hair that swept away from his temples and fell below the collar of his buckskin jacket in back. And his eyes... they were a clear, farseeing hazel, framed by a startling luxury of dark lashes and brows. Looking at him, Elizabeth felt a flutter of nervousness begin in her stomach, simply because he was unlike anything she had ever seen before.

Quickly, afraid to be caught staring, she lowered her eyes to her cup. The mixture inside was green and sprinkled with bits of debris; it did not look at all appetizing. Trying not to sound ungrateful, she asked, "What... is it?"

"An herb. I don't know the English name for it. The Indians use it as a restorative."

She looked up at him, her curiosity struck. "How do you know?"

Jed lowered himself to the ground in front of her, sitting

with one knee propped up and his elbow looped loosely across it. "I lived with them for a while."

Elizabeth's eyes widened as she absorbed his statement, and she couldn't help blurting out, "Indians? Here?"

A soft smile gentled his lips and he responded, "No, ma'am. Out West."

The West. The word itself sounded like a fairy tale, like a promise to her. The West was that distant, romantic land, home of savage redskins and mammoth buffalo, home of Sam Houston and his gallant freedom fighters, of unclaimed wilderness and vast, rolling plains. Of course he had come from the West.

Her thoughts began to race, for within the past week her imagination had been fueled by talk of that distant land and the brave adventurers who mapped and conquered it. That she should meet, in this remote patch of Alabama hillside, one of those very men seemed at the same time to be too incredible to be true, and preordained. So struck was she by the sheer storybook quality of it all that she couldn't think of a single one of the countless things she had always wanted to ask about that magical part of the country.

And then she realized she was staring in a most impolite way, and blushed. He met her gaze with tolerance and, perhaps deep down, even a flicker of amusement in his own eyes. Disconcerted, Elizabeth took a quick sip of the tea. It was hot, but the taste was woodsy and not entirely unpleasant. When she looked up at him again, shyly, she smiled.

"I . . ." She faltered, caught again in the warmth of his clear hazel eyes. She continued with the only thing her rattled brain could think of to say at that moment. "I'm afraid we haven't been properly introduced."

He smiled again, struck perhaps by her obvious effort to remember her manners. "My name is Joshua Fielding, ma'am," he answered. "But most folks call me Jed."

Elizabeth's eyebrows rose with interest. "Why?"

He lifted a single shoulder. "My second name is Edward. Folks just started slurring it together, I reckon, when I was a youngster, and it stuck."

Jed was amazed at how easy he felt with her. Most times he was uncomfortable around females and never knew what to say. Not that the women he ran into were much interested in talk, when it came to that. Maybe it had something to do with the fact that she was sitting on the grass with twigs in her hair and dust on her cheeks, drinking from his battered tin cup. Maybe it was remembering the way she had looked at him when she first came to, stiff with terror but bravely refusing to cry. He only knew he was comfortable, sitting with her like this, and that was a peculiar thing.

She flashed him another one of her quick, shy smiles, and said, "Well . . . thank you, Mr. Fielding, for taking care of me. It's very gallant of you."

Funny thing, that. He had never done it before, but it was a good feeling, to take care of a woman. He frowned a little, thinking about it. "If you don't mind my asking, ma'am . . . what are you doing way out here on a horse like that? You're not in any trouble, are you?"

Her eyes flew to him in quick denial. "Oh, no! That is . . ." Her eyes clouded as she remembered. "Well, yes, I suppose I am in trouble. You see," she explained quickly, "I didn't want to disturb the groom, and I didn't intend to be gone long, but the dog ran away and I had to try to retrieve him because it is Mr. Bledsoe's favorite and . . ." She was forced to admit honestly, "If he discovers the hound is missing, I *will* be in all sorts of trouble, for riding alone and without permission. I never intended to be gone this long or come this far, but . . ." With a little breath and a despairing glance at the surrounding woods, she let the sentence trail off.

Jed felt momentarily disoriented when he realized the seriousness with which she regarded her circumstances. Nothing in his background helped him to understand the world from which she came—a world in which a lost puppy was a monumental crisis. Part of him could only stare in incredulity even as another part caught the genuine distress in her eyes and wanted to comfort her. Of course, he never would have voiced his scorn out loud, but what surprised him was that, looking at her, he couldn't really feel scorn. She was upset, and it didn't matter why. He wanted her to feel better.

He said, following the direction of her worried gaze, "Likely he'll catch your scent or that of your horse and catch up with you. Or he'll hightail it back to his kennel when he gets hungry."

She was immediately swept with a feeling of relief. Of course, he was right. When he said it, it sounded like the most natural thing in the world. Why hadn't she thought of it herself before? She took a sip of her tea, suddenly able to smile a little at her own foolish worry. "You sound like a man who knows dogs, Mr. Fielding. Do you have one of your own?"

"No. But I had a wolf one time." Then, seeing the astonishment in her eyes, he amended, "It might have been part dog, I guess. I caught it trying to steal some meat out of my camp, and that's not a natural thing to do...most wolves will stay well away from the scent of man. I figured it must be desperate, so I let it have the meat, and sure enough, it was hobbling from a hurt leg. When I left the next day, I left some more meat behind for it, and before I knew it, he'd taken right up with me. Started sleeping in camp and running along with the horses when his leg got better. That's what makes me think he must've been part dog. A wolf will get along easier with a man than it will a horse."

Lost in the story, Elizabeth asked, "What became of him?"

Jed hesitated, a wistful expression crossing his features as he remembered. He hadn't thought of that old wolf in years. "He took off one day. Went back to his own kind, I guess. Or got killed." And Jed had been alone again. He hadn't realized until now how much he had missed the dubious companionship of that scraggly old wolf in those first few days. Or maybe it was just the fact that he was telling it to her, and the company of a woman tended to bring out the sentimentality in a man. Or made him remember how bad lonesome could feel.

Elizabeth took another sip of the tea, marveling over the tale. She thought she was beginning to understand something of the power he exuded, the strangeness and difference that separated him from any other man she had ever met.

Some might have said it was his clothing, roughly stitched and fashioned from the hides of animals, that gave him the aura of something wild and uncommon. But she knew now that was only part of it. It was all of him—his clothes, his face, his eyes, his figure, the way he moved and breathed and perhaps even thought—that announced he was a man like no other. She watched him as his fingers absently and gracefully wove a stalk of grass into a braid. She found the sight of those large, blunt fingers engaged in such delicate work fascinating, as amazing and intriguing as every other part of him.

Elizabeth had lived the most fertile period of her girlhood in relative seclusion, isolated from normal social interaction while in mourning for her mother's death. While other young belles were making their debuts, learning to flirt, and gathering marriage proposals like mayflowers, Elizabeth had filled her hours with daydreams and her eager imagination with novels. But this reality was far, far more stunning than anything she ever could have imagined.

Joshua Edward Fielding was a man who had known danger, mysteries, and challenges; he lived a life so far removed from all that was familiar to her that the men of her world could not even imagine it. He had done and seen things of which he would never speak. He came from another world, and whether that world had fashioned him or he had molded it never would be known. He was more than a storybook hero. He was real.

Making no effort to hide her enthralled curiosity, Elizabeth said, "I've always wondered what type of men go West."

Jed laughed a little, without realizing how long it had been since he last had. "Well, I don't rightly know. In Texas it seems we just get the kind of men that don't know any better."

"Texas!" Elizabeth's eyes were bright and eager, her imagination so awakened now that she was no longer speaking to him as much as she was weaving a lustrous tapestry inside her own head. "Tell me truly what it's like. Who are the men who go there? What makes them strike out for such a far and savage land? What courage and daring they must possess, what grand visions for tomorrow!"

With a half-amused twist of his lips he answered, "Well, I don't know how daring they are, or courageous. Some of them are, I reckon. Mostly they're just folks looking for space to settle or something to do. Shopkeepers, drifters, stockmen . . . farmers, lots of them."

"Is that what you are?" She held her disappointment cautiously at bay. Somehow she could not imagine this larger-than-life man as a simple farmer.

"No." Briefly Jed's eyes went over the ragged patch of ground that was all his family had to show for thirty years of backbreaking work. Elizabeth could see the shadow that crossed his face, but she did not understand it. "I'm not a farmer."

"What, then?" she insisted.

He looked back at her, puzzled by how hard that question made him think. Perhaps it was simply that when telling the story to a beautiful woman, a man wanted to have more to show for his life than twenty-five years of memories. Perhaps it was that he had always expected to have more by now. There was the small ranch in Texas, but after three hard years that was still just a dream, and he couldn't bring himself to mention it. How could he explain the backbreaking labor, the brutal conditions, and the wonderful future he hoped it would all lead to . . . ?

When he answered at last, he just put it the simplest way he could. "I'm a fighter, mostly."

Elizabeth nodded, not understanding but intrigued. "I've heard it's a savage land. There must be an awful lot of desperate characters out West."

"I've heard it said," he answered with an easy shrug, "that there's only two types of men in Texas . . . those with the devil nipping at their heels and those with a bit of the devil in them."

Elizabeth's eyes sparkled with mischief. "And which type of man are you, Mr. Fielding?"

He glanced at her, his eyes crinkling as an easy grin transformed his face. "Both," he answered without hesitation, and she laughed.

Her laughter was like the first sip of whiskey after a long drought, only sweeter, subtler, infinitely more warming. Jed had never flirted with a woman before in his life and was dimly astonished to find himself doing it now. But he wouldn't have stopped for the world.

Elizabeth looked up just then and their eyes met. What

she saw in his gaze she couldn't name, but for a moment it took her breath away. He was looking at her, and his eyes, so strikingly laced by those thick dark lashes, seemed lit by an alien fire that, when she looked at it, did not seem to allow her to look away. Her pulse beat faster, and there was a shallowness to her breathing. She felt as though her skin were opening, cell by cell, in rapid rippling motions, to a new level of awareness. It was only for a moment, the very briefest of instants, but in that moment Elizabeth thought, *He is going to kiss me.* She did not know how she knew that, but she knew it was true. The thought brought her a thrill of excitement and anticipation that was so swift and intense, it was almost dizzying.

And Jed might have kissed her. In that moment during which his eyes were captured by the sweet, soft luminosity of hers he might have done anything, for the world as he knew it ceased to exist. The gentle drone of the insects, the grass whispering with the breeze, the motes of dust drifting in the sun-washed air...all of it faded away. There was only himself, poised on the edge of he knew not what—and her, looking at him with eyes as rich as jewels, her face tinged with the sun, her lips soft and rouged and slightly parted....

A crashing in the undergrowth brought Jed to his feet an instant before the loping, grinning dog came bounding out of the woods. Elizabeth gave an ecstatic cry as the animal flung himself upon her, a tangle of muddy paws, matted fur, and slobbering tongue.

"Caesar!" She was laughing and scolding at the same time, hugging the animal fiercely around the neck. "You bad, bad dog!" She looked up at Jed, her eyes sparkling with relief and joy. "You were right—he found me!"

Jed smiled and didn't know when he had been so sorry to be right.

Elizabeth spent the next few moments trying to pluck the cockleburs from the fur of William Bledsoe's prize hound while attempting to keep him from doing further damage to her riding habit. When Jed slipped a loop of rope around the dog's neck, she exclaimed breathlessly, "Oh—thank you! This should keep him from getting into any more mischief."

And then she noticed Jed was also holding the reins to her horse.

She took up her jacket and stood, smoothing her skirts with quick, nervous motions and rearranging her bonnet. It was time to go. In all that had happened in the past half hour she had not thought once—it had simply never crossed her mind—that soon it must end. She glanced at him and said, rather unnecessarily, "I guess . . . I should be going."

"Yes, ma'am. They'll be missing you."

Those tiny lines around his eyes were softened with a smile and his magnificent mane of golden hair glowed in the sunlight. Standing, he was so much taller than she had imagined, and she had to tilt her head to look at him. Suddenly she felt almost panicky. How can it end now? She wasn't ready to go. How could this lovely, dreamlike interlude come to such an unremarkable end?

Her best friend had fallen in love with a man she had glimpsed only once, as he lay wounded and bleeding on the deck of a ship, a hero from the wars. For three years Margaret had remained true to her one and only fantasy love, and for three years Elizabeth had unabashedly envied her friend the beauty of her secret romance. But even Margaret's story, as noble and lovely as it was, could not compare to Elizabeth's adventure that morning. How could she simply ride away from him?

And as she hesitated, looking at him with those wide green eyes, Jed heard himself volunteering, "I'll ride along with you, to make sure you get home all right."

For a moment Elizabeth's heart leapt and the joy was reflected in her eyes—and then, just as quickly, her smile was doused with the cold water of reality. She imagined herself coming out of the woods with this man and riding up to Spring Hill, her clothing in disarray and her hair tumbling down. . . .

With this man she had shared more than a few moments of romantic fantasy and talk of faraway lands. He had unfastened her clothing, he had glimpsed her petticoats and touched her intimately; even remembering that, she went hot all over with embarrassment. If Miss Nancy ever found out—if *anyone* ever found out—she would be ruined.

The very thought made her gasp. "Oh, no! You *mustn't*." Her eyes grew dark with alarm. "It—it wouldn't be at all proper, and if anyone ever found out . . . oh, it simply wouldn't do!"

Once again Jed felt that little twinge of confusion and annoyance for his inability to understand the things that were important in her world. But it only mattered, he supposed, that they were important, and he did not argue with her.

"If you follow this trail about a hundred yards," he said, nodding, "it will take you to the Mobile road. Will you know where you are from there?"

"Oh, yes." Relief flooded her, as well as embarrassment for having become lost almost in her own backyard. "I-I'm quite familiar with the countryside, only I didn't realize the road was so close."

He looked at her for another moment, and the softness of those lines around his eyes made Elizabeth's heart beat faster. She found she couldn't meet his gaze for very long. Instead she busily began pulling on her jacket, buttoning it to the throat, and retying her bonnet strings to tuck in the straying wisps of her hair. Jed looped the dog's lead around the pommel of her saddle, and at last there was nothing she could do but mount.

He linked his fingers together, and she placed her small, booted foot in them, swinging into the sidesaddle with such grace and modesty that not even a whisper of lacy undergarment was allowed to offend the human eye. He moved to hold the bridle while she gathered up the reins. Caesar, for once, was obedient, sitting on the ground as he waited.

She was mounted, reins in hand, horse eager to be off, dog safely in tow, and there was no more reason to linger. But only now did she realize the thousand things she had wanted to ask him, to say to him. There was so much she wanted to know about him, so many empty spaces in her life that needed to be filled with the memory of his voice, the movement of his hands, the intimacy of his smile. The quickness of rapport they had shared, the easy bond of comfort that had grown between them was something Elizabeth had never experienced before, and she knew instinctively that it would not come again. . . . Yet it was gone too soon. He had told her everything yet nothing, and there were a thousand, thousand things more she wanted to hear from him. But now it was too late. She had to go.

Jed did not know what to say to her. From the height of the saddle atop her thoroughbred horse, in her prim riding jacket and kid gloves, she looked regal and untouchable. Words, which once had flowed so easily between them, now seemed awkward and stilted. He wondered if she had guessed how badly he had wanted to kiss her a moment before. He hoped not.

At last the only thing that came to him was "I'm sorry, ma'am, for scaring you before. I'm thinking maybe if I hadn't shot when I did, you might not have been thrown."

"Oh, no, Mr. Fielding," she answered swiftly, bright

with an emotion Jed could not define. "It was not your fault at all. You acted most courageously."

For most of her young adulthood Elizabeth had heard warning against wearing one's heart on one's sleeve, but she had never understood the phrase, nor did she have the temperament with which to prevent it. She had not been trained in the art of flirtation, and she did not understand duplicity. She knew no other way than to speak exactly what she felt, and even though shyness colored her cheeks, she said softly, "It is the dream of every young lady, is it not, to be rescued in the wood by a gallant stranger? You have been a hero to me today, sir, and I will never forget you. Not ever."

And then, quickly, before her own weakness and foolishness persuaded her to stay, Elizabeth jerked the reins and rode off.

Jed watched her go, a faint cloud of puzzlement and wonder shadowing his features and slowing his reason. A hero? He never had thought of himself in those terms before. And he never had expected to hear a lady use that word to describe him, especially with such shy and rapt sincerity in her eyes.

He stood for a moment longer, listening to the sound of her hoofbeats growing fainter in the distance and was surprised by how much dimmer the day seemed without her in it. Then, scowling a little at his own foolishness, he turned away, walking back toward the house to pick up his saddlebags.

Without turning, he called out, "Come on down, Sam." He didn't raise his voice above a conversational tone, and the rider who had been waiting in the cover of the trees behind the house nudged his horse forward.

"Didn't want to interrupt your good-byes," Sam Houston said, grinning. Leaning on the pommel, he walked his horse to a stop a few yards before Jed. "Thought the lady might be embarrassed to see me riding up in the middle of them."

Sam Houston was Jed's oldest friend and, whether on the plains of Texas or in the hills of Alabama, the only man in the world who could feel safe riding into his camp without hailing first. Nonetheless, Jed had never been less pleased to see anyone in his life.

Still not turning to look back at Houston, Jed muttered, "Considerate of you," and started into the house.

"I must say, I'm impressed." Sam pushed his hat back on his head, dark eyes crinkled with laughter at his friend's discomfiture. "You could do worse in the female department. Lord knows, you have before."

Jed said nothing. In many ways Sam Houston was the most admirable man he knew, but he had two great weaknesses—a fondness for both the bottle and pretty young women. Advice on women was the last thing in the world he would ever accept from Sam Houston.

Jed went inside, doused the fire with the water left over from Elizabeth's tea, picked up his saddlebags and rifle, and went back out to his horse. There was no need to linger any longer. He was ready to go home.

Sam turned his horse toward Jed. "Are you heading back to Texas, then?"

Jed bent to check the cinch. "Yep. I'm finished up here."

"Well, looks like I caught you just in time."

"I told you, Sam, I've got no truck with your politics or your speeches. You come back out to Texas and we'll ride the trail together, but out here you're on your own. I'm going home."

Sam said, "I've got a man I want you to meet."

Jed swung into the saddle. "Not interested."

"An important man—to Texas, to all of us. He has a proposition for you, and all I ask is that you listen."

Jed had known, from the moment he had met up with Sam on his way back to Alabama, that it would come to this. Sam had it in mind that the more people he could get to bring their money into Texas, the better chance they would have in Washington for annexation, and he held that it was every Texian's sworn duty to take up his cause. Nobody knew better than Jed how badly American money was needed in Texas, but he wasn't much for causes, and as far as he was concerned, Texians could take care of themselves, without any help from outsiders.

Lifting his reins, Jed said, "No point in listening. I'm putting this place behind me."

Sam's face grew quiet. "I gave the man my word, Jed."

Jed looked at him, irritated and resigned. The two of them had ridden many a long trail together, and nothing could bind men together faster than a stretch of Indian-infested country where your next step was only as sure as the man who rode in your shadow. Sam Houston had taught Jed to read and to write his name. They had fought side by side against General Santa Anna and had saved each other's lives many times over. If there was one thing Sam Houston knew for sure, it was that Jed could not refuse him anything. Especially when the other man had given his word.

"Blast it all, Sam, you know I'd rather walk barefoot through a nest of rattlers than go sashaying into one of your fancy house parties." He was scowling, but both knew the protest was superfluous. "What the hell did you want to go rope me into something like this for?"

Sam grinned, laying back easy in the saddle. "A little culture and refinement won't do you a bit of harm, young friend." Then, "All I ask is that you listen to what the man has to say. Nobody's tying you into anything."

"Good. Because listening is all you're going to get. I'm going to be in Mobile before the sun hits the water." Jed lifted his reins and moved out around the house. "Who is this man, anyway, and what's so all-fired important about him?"

"His name is Lord Hartley, and he's from England. You'll see what's so important about him when you talk to him. He's visiting Spring Hill Plantation, just up the road a bit. It's even on your way to town."

Jed knew where Spring Hill was. The most gracious and prosperous plantation on the bay, it had been a symbol throughout his boyhood of all he wanted to be, all he expected to obtain. There was a certain sort of irony in the fact that now, just as he was preparing to ride away from all his boyhood dreams, he would be walking for the first time through the gates of Spring Hill. Maybe it was even fitting.

"I'll go," Jed said, though his tone was still dark with reluctance as he urged his horse around to lead the trail. "But I'm not staying."

Sam cast him a sly look. "Oh, I don't know about that. Seems to me you've got some old acquaintances to renew."

Jed glanced at him suspiciously, and Sam's eyes flashed with amused astonishment. "You don't mean to tell me you don't know who that lady was?"

Jed realized for the first time that she had never gotten around to telling him her name. He had an uneasy feeling he was not going to like what Sam was about to say.

Sam chuckled out loud. "Her name is Elizabeth Coleman, of Larchmont Plantation," he informed Jed, eyes twinkling confidently. "And she's staying at Spring Hill. You'll be *sashaying*"—he put deliberate emphasis on the word for Jed's benefit—"up to her front door in less than an hour."

CHAPTER
Three

___

On this bright May afternoon in 1839, Spring Hill was living up to its name in all its glory. An endless froth of tree azaleas in fuchsia, white, and petal-pink lined the twisting walkways, while yellow beds of daffodils and jonquils alternated with lacy designs of white ice plant and lavender thrift throughout the expansive gardens. Climbing roses twisted through a central arbor, their pale pink buds just beginning to unfurl, and the graceful drape of the willow branches was just a shade lighter than the hue of neatly cropped spring grass that carpeted the pathways between the formally shaped hedges of yew and boxwood.

Lace tablecloths fluttered in the breeze beneath silver bowls piled high with strawberries, trays laden with delicate cakes and other confections, and crystal punch bowls offering fruit punch. Magnolia-complexioned young ladies, dressed in the pastel silks, taffetas, and lawns of spring finery, strolled through the gardens with gentlemen in frock coats and satin stocks, the ladies' parasols twirling with lazy ribbons of color above their heads, the gentlemen's polished walking sticks tapping out lazy rhythms on the flagstone.

It was a scene of luxury and indolence, of gentle festivity and refined gaiety. In a corner of the lawn a group of ladies played croquet. Beneath a spreading oak, three of the state's most successful planters lit cigars and launched into a discussion of the future of the South and the nature of aristocracy. Nearby a handful of children was playing with a ball and hoop, ever mindful of their Sunday clothes and their Mammy's watchful gaze.

Caesar dozed contentedly in his pen, and a certain temperamental stallion, groomed and curried, munched at his feed bag. Inside the airy, white-columned house, Elizabeth Coleman and Margaret Lea sat side by side on the striped silk settee in the drawing room. Their spines straight, hands folded in their laps, and heads bowed demurely, each was wishing desperately to be anywhere else.

Miss Nancy Lea, with barely a whisper of her black silk skirts, moved behind the escritoire and took her seat. Elizabeth, swallowing the lump of dread in her throat, ventured a glance at her. She couldn't imagine how she had been found out. She had bribed the stable boy with a strawberry tart to curry the stallion, groom Caesar, and say nothing to Mr. Bledsoe's groom about her early-morning ride. She had crept up the back stairs without alerting a soul and had successfully bathed, changed, and arranged herself in the morning room before anyone ever thought to look for her. Her soiled riding habit and scarred boots were safely bundled away in the bottom of her trunk, and she could not imagine how anyone could have guessed her misadventure. Miss Nancy Lea must have eyes in the back of her head.

Miss Nancy said now, "I thought it appropriate, ladies, that we discuss some of the finer points of civilized behavior before joining our guests this afternoon." Her voice, for all its sweetness, wielded more power over the two girls in her charge than the roar of a bull. "And I also thought, since the behavior of the one invariably mimics that of the other, that both of you should be present for this discussion."

Margaret and Elizabeth met each other's eyes in a swift glance of anxiety and chagrin. Elizabeth's heart began to pound, and she wondered if it might not be best to throw herself upon the mercy of Miss Nancy's disappointment. How, oh, how could she have ever been so foolish this morning? And how had Miss Nancy ever found out?

Miss Nancy Lea was Margaret's mother, the widow of a Baptist minister and the symbol of all that was good and perfect about Southern womanhood. Miss Nancy's youngest daughter, Antoinette, had married Mr. William Bledsoe and become mistress of the magnificent Spring Hill Plantation about the same time Elizabeth's mother had died. At that time Miss Nancy had turned her full attention to the future of her older daughter, Margaret . . . and that girl's best friend, Elizabeth Coleman.

With the death of Elizabeth's mother at the most crucial hour of her young womanhood, her father, Abraham Coleman, had turned the upbringing of his daughter almost completely over to Miss Nancy Lea. Since Elizabeth's home of Larchmont was only eight miles distant from Spring Hill and twelve miles from town, Elizabeth had been a familiar figure in the Lea/Bledsoe household for many years. In the last two years, secluded by her formal period of mourning, Elizabeth had divided her time exclusively between Larchmont with her father, Spring Hill, and the parsonage in town with Miss Nancy and Margaret. All in all, the arrangement was most fortuitous, and Elizabeth never had cause to regret it...except at moments like this.

Miss Nancy was a severe-looking woman, the black widow's garb accentuating her thin figure and sharp features. Her coal-black hair was pulled back tightly from a stern widow's peak and sharply contrasted with her flawless white skin. A look from her, it was said, could stop the devil in his tracks, but her real power lay not in her formidability but in her gentleness. All she had to do was say quietly, "I'm most disappointed in you, my dear," and Elizabeth wanted to cover her head and never have to face the kind, sad eyes of the other woman again.

Elizabeth gathered her courage, unsure she could bear to hear those words today. She cast another swift glance at Margaret and then turned to Miss Nancy. "Please, ma'am," she ventured, "if I might explain."

Miss Nancy returned a glance filled with gentle reprimand. "It is impolite to interrupt, Elizabeth. It is not to you I address myself this afternoon, but"—she fixed her eyes on her daughter—"to Margaret."

Elizabeth was swept with such great relief that she did not even hear the words that followed. Margaret! Miss Nancy did not know; she hadn't discovered Elizabeth's disobedient adventure. Providence was still with her, for it was Margaret, not Elizabeth, who had incurred Miss Nancy's disapproval today!

And then swift chagrin gripped her for reveling in her own success to the exclusion of her friend's troubles, and Elizabeth turned her attention back to Miss Nancy.

"...but this childish infatuation has quite gotten out of hand," Miss Nancy was saying, her voice soft but firm. "I was told that you were even so bold as to walk in the gardens with him yesterday, having only been just introduced and quite unchaperoned. This simply will not do, Margaret.''

Elizabeth cast a quick, sympathetic glance toward Margaret, but her friend's chin was held high, her face composed and immobile. Elizabeth started a little when Miss Nancy inclined her gentle eyes upon her.

''And you, Elizabeth, are not entirely blameless in this matter. I understand a young girl's need for romantic fantasies, but I'm afraid you have indulged your fondness for questionable literature of a romantic nature to such an extent that common sense has quite been overruled. You have encouraged Margaret's obsession with General Houston, openly and quite often, and I must tell you now that you have done her no favor. It is past time, I fear, that you understood that the stuff of which novels are made rarely have a place in the life of a properly brought-up young lady.''

Elizabeth nodded, casting her eyes downward demurely. ''Yes, ma'am.'' In truth, she thought Margaret's adoration for General Houston far more romantic than anything ever written in a novel and doubted whether her enthusiasm for the romance had affected Margaret's thinking one whit. But she was relieved to have gotten off so easily and dared not object whatever the circumstances.

Miss Nancy turned back to Margaret. ''Your inexcusable behavior of yesterday afternoon to one side, my dear, I think it's best that you understand now that the man is completely unsuitable. His reputation is widely known, as is his propensity for the bottle, and no young lady of good repute would even consider entertaining his affections. I suggest you put whatever notions you might be harboring of your own along those lines completely out of your mind.''

But Margaret, it was plain to see, had no intention of doing any such thing. ''He is a hero of the wars,'' she asserted, her color growing high, "a general and the president of a nation! He has been governor and—"

"None of which," insisted Miss Nancy firmly, "has any bearing upon his status as a gentleman. He is a divorced man, my dear, and surrounded by scandal of such a nature that it must not even be whispered about among those of delicate sensibilities."

"I don't care!" Margaret's eyes were glittering with a sudden rush of unshed tears, and her small fists clenched in her lap. "I love him. I have loved him since the moment I saw him, wounded and fainting on the ship at New Orleans, the hero of San Jacinto—I have held that picture of him in my mind since that day, and prayer and providence have at last brought us together! I shall never cease loving him!"

Elizabeth felt such a strong rush of pride for her friend that she wanted to shout encouragement. She knew how Margaret felt because of her own adventure that morning, the memory of which still danced in her brain like a dream too wonderful to be dismissed. Elizabeth understood more than ever how Margaret felt about General Houston. For years he had been a fairy-tale hero to her, but she had loved him unwaveringly, until, at last, a mere two days ago, destiny had brought him to Spring Hill and Margaret's side. His affection for her had been as instant and as devout as had hers for him, proving only that sometimes fairy tales did come true. Perhaps someday Elizabeth's fantasy might have the same happy ending.

Miss Nancy looked at her daughter in sympathy and tolerance. "My dear, you were but a child then, and General Houston is as old as I. As for providence having brought him here, I'm sure you must admit it was Mr. Bledsoe's business interests, and nothing else, which brought him to Spring Hill this weekend . . . a circumstance I devoutly hope I will have no further cause to regret."

Margaret was staunchly silent, and Miss Nancy rose, moving gracefully toward them. "My girls," she said kindly, "attend me well, for it is unlikely you will hear anything of more importance to the consequence of your futures than what I am about to say. It is necessary always to remember your station and to invite no associations outside your own social class. To do otherwise will only bring unhappiness and heartbreak to all parties concerned. There are certain codes that govern gentlemanly behavior, of which men like General Houston are doubtless unaware and by which he is not bound. He is a fine man, to be sure, but his world is so apart from yours, my dear, that each of you would find yourselves lost should you try to seek common ground. I do you a kindness in telling you this, for your pain would be inconsolable should you discover it for yourself."

"But surely," Elizabeth objected, losing herself in concern for her friend and in horror over the possibility of seeing such a beautiful love story dashed to the ground before it had barely drawn breath, "you don't intend to forbid her to see him? After she has waited so long and loved so truly, and he has only just arrived. . . ."

Miss Nancy's patient look of quiet reproval silenced Elizabeth, giving her cause to retract—though not regret—her interference. She *did* try to be soft-spoken and retiring, to keep her opinions to herself and to speak only when addressed. But sometimes, when a truth needed very badly to be told, Elizabeth forgot the rules of ladylike deportment. None to her credit, that happened more often than not.

Miss Nancy, satisfied that Elizabeth had taken her unspoken point to heart, answered her question. "If General Houston has wish to address my daughter, he will come to me, as a gentleman should. Until that eventuality, however," she added, turning back to Margaret, "I forbid you to seek him out, for such behavior will do nothing to enhance your virtue or garner the respect of any gentleman present. A lady never puts herself forward to draw the attention of a gentleman,'' she pointed out calmly, and to both girls. ''She must at all times remember modesty and decorum, and should attention come her way, she should accept it quietly, ever aware of the great honor that is being bestowed upon her. A lady's reputation is her only dowry, and one must at all costs strive to keep it intact.''

She smiled and extended a benevolent hand to each of them. ''And now, my dears, we have guests to attend to. You will each go out and extend the best of our hospitality, conducting yourselves at all times like the proper ladies you have been bred to be. I demand nothing more, and I expect nothing less.''

At forty-six, Sam Houston was still a commanding figure, towering over his companions in breadth and height. Though dissipation had caused a slight sag in his face and easy living had left his muscles less firm than they should have been, he was not in any case a figure to be taken lightly. His very presence seemed to command respect, and his voice, even in conversational tone, boomed with authority.

''Well, sir, I must say I couldn't be more pleased.'' He addressed William Bledsoe now, lifting his glass to him with a beaming smile of approval. ''I'm sure you'll find Texas to be all that I've promised—and more.''

''Well, I must confess your talk of expansionism and investment in Texas has us all intrigued,'' answered Bledsoe. ''My mother-in-law even more than myself. We decided the only sensible thing to do was to go to Texas and see for ourselves.''

''Mrs. Lea will be accompanying you, then?'' Houston inquired, trying, rather unsuccessfully, to hide his surprise.

William noticed his confusion and responded with a grin. "My mother-in-law is the shrewdest businesswoman I've ever known, and I would almost trust her judgment before my own. As for the rigors of the journey, have no concern on her part. The Lea women are all quite remarkable in that respect—stronger than they ever would have anyone guess, in mind as well as spirit."

"Indeed," Houston murmured, and into his eyes came a spark, which he hid by taking another sip of his bourbon. The Lea women were most indisputably remarkable, and one much more than the others. He added mildly, "And will her lovely daughters be accompanying her?"

"I rather doubt it. My wife disdains to travel, and Miss Margaret . . . well, frankly, sir, I believe Mrs. Lea is concerned that Margaret's temperament is too unsettled for the journey."

"But surely the good lady does not intend to travel without female companionship?"

Bledsoe hesitated, giving that some thought. "I'm certain not." Then he smiled. "But Miss Nancy can be relied upon to make her own arrangements, and I'm sure that they will be eminently suitable."

Sam was disappointed that Margaret was not, after all, likely to see the land he had described for her at such glowing length last evening—and that his reunion with her would not be in Texas, as he had hoped. But he had come to court American investors, not a wife, and he had little cause for complaint.

He turned to his companion on the left. "What of you, Mr. Coleman? Surely you'll be joining your friends for the grand excursion."

Abraham Coleman shook his head. "Regretfully, I am unable to leave the plantation at this time. But I am happy to rely upon Lord Hartley and Mr. Bledsoe's advice in business of this nature. Since Lord Hartley is more or less leading the expedition, I'll doubtless consent to any report he brings back. Taking into consideration, of course,'' he added, flashing William Bledsoe a grin, ''Mrs. Lea's most excellent judgment.''

''Then the deed is practically done,'' declared Houston. ''Lord Hartley has already obtained vested interest in Texas, and in fact, I expect him to be one of the leaders in colonization. Soon, perhaps, you will be joining him, Mr. Coleman.''

''Cotton is my business, sir,'' responded Coleman, ''and it's been good to me. If the Texas soil is only half the friend to the planter you have promised, then I shouldn't doubt that a great many of us will be joining him.''

''Cotton,'' asserted Houston grandly, ''is the kingdom upon which Texas will be built. From the Gulf to the Rio Grande, the hills will be white with it. And we will all be rich men.''

''A toast, then, sir.'' William Bledsoe raised his glass. ''To our very good fortunes.''

Sam Houston, never one to miss an opportunity, added with gusto, ''And to Texas—where your fortunes await you.''

Charles Edgecomb, Lord Hartley, was a fine-looking man in his early thirties whose pale blond hair had not yet begun to thin and whose sharp, aristocratic features announced centuries of breeding and superiority. He had the lean, long build of a fencer and the impeccably groomed style of a dandy. His eyes were gray and heavily lidded; his lazy grace was an innate disguise for a shrewd mind; and his reflexes were as quick and cunning as a desert snake's.

He had left behind a wife and son in England, a tea plantation in Ceylon, and a sheep ranch in Australia. For generations the name of Hartley had been synonymous with exploration, conquest, and colonization. In Africa, India, Malaysia, the Caribbean, and the Pacific, the heirs of the Hartley dynasty had gone forth to leave their mark, blazing the trail for civilization and manifesting the destiny of dominance of the superior. Charles Edgecomb was a man in whom the thirst for adventure was inbred, the right to conquest an unquestioned imperative. Texas, he believed, was the destiny of his generation.

William Bledsoe had graciously offered the use of his library for Lord Hartley's private business, and he was as at home within it as he was in his own private study at Edgecomb Hall. The room was dark, furnished with heavy chairs of Corinthian leather and rugs imported from Persia. The walls were lined with books, and the desk was as big and heavy as it was imposing.

When Jed knocked on the library door, Edgecomb let him in with a formal greeting. He then strolled around the desk, flipped open an intricately frescoed humidor, and offered his guest a cigar. Jed took it because he was not a man to refuse a good cigar, but at that moment he would have preferred, on the whole, to be anywhere else. Hartley sank casually into the chair behind the desk, leaving Jed to find a seat in one of the big leather chairs opposite him. Jed had never found it wise to trust a man who arranged himself with his back to the sun. He had used that trick too many times himself.

West of the Sabine, the land was big and the people few, and for that reason most everyone got to know or hear of everyone else eventually. Lord Hartley had been through Texas in '34 and again in '37, and his reputation had preceded this meeting with Jed. He fancied himself a cardsharp, it was said, and was known to carry a knife in his waistband. He asked a lot of questions and remembered what he was told, and he was nobody's fool. He hired the best guides and paid them well, and he wasn't afraid of much. Once a trapper had accused him of dealing seconds and had walked away from the dispute minus an ear, which put out that Hartley was not a man to be reckoned with lightly.

The minute Sam Houston had introduced Hartley, Jed became aware of that prickling sense of uneasiness again. He was dimly amazed that he had had to come this far from Texas to find trouble lying in wait for him.

Hartley leaned back in the chair, the cigar smoldering between his slim fingers, and smiled that cool British smile that never seemed to reach the eyes. He said, "Let me get right to the point, Mr. Fielding, for you strike me as the sort of man who does not appreciate wasting time. General Houston has recommended you highly, and I can see now he was right. You are exactly the kind of man I need."

Jed regarded him expressionlessly, waiting. The sun, pouring in over Hartley's shoulder, glared in Jed's eyes and blurred the other man's features, but it didn't matter. Jed knew all he needed to know about Hartley already.

"You're a woodsman," Hartley said. "A tracker, a soldier, and a good man with a gun. I want you to ride for me."

Jed tasted the cigar, enjoying its rich, full fragrance, regarding Hartley mildly. "Where?"

"Texas," Hartley answered, letting the word hang there for a minute. "A big land made for big men with big dreams. You and I, Mr. Fielding, are such men. We were destined to make Texas our own."

Jed was silent for a moment, watching the blue smoke from his cigar curl toward the ceiling. He wondered, not for the first time in the past hour, what he was doing there.

He looked back to Hartley and answered, casually, "I ride for myself."

Hartley's mirthless smile did not fade, but Jed could sense a sharpening in him as he reassessed the situation. Clearly he realized Jed would be a bit more difficult than he had imagined at first. "You haven't heard my offer yet."

"Don't need to."

Hartley took another look at Jed, and the leather chair crinkled as he stretched out his long legs beneath the desk. Jed was wondering where Miss Elizabeth Coleman was, and if he would see her before he left. Part of him hoped he would; the other part knew better. The best thing he could do was get back where he belonged. This world of Spring Hill, of pale, well-groomed men who, like Hartley, were too used to getting their own way, was not for him. Sam Houston had managed to live with one foot in Alabama and one in Texas, without doing himself any visible harm, but Jed had no interest in ever trying that difficult, fence-straddling act.

"I hear you're a landowner in Texas," Hartley said pleasantly.

Jed had been awarded sixteen hundred acres for his service in the Mexican war, and he had spent the past three years rounding up and fattening a small herd of wild Texas cattle. It wasn't exactly a fortune, but he had staked his claim on some of the richest, prettiest land in East Texas, and it was a beginning. He answered, "That's right."

"So, you see, we have something in common." Hartley's manner was easy and expansive. "I, too, have invested my future in Texas land coupons."

Land coupons were about the only negotiable commodity Texas had to offer at that point. They were as cheap as dirt and going fast, but as far as Jed was concerned, they were a sucker's bet. They didn't apply to any specific land but just represented acreage that could be claimed. Until the land was claimed, the coupons were good for wallpaper but not much else, and that was exactly how most of them ended up being used.

Jed chewed on his cigar. "That right?"

Hartley leaned forward a little, his fingertips touching on the broad surface of the desk. "Two hundred thousand acres." He pronounced each syllable slowly and with definition. "And that is only the beginning."

"Quite a spread," Jed commented, and his tone revealed nothing but a passing interest. "What are you going to do with it?"

"I am going," pronounced Hartley quietly, with a smile at the corner of his lips that left no room for argument, "to build an empire. A kingdom that will stretch from the Brazos to the Sabine, from the Red River to the Gulf. That's the very best land in Texas, and it's the land I plan to have. You see, Mr. Fielding," he said, leaning back in the chair again as he picked up his cigar, "the name Hartley has always been associated with greatness. My family has been responsible for bringing conquests into the British Empire as far back as the Normans. Wherever there is a frontier to be gained, there has been a man with a vision. Texas is my vision."

Jed let his ashes fall carelessly into the brass spittoon at his feet, but he did not take his eyes off Hartley. "Might be a bit harder to do than it sounds. For one thing, my spread sits right in the middle of your so-called empire."

"Precisely why I came to you." Hartley fixed him with his cool and confident gaze. "Wherever there are empires to be built, there must be men willing to fight for them, and you strike me as a fighter, Mr. Fielding. Besides being the best man for the job I have in mind, you already have a vested interest in Texas. I am quite willing to buy your acres to ensure your loyalty, but more than that, Mr. Fielding, if you work for me, you will have a chance to *be* someone in this country. I can make you a rich man, and I'll make you a powerful one. That's not a combination many men could refuse."

"No," agreed Jed, "I reckon it's not." He watched and waited, amazed by the scope of Hartley's arrogance.

There were some who said a smart man sizes up a situation in terms of right and wrong, black and white, and doesn't waste time trying to read what lay between. Maybe Jed wasn't very smart, but he had never been able to ignore the shadings of a man's character, the little nuances of weakness and strength that defined an opponent's behavior. Hartley was not so different than a lot of others who came to Texas. They all knew what they wanted and didn't much care what they had to do to get it, but that didn't make them evil. Hartley hid his ruthlessness beneath a veneer of civility, but everybody used what weapons he had. That did not make him a purely bad man.

Jed saw Hartley as quick-thinking, courageous, and determined. He was the kind of man who could cheat at cards without a qualm but would blow a man's head off for insulting a woman he didn't even know. He would defend you to the death if you were on his side, but if you weren't, he would sooner or later find a way to step over your body. Most importantly, he went through life with never a doubt that what he did and the way he did it was right. He was neither good nor bad but a peculiarly twisted combination of both. And that was precisely what made him so dangerous.

"You're a cautious man," Hartley observed, twirling his cigar between his fingers. "I like that."

"A thoughtful man," amended Jed. "And what I'm thinking now is that there's a lot of folks between the Brazos and Sabine—me included—that won't take too kindly to your plans for an empire. Folks that got there before you."

"Indians, Mexicans, drifters," dismissed Hartley.

"Some. But there are settlers too. Farmers. Townbuilders, even. Folks that came looking for a place to call their own. What do you propose to do about us?"

Hartley smiled. "Well, I imagine those others will just have to move out of my way, don't you? You, of course, could join me."

"Or fight."

Some of the smile faded from Hartley's eyes, though his tone remained casual. "You're a military man, Mr. Fielding. You're doubtless familiar with the great generals of history—Alexander the Great, Caesar, Napoleón. Men of vision and destiny bring civilization to barbarians. They conquered because they were meant to do so. They built empires, and so will we."

Jed regarded him calmly. "Texas is a big land, and folks thereabouts can get mighty stubborn when riled. I think even Alexander the Great would have himself a tussle if he came upon Texians in a temper."

Hartley's confident, shadowy smile was back. "Even the strongest—and most stubborn—must eventually submit to the dominance of a superior force. It is the law of history itself."

"For a man who talks so much about history," Jed pointed out, "seems to me you've learned mighty little from it. About a hundred years ago some other folks came over here with notions not too different from yours, parading their red coats and blowing their bugles. As I recollect, they turned tail and ran as soon as they got a whiff of what they were up against."

Not a trace of good humor remained in Hartley's eyes now, and his tone went rather stiff. "Your point?"

Jed shrugged. "The point is, kingdoms and suchlike don't seem to work on this side of the ocean. It's in the land, for one thing—too big and too rough. It's in the way we think, for another. We just never got used to living in another man's shadow, and I don't reckon we're likely to start doing it now."

"You forget, Mr. Fielding," Hartley pointed out coolly, "that Texas is a separate nation. New, struggling, in need of discipline. I will bring prosperity and order, the very things of which civilization is made."

Jed shook his head a little, half smiling, and tossed his cigar into the spittoon. "Just don't expect anybody to be holding out the welcome mat for you. Texians are a mighty peculiar lot when it comes to interference from outsiders."

Hartley's face went smooth and blank, and though his tone was negligent, Jed could see his muscles tighten. "We have ruled before. Africa, India, Australia, the West Indies...I rather doubt I shall run up against anything in Texas I have not known before."

Jed smiled and got to his feet. "Well, sir, I don't know about them Africans and Indians, but in Texas we just got through throwing out a bunch of folks who thought they had the right to tell us what to do, and I wouldn't be surprised if we went and did it again, given cause."

"I see." Hartley rose gracefully, but his manner was no longer hospitable. "Might I take it, then, that you're refusing my proposition?"

"You take it right. I'm no man's hired gun. I'm keeping my land, thanks all the same. And nobody's going to buy me out or push me off."

"Pity." Hartley observed him for a moment, giving no hint of what might be going on behind his bland eyes. "Those who aren't with me usually find themselves coming against me at one time or another and live to regret their choice."

Jed met his gaze calmly. "I figured as much."

"You may have cause to change your mind." His voice was very quiet. "I should hate for you to be one of those I have to move out of my way."

"So would I," Jed agreed pleasantly. "For your sake."

Hartley's eyes went hard. "I will do it, you know."

Jed replied, without a flicker. "You can try."

For a moment the challenge, quiet and steely, hung in the air like a naked blade. The eyes of the two men met and held, the thin mask of civility evaporating so that, for the briefest of instants, only a flash of something primitive and savage remained.

And then, as quickly as it had vanished, the polite mask reappeared. Hartley walked around the desk, his smile in place, his manner polite. "But let us not spoil such a fine day with so much business talk." He opened the door, extending a hand for Jed to precede him. "Come outside, let me find you a drink. Mr. Bledsoe's hospitality was not meant to be wasted in the library, and I'm sure we'll find much to talk of besides Texas."

"Margaret, have you lost your hearing as well as your good sense?" Elizabeth demanded, casting a quick glance across the lawn to Mrs. Lea, who was conversing with a group of young matrons. "I specifically heard your mother forbid you, in no uncertain terms, to seek out General Houston. Would you defy her right beneath her nose?"

Margaret returned a look of impatience. "Fie, Elizabeth, since when did *you* become such a coward?"

Since, Elizabeth thought silently, *the Good Lord spared me my secret this morning.* Elizabeth did not believe in tempting fate and had resolved firmly to be a model of deportment from the moment she had escaped Miss Nancy's presence. But then, Elizabeth made that very same resolution at least twice every day. Something always seemed to come along to stray her from the path of righteousness. . . .

The weakening factor this time was Margaret's eyes, wide and blue and filled with pleading. "Elizabeth, please, where is your sense of romance? Mama cannot possibly object if you come with me, for your papa is standing right there with him, and we can only pretend to ask his permission for some little nonsense or the other. Mr. Houston dares not break away from his group to seek me out, but if we went over to them, nothing could be more proper, don't you see?"

Elizabeth did not see, but Margaret had appealed to her sense of romance, and she was weakening fast. "It is impolite to interrupt a gentleman's conversation," Elizabeth said, warily watching the three men—her father, Mr. Bledsoe, and General Houston as they waved their cigars in the enthusiasm of discussion.

But her voice lacked conviction, and Margaret seized on her vacillation immediately. "Gentlemen love to be interrupted," she insisted, and grabbed Elizabeth's hand. "Especially," she assured her with a twinkle in her eyes, "by young ladies!"

They were not more than ten feet away when two more men rounded the curve of the spreading oak and joined General Houston's group. With more than a little astonishment Elizabeth recognized Lord Hartley, an old friend of the family, and with him the tall, golden-haired man in fringed buckskins.

For a moment everything froze; Elizabeth couldn't hear a bird twitter nor feel a breeze. It was only an instant—no, less than an instant—but it was time enough for the entire world to tilt crazily on its axis and let reason slip completely away. And in that frozen instant a thousand, thousand things raced through Elizabeth's mind.

Joshua Edward Fielding, hero of her fantasies, conspirator in adventure, symbol of all that was wild and free and unobtainable, was here. It was impossible. How could he have come here, in this place, in this time? Impossible but undeniably true. He was here.

She remembered his hands, so strong and sure yet strangely graceful, working an intricate pattern into woven grass. She remembered the glint of sun on his untamed hair and the shadow of a moving branch on his bronzed cheek. She remembered his eyes, clear and bright and perceptive, soft and dark with unnamed thoughts, and remembering made her flush.

She remembered his voice, lazy and oddly musical at times, stirring the imagination with the words he spoke. She remembered the way he had looked at her when she was certain he was thinking about kissing her.

And then she remembered other things. Jed Fielding, alone in a tumbledown shack in the woods. Jed Fielding, who had unbuttoned her blouse and touched her skirt and glimpsed unmentionable parts of her anatomy . . . Why had he come here, how had he found her, what did he intend to do now that he was here?

The codes of gentlemanly behavior do not apply. . . .

She stumbled, but Margaret did not even notice. And what could she do, with only a matter of a few steps separating them, but wordlessly allow Margaret to pull her along? His eyes were turned on her father, acknowledging introductions, and he had not yet seen her. If she broke from Margaret and ran . . .

It was too late. Seeing them, Elizabeth's father had turned and with a pleased smile he welcomed them. "Well, young ladies, you look as though you've a pleasant secret or two to tell! Come, tell us what you've been up to."

Her father was drawing them in, and it was only a matter

of moments until her fate was sealed. Dread pounded in Elizabeth's heart and weakened her knees. She could not meet Jed Fielding's eyes, and his presence, so large and so vibrant, was twisting her stomach into a thousand knots.

"Mr. Fielding, I don't believe you've met Miss Margaret Lea. . . ."

Margaret curtsied, but she had eyes only for Sam Houston. The seconds until Elizabeth's doom ticked carelessly down.

"And my own lovely daughter, Miss Elizabeth Coleman."

Elizabeth held her breath. Now it would be over. He would make a careless remark about their previous meeting, a simple gesture of recognition or surprise, and all would come out. He could not be expected to understand how desperately her fate rested in his hands at this moment.

Bravely she lifted her eyes to him and waited for the ax to fall. But his face was very bland, his manner perfectly composed. There was nothing—nothing except a far-off twinkle, perhaps, in the very depths of those clear hazel eyes—to imply any kind of recognition at all. And as she waited, heartbeats suspended, for the words that would ruin her reputation and seal her fate, he smiled, faintly and distantly. And all he said was, politely, "It's a pleasure to meet you, ma'am."

CHAPTER
Four

Jed couldn't help but think it strange, the twists and turns life took. He propped his foot up on a stone bench, gazing toward the big, beautiful house where the pretty ladies and courtly gentlemen of Alabama's aristocracy were gathered. A half-cynical, half-wondering smile curved his lips downward. Of all the places in this great, vast land he might ever have expected to find himself, this was the last.

And of all the women in the world whose path he might have ever expected to cross his own, the likes of Elizabeth Coleman had never even been under consideration.

It had been an odd thing, seeing her this afternoon, all dressed up in a snow-white frock and picture hat, not a hair out of place, walking like a princess and looking like something out of a fancy ladies' magazine. And remembering her this morning with twigs in her hair and stains on her shirt, sitting in the tall grass beside him. It was a shock, trying to put the two pieces together, but it was not something for which he was unprepared. He had known from the beginning the kind of world from which she came, and how ill-suited he was for it. He simply had not expected it to be so awkward, meeting her again.

When she had looked at him, agonized embarrassment staining her cheeks and helpless shock in her eyes, he felt big and clumsy. All he had wanted to do was apologize for his presence. Of course, she had never expected to see him again; he had no business there. What had seemed so easy and natural in the spring-dappled farmyard suddenly seemed reprehensible conduct on both their parts, and all it took was seeing her in her own environment to take all the beauty out of the memory. He was as embarrassed as she was, and he had been almost relieved when, after a few agonized moments of awkward small talk all around, she had made some excuse and hurried away.

The sun was dipping behind the horizon, and Jed was no closer to Mobile than he had been when he had started out. The Bledsoes had asked him to stay to supper—they were a gracious lot, for all their fine airs—but Jed wanted no part of that. There was no excuse for his having stayed this long, except that there was pleasure in lingering in the shadows of this luxurious life-style, and perhaps, far back in his mind, he was hoping he might catch one last glimpse of Elizabeth Coleman before he left.

He had met Miss Nancy Lea, a sharp lady for all her pretense of modesty, who listened alertly and questioned intelligently all he had to say about Texas. She talked about making the trip West with her son-in-law and Hartley, and though it wasn't Jed's place to interfere, he hoped someone would talk her out of it. Texas was no place for a fine lady like her, and he couldn't imagine what interest there would be.

Abraham Coleman, who was involved somehow with

Hartley, wanted to talk about the cotton plantations along the Brazos. There wasn't too much Jed could say about that. He liked Coleman, though it was obvious his notions had been influenced by Hartley too much for Jed's taste, and somehow knowing that he was Elizabeth's father made him nervous. It was Bledsoe who finally rescued him, insisting upon showing Jed the gardens. They had shared a pleasant walk, and when Bledsoe had excused himself to attend to another guest, Jed lingered on the flowered path in the fading twilight. Folks were starting to wander inside now, and he thought it was about time he hit the saddle. But mostly he thought about Elizabeth.

It had been one day to mark down in memory: himself, welcomed as an honored guest at the renowned Spring Hill Plantation; a fancy English lord offering to make him a rich man; and Elizabeth Coleman...always his thoughts returned to her.

With a small hiss of impatience he ground out the cigar Bledsoe had given him and turned to make his way toward the stables. He was foolish to get so tangled up by a woman he would never see again. She was something to remember, all right, and he would remember her often and at length. But right now he had places to go and things to do, and all of them were far away from this place.

He heard the light step on the path before him and stepped back a little into the shadow of an azalea tree, not wanting to have to make explanations to anyone for his abrupt departure. He had already thanked Bledsoe for his hospitality, and Sam knew him too well to look for him when it came time to go.

His chest felt as though it had been dealt a blow with a sledgehammer when the figure rounded the corner and he saw that it was Miss Elizabeth. She was all alone, looking pensive and more lovely than it was right for any woman to be. For a moment Jed couldn't even move to make his presence known.

She had changed for evening into a deep rose-colored dress that rustled like silk when she walked. Its small puffy sleeves were off the shoulder and trimmed with a little froth of lace, showing off her slender arms and white shoulders. She didn't have a hat, and her hair was shiny and puffy around her face, with a perfect ringlet falling over her shoulder.

For a while he was so taken by the sight of her that he forgot where he was. But as she drew closer he realized that she might be startled to come upon him lurking in the shadows like that, and he stepped forward.

"Good evening, Miss Coleman."

She made a soft sound of surprise, and her face grew pink as she stammered, "Oh—Mr. Fielding. I—good evening. I—I was told William was here."

That was the truth, though not entirely so. She had been told William had taken Jed to the gardens, and she had come deliberately in search of them. She told herself she had only come to thank him for keeping her secret, but seeing him now, she knew it was more than that. Fate had brought him into her life, magnificently and miraculously— just like it had brought Sam Houston into Margaret's—and how could she turn away from what was so obviously meant to be? She had to see him again. There simply was no choice.

She had been deep in thought, trying to find the right words to say to him, and she hadn't expected Jed Fielding himself to step out on the path, without William. He made such a striking figure against the delicacy of pink azalea blossoms and violet twilight shadows that she was completely caught off-guard. She could barely get her breath.

Jed said politely, "He was, ma'am. He just now went back to the house. You'll probably find him there."

And all Elizabeth could say was "Oh."

Seeing how embarrassed she was, Jed didn't know what to say. He swallowed a lump in his throat that felt the size of a pumpkin, but his voice was still gruff as he said, "Well. Excuse me, ma'am." He started to move past her.

"Oh, Mr. Fielding, please," Elizabeth blurted out, reaching out her hand as though to catch his arm. Jed turned, and she didn't know what else to do except to spill out the words. "I—please, I wanted to . . . thank you for this afternoon." Her expression was pained, her eyes pleading. "For keeping our secret . . ."

Jed smiled a little. *Our secret*. That had a good sound. He answered, "Seemed only gentlemanly, ma'am."

Elizabeth flashed him a look filled with gratitude, and his smile lingered. How gentle his face looked when he smiled, and what a contrast that sensitive expression was to the power of his stance. It was a smile Elizabeth would remember forever, for just looking at it made something inside her seem to want to blend toward him. He was a gentleman. She had always known that. Was that not the nature of a hero?

But then he glanced away, and Elizabeth knew he was getting ready to leave. Strange to think that less than eight hours ago she could have poured out her heart to him, and now it was an effort to find anything at all to say. But she couldn't let him go.

She said quickly, lacking anything better to detain him, "How . . . do you like Alabama?"

It was an obvious ploy to get him to linger, but he was polite enough to pretend not to notice. "I like it just fine, ma'am," he replied. "Though it seems a little smaller than I remember."

"Oh." She seized on that as a way to continue the conversation. "You've been here before?"

His smile was oddly strained, as though the memory weren't entirely pleasant. "That was my folks' farm we were at this morning," he confessed.

Jed watched her carefully for signs of disdain, but all he

saw was bright curiosity. "Imagine," she murmured with a kind of wonder in her voice. "You grew up right here, not ten miles from my own plantation...and we never met until now. How strange are the workings of fate, don't you agree, Mr. Fielding?" Not giving him a moment to answer, she hurried on. "What caused you to leave Alabama for the western lands?"

Jed hesitated, but he was beginning to feel easier with her again, almost like he had that morning. She possessed the most uncanny ability to make him forget how difficult it usually was for him to talk to women. She looked at him with those big bright eyes, and he suddenly seemed to be a font of information, and all he wanted to do was share it with her.

He lifted one shoulder in a shrug. "I always had the restlessness, I guess." And he still did. It was a hollowness in the pit of his stomach, a determination that set his sights on being more than he was. "My pa always wanted me to have better than he could give, so when Ma died, we agreed it was time for me to go out and see what I could find for myself. I took off west and ended up in Texas."

Elizabeth was fascinated. "And you've been there ever since?"

Jed shook his head. "No, I did a bit of wandering in between. I crossed the Big River, made it all the way to the Rockies once. I had a lot to see."

There was a bench nearby, and Elizabeth sank onto it, hoping he would join her. It wasn't really improper, for there were other people around—occasional murmured voices and soft laughter wandering on the other side of the flowered path—and it was not full dark. But Jed looked uncertain, and she knew if she gave him a chance, he would try to leave again. "You said you had lived with the Indians," she encouraged.

"That's right." He felt almost completely relaxed now, at

home with her. He even thought about sitting on the bench beside her but changed his mind. That might be going too far. "The Cherokee, in Texas. I found myself in a bad way one time—out hunting meat, I went into a gully and broke my leg. By the time I made it back to where I'd left my horse, the animal had wandered away—he was a half-broke mustang, anyway, and it's their nature to keep moving."

He caught himself, fearful he might be boring her, but her eyes were so rapt and attentive that he was encouraged to go on. This was probably the way a woman was supposed to make a man feel while he was talking: as though there were nothing more important in the world than what he had to say.

"I found shelter in a hollowed-out bank," he continued, "with the nearest stream a fifty-yard crawl over rough ground and me not in any shape to search out anything better. I had my gun, but the only game I could get was whatever happened to wander up to the cave, which was precious little. I must have holed up there a week, and prospects looked mighty grim. I took fever and got so weak, I couldn't even go for water. I thought my time was about up when I opened my eyes and there was the biggest, fiercest man I'd ever seen bending over me." Elizabeth's eyes went even wider. "I thought it was delirium," Jed said, "but he picked me up, strapped me to a travois, and carried me to the Cherokee village."

He smiled a little, letting his mind travel back over that distant time. Then he told her simply, "The man's name was Sam Houston."

Elizabeth could barely contain her wonder. "And they took you in—just like that?"

Jed nodded. "Sam was a member of the tribe, the adopted son of Oo-loo-te-ka. I was welcome in his lodge, and I stayed through the winter, hunting for them and learning from them."

Elizabeth's eyes were wide, her voice almost breathless. "But—Indians are such savage creatures! Weren't you afraid?"

Jed smiled a little. "To the Cherokee we're the savages. They were living in log houses and farming the land long before the first white man set foot here. Before the Trail of Tears, when the government pushed them off their land, they owned some of the biggest plantations in Georgia and North Carolina, with slaves to work the fields and warehouses full of goods. Most people make the mistake of lumping all Indians together, confusing the Cherokee with the savage Indians in the far west. They're nothing alike at all."

A slight bitterness crossed his face, or was it sadness? He spoke almost as though to himself. "Of course, now they are living like savages, I guess, a lot of them. Crowded on small reservations, poor and hungry . . . and some of them who can't take reservation life have moved out into the wilderness, living off the land just one step ahead of the white men who'd like to round them up and push them even further. It can make a man sick inside, to see what they've come to. They're good people, better brought up and better educated than most white men, and all they want is to be left in peace."

And then he seemed to recall her presence. "That's not to say they won't fight," he added. "Fighting is a way of life to the Indian, just like it would be to anybody who's lived against the land as many generations as they have. There's some tribes that will invite you into their village, hunt with you, share their tepees, and then kill you when the notion strikes—just because that's the way they're used to living, and they feel different about killing than we do. Most times it's not too smart to trust an Indian out of your sight, because there's just no way a white man can think like they do. But the Cherokee are different. They're what the government calls civilized."

He said the word *civilized* with a slight twist to his voice, as though there were something amusing about it. But Elizabeth, with so many new ideas and grand, exciting concepts rushing through her head, did not pause to question his tone. She wanted to know more about Jed, to absorb and experience everything that made him who and what he was. She wanted to hear him talk.

She said eagerly, "You must have served with General Houston in the War for Texas Independence."

Jed nodded. "I was there before he was, of course. But when Sam came down to take over the command, we rode together from Goliad to San Jacinto."

Elizabeth could hardly believe it. A real war hero, in every way as exciting and glamorous as Margaret's own General Houston . . . but a dozen times more appealing to the eye. She would have asked more about the war, but he tactfully changed the subject.

"That's how I got into ranching," he said. "After the war Sam needed cattle to feed the army, so some of us started rounding up the wild steers that were roaming about. It turned out, though, that there were more cattle than men to feed on them, so I ended up keeping my share, to sell."

"So you have your own ranch?" An independent businessman, not unlike her own papa in that respect. The possibilities were broadening.

"Just a small spread," Jed agreed modestly. "Not much to speak of."

She suggested, "It must be very well-run for you to be able to leave it alone. What brought you back to Alabama?"

Jed hesitated for just a moment. There was an aura of unreality about all of it—Elizabeth Coleman in her rose silk dress sitting before him alone in the garden, talking to him, her moss-green eyes, wide and intent, turned up to him. He knew he should say good night and put this place behind him as fast as he could. And he knew he wasn't about to do any such thing.

He answered, "I got word that my pa had died."

"Oh." Her sympathy was quick and genuine. "I am so sorry."

"That's all right. He'd been gone a year before I got back here. He was a good Christian man," he added simply, "and he did his best with what he had, which is about all you can ask, I guess. Trouble was, he never had much to do with." He forced his eyes to wander away from her, sitting so pretty and proper before him, her hands folded in her lap, her skirts draping gracefully to the grass, her eyes upturned and filled with interest. He had never known a woman could be so alluring just sitting there. And all he could think about was how close he had come to kissing her that morning.

"Anyway," he finished, "I had in mind to sell what was left of the farm and put it into my ranch, and I met up with Sam on the way across. He wanted me to come along today, so I did." He allowed his eyes to wander back to her, and she was smiling.

"I'm awfully glad you did," she said softly, and the way she said it made Jed's heart jump. She sounded as though she meant it.

Jed glanced at her, the beginning of a smile on his lips. "You didn't look so glad when you saw me this afternoon."

She blushed. "I . . . was surprised. I never thought to see you again."

Her eyes seemed to be filled with a hint of something—a plea for understanding, a sharing of wonder, even an invitation. Whatever it was, it made Jed's throat tight; his half smile faded, and his voice grew a little husky as he answered, "I didn't think I'd see you again, either."

There was a silence, and then the soft song of a lone cricket. The voices in the garden, the rustling movements, seemed farther away. A lamp went on in the window across the way and cast a misty beam of dim yellow light across the path, near to where she sat. Jed thought he'd better suggest she go inside. But he wanted to look at her for just a little while longer.

She said, almost reluctantly, "I suppose people have been asking you all day to tell them about the West. It must be tiresome for you." She hoped he would deny it, for she wanted to hear everything—everything about him and the life he had led; she wanted just to hear the sound of his voice.

Jed answered, "There's no point in a man going wandering if he can't bring back what he's learned to other folks. In the West the only things we know are what other people tell us. If there's a war party on the border or a poison water hole in the canyon, you need to know it, so you listen and you talk. It's a man's duty. Same for the folks back East. How're they going to know unless somebody tells them?"

Elizabeth said, almost breathless with the promise of adventure to come, "Will you tell me about Texas?"

Jed couldn't imagine why a pretty girl like her would want to hear about the frontier, but there was nothing he wanted to do more in the world than talk to her. It didn't matter what about.

He took a step forward and sat down beside her. Once it was done, it didn't seem so bad. He made sure he was far enough away so that the full folds of her skirt did not even brush his leg. But even so, he could catch the trail of her perfume . . . warm and sweeter than roses.

He said, "In East Texas, where I staked my claim, it's not so much different from here, to look at. There's trees and flowers and rolling hills and creeks that bubble out from under rocks with the sweetest water you ever did taste . . . but it's big. Bigger than you can even think of. It's the air, I guess, with not so many people clogging it up, but when you look at the sky, it seems to go on forever, and it's a blue like you've never seen before. And at night, camped out on a hillside, the moon seems to take up half the sky and the stars are so close, it looks like you could just reach out and scoop up a handful.''

Jed forgot that he wasn't much with words and that he didn't know how to talk to women. He listened to the lazy chirp of the crickets, felt her warmth beside him, savored her perfume mingling with the scent of roses, and he talked because it felt natural and good.

''It's a wild place, though. Nothing manicured about it. The towns are mighty few and far between, and all it takes to call a place a town is a saloon or maybe a trading post. Mostly it's a land fit for what it's got—longhorn steers, mustangs, bears, and Indians. The white man is still an intruder, though we've been there and settling heavy for nigh on to a hundred years.''

''It sounds . . .'' Elizabeth struggled for the right words, her imagination racing. ''Exciting,'' she said, but the word was inadequate. The land he spoke of was as unique as the man himself.

Jed chuckled. ''I guess you could say that,'' he agreed.

The glance she cast his way seemed peculiarly coy. ''And the women in Texas—are they pretty?''

Jed wanted to turn that into a compliment, to tell her that nothing and no one had ever been as pretty as she was, but he felt clumsy even trying to form the words. So he simply answered, ''The women in Texas are mighty few and far between, ma'am.''

Her smooth, white brow knitted a little, and Jed watched the expression with fascination. ''Mrs. Lea is planning to make the journey, you know. I overheard Lord Hartley telling her it would be perfectly safe.''

The last thing Jed wanted to do was to dispute Hartley's

word, especially on a subject that didn't concern him. "I was talking about the frontier," he explained. "Now you take Galveston—its a fair-sized little town and there's families there, though I wouldn't exactly say it's a place for a proper lady to live. But mostly, as you move away from the coast, you're moving into wilderness. Some settlers, they bring their wives and try to raise a family, but it's a rough land and . . ." He started to say that not many of them survived but thought that might be too blunt. Instead he finished by saying, "Most females don't cotton to it. It's not much of a life for a woman."

"I wouldn't care," Elizabeth said softly, her eyes glowing with the deep conviction of a rampant imagination. "It sounds like the grandest adventure that could ever befall a woman. I would go in an instant if I had the chance." And already, in the back of her mind, an idea was forming. Miss Nancy was going to Texas. She had already refused Margaret permission to go. Perhaps if Elizabeth was very, very good, if she was a model of deportment and the sweetest of companions . . . if Papa could be gotten around and Miss Nancy persuaded . . .

Jed looked at her, wondering what was going on behind that prettily wrinkled brow. Somehow during their conversation she had moved closer, or he had. Her skirts were folded against his thigh, and he imagined—it made his stomach go tight—that he could almost feel the press of a small knee. He could see the soft rise and fall of her chest, the creamy skin just above the gentle swell of her breasts, and he almost thought he could feel the brush of her breath, she was so close.

Her hair glinted in the light from the window in the same way moonlight shines on the wing of a crow as it dips toward a stream. He wondered what it would feel like to the touch, and he had to close his fist at his side to keep from finding out. She was so incredibly close, her eyes so bright and her face so avid and intent upon him, he had to look away. But he could not make himself stand up. He wanted to kiss her. He had wanted to do nothing else almost since the moment he had met her.

Elizabeth could sense the change in atmosphere between them, and though she could not define it, her heart beat a little faster in unconscious recognition of it. She knew nothing of men, but she knew that by sitting with him like this in the shelter of the fragrant, obliquely lit garden, she was more aware than she ever had been of what was meant by the word *masculine*. The awareness made her feel weak inside, fluttery and uncertain, yet excited and anxious, like she had felt as a small girl on Christmas morning.

She didn't even notice it was growing dark, much less realize that if they were discovered, her circumstances could in no way be explained as proper no matter how innocently they had begun. She only thought that she wanted to stay with him, to experience his big, bold presence, and to cautiously explore the excitement that hovered just out of reach like the promise of a wondrous surprise. Yet part of what she sensed in the changing of his mood was restlessness. The silence between them had been going on too long and was becoming uncomfortable. He was only being polite by sitting with her. What was it Miss Nancy had said? "A lady never puts herself forward. . . ."

She said, reluctantly, dropping her eyes, "But I'm boring you, keeping you here talking about yourself."

The last thing she was doing was boring him. He could have sat for days doing nothing but watching the way her lashes formed perfect little crescents of shadow on her ivory cheekbones, but Jed did not know how to tell her that. So he said only what was polite. "No ma'am. You're not boring me at all."

From inside, the first lilting strains of a waltz drifted out and Elizabeth knew that soon she would be missed. But the evening had only begun, and leaving this secluded romantic garden did not mean all was lost. Once they went inside, he would surely ask her to dance and perhaps even take her in to supper.

She got to her feet, smiling demurely. "But you are only being kind. You have come to a party and I am keeping you from it. See, the music has started, and I know you are anxious to go in and join the dancing."

Jed stood immediately as she did, and his heart had begun to pound with something like alarm at the thought of her leaving. That was foolish. He should have left long ago. He should leave now, before he started looking at her and thinking things she made it entirely too easy for a man to think. . . .

He smiled and found himself admitting, "No, ma'am. I don't know how to dance." He wondered if he should offer to walk her back to the house or simply say his good-byes here and now. He tried not to think about how long it would be before he saw such as she again.

Elizabeth looked at him, astonished. "You don't know how?"

Jed's smile deepened just a fraction at the corner. She made it sound as though he had just confessed to not knowing how to strike a match or tie a knot. "Not the kind they're doing in there," he qualified. "Not much call for it where I come from."

Well. That did put a crimp in her plans. How could he ask her to dance if he didn't know how? Her brow furrowed thoughtfully and then cleared with inspiration. "It's quite simple," she volunteered. "I could teach you in a moment."

Jed took an automatic step backward. "I don't think—"

But what could he do when he felt the touch of her soft, warm hands on both of his, when she stepped toward him, looking so flushed and childishly confident? Try as he might, he could not find a way to say no, nor even a reason for it.

Elizabeth had practiced the steps with Margaret and Antoinette for hours on end in the schoolroom. Sometimes they practiced what they had learned with the neighbor boys under the shade tree, and she had absolutely no doubt of her ability to teach this man to dance.

"All you do," she instructed him easily, "is take my hand, like so...and place your other hand here..." She clasped one of his large, rough hands in hers, at some distance from her shoulder, and guided the other to her waist, intent upon the music. "The rhythm is very simple, step-slide-turn, step-slide-turn, just let the music guide you. Are you ready?"

Jed felt her small white hand, swallowed in the largeness of his. Her tightly corsetted waist was beneath the fingers of his other hand, and the brush of her skirts was against his knees. His throat was so tight, he could barely swallow. He nodded.

Elizabeth became suddenly aware of how very large he was, how rough and powerful was the hand that held hers. They touched at no part except their joined hands and his fingers, tenuous and light upon her waist, for her other hand swept up her train and held it away from her body. They stood almost two feet apart. Yet he was close, so close, and his eyes were shaded and strangely lit. Her heart was beating madly. For a moment, standing there with him, her thoughts careened dizzily and the night seemed to throb with promise. And then, quickly, giving him a faint and tenuous smile, she moved into the steps of the dance.

He was not prepared, and even if he had been, he doubted if he could have remembered what she had told him barely two seconds before. His clumsy feet stumbled, and so did hers, and they fell against each other. She laughed, and so did he, as his hands came down to steady her. Jed never knew what possessed him to do it. Perhaps a man never does.

She was looking up at him, her eyes sparkling and her lips parted with laughter. His hands were on her bare arms, her breasts were brushing his chest, and he bent his head and kissed her.

Elizabeth had read about it, dreamed about it, talked about it—but never had she imagined it would be like this. His arm came around her waist, his hand lightly cupped her bare shoulder, his lips covered hers, and it was as though everything she had ever known in familiarity about the world were suddenly cut loose and set adrift.

The night faded; the music died into a dim and heady roaring in her ears. Something was released within her—a gush of awareness, terror, excitement—a warm, melting sweetness that whirled and danced and blocked out all else. His lips were upon hers, soft, heated, strange, invading her senses with alien tastes and scents and sensations. His body was hard and large and enfolding her with a peculiar gentleness that made her feel as though her muscles and bones were melting into the shape of him. Her heart pounded and her breath grew shallow and she was trembling, helplessly, all over. He was kissing her, and it felt wonderfully, gloriously, like dying.

Jed knew he should stop. With every passing thud of his heart he intended to stop. He tried to remember who she was, and who he was, and he could not believe that he held this beautiful creature in his arms. Her perfume—sweet, warm, intoxicating—invaded every pore of his body, heating his skin, pounding through his blood. She was so soft, and he was so weak. Her lips, her smooth skin against his fingertips, her breasts pressing into his chest, the tiny waist . . . the rustle of silk and the taste of strawberries. He tried to stop, but his blood was thrumming and his head was spinning, and he did not know how he would ever be able to stop.

Arousal, hot and heavy and unpreventable, flooded through his veins and swelled in his loins, drugging him. She was a lady and he should not be feeling this way, thinking these things. He should not even be touching her. But flames were growing, helpless excitement and heady desire, and all he could do was hold her, taste her, feel her against him as reason fast slipped away. He was ashamed, but he was ensnared. It took all the will at his command to lift his face, to step away.

He was breathing hard, and his skin was on fire. That this innocent, lovely creature could do that to him . . . Her face was flushed, her lips swollen from his, her eyes luminescent. He could see the rise and fall of her chest, the little tendrils of hair that clung to her newly dampened cheeks. He wanted to touch her face, to smooth her hair, to draw her against him and taste her lips again . . . and he knew that if he did, he would never stop.

So, with an effort, he took his hands away from her. He said, somewhat unevenly, "You'd best be getting inside now."

Elizabeth nodded, barely able to whisper a response. "Yes."

She could have no idea what a temptation she was, standing there so close, breathing so shallowly, looking at him. Deliberately Jed closed his mind, refused his instincts. He said, "Good-bye, Miss Elizabeth. It's been . . . a real pleasure meeting you." He lowered his eyes and moved quickly past her onto the path.

Elizabeth turned just in time to see his figure disappear into the shadows, and she called, "Good night, Mr. Fielding."

She stood in a sort of dazed wonder, her fingertips pressed lightly to her lips, a warm and incredible joy pulsing through her veins and stunning her senses, until Margaret's voice, calling out to her, jolted Elizabeth back to her senses. She made repairs to her appearance but knew there was no way she could hide her wonderful secret as she followed her friend back inside.

It wasn't until much later that evening that she realized Jed Fielding had not said good night. He had said good-bye.

CHAPTER
Five

J ed stood with his foot propped up on the ship's railing, looking out over the landing. It was a warm spring day, and the planks of the deck, heated by the sun, felt warm beneath his moccasined feet. His gaze was absent, but there was a soberness in him. He knew that he was, in all likelihood, seeing it all for the last time.

Captain Mercer Chapman leaned his elbow against the rail beside Jed and followed his gaze to the landing below. He was a big, florid-faced man, easy-moving despite his bulk. His window on the world was the run from Mobile to Galveston, but through it he absorbed a store of knowledge that could fill a history text. He never tired of watching the endless flow of passengers and reading their stories in their faces.

He inquired of Jed now, casually, "How long are you going to be gone for?"

Jed replied, not glancing around, "Forever, I guess."

He had been cooling his heels in Mobile for two weeks, waiting for the steamship to Galveston, and he had had a chance to do a lot of things for the last time. He had slept in a bed with a feather mattress, eaten food that wasn't of his own cooking, sat in taverns and listened to men talk about what was going on in New Orleans and Philadelphia and Richmond. He had bought himself a newspaper and a new set of clothes and a good leather hat to keep the Texas sun and rain out of his eyes. He had stocked up on foodstuffs and dry goods to take back to the ranch, and enough ammunition to make the store clerk look at him suspiciously. In the afternoons he had sat in front of the dry-goods store and listened to the talk and watched the pretty girls go by. And he had done a lot of thinking.

If there was one thing this trip had taught him, it was that he wasn't meant for a place like this. All of his life Jed had dreamed of cottonfields, thoroughbred horses, white-columned mansions. He had left here vowing that someday it would all be his; he had returned to discover that this was not what he had ever really wanted at all. He didn't belong here, and he was ready to go home.

Jed's reply did not surprise Chapman. He knew a frontiersman when he saw one, and it had to do with more than the way a man dressed. He commented, "You look like a born-and-bred Texian."

Jed answered, "No. I was born here in Alabama, but I reckon Texas is my home now." It occurred to him what a pity it was, that he had spent all those years yearning for something he didn't even want. Texas was his home, and the childhood dreams had lost their appeal.

The captain chuckled. "Went West to seek your fortune, eh?"

"Yep."

"Did you find it?"

Jed felt a grin of ruefulness tug reluctantly at his lips. He had set out ten years ago to make his fortune, all right, and he had always figured that by now he would be living in a fine house like the one at Spring Hill. Now he realized how much happier he was with what he did have.

He had a log cabin in the Texas wilderness, and most of his possessions he could carry on his back—a Kentucky long rifle, a bowie knife, and a Patterson Colt five-shooter that Sam Houston had brought back from the States last year. He had twelve dollars left from the sale of the farm after putting the rest into supplies for the ranch. He wouldn't exactly call that a fortune by anybody's standards.

But he answered, "I guess I found what I was looking for."

Because, Jed realized now, he had more than what could be added up in a tally book. What he had might not seem like much to most folks, but it was a start better than his pa had had, and there was room to grow. His was the life of the future, and he had no regrets.

He was a man of the plains and valleys, the wooded slopes and sweeping canyons. He had walked the path of the wolf and slept where the eagle nested, and he would never be able to come back here. He had no patience with the foolishness and fripperies of William Bledsoe's world; he wasn't meant to while away his days in polite conversation and his evenings over a glass of imported wine. He had no place among the conventions of the society of Southern gentlemen, nor the gentle beauty of the aristocratic lady, like Miss Elizabeth. He knew that now.

"You're lucky, then," commented the captain soberly. "Most of 'em don't."

"Reckon that's because they don't know what they're looking for."

"Life out West can get lonely," Chapman said. " 'Bout as lonely as life at sea."

Jed nodded.

"Kind of scarce on females, aren't they?" Chapman asked.

"Not too many women can take the life out there."

"I reckon so," the captain answered.

Jed thought best about women when there were no women around, and now, from a distance, he understood it all quite clearly. Elizabeth Coleman was a fantasy, a symbol of something too good to be true, the living representation of a man's most treasured childhood dreams.

Oh, Miss Elizabeth was a fine woman. She knew how to waltz and which fork to use at the dinner table. A glimpse of her smile could set his heart to pounding, and the softness of her movements were like poetry to watch. But on the frontier there was precious little time for waltzing, and most people ate with a knife, if they could find that. A pretty woman was a fine thing to look at, but looks meant little when there was game to be skinned and firewood to be cut and rows to be plowed. Jed knew all that, and he tried not to be sorry he had walked away.

But he couldn't seem to get her out of his mind.

The captain said, "Worst part about being at sea is not having a woman. Guess it's not too different for you."

Jed glanced at him. "You a married man?"

The captain shook his head. "Never got around to it. Many's the time I wished I had."

Jed nodded. It was a bad thing for a man to be alone. Nature had never intended it to be that way, and Jed was more conscious of this fact now than he had ever been in his life. A man could spend all his years learning and growing, building and improving; he could map out the mountain and learn the ways of the buffalo, he could tame the land and build his fortune; but what good was any of it if he had no one to leave his knowledge to, no one to share his accomplishments with? He would die, and all that he was, all that he had gained, would die with him. A man was nothing until he had a woman to walk by his side and sons to follow in his footsteps.

He was twenty-five years old, and most of those years had been spent just trying to keep himself alive. He hadn't spent much time thinking about a wife, a family, or needing such things. But since meeting Elizabeth, he hadn't thought much of anything else.

"Takes a special kind of woman," Jed agreed thoughtfully, "to live with men like us."

Where would Jed find a woman willing to live the type of life he had chosen? Across the Sabine there were tavern girls and squaws, sometimes a loose-skirted señorita in the borderlands, but no decent women living alone. No marrying women. And back East . . . well, back East there was Elizabeth.

"Just like it takes a special kind of man to live like we do."

Jed nodded. "It's not everybody that's cut out for it."

Chapman squinted his eyes against the sun. "Hell, I've seen 'em all," he answered. "They go West thinking it's going to be an adventure, something exciting to write home about. They hear about the free land, the buffalo plains, the beaver creeks, and their blood gets all stirred up and nothing can keep 'em at home. What they don't think about is the storms that can shake the prairie or the silence that can drive a man mad. They don't think about the Comanche or the dust or dying of thirst ten feet from a water hole. I've seen 'em come and go, all kinds. Some come back broken men; sometimes all that's left is a few possessions to ferry back to the widow.

"Now you take them two over there." Chapman nodded to Jed's fellow travelers, who were standing on the upper deck, gazing out toward the sea. "Peterson there, he's got him a nice little business in Galveston. Storekeeper, taking back goods for his shop. He's doing just fine, 'cause he sticks to what he knows. Wouldn't be surprised but he turns up a rich man someday, the way Galveston's growing.

"But that whey-faced little pilgrim, the schoolteacher. I'll lay you American dollars to Navy beans he left a little gal behind somewhere, maybe even a wife and kids, and he's got it in his mind that the West has the answer to all his problems. We'll be seeing that one next in a pine box."

Jed nodded. He, too, had seen them come and go. The schoolteacher had the mark of death on him so clear, he could almost smell it. He felt sorry for him, in the vague way he did for all pilgrims, but it was basically none of his concern. Jed had problems of his own.

Both men's attention was drawn then to the sound of an approaching carriage. "Well, then, that's the last of them," said Chapman, grinning. "Best paying too. I'd better get ready to cast off."

He walked up deck, and Jed watched the arrival of the last group of passengers.

Jed had not known any others would be traveling to Galveston this trip, but when the carriage drew up at the landing, followed by a wagon loaded with trunks, he mentally adjusted his own space on the small steamer to make room for a crowd. It looked like a family, and from the amount of luggage they were carting, there were womenfolk along. He could see Sam Houston's hand in this and allowed himself a brief flash of irritation at his friend. The way Houston had been preaching, the Pearly Gates lay just the other side of the Sabine, and he was a damn convincing man. Before long every sodbuster and fancy-talking stick-walker with a penny in his pocket would be pouring across the border.

Jed's attention sharpened as a familiar figure climbed out of the carriage, and a flicker of amusement deepened the corner of his mouth. It was William Bledsoe, pretty as a picture in fawn breeches and a blue satin stock tied in a bow. Sam had worked even faster than Jed had thought. The figure alighting beside Bledsoe was none other than Charles Edgecomb, Lord Hartley, resplendent in tailored blue wool and mirror-bright boots. For a moment Jed's amusement faltered, then deepened. He didn't know why he was surprised. It was shaping up to be one hell of a trip.

They hadn't noticed him yet, and Jed did not go out of his way to draw their attention. His ribs had begun to ache dully with a peculiar, suspended question as he focused his eyes on the remaining two occupants of the closed carriage. He could see the shape of two bonnets inside, and there was no reason for him to think that one of them might belong to a young girl with dark hair and green eyes. Even Bledsoe would not be such a fool as to bring a young girl on a trip like this. What reason would he have for doing so? It was insane. It was impossible. And it only went to show how badly she had addled his thinking, to imagine . . .

Without realizing it, he held his breath as Miss Nancy Lea took the proffered hand of Lord Hartley and stepped from the carriage. Bledsoe had noticed Jed now and lifted a hand in greeting, but Jed did not respond. His eyes were fixed on the carriage, on the small gloved hand that was placed in Lord Hartley's, and finally on the slim, delicate figure of Miss Elizabeth Coleman as she stepped down lightly onto the muddy pier.

He watched as Bledsoe gave orders to hefty black men regarding the disposal of the luggage. Finally, with feet that felt as though they weighed twice as much as they were supposed to, Jed went forward to greet the newly arrived party.

"Well, Mr. Fielding, what a pleasant surprise!" Bledsoe's hand clasp was enthusiastic, his beaming smile genuine. "Mr. Houston didn't mention you'd be taking this ship. What a reassurance to know we'll not be traveling to Texas completely on our own recourse. You remember my mother-in-law, Mrs. Lea."

Jed nodded politely. "Pleasure to see you again, ma'am."

Mrs. Lea returned his greeting with an aristocratic coolness in her eyes that belied her wilted, overheated appearance in her widow's garb. She didn't actively dislike Jed, he knew; frostiness was just part of her breeding.

"And Miss Elizabeth Coleman..."

Jed met Elizabeth's eyes but just for a moment. Her cheeks went hot, and her eyelashes dropped when he said, "Miss Coleman." She murmured something so softly that he didn't hear it.

Jed knew he should look away, just as she did, but no amount of strength of will could compel his eyes not to linger. Just standing beside her was like bathing in a shower of summer rain after a long drought, feeling droplets of new life sting through layers of dust and neglect, awakening dormant senses that were aching with thirst. He looked at her, but she refused to look at him. The things they were trying not to think about were so loud between them, they practically throbbed. For two weeks Jed had done nothing but think about her, fantasize about her, wish for her. And now that she was here, he wished to be anywhere else.

Forcing his eyes away felt like the hardest thing he'd ever had to do, and when he looked up, Hartley was smiling at him. It was a lazy expression that had nothing to do with friendliness. He said, "Somehow, Mr. Fielding, I was sure our paths would cross again. But I didn't think it would be so soon."

The Cherokee had a saying: The path of the enemy never wanders far from your own. Jed had learned to count on that for a fact. He answered with the English equivalent and with a negligence that disguised his suddenly increased wariness: "Small world." He turned back to Bledsoe. "I didn't know you folks would be making the trip so soon."

"Lord Hartley has urgent business there," replied Bledsoe, little to Jed's surprise. The man had an empire to build, and he was not one to waste time. "Naturally we were glad to move our own plans forward a bit."

None of that explained why Elizabeth was there. Jed forced himself not to look at her. "Rough trip for women-folk," he commented.

Bledsoe looked surprised. "Why, we were assured it was quite safe. After all, Galveston is but a short distance from here, and I understand steamers navigate the Trinity quite regularly. We anticipate no difficulty."

Jed said nothing, but he was sure Sam Houston hadn't given them that advice. His eyes slid toward Hartley and then moved back to Bledsoe.

Jed said, "I guess the ladies will want to get to their cabins." He caught the attention of the steward, who escorted the ladies toward their somewhat primitive accommodations.

Only when her back was to him did Jed dare look at Elizabeth again, and then he didn't seem to be able to look away. He filled his eyes with her shape, the flow of the pale gray traveling suit over her shoulders, the tiny waist, the flash of a kid slipper as she lifted her skirt to step over a coil of rope. She walked without seeming to move at all, even on the uncertain deck, and she held her head up high. He had always admired a woman who held her head up.

Bledsoe had stepped over to speak with the pilot, and Jed

and Hartley were left alone. Elizabeth disappeared behind the bulwark, and Jed let his eyes wander back to Hartley. As far as he was concerned, they didn't have anything else to say to each other, but he could see Hartley disagreed. So Jed leaned his arm on the rail, propped his foot on a keg of nails, and waited.

Hartley said mildly, "I can't help but think how fortuitous it is, our meeting like this. I don't like to leave things unresolved."

As a matter of fact, neither did Jed. Outside of Comanche territory, he had never gotten in the habit of sleeping with his finger on the trigger, and he wasn't inclined to start now. But something had begun between them that afternoon in Bledsoe's library that would be a long time in settling, and that little prickling feeling of trouble ahead was nagging at Jed's scalp again.

Jed looked at the other man for a long time. He said simply, "It's a pity."

Hartley was caught off-guard momentarily. Caution showed in his eyes. "What is?"

"A man like you." Jed let his eyes wander back to the landing where the last of the newly arrived luggage was being hefted toward the gangplank. "Smart, book-educated, not afraid to take chances—the West could use men like you, I reckon." Absently Jed plucked out a strand of hemp from the anchor line and tossed it overboard. "But the way things are going, you're not going to live long enough to be much use to anybody."

Hartley quickened and his eyes narrowed. "Was that a threat?"

"Nope." Jed looked back to him mildly. "Just a fact. A man goes looking for trouble, he's bound to find it. And in a place like Texas, trouble comes in big doses." The sun glinted in his eyes, and the breeze whipped a lock of hair over his forehead. Jed's expression was calm, his stance relaxed. He added, "It comes to me that the best thing that could happen to you would be for you to stay out of Texas altogether."

Hartley chuckled. "You can get that idea out of your head, Mr. Fielding. I've got two hundred thousand acres of Texas land, and there I intend to stay."

Jed only smiled. "Well, you're not there yet. And them coupons of yours aren't worth the paper they're written on until somebody puts down a stake."

"You needn't fear for that, sir," replied Hartley carelessly. His heavy eyes, crinkled with the sun, were as cold as ice. "I know what I'm about."

"I'm sure you do," answered Jed smoothly.

Hartley said nothing, and the two men stood and looked at each other for a long time. Hartley was the first to turn, stiffly and silently, and Jed watched him walk away. When he was out of sight, Jed turned to gaze back out over the railing, but he was no longer looking at the activity on the landing they were about to leave behind. His eyes were turned toward the sea that awaited them, and his thoughts were on Elizabeth Coleman.

CHAPTER
Six

The ship was small, built to transport both cargo and passengers, but neither one in comfort. Most of the cargo was stored on deck, crates sometimes piled higher than the pilothouse, but personal belongings were protected in the hold below. There were two rows of cabins with doors opening into the main cabin that separated them, where meals were served and passengers might mingle. Elizabeth and Miss Nancy were fortunate, by standards of the day, to have private cabins, each small, dark, claustrophobic, and barely bigger than a bandbox. The men were not allowed aft of the mid-ship gangway and either shared cramped communal sleeping quarters or slept on deck. There was nothing glamorous about steamship travel, but no one had promised her there would be, and Elizabeth was so dazzled by all that had happened to her in such a short time, she barely noticed the discomforts.

The sun had set an hour earlier, and Elizabeth was standing on deck, rocking with the motion of the ship, gazing out over the silvery wake left by the paddles in the dark fabric of the sea, listening to the throb of her own heartbeat. He was here. Jed Fielding was here, and tonight she would be with him.

If ever she had doubted the nature of what was happening to her, she did no longer. Like a modern-day Galahad, Jed Fielding had swept into her life, inspiring fancy, lodging in her dreams. By all reason what she should have expected to be no more than a brief interlude from a storybook had turned into more, and he had come into her life again. He had kissed her. He had left her, but sweet providence, as it always had done, had conspired to bring them together again.

She had not known he would be on this ship. She had hoped, she had prayed, but how could she have been certain? When, by gentle suggestion, subtle hinting, and perhaps just a bit of wheedling, Elizabeth had persuaded Miss Nancy that she would be the most desirable of companions for the journey west, especially since neither of her own daughters wanted to or could go—and when, by judicious use of wit, reasoning, and tears, she had convinced Papa that the trip would not only be educational, but also that she would in fact be doing him a favor by representing his interests in Texas, Elizabeth had not dared to dream she might meet Jed again. She had had nothing more in mind but that she would at least be allowed to see the land of which Jed had talked. Perhaps, deep in her most secret longings, she had even thought that, if the good Lord were willing, they might meet again, in Texas. But Texas was a big land, and how could she have known?

But the Lord had been willing, and Jed was here. She

could not deny, even had she desired to do so, what was meant to be.

What she had done was bold, far too bold for one as gently reared as Elizabeth, and if Miss Nancy found out she would have Elizabeth confined to her cabin for the rest of the voyage. Elizabeth shivered a little and pulled her shawl more tightly about her shoulders, almost regretting her impetuosity. But what else was she to have done? Life had taught her little of matters of the heart, and she knew only what she felt. She had to see him again.

The ship's timbers creaked and groaned, the throb of the steam engine and the rhythmic rush of ocean in its wake seemed to mimic the dry and anxious pounding of Elizabeth's heart. What would she say to him? Had he guessed already how she felt, or would he think it brash of her to have sent him that note? Would he come at all?

She knew that there were men who could engage in unspeakable intimacies with a woman and never give it a second thought—at least that was what she had garnered from some of the more risque novels in her father's library— but those were men of bestial appetites, amoral rogues and evil devils, and Jed Fielding was not like that. Of course he thought of her. He would never have kissed her had he not felt for her as she felt for him. Then why had he left her?

She should not have sent him that note. She should never have asked a gentleman to meet her on the deck of a ship after dark. It had sounded so dashing and romantic at the time, but she was sure now it was a dreadful mistake. A lady never puts herself forward. He would look upon her with contempt. She would never be able to meet his eyes again. And he might not come at all.

But she could not make herself turn and go back to her cabin.

Elizabeth lifted her eyes helplessly to the inky sky, and

then she caught her breath. A single star hung suspended against the vastness, twinkling courageously. Sam Houston's Texas, the lone star of which he spoke so eloquently. Slowly, as she looked at it, she felt a stillness creep through her, a warmth and a certainty. The ship climbed a swell, and in the distance a night fish jumped; from inside the main cabin she heard a burst of masculine laughter. But Elizabeth's eyes were fixed on that star, and within her a glorious calm grew. It was an answer written on the heavens by the hand of providence, a sign to guide her fate and soothe her anxious spirit. It was her destiny. Texas . . . and Jed Fielding, the man she was going to marry.

She did not hear the footstep behind her. There was no breath, no movement, no small sound to warn of his approach. He was simply there, his strong dark hands resting on the rail beside hers, his warm shadow falling over her, his solid presence registering in the quickening of her pulse and the sudden shallowness of her breath. And for a long time he did not speak or look at her.

And when the words came, they were not at all what she expected. He said, gazing out over the frothy sea, "You must read a lot of books, Miss Elizabeth."

She had not realized it would be so hard to speak. Her eyes went to him, startled. "I—why— What makes you say that?" she managed.

Jed pulled out the folded note. Her penmanship, spidery and flowery, had been hard to read for a man unused to letters, but he had only to see the single initial *E.*—which doubtless she had meant to be cryptic—to know the content and the motivation. The note had made his muscles tighten and his palms grow heated, but he had had no intention of obeying its summons. He had folded it into his pocket knowing he shouldn't even keep it, and he had determined to put it—and her—out of his mind. And at the first opportunity he had left the others to their cigars and their cards and he had come out on deck.

He offered the note to her now, and he said gently, "That was a foolish thing, Miss Elizabeth. You shouldn't be meeting with me like this."

The folded square of pale blue paper held her scent and words written by her own hand, and he was sorry to have to return it. But that was what he had come for, he told himself. To return it and to advise her to go back to her cabin. Then why was he standing here with his eyes fixed upon the curve of her delicate white neck? Why was he breathing a bit more deeply, as though trying to draw in the whisper of her perfume one more time?

Elizabeth slowly took the paper he offered between thumb and forefinger, and their hands never brushed. Her thoughts were racing and colliding, and she was afraid he would notice the way her fingers were trembling. Anxiety fluttered in her throat, but alertness, quick and hot and poignant, flowed through her veins. She said with as much steadiness as she could manage, "I don't . . . understand what that has to do with reading books, Mr. Fielding."

He measured his words, trying to be kind. Didn't she have any idea what she was doing? It all had been fine and good, to look back upon the memory of a kiss and remember a pretty girl in a rose garden. But she was here, tempting him with everything at her disposal, and he couldn't allow himself to get caught up in her fantasy again.

He said carefully, "I don't mean to sound hard, but a lot of times things sound good in books that turn out to be pure foolishness. And seems like sending that note might have been one of them."

Elizabeth swallowed hard, and her hand closed around the paper and tightened on the rail. With an effort she said, "So you think I am foolish."

"No, ma'am." His voice was low and gentle and touched with the softness of that easy drawl that seemed to make her heart expand in her chest whenever he spoke. "I think sometimes you do foolish things. But then, don't we all?"

Was he thinking about the night in the rose garden? She ventured a glance at him, but his face, turned now to gaze out over the ocean again, was still and unreadable. She wondered, if she touched it, whether his skin would be as hard as it looked. His lips had not been hard. . . .

She said, perhaps a bit too quickly, "I get the impression you think all of us are a bit foolish, Mr. Fielding. For coming on this trip, I mean."

He looked at her. How tiny she was, even smaller than he remembered. He answered, talking to keep himself from thinking about how alone they were and how close she was. "I was surprised. Why did you come?"

To be with you. To see you again. . . . Because it was my destiny to walk where you had walked and love what you have loved. . . . "Mrs. Lea . . . needed a companion" was all she could manage, and she lowered her eyes briefly. "Her own daughters were . . . disinclined to make the journey, and I . . . wanted to see Texas."

A faint smile softened his features only fractionally. Even though it was half cynical and very brief, it was to Elizabeth beautiful. *You remember,* she thought on a rising breath of hope. *You do remember how it was in the rose garden. You have not forgotten me.*

"I hope you won't be sorry," he said. He wondered if all those things he had said about Texas had influenced her to come. He tried to remember what they were, but he could not remember anything about that night except how it had felt when her lips were beneath his and his arms were holding her. "The frontier is not a very hospitable place for delicate ladies like you . . . and Mrs. Lea,'' he remembered to add.

Why was he standing here, prolonging the torture like this? He shouldn't be talking to her at all. If he had any sense at all, he'd go back inside right now and tell Mr. Bledsoe to keep his ward locked up for the rest of the trip. She was far too great a danger to be allowed to run loose like this.

''I shan't mind.'' Her voice was barely a breath, for her throat seemed to be growing smaller. His hand was just an inch from hers on the rail, and his arm almost brushed her shoulder. Tonight he was wearing a broadcloth jacket that looked new, but obviously it was not tailor-made. The breadth of his muscular upper arm was plainly outlined by the too-tight material.

She moved her eyes away, back to the length of his hand so near to hers. There were calluses on his palm and fingertips, she remembered, but the back was smooth, strong-boned, and lean. She knew every ridge and pad on that hand, as one might commit to memory the map of a longed-for and faraway place. She almost could feel its warmth.

From inside the cabin, someone coughed. The ship rolled and swayed, and Elizabeth tasted sea salt on her lips. The gentle, steady wind gusted slightly and fluttered her shawl away from her skirts. Jed's eyes followed the movement.

She said, touching her tongue lightly to her lips again, ''When we get to Galveston, will your route be different from ours?''

''Yes, ma'am. I'll be going up the Brazos, on a smaller ship. You folks will likely take the Trinity.''

''I see.'' That tightening began in her chest again. Three days and their paths would part. Didn't he understand what that meant? Couldn't he hear the pounding of her heart, even from where he stood?

She looked at him and tried with all her might to control the shallowness of breath that weakened her voice and affected her reason. His hair, thick and lustrous, waved away from his face at the temples to fall heavily over his collar, seemed almost silver in the night.

Her voice seemed very small as she said, forcing her eyes to look away, "That's . . . unfortunate. I think we would all feel more comfortable . . . were you to accompany us to our destination."

Jed looked at her, surprised by the sudden jerking in his chest with the mere possibility. To stay in her company for weeks, to travel with her, to protect her, to hear the sound of her voice and watch her gentle movements . . . It would be insane. He would be insane to consider it, even if it was possible. Look what she was doing to him, in just these few minutes alone under the starlight. . . .

He answered, "I've got a ranch waiting for me, and some good friends depending on me to bring back supplies. Besides," he added, though it grated him to say it, "Hartley knows the country."

"Yes, of course." She dropped her eyes to their hands again, so close, not touching. The sea breeze played with a wisp of hair over her forehead. She could not even lift her hand to push her hair back into place. She could only look at his hand and feel his quiet power beside her, and the warmth that seemed to radiate from his body. He was so near. But they did not touch.

Jed followed her eyes to the rail. Her small hand, white and delicately veined in blue, rested near his. He remembered how soft her skin was, like rose petals or the texture of a cloud if one could touch it. Her waist had been so small beneath his hand that he could almost encircle it. A simple move, a mere turning and touch, would bring her into his arms again. His throat went dry with the thought of it.

If he should move and slip his arm around her waist and bring her gently—ever so gently—against him . . . if he should look down and see her face upturned to his, those eyes as green as the bottom of the sea, the lips slightly parted and breathless, the ivory skin tinged with the pink of shyness . . . if he should cover her lips with his and taste, just one more time, the beauty and the softness of her . . . Would her eyes drift close, would her hands touch his shoulders, would she sway against him and breathe her fragrance into him? Would she come to him in joy and gentleness, or would she be shocked and frightened and move away? Would she welcome his touch, his kiss, as she had the last time?

Yes, he knew instinctively, she would welcome him. All he had to do was move slightly, lift his hand, touch her waist, turn her to him. She would welcome it because she was a sheltered young girl whose head was filled with romantic notions, an innocent who arranged secret trysts by perfumed notes and sought out men in twilight rose gardens. . . . But Jed was a man who had lived some of life, and he was old enough to know better.

His heart was pounding slowly and steadily, and his hands had tightened, without his even being aware of it, on the rail. He knew he should go in. He should say good night and see her safely on her way to her own cabin, and neither of them should ever think of this again. And knowing that, he stood still. Knowing it was the worst possible thing he could do, he looked out over the ocean and asked her quietly, "Why did you want to see me, Miss Elizabeth?"

Elizabeth's eyes went to him with all the helpless hope that was in her heart. It was too late for dissembling, too late for pretending. She stood upon the rocking deck of a small ship in the middle of an ocean on her way to a far-off destiny in a strange new land, and none of the conventions of proper behavior seemed to apply. There was only the man she loved and the desperate need that lived in her heart.

She whispered, "Can't you guess?"

Her eyes were dark and aching with sweet vulnerability. Her face was turned to him, so close that her lips parted on a hesitant breath. All he had to do was lift his hand . . .

He knew. And the knowledge drained away the last of his patience.

He looked away. He breathed deeply of the salty night air and said firmly, "You should go inside now, Miss Elizabeth."

"I don't want to go inside." She could barely hear her own words over the staccato leaping of her heart. "I want to be here—with you."

Jed's hands tightened on the rail. "This is not some fancy garden party, and you've got no business out here with me."

Elizabeth's pulse was pounding strongly in her throat. Her chest felt crowded—with anxiety, with fear, with desperate, demanding hope. Her fingers tightened next to his; she felt the damp paper of the crumpled note beneath one palm and the smooth wood of the rail beneath the other.

From deep within her she garnered boldness she never knew she possessed, and urgency quickened her voice: "I thought—that first day—I would never see you again. But then you came to Spring Hill with Mr. Houston and . . . and I knew it was meant to be. Don't you see?" she insisted breathlessly. "Fate has brought us together. Can we ignore that?"

His tone was as calm as he could make it. "Fate doesn't have a thing to do with it. It was William Bledsoe's fool idea to bring women to Texas, like it was some kind of sight-seeing trip to New York City. If you want to blame it on anything, blame it on him."

Elizabeth searched his face but it was so difficult to read, and all she had to go on were her own feelings, deep and powerful and overriding. Her voice was not quite steady as she said, "Could it be . . . that I've mistaken you, and—the way you think . . . toward me?"

He looked at her then, and the expression on his face was carefully controlled, as was his tone. "You don't have the first notion what a man feels at a time like this."

There was a light in his eyes, a burning that hid some male mystery, and it frightened Elizabeth, even as it made her pulses patter with excitement. There was danger in the way he looked at her, and something alarmingly intimate and forceful, but there seemed to be a kind of promise, too, and she could not back away from it.

She felt flustered, hot, and uncertain, yet frightened. But how would he know if she did not tell him? Boldness propelled her; she placed her hand over his. "But don't you see?" she blurted out helplessly, and all her heart was in her eyes. "I love you! I think I must have loved you from the moment we met, for what else could have given me courage to follow you here, to speak to you like this? I shall love you forever!"

Love. The word hung in suspended beauty on the gentleness of the night, glimmering with promise and beckoning with hope. But it was, to Jed, a sobering word.

Jed had known passion for a woman, and dazed romantic daydreams, and emotionless, matter-of-fact urges for physical release. He had never known love. What Elizabeth Coleman did to him was more than passion; it was deep and debilitating and obsessive. It worked itself inside his head and shamed him for his thoughts and weakened him with its power; it sometimes made him feel as though he didn't even know himself anymore, and no, he had never known anything like it. But it wasn't love.

Love was making one life out of two. It was when two people walked the same trail and neither one ever had to look to see if the other was following, because they walked side by side. It was not something that came easy or swept down upon you in the dark of the night and seized you like a fever. It was something slow and hard and rare to find. But when it came ... when two people stood together through the storms and droughts of life with heads held high, equal partners sharing and protecting and providing for each other ... When it happened, it was the most beautiful thing in the world. It was what Jed wanted for himself, someday. But it was not what he and Elizabeth Coleman had now. Nor did he see how it was something they could ever have.

But her hand was soft and warm on his, and there was a tightness in his throat and a fullness in his groin he could not ignore. Impatience churned, and his voice grew harsh. "You don't know me," he said curtly, but he could not pull his hand away. "You don't know anything about love."

Breathless, Elizabeth moved closer, tilting her face up. If only he would kiss her, if he would take her in his arms as he had done before, then she would know, then everything would be all right. "I know all I need to know," she said softly.

Her breasts brushed against his chest; her skirts rustled on his thighs. Her lips, parted and eager and as soft as dew, were below his, and her eyes were glowing like a hundred fireflies in the dark of night. The human male was a frail creature after all, and it would be so easy ...

His heart was beating, hard. His eyes touched her face, the delicate sweep of her throat, the ink-black hair with its thousand lights. He let himself imagine, just for the briefest of moments, the texture of her hair, the scent of her skin. If she was his woman, he would reach up and loose that hair and gather it by handfuls, drawing its silkiness over his face, through his fingers, touching it to his skin. . . . If she was his woman, her hair would be a dark and glistening aureole on the pillow beneath him, her skin like heated silk against his fingertips . . .

But she was not his woman. And she could never be. A harshness rushed through him—a brief, irrational anger for things he couldn't control—and he pulled his hand away from hers. He looked at the ocean they were leaving behind and the miles that were disappearing between the place that had never been his and the land he now called home, and his voice was rough as he answered curtly, "Miss Elizabeth, you're messing in something you don't understand, and you're going to get in trouble if you don't stop it. I'm not one of your wet-behind-the-ears beaux. I'm a grown man, and when a woman like you throws herself up against me, I don't exactly think about dancing."

She could barely get her breath; she searched his face in the starlight anxiously. "What—what do you think about?"

He turned back to her. His voice was very low, almost a growl. "I want you, Miss Elizabeth," he said bluntly. "I want you in the way a man wants a woman that has nothing to do with love."

She said nothing. She just stood there looking at him with those wide, brilliant eyes. Her breasts were rising and falling softly, her lips were no farther away from his than the bend of his head, and there was only so much a man could be expected to endure.

"Listen to me, Miss Elizabeth Coleman," he said harshly, his eyes churning. "I'm not a gentleman. If you keep on at me like this, I'm going to forget where we are and who you are and you're going to find yourself flat on your back with your skirts up over your head. That's what I want." He ground it out like a challenge. "Is that what you want?"

Elizabeth felt the blood drain from her face, and the skin

across her cheekbones went dry and taut. She took an automatic step backward, and horror pulsed through her with the same blinding force as had passion only a moment ago. No one had ever spoken to her like that before. That he should *dare* . . .

The ugly, crude words reverberated through her. Disillusionment, repulsion, and anger collided within her and left her speechless, shaking with rage. On a broken breath she drew back her hand to hit him across the face.

He caught her wrist in midair, his grip rough and his face dark. "The game is over, Miss Coleman," he said quietly, and he spoke as he might to an impetuous child, with restraint and a touch of pity. "If you want make-believe, you've come to the wrong man. My advice to you is to go back home where you belong and count your blessings."

He released her wrist abruptly and walked away.

CHAPTER
Seven

Captain Mercer Chapman folded his cards and pushed away from the table. "Looks like it's between you two boys now," he said around a mouthful of cigar. "If I quit now, I just about break even, and to tell the truth, Hartley," he added, his movements casual as he stood, even as his eyes moved alertly from Hartley to Jed, "I kind of believe Fielding's holding that third ace."

Jed smiled mirthlessly, but he never took his eyes off the man across the table. Captain Chapman had been the last to fold, and it was between the two of them now. "What about you, Hartley? You believe it?"

Lord Hartley's lips curled upward in a negligent gesture of dismissal, but his eyes were hard. "You've had the devil's own luck tonight, Fielding, but as a matter of fact, I'm not that easily impressed."

"You just might be right." Jed's voice was deep and

smooth. "Everybody's luck's got to run out sometime, don't it? But it's going to cost you to find out."

The main cabin was dim, smoky, and thick with the taste of burning cigars and oil lamps, as it had been every night after the supper table was cleared. The ladies had gone to their cabins, and the gentlemen had gathered around for a friendly hand of cards, and for a while that was all it had been. Then Jed Fielding got into the game.

For the past two nights of the voyage Fielding had done little but watch. Hartley had won consistently—too consistently for some of the men's liking—and emotions had begun to run high. But when Jed Fielding had sat in tonight, the tables began to turn. The other players had recouped their losses, and a couple of them were even ahead by a few dollars. This being the last night of the trip, all were happy to quit while they were ahead, and if anyone suspected what was going on, no one said anything. This was now between the two men, and it was, from the looks of it, a duel to the death.

Before Jed was a pile of currency, most of it Hartley's. A cigar smoldered in the saucer at his elbow, and his expression was cool and unconcerned. Someone mumbled something about "damnedest run," but for the most part no one spoke. The tension was as thick as the smoke, and everyone present had a stake in this. They watched.

Hartley glanced at Jed's holdings and then at the pot in the center of the table. His eyes were as unreadable as ever, but his smile was slightly apologetic. "I confess my weakness. I am curious. But as you see"—he nodded to the pile of money on Jed's side of the table—"I seem to be temporarily short of funds. You will take my IOU?"

He was already moving for his breast pocket, but Jed's voice, mild and flat, stopped him cold. "No."

Hartley's eyes flashed with the shock of the insult, but Jed explained simply, "Where I'm going, there won't be much chance to collect. I'm afraid I'm going to have to ask for cash or close it out right here.''

Hartley leaned back, watching Jed thoughtfully. Jed had over two hundred dollars of his money, and there was another hundred in the pot. It wasn't that Hartley couldn't afford to lose, it was that he did not intend to. Most especially not to Jed Fielding.

And Jed knew that.

Hartley could not explain Jed's previous run of luck, but he knew it would end here. No one ever walked away from his table a winner. And more was at stake now than three hundred American dollars.

Hartley smiled faintly. ''Perhaps I have something else that would be of interest to you.''

Jed chewed on his cigar. ''You might.''

Hartley reached into his breast pocket and withdrew a leather folder. He placed it on the table beside his hole card. ''Two hundred thousand acres, Mr. Fielding. Does that improve my credit any?''

Jed looked at him for a moment, then removed his cigar and absently flipped through the stack of bills before him. ''I'll cover you at a penny an acre,'' he announced.

A murmur went through the crowd, and Hartley's eyes went flat. ''That,'' he replied coldly, ''is preposterous.''

Jed shrugged. ''Your choice. But seems to me that land ain't doing you much good sitting in your pocket. Was I you, I'd put it to work for me.'' And he smiled. ''But then, I'm not you.''

Hartley was silent. Even at one cent an acre he would have the equivalent of two thousand dollars for the game. He could easily afford to cover Jed's bet and raise enough to recoup his own losses. It wasn't as though he intended to lose.

He said, stretching his lips into that cool smile again,

"Very well, Mr. Fielding. A penny an acre." And he began to count out coupons.

Jed glanced up at the spectators. "You boys hear that?"

"Legal in front of witnesses," agreed the shopkeeper.

"Captain, you want to write out a little note to that effect?" When Hartley cast him a sharp look, Jed explained pleasantly, "Just in case there's any questions later."

Mercer called for a pen and paper and looked at Hartley. "You understand what you're agreeing to?" he prompted. "If you lose, Fielding will have your coupons at full value. But if Fielding loses, all he has to do is cover your bet at a penny an acre."

Hartley gestured impatiently for the agreement to be drawn up. "I can perform simple mathematics, sir. Get on with it."

The captain wrote and witnessed the agreement and passed it to Hartley for his signature. With a hasty scrawl of his name Hartley pushed the paper over to Jed and placed thirty thousand acres of prime Texas land on the table to match the three hundred in cash Jed had put up. Then he leaned back and smiled. "Now, sir. Let's have a look, shall we?"

Without further ado Jed turned over the third ace.

A ripple of grins and excitement went through the spectators, but Hartley's face remained blank as Jed raked in his winnings.

Captain Chapman watched both men through the smoke of his cigar, careful of what he knew was coming. He knew they would be coming into harbor soon, and any other time he would have returned to his post to conduct the tricky maneuver himself. The Galveston harbor was notorious for its hidden dangers. But his navigator had assured him he was experienced, and Chapman expected no problems. Besides, the way things were going in this cabin, he suspected his presence was needed more here than on the bridge.

Jed folded up cash and coupons and pushed his chair

away. "Well, sir, I do thank you. I never like to go home empty-handed."

Hartley, his heavy eyes lowered, began to gather up the cards. "Surely you don't intend to leave me without a chance to recover my losses?"

"It's getting late." Jed tucked his winnings into his coat pocket. "Think I'll stretch my legs a bit and turn in."

Hartley tapped the cards on the table and began to shuffle. His eyes met Jed's, his expression mild. Jed Fielding had surprised him. He had known he was tough but had not expected him to be ruthless. He would not make that mistake again.

He said carelessly, "One more game, same stakes. A mere point of etiquette, dear boy. You can't refuse me." He shuffled once more and passed the deck to Jed.

Jed had watched Hartley for two days and knew his game. He could not explain what had made him decide to try to beat him at it tonight . . . unless, perhaps, it was the fact that he knew he could. Or it might have been the fact that he did not think he could spend one more night staring at Elizabeth Coleman's closed door.

He saw her in the day, sitting with her chaperone in the main cabin, sewing or reading. He saw her at mealtimes, and her eyes never met his. He walked on deck, and her scent mingled with the taste of salt air and drifted on the breeze that tangled his hair until he thought he would go crazy. After supper she excused herself and went to her cabin, and from where he sat, Jed could see the door, could almost hear the rustling sounds she made as she moved around inside, and whenever he looked, his throat tightened up. He had to do something.

So he had decided to teach Hartley a lesson.

All he had wanted to do was see that the other men got

their money back. They were settlers and working men and couldn't afford to lose. Jed hadn't intended to get involved.

But he thought about Elizabeth, and he kept playing. He saw Hartley's bottom deal, and he got mad. Not that he needed much of an excuse to go after Hartley. From the moment they had met, an instinctive challenge had been there, like something between two animals bristling at the scent of each other. He didn't know, or care, why it was he despised the man so; the enmity between them was something that had started out small and was now escalating out of control, but beyond that he couldn't explain it and didn't try. It was simply a fact, and neither of them would ever meet the other without facing the need to rise up to that challenge and do something about it.

Jed had no intention of walking away from this hand, and he suspected Hartley knew it. He pulled up his chair again and cut the cards.

Coleman watched as Jed passed the deck back to Hartley. He knew what was going on, and he knew how it was likely to end. He knew he should stop the game. But Hartley had taken him for a lot of money, and only Jed Fielding's intervention had gotten it back for him; the captain was sure of that now. He had no complaints, and neither, he suspected, did anyone else at this point. He settled back to watch.

Hartley dealt out the cards for five-card draw. Early on he had begun to suspect—nothing more than a niggling uneasiness, really—that Fielding knew about his bottom deal. He had edged away, and this was what had happened: he was out of cash, and Fielding held thirty thousand acres of his land. Now he was pulling out all the stops, and if Fielding called him on it . . . well, so be it. He would as soon deal with Jed Fielding away from the table as over it.

Charles Edgecomb, Lord Hartley, had accumulated his great position of power and wealth through aggression, determination, and confidence. Generations of breeding and years of experience had taught him strategy, patience, and courage. The one thing he had never learned was how to lose.

Perhaps if he had, things might have been different.

Jed looked at his cards, his face impassive. Absently he fingered his cash and pushed some bills forward. "I'll open with a hundred in cash. That's ten thousand acres to you, Hartley."

Hartley smiled. "Well, we are off to a roaring start, aren't we?" He reached into the folder and counted out some coupons. "I'll cover that and raise it another..." He glanced at Jed. "Twenty-five thousand acres. Not too steep for you, I trust, Mr. Fielding?"

Jed covered his bet with two hundred in cash and five thousand acres. "I'll call." His eyes strayed to the closed door on the other side of the cabin. Was she sleeping? Was she lying in the dark, listening to the sea? Was she thinking about him?

Hartley glanced at his hand. Already he had a pair of tens, but he was taking no chances. "Dealer takes three." He discarded three cards and deftly dealt himself three of a kind. He would win easily with a full house, but he dared not be too obvious, so he made certain the cards he gave himself were not too high. He turned the play over to Jed. "Sir?"

Jed moved his eyes away from the closed door and back to the cards in his hand. A quick irritation burned in his stomach, but it was anger at himself this time, not at Hartley. Perhaps it had always been.

Negligently Jed tossed a single card on the table. "Deal me one."

Hartley lifted a cool eyebrow. "My, you are a daring young man, aren't you?" Either Jed was the biggest fool alive or he was holding a hand for which the luck of the draw could never begin to account. Hartley decided not to take any chances. From the bottom of the deck he dealt Jed a two of clubs. "Your bet, sir." He smiled.

Quick and cautious glances went through the gathering of spectators, and Jed's eyes wandered, just once more, to the closed door.

In a few hours they would disembark in Galveston and he would never see her again. It would be the best thing that could ever happen. Maybe then he would be able to get her out of his mind.

He turned back to his hand.

William Bledsoe was worried. He, too, had lost heavily and was enough of a gentleman to know that his sudden and recent turn of luck had been inspired by something slightly more calculated than the luck of the draw. He had not liked the turn his thoughts were taking when he retired from the game, nor did he like the undercurrent of tension that had been escalating between the two men since then. The sportsman in him liked Fielding and admired his intent, if not his methods, but the gentleman did not want to be confronted with the truth of his suspicions—nor did he want to see ugliness spring from a game of cards.

Both men were playing their hands close to their chests, and it was impossible to guess the outcome of this game. A veritable fortune rested on the table already, but more than money was at stake, and everyone in the room knew it. Before this night was over, someone would be called to an accounting, and violence hung like a suspended breath over the table.

William said, forcing a smile in an attempt to lighten the moment, "One of you has got to be bluffing, but damn me if I can guess who it is. I would say you are well matched, gentlemen."

Neither man replied.

Jed studied his cards for what seemed like an eternity—or at least he pretended to study them. Hartley had a feeling that Jed was not the least surprised by what he had drawn. When Jed's cool eyes met his across the table, Hartley was sure of it.

Jed reached down and pushed another stack of coupons across the table. "Twenty thousand acres."

Hartley did not like a confident man, especially when there could be no possible reason for such confidence. Jed had only five thousand acres left, and he could not possibly beat Hartley's full house with a two of clubs in his hand. Then why was he taking such a chance?

Hartley smiled. "As much as I hate to take advantage of my fellowman, Mr. Fielding . . ." He reached into the folder and counted out a stack of coupons, never taking his eyes off Jed. "I'm afraid I must put my faith in the laws of probability. I'll cover your twenty thousand and raise one hundred thousand acres."

Jed lifted an eyebrow, glancing at his own remaining five thousand acres. "Well, now," he drawled, "that's mighty generous of you, mister, but I'm afraid I can't cover that kind of bet, even at a penny an acre."

There was venom in Hartley's smile and deep within his dark eyes a dangerous spark of intoxicated triumph. "Then allow me, please, to be of some assistance. You see, my curiosity is piqued now too." He leaned back in his chair, his long fingers absently playing over the three acres that rested before him. "I believe you mentioned your sixteen-hundred-acre ranch. And cattle?"

"Three, four hundred head." Jed's face was expressionless.

Hartley looked thoughtful. "Then I've a sporting proposition for you. Winner take all—your ranch and stock, plus the remaining five thousand you've got in front of you, against everything I've got on the table. I believe that's a fair offer, don't you?"

"More than fair," agreed Jed mildly.

"Lord Hartley," intervened Bledsoe quickly, "you can't be serious. That's far more than Fielding's land is worth—"

But Hartley waved a dismissing hand. "One cannot put a price on goodwill, sir. I've made this gentleman a fair offer, and I think we all agree it will be worth it to see what he has."

Jed said quietly, watching him, "Seems to me you're going to an awful lot of trouble to ruin me, Hartley."

There was a heartbeat's silence, and there was nothing but ice in Hartley's eyes. There was no longer any pretense of pleasantness in his manner, and Jed thought briefly that he had seen that same expression in the eyes of a Texas bad man once, in the split second before he drew his gun and killed a man for spilling his drink.

Hartley drawled lowly, his gaze never flickering. "Perhaps. But it has recently occurred to me, Mr. Fielding, that not even Texas is big enough for the two of us."

Jed added his five thousand acres to the pot. "Captain? You want to write up another one of them agreements?"

The hastily scrawled agreement of value was signed by both parties and placed on top of the land coupons. In the center of the table rested one hundred eighty-five thousand acres of Lord Hartley's empire, and all Jed had in the world.

Hartley tossed his cards on the table—two tens and three fours. "There you have it, my friend. I'm afraid the only thing that can beat that hand is four of a kind—unlikely, I think we'll all agree, as you only drew one card."

Jed admitted, "Well, I don't have four of a kind." He put down a pair of sevens, watching Hartley's eyes. Then he added the queen of clubs and the queen of spades, keeping one card in his hand.

Hartley visibly relaxed. He knew that last card was a two of clubs. "Those queens are quite lovely, of course, but I'm afraid even they will not beat a full house." He reached for the pot.

"Won't they?" Jed laid down his last card, and his eyes never left Hartley's. "Never bet against the queen of hearts," he said.

Hartley's eyes went to the card and then froze. It was the queen of hearts.

"Full house," breathed Bledsoe. "Queens high. Fielding wins!"

The silence that followed was like an explosion. It lasted just long enough for Jed to see Hartley's face go sallow, his eyes seeming to retract in his head, his fingers clench. His throat worked convulsively, he started to speak, and then came the burst of amazement and congratulations from the spectators, and Hartley went tight. He could say nothing, and it was impotence, perhaps, as much as anything else, that was churning him into a fine rage.

Jed began to pull in his winnings, and he met Hartley's eyes calmly. "Well, sir," he said, and smiled, "looks like I just won me an empire."

Hartley's fist went tighter on the table, and his nostrils flared. He wanted to speak. But he could hardly object to the queen of hearts without revealing that he had cheated to deal Jed the two of clubs. A man like him didn't like to lose, but being beaten at his own game was beyond all tolerance. He wanted to do more than speak. He wanted to kill.

Jed folded the land coupons into a neat stack and rose to tuck them into his pocket. "Well, gentlemen, it's been a real pleasure, but I've got me a busy day ahead. I'll be saying good night."

He was half turning from the table when he saw Hartley rise. In the same moment Jed's peripheral vision caught the movement Hartley's hand made toward his waistcoat. He had been expecting that and did not hesitate a second. In a simple, fluid motion Jed completed his turn into a roundhouse kick that caught Hartley hard just above the ankles.

Hartley's feet went out from under him and he sprawled backward. The knife he had drawn clattered to the floor.

Jed stood above him, meeting the hatred and shock in Hartley's eyes with calmness in his own. "Now, that wasn't very smart, was it? In front of witnesses and everything. Now your friends are going to start wondering what kind of man you really are."

Until Jed spoke, the spectators had been arrested in disbelief; now the captain moved forward quickly to retrieve the knife. "You know the rule against weapons on board this ship, Lord Hartley," he said.

Bledsoe interjected, outraged, "Now see here, Hartley, this is hardly gentlemanly behavior. I hardly see the call for—"

Hartley pushed himself to his feet, his fists clenched and his eyes black with malice. His voice was choked and ugly. "No one takes what is mine."

"Dealer's choice," Jed replied calmly. "Seems to me you set the rules when you sat down to play." Hartley opened his mouth to speak, and Jed could see the strong muscles of his arms tremble with repressed rage. Jed cut him off quietly. "Now you just think a minute before you say what I can see you're dyin' to say. Looks to me like you're ahead of the game at this point." He cast his eyes casually around the room. "Now, these boys look pretty satisfied with the way things turned out. Are you satisfied, boys?"

There were a few murmurs and nods, but the men were not immune to what was building. They began to move back.

"You've still got a nice little nest egg for yourself," Jed told Hartley. "Not exactly an empire, but"—his lips curved faintly—"with a little sweat and know-how, I'm betting you could turn it into a modest little spread. Of course"—he inclined a polite nod to Hartley—"there's plenty of land to be had in Texas. If you had a mind to, I reckon you could always go out and buy yourself some more of these coupons."

Hartley's eyes were deathly still. "I'm not in the market for deserts and Indians. And we both know you plan to use the coupons in your pocket to claim the only part of Texas worth having."

Jed smiled. "Can't say that I disagree with you." He touched his pocket lightly. "Seems logical to just hook these coupons right onto my spread and kind of let it stand, as a monument to what a man can do when he puts his mind to it. You can take a lesson from that, Hartley, as to how far you can come when you start from scratch."

He paused questioningly, and Hartley's face was like stone—volcanic stone—a cold fire in his eyes. He said quietly, "I don't have to start from scratch. I'm going to get back what you stole from me."

"I kind of doubt that," replied Jed easily. "You see, I'm not really a gambler at heart. I know when to quit. Maybe that's another thing you ought to learn."

Jed turned away. "Good night, gents."

He knew he wouldn't get far, and he calculated his steps perfectly. Hartley lunged and Jed spun around, sending him stumbling back against the table with a hard blow to the midsection. The table crashed against the wall, chairs tumbled, and Hartley barely paused. He came at Jed with the rage to kill.

Elizabeth heard the crash of tables and was across the room of her cabin before she heard the second blow crack the air. She flung open her door just as Miss Nancy burst from her cabin, and what she saw caused her hand to fly to her lips and the breath to freeze in her throat.

Jed was flying at Lord Hartley, his fist impacting against the other man's jaw with a brutal force. The returned blow was so swift, she did not even see it, but she heard the sickening sound of flesh against flesh, the soft grunt of lost breath. Jed lunged and Hartley reeled backward, and droplets of blood splattered on the wall.

Miss Nancy grabbed the captain by the arm. "My good sir, do something! Stop them!"

The captain drew his eyes away from the fight with great reluctance and looked at Miss Nancy. There was another crash as Jed tumbled back against the wall, then lunged forward again. Miss Nancy raised her voice; Elizabeth had never known the woman to raise her voice before in her life. "Are you just going to stand there?" she cried. "Do something! Stop them."

The captain took his cigar slowly from his mouth and answered politely, "No, ma'am. I don't guess I will. Now, may I suggest you and the young lady there go on back to your cabins? This is between men."

Miss Nancy crossed to Elizabeth's side. Her face was white and splotched with two dark dots of shocked color. She slipped her arm through Elizabeth's and tried to turn her. "Go inside quickly, dear," she insisted. "This is no fit sight for a lady's eyes."

Elizabeth barely heard her. She couldn't move. She stood, transfixed with horror, and watched the animal brutality that urged male against male, the flying droplets of sweat and blood, the crashing blows, the naked violence. She heard the heavy breaths, the grunts of furious effort; she tasted savagery in the air and she was sickened, horrified . . . and mesmerized. She stood with her hands at her mouth and her eyes wide with shock, and she could not move.

In size the two men were well matched. Though Jed had by far more power in his arms and hands, Hartley was a trained boxer, and what he lacked in strength was more than compensated for by sheer rage. Jed had taken a couple of hard blows before he caught on to Hartley's technique, and by that time his own adrenaline was pumping and he knew this was not going to end until one of them couldn't get up again. And Jed had another advantage. He had never learned the rules of the ring.

He ducked below a vicious blow aimed at his jaw and swung up and to the right. He felt the crack of a bone and the gush of blood, but the impact of his own blow swayed him off-balance and made him a perfect target for Hartley's next punch. Hartley's fist stabbed with a cruel force into Jed's midsection, and the pain was excruciating. He staggered backward and lost his breath, and for a moment his vision blurred.

Hartley, resting in his victory, took a moment to catch his breath and didn't anticipate Jed's next move. As swift as a panther, Jed swung his foot hard around into the other man's hamstring. Hartley doubled over, and Jed landed two long punches to his kidney, then brought his doubled fists down on Hartley's neck. Hartley was on the floor, but with a man like that, as mad as he was, Jed knew better than to turn away. He came in on him, methodically and determinedly. There was no satisfaction in him, no fury. Just a job that had to be done. Dimly he heard a woman's scream as Hartley's head lolled on the floor beneath the power of Jed's fist.

There were hands on his shoulders, but Jed needed no one to tell him when it was over. He stepped away.

His muscles were aching, and his vision was blurred with sweat. He stood with his feet planted apart, breathing hard, his nerves alive with residual energy.

Hartley's face wasn't so pretty anymore. His lip was split and his nose was gushing blood, and violent red bruises were already beginning to rise around his eyes and under his jaw. But when the captain knelt beside him and made a cursory examination, he said flatly, "Well, he's not dead." He looked up at Jed. "Though you might live to wish he was."

Chapman left Hartley to William Bledsoe and crossed over to Jed. "He didn't strike me as the type to forgive too quick." He looked down at Hartley's knife, which he still held for safekeeping. It was a fine-looking piece, ebony-handled and ivory-studded and sharp enough to cut hair. He looked back at Jed. "If I was in your place," he advised soberly, "I'd mind my step."

Jed managed a smile, though it hurt his face. "Do me a favor." His words came choppily, for he was still out of breath, and he indicated the knife. "Hold on to that thing until we're in port. I need some sleep."

The captain blandly tucked the knife into his pocket. "Seem to have misplaced it already."

And then Jed saw Elizabeth.

Victory, energy, and residual savagery were pumping through his veins like a living force, and all he wanted to do at that moment was to crush her to him and devour her lips with fierce and triumphant possession. An instinct as old as the nature of man had him in its grip, and fighting it was all he could do. He wanted her. He wanted her now, forever, and with such an intensity that his strained and aching muscles quivered with the need to reach for her.

She stood there, white-faced and bewildered, and something twisted inside Jed's gut. Delicate, fragile Elizabeth, with horror in her eyes and shock in her face, looking at him as though she had never seen him before. His hair was plastered to his skull, his shirt wet with sweat and flecked with another man's blood. His hands were torn and bruised, and she was seeing him exactly as he was. Now she had seen it all, and he was swept with a wave of self-disgust so powerful that it almost choked him.

He turned quickly and left the room.

CHAPTER
Eight

Jed paused on deck, wrapping his fingers around the cool wood of the rail, breathing deeply of the damp salt air. In the distance he could see the faint lights of shore. Texas. Home. And not a moment too soon.

His shoulders ached and his torn knuckles stung, but deep inside him was another hurt, a hollow, bruised sensation that had nothing to do with the physical. In his pocket he had more than three hundred dollars—more money than he had ever called his own at any one time in his life—and that should be enough to make any man happy. He had fought a good battle and seen justice served, and he should have felt nothing but satisfaction, contentment, and eagerness. He was home. He was returning home, victorious. All he had ever wanted, and dreamed of, was now at his disposal.

Then why did he feel as though he were leaving the only thing of any importance behind?

He pushed away from the rail and began to pace again, working off restless energy, trying to outdistance the pull of his mind. The irony of it was that to a stockman like Jed the land coupons were little more than elaborately decorated slips of paper. Only the farmer needed to possess land; a range man understood that the land was there to borrow, to pass through, to use when he needed it, and to leave behind when it was time.

There were no fences in Texas, no boundary lines that a man couldn't drive his herd over with a polite word and a tip of his hat. But to a man like Hartley, with his cotton plantations and his building sites, owning land was the most important thing in the world. Maybe it was worth it, to keep men like that from thinking they could divide up and parcel off Texas for their own profit. Certainly it was worth it to keep the farmers and fences away from Jed's own range. The future of Texas would be built on nothing more than what Texas itself had to offer: land and cattle, and it had plenty of both. Texas did not need the Hartleys of this world improving its future.

Jed should be satisfied. He had done what he had to do. But all he could see was that look in Elizabeth's eyes.

He measured his strides with eyes that were fixed and grim upon the deck beneath his feet. It was best. She had seen him for what he really was, a man as ruthless as the land that had bred him, tough and violent and raw. She had no place with him, just as he did not belong in her world. She must know that now.

But he had never meant to hurt her. That night when she had stood on this very deck and poured out her heart to him, he had fought one of the biggest battles of his life. He did not like being cruel, but how else could he make her see? He had only done the best thing for her; couldn't she understand that? There had been no other way. But he hated to have hurt her.

He should go to her and apologize. How could he live the rest of his life with that look in her eyes as his last memory of her? How could he leave her, knowing she hated him?

His eyes strayed to the door of her cabin, which opened onto the deck. A faint thread of light shone beneath, and his heart began to beat heavily. He should go and tap lightly on the door. But when she opened it, would she be clad in a delicate white nightdress, her hair streaming down her back . . . ?

No. He would only see her to apologize. She deserved that. She was a lady and he had hurt her, and she deserved an apology.

To go to her now would be insane.

His eyes rested on that door, on the stream of light beneath. He could feel the rustle of wind in his hair and the pulse of blood in his chest. Only a few steps would bring him to her. He took the first one.

The young officer at the helm was a good navigator, but he knew little of piloting a ship into harbor. Perhaps he had overqualified himself to the captain, but he needed the experience and had no reason to doubt his own ability . . . until now.

He had heard Galveston was a tricky harbor, but he had not imagined anything like this. The waters seemed to be littered with the skeletons of ships run aground on hidden sandbars; they floated past his line of vision like spectral monuments to the overconfident. The lighthouse flashed its beacon on his face, and his nerves were as tight as the twinkling lights of the city that grew closer by inches. The captain had promised to return before they entered harbor.

Something had detained him, but he could have no idea how urgently he was needed at the wheel. . . .

The navigator felt a fine sweat break out on his upper lip as he turned the wheel cautiously, plotting to avoid the sagging mast of a broken ship to starboard. The steam engines throbbed and hummed; the lighthouse swung its slow arc across the graveyard of other departed vessels. He did not know how much farther he could proceed with any margin of safety, and he wished desperately that he had not bragged so to the captain, and that the man would soon return to the bridge. But until then it was up to him, and he could only hope luck would be with him tonight . . . and that luck would be enough.

Jed paused outside Elizabeth's door, his hand half lifted to knock. What made him think she would even want to see him? She might not open the door. Was she thinking of him and despising him? How could he face that look in her eyes again?

He should go. If he was caught here, there would be trouble, and he had had more than enough trouble for one night. Besides, he was sure she did not want to see him.

But he wanted desperately to see her.

All he wanted to do was say good-bye to her, to tell her he was sorry, perhaps to touch her face, or the silkiness of her hair, just once. . . .

And he knew if he went inside that cabin, he would never leave.

In his pocket was the key to a dream, in his muscles the ache of justice hard-earned. It was enough. He should be happy, he should be satisfied with this night's work. If he knocked on her door now . . .

He hesitated, his breath dry in his throat, his blood tight in his veins. His hand lifted another fraction and then paused just before the smooth wood panel. The heartbeats ticked off.

And then, slowly, his hand dropped and clenched into a fist. Jed swung around and directed his footsteps up the deck, away from her door.

It was never easy to walk away when you were winning. But when the stakes were this high, it was the most important thing in the world a man could know how to do.

The young navigator heard the heavy steps approaching the pilothouse, and he breathed a sigh of relief. The captain was on his way, and the officer had learned his lesson. Never did he want to live through a night like this one again. He stepped back, preparing to relinquish the wheel, but his relief was premature, the captain's arrival a moment too late.

The captain's form appeared in the doorway as an indistinct blur of blue and white only a split second before they heard the grinding, tearing jolt. The captain screamed, "What the hell are you doing? Hard to port!" and he lurched forward.

Dust drifted from the overhead timbers, the motion of the ship slid and dragged; a moment of utter paralysis gripped the young officer as he knew the horror of what was happening. He jerked the wheel but there was no response, and the impact of the unseen collision flung him from his post. The captain grabbed the wheel, bracing himself against the bulwark, frantically trying to turn but to no avail. The vessel shuddered and ground to a halt, listing violently to starboard.

Elizabeth had just doused her lantern when the impact struck. She was standing beside her cot, preparing to crawl in, when she heard the awful tearing sounds. Even as she turned in alarm, the floor tilted beneath her. She lost her footing and fell hard, crying out as she struck her hip against something blunt. She lay for a moment in the grip of disorientation and terror while the timbers overhead groaned, sounding as though they would come crashing onto her head at any moment. The boards beneath her heaved and trembled, and a horrendous, screeching, rending sound blotted the air. Sweeping her hands around frantically, Elizabeth tried to find her position in the dark. Her fingers scraped against the bottom of her trunk, and she pulled herself to her feet, lurching toward the outer door. Sobbing with dry breaths of terror, she found the latch and pushed, and then the floor went out from under her again and she cried out as she was thrown to her knees.

The second violent settling of the ship caused it to list at an almost perpendicular angle, flinging passengers to and fro, toppling cargo, tearing furniture from its bolts. In the main cabin two lanterns spun from their brackets and were joined by a third, shattering glass and spilling puddles of burning oil over the floor. The greedy tongues of flame licked and crawled, converging against the walls, traveling up the table legs, spreading like a living carpet over the crisp pine flooring. Fanned to eagerness by the open door to the deck, sparks drifted upward to the ceiling and caught; fingers of flame grabbed at the walls and found hold, crackling and spitting and devouring everything in their path.

On deck there was panic. Passengers had spilled out at the first grinding crash, and a frantic crew was doing its best to direct them. Bales and kegs and crates littered the deck. Captain Chapman, cursing his luck and his inept officer, climbed over the wreckage and tossed aside broken merchandise, shouting, "No need to panic! We've just run aground and will go ashore by longboat. There is no danger of sinking!'' He repeated that for the benefit of those just climbing out of their cabins. "We are in no danger!"

William Bledsoe was leading Miss Nancy Lea up the deck, and the shopkeeper was desperately running from broken bale to damaged crate, loudly bemoaning his lost merchandise. A crewman ran by in a blur, and the school-teacher was frantically grabbing at Captain Chapman's arm.

"Leave your possessions!" the captain commanded, his voice ringing over the chaos. "The crew will unload them later. We are in no danger! Proceed to the longboat; there's plenty of room—''

And suddenly Miss Nancy screamed, "Elizabeth!"

The captain looked around and did not see the youngest member of their party. Miss Nancy was looking around frantically, tugging on William's arm, crying, "Elizabeth! Where is she? I don't see—''

Quickly the captain made his way around the spilled and broken cargo to the young lady's door, which he could see, at a glance, was blocked by several large crates and a spill of unlashed cherrywood timbers. He pushed the smallest of the crates aside, which just allowed him access to the door, and shouted, "Miss Coleman! Are you all right?"

Miss Nancy Lea was like a tigress behind him, crying out for Elizabeth, trying to pull away from Mr. Bledsoe's restraining grip. From behind the blocked door Elizabeth's voice, choked and panicked, cried, "Yes! I can't—my door—''

"This door is blocked," the captain called back. "Go to the other door, Miss Coleman. I'm on my way to the main cabin to meet you!"

Over his shoulder he instructed, "Get Mrs. Lea to the boat. I'll take care of Miss Coleman." And then, louder,

"All passengers to the longboat! We will be departing as soon as all are on board!"

Elizabeth, reassured by the captain's calm orders, fumbled through the dark toward the main cabin door. The deck was at an awkward angle, causing her to cling to her bunk for balance and grab for the wall to keep from falling. At last she reached the door and, bracing herself against the edge of the bunk, searched for the latch. The captain had said they were not sinking. There were people outside; she could hear them running and shouting. They were going to be all right. She wasn't hurt, there was no danger, there was no reason to be afraid.

She found the latch and, with a sob of relief, pushed it upward. The door swung open to a wall of flames, blinding her, leaping at her, singeing her face and scorching her lungs. . . .

Her scream was choked off in her throat. With all her might she pushed the door closed and fell against it. Panic cut off her breath; she couldn't even sob. All she could do was cling to the hot boards and stare wildly into the darkness.

With the first grinding lurch of the ship Jed knew what had happened. He had been run aground before, and he knew what to expect. He could hear the captain reassuring the passengers, he saw the rush of activity as the crew prepared the longboats, and he knew there was no danger, except to the cargo below the waterline. Most of what Jed valued he carried in his pocket, but he hated to lose his guns. Given recent developments, he might have more than one reason to regret their loss if he left without them.

He saw the captain rush past, and the crew guiding the

passengers toward safety. Everything seemed to be under control. He moved toward the cargo hold.

It took but a few minutes of searching through the rubble to find a length of pipe with which to break the lock, and then he took a lantern from the bulwark and descended the hold. Trunks had been scattered everywhere, some of them broken open, others piled atop one another. He found his long rifle flung into a corner and his saddlebags beneath a scattered stack of books belonging, no doubt, to the schoolteacher. He tossed the saddlebags over his shoulder and then, as an extra precaution, removed his five-shooter and tucked it into his waistband. His Bible, which was the only thing from home he had thought worth saving, was lying beneath it. Without pausing to consider why, he took it out and buttoned it inside his shirt. Then he climbed out of the hold.

All told, he must not have been below decks ten minutes, but in those minutes the scene had been transformed drastically. He could smell the smoke and hear the crackle before he emerged on deck, and a bolt of alarm propelled his last few steps. Swiftly his eyes took in the scene. Billows of smoke poured from the forward section, and breaths of flame lapped at the bulwark and dug greedily into the timbers. A keg of kerosene had broken open, and fire swirled and poured over the deck. Dancing sparks drifted upward and smoldered on the mast. Jed ducked quickly as a flaming torch broke off overhead and plunged past his face. He swung around and hurried toward the aft where, from the shouts and cries of panic, Jed knew the captain would need all the help he could get.

The timbers were dry and quick to fuel, but it was the cargo—bolts of dress goods, cured timbers, whiskey, and oil—that was feeding the flames with such astonishing rapidity. Fanned by the sea breeze, the fire swelled and danced, separated and leapt, filling the air with noxious fumes and blinding the eye with its greedy brilliance. Jed slapped at sparks that singed his jacket and wiped the sooty smoke out of his eyes, leaping over a smoldering timber that blocked his path. And then, above the roar and snap of the fire, he heard the moan.

Drawing his arm over his eyes again, he looked around, ears alert, eyes sweeping. There, on the deck a few feet away, he saw a hand. He pushed aside a smoldering crate of dried goods and made his way over to it.

Lord Hartley, his face swollen from Jed's blows and smeared with soot, lay pinned against the bulwark by a heavy post. His eyes, on meeting Jed's, were alert and expressionless. He gave up his efforts to move the post when Jed dropped down beside him. He sank back against the bulwark, his nostrils flaring for breath, and watched.

Jed let his rifle and saddlebags fall to the deck and positioned himself against the post. It had fallen at such an angle so that it had not crushed its victim but merely had rendered him helpless. Jed braced his shoulder beneath the weight and pushed upward; Hartley lifted with his hands until the post tumbled to the side, and he was free.

For a moment the two men rested, breathing hard, then looked at each other. Hartley said quietly, "You, sir, are a fool. You have just saved the life of the man who is going to destroy you. It is a matter of honor with me, you see."

A length of burning plank hit the deck beside them, and Jed reached forward and grabbed the other man's arm firmly, hauling him to his feet. "Well, then," he replied curtly, "let's just hope we both live long enough to satisfy your *honor.*"

He turned to retrieve his rifle and his saddlebags, but a crate of foodstuffs toppled over them and began to burn. Jed turned and, coughing, made his way up the deck after Hartley.

The ship was listing at such an angle that the longboat was resting in the water, only a few feet below the deck rail. Jed saw Miss Nancy already in the boat, her white, lined face streaked with soot and tears, her fingers pressed to her lips to repress cries of distress. The crew and male passengers were frantically trying to keep the flames back, beating the deck with coats soaked in seawater, fragments of blankets, anything they could find. Drifting sparks and burning debris sizzled on the water and smoldered against the rail, coming dangerously close to igniting the longboat.

Hartley shouted, "Why aren't we pushing off! We'll all be killed!"

A feeling as sharp and deadly as cold steel went through Jed's chest, and he grabbed Bledsoe's arm. "Where is Elizabeth?" he demanded.

William Bledsoe, coughing violently, swung his coat at a sliver of flame creeping toward his boot and turned to Jed with wild, distressed eyes. "Trapped!" He gasped. "The captain—"

He gestured weakly, and Jed spun around, losing not a step as he rushed through the smoke toward the dim silhouette of the captain.

Chapman was desperately trying to pry away the smoldering crates and kegs that blocked Elizabeth's door. Every breath he took was a gasping cough, his face raw and brilliant from close proximity to the fire, his hands blistered and bleeding. When Jed reached him, the captain turned to him frantically. "Tried to get through—main cabin." He gasped. "The flames . . ."

Jed lifted a bale of smoldering cloth and tossed it aside. "Go!" he shouted. "Get those people ashore!"

"Can't—"

Jed grabbed his arm and furiously spun him around. "You're no good here! Look at your hands! Get those people ashore while you've still got the chance!"

Ravaged uncertainty was clear on the captain's face. A woman lay trapped, possibly already dead, while a dozen others might lose their lives if he delayed. He gasped. "I can't leave—"

Jed's fingers tightened on his arms with a brutal force, his eyes dark and his face fierce. "Damn it," he shouted hoarsely, "it's Elizabeth! Do you think I'm going to let her die? Go!"

He flung the captain away from him and furiously began to pull away the burning debris that kept him from Elizabeth. He did not feel the pain in his scorched hands, the agony that seared his lungs, the sparks that smoldered through his jacket and burned his skin. All he thought of was Elizabeth.

She lay on the floor where the air once had been better but now was only a choking carpet of black and poisonous fumes. Consciousness came in ever dimmer breaths, tossed like a life rope that she was too weak to grasp. Her lungs were singed and aching, her coughs more of a reflex than any genuine effort to breathe. Her mouth, her nose, her eyes—all were afire; nausea choked and roiled within her; and she thought, after all, that this was the most horrible of ways to die. . . .

When last she had been able to turn her head, she could see the tendrils of flame licking through the door that opened onto the main cabin, and she knew that soon it would fall inward and she would be consumed by fire. Her fingers were bloody from clawing at the outer door. She knew they were trying to reach her, but there was no time. She could not hold on to consciousness much longer.

*   *   *

Jed shoved away the last heavy crate with his feet and pushed open the door. The gust of air fanned the flames on the opposite side of the wall, and the door burst in, crashing fire and sparks onto the floor. Frantically he looked around, panic throbbing in his chest, smoke and flames blinding him, and he couldn't see her. *He couldn't find her. . . .*

A sound of rage and terror rolled in his throat, and he lunged into the room, toward the flaming mass of door that blocked most of it. He caught a glimpse of white—there, in the corner beside the bunk—and in an instant he was on his knees beside her.

He saw her eyes, blurred with tears and wide with wonder, her face smudged with smoke and ashes. He heard the small choked coughs of her breath, and the relief that went through him was like an explosion. He scooped her up; he felt her arms lift weakly to go around his neck, and for a moment all he could do was hold her tightly, crushing her against him, burying his face in her hair and whispering things she did not hear and he would not remember. He squeezed his eyes tightly closed, his lips touched her face and her hair, and she was breathing, she was sobbing and coughing, she was alive. . . .

He slipped his arm beneath her knees and turned her face to his chest, then swiftly was on his feet, carrying her outside. The breeze was cool, and he drank deeply of it, for even tainted with smoke as it was, the air was a restorative after the inferno of Elizabeth's cabin. She began to cough more vigorously, dragging in breaths, and he held her tightly.

A wall of flame stood between him and the longboat, and he did not hesitate. He turned quickly toward the opposite rail. "It's all right, Elizabeth," he whispered, "I'm with you. I'm not going to let anything happen to you now."

* * *

Captain Chapman unloosed the rope and tossed it into the longboat but hesitated on deck, looking back. He would not leave until all passengers were safe, but he could not risk leaving the boat tied up any longer. Sparks were dusting the air, fiery timbers were falling, and the passengers were frantic as they fought to keep their clothes and hair from catching fire. The disaster had been spotted from shore, and already rescue boats were setting out, but they would arrive too late.

Lord Hartley was shouting to push off, and Miss Nancy was screaming frantically for Elizabeth, refusing to accept the comfort of William Bledsoe. Chapman knew he could not delay much longer, but his loyal crew held the boat still in the water, refusing to desert their captain until he gave the order.

Bledsoe, pushing his mother-in-law into the arms of a crew member, was clambering over the other passengers, calling, "Captain! Let me go back! Two will have a better chance than one!"

"No!" Chapman snapped back. "I've got two passengers to worry about already!" Despite his weakened condition he would go back as soon as the boat was safely launched, but he held little hope for rescue. If anyone could get to the girl, Fielding could, but Captain Chapman was very much afraid she was already dead.

He had never lost a passenger before. The horror was sickening, debilitating.

Miss Nancy cried, "We can't leave her! You must—"

Suddenly Chapman's attention was riveted on a movement within the cloud of smoke. "Look!" he shouted.

Silhouetted against the glowing wall of fire was Fielding, the girl in his arms. He made it to the rail, and Chapman knew what he was going to do.

He turned back to the boat. "They're safe!" he cried, and leapt in. "Push off!"

Miss Nancy grabbed his arm, her face wild and her clutch desperate. "What are you doing? You can't—"

"There's no way we can get to them from here," he told her, and the effort to keep his voice soothing was not so great as it once had been. "Fielding knows what he's doing. They'll be picked up by rescue boats, and if not, it's only a short swim to shore. They made it this far, ma'am. They're going to be all right."

Miss Nancy screamed, but he firmly gave the command to row. He looked back just once, but whatever uneasiness he harbored was invisible on his face. He knew that the likelihood of their being found in the dark by the rescue boats was slim. But if Jed Fielding was half as determined as he seemed, the swim to shore was not impossible. As soon as he landed, Chapman would organize search parties to look for them on shore, but until then, there was nothing else he could do.

He murmured, "God go with them," and picked up an oar.

Jed hesitated at the rail, holding Elizabeth tightly one last time. She was still coughing, but her breathing seemed easier now, and he knew he could not delay much longer. He cast a quick glance behind him, and as he did, a support piling creaked and fell with a flaming crash not two feet from where he stood.

"Listen to me." He looked down at her, his voice stern and his face grim. "You're going to be all right. Don't be afraid." Her eyes were wide and attentive, her shoulders shaking with repressed coughs, but whether she heard him, or understood, he could not be sure. His fingers dug into the soft flesh of her thighs and pressed against her ribs, and he had a brief, agonized awareness of how small she was, how light and how very fragile. . . .

"Breathe deeply now, as deeply as you can."

She obeyed shakily, watching him with the wide eyes and absolute trust of a terrified child, and it pulled at his heart.

"It's important." Emotion gruffened his voice and tightened his fingers against her flesh. "Keep your eyes and your mouth closed. Can you do that?"

Her eyes went wider, but she nodded.

"Promise me," he commanded urgently, and made himself loosen his grip. "Promise you won't be afraid."

Elizabeth nodded slowly. Her voice, through cracked and parched lips, was but a croak. "I promise . . . as long as you're with me."

Jed looked at her, and anxiety raged in his eyes. All he wanted to do was hold her, kiss her, hold her close and never let her go. . . . And even at that last moment he wasn't at all sure that he would be able to do what he knew he had to do.

But he closed his eyes briefly and made everything within him be still. "I'll be with you," he whispered, and brushed her cheek with a kiss. "I promise."

He walked to the rail and opened his arms. Even before she struck the water he was diving in after her.

CHAPTER
Nine

T he water dragged at the hem of Elizabeth's nightgown as Jed, with one strong arm around her waist,
found footing in the sand and pulled her on shore.
She stumbled, but he held her firmly, just as he had all
through the journey through death.

The moon had set, and it was that darkest, most isolated
hour before dawn. They had emerged upon the beach at
some distance from the city, in an area occupied by a
tumbledown fisherman's shack, a few deserted squatter's
lean-tos, and the remnants of an occasional canvas tent.
Through the heavy shadows of the trees and scrubby dunes
they could see the faint twinkle of lights from the city; in
the background the dying ship cast an eerie aura of false
sunrise and skeletal limbs. Through the roaring of their own
ragged breaths they could barely make out the shouts and

movements from the opposite shore, but sound carried well over water, and the city was still an hour's walk away.

The night air was warm and humid, as still as a muffling blanket, as welcome as a soft bed. Elizabeth was trembling violently all over, but not from cold. Residual terror and sweet, strong rhythms of victory surged through her veins with ever-increasing rapidity and left her weak. She was dizzy, intoxicated with wild triumph and yet more aware, more powerfully attuned to life and all living things than she ever had been before.

They had survived. They were here, together, and they had survived. . . .

In flashbacks the horror came, and with each reliving, the memory became more real, more present and alive than it had been before: Jed's face, appearing in the haze of her fading consciousness with such distant wonder that she had been certain it was a death dream, his arms enfolding her, crushing her to him, imparting strength and wonder and new life, lifting her, carrying her; air, flowing once again into her lungs; his voice, his face, her lifeline; and then the dark, thick abyss of a watery grave, that moment of sheer and rigid terror when she was certain she would die; fighting the blackness, fighting the helplessness, desperate for air; and then Jed's arms around her, lifting her to the surface, and precious air filling her lungs again, his face filling her eyes; Jed holding her, pulling her with him even though doing so endangered his own life, through the long and arduous swim toward safety.

Tonight she had lived through what few people ever would, or should. She had survived an ordeal unlike any she ever could have expected or prepared for. Elizabeth Coleman knew gracious manners and delicate needlework, orderly gardens and elegant sitting rooms; from birth she had been accustomed to having her every want supplied before she voiced it, for that was the nature of her world. She knew nothing of terror or danger or death. She had faced and survived all tonight, and nothing would ever be the same again.

Stumbling and leaning on each other, they made their way across the stubbly, grass-strewn shore toward the nearest shelter, a rough-planked lean-to that was open on one side and seemed to have once served as a scavenger's hut. There was a pile of canvas sail in a corner, as well as fishing nets, cooking pots, and scattered over the floor was a litter of other discarded cargo, doubtless rescued from previous abandoned ships.

But the walls, as flimsy as they were, provided some protection from the coolness of the sea breeze against their soaked clothing. Once inside, they fell as one to their knees, overtaken by exhaustion and relief. Automatically, hardly even aware of the movement, Jed reached inside his shirt and with leaden fingers removed the heavy weight of his gun and his Bible, placing both items on the ground next to him. Then they were both still, the only sound they heard the lapping of waves and the heaviness of their own breathing.

For a long time they stayed like that, kneeling across from each other, breathing hard and reeling with the impact of the moment. Their eyes could not leave each other, and the very air around them seemed to be charged with the electric thrill of conquest. They had survived. They had fought death and won and they were here, together.

And then, with a smothered cry, Elizabeth flung herself into his arms, burying her face against his chest. Deep, searing breaths racked her, and her face went to his neck. She tasted salt against his skin, and the muscles of his shoulders trembled as he wrapped his arms around her.

Her arms tightened around his neck, and her voice was

breathless and ragged, muffled against his clothing. "I thought I would die! But I didn't, I—"

His whisper shook with emotion. "I couldn't let you die." He turned his mouth to hers and he drank of her, fiercely, urgently, endlessly.

The pent-up tension burst between them like star fire; the throbbing wonder, the desperate need to hold and touch exploded in a rush and swept over them, consuming them and carrying them away with its power. Their embrace was urgent, wild and frantic and intense, but it was fed by joy, a flood of relief and wonder that demanded blindly, thoughtlessly, to be expressed. Jed's hands were hard on her back and his mouth demanding, consuming; Elizabeth's arms strained and ached with the effort to draw him closer, to hold him tighter, never to let him go.

She was kissing him back with the frantic, instinctive thirst of unnamed need. His mouth drew from her, tasting, commanding, taking from her as though seeking his very life's breath. She took from him with the same frantic, dizzying need, knowing only the hungry demand of what she must have . . . his touch, his heat, his power, and his strength.

She was drinking of him, infused with him, and she felt herself sinking, floating backward, until the rough texture of canvas was beneath her back and Jed's weight, warm and strong and invincible, was sheltering her.

A splash of rigid awareness burst through the cloudlike quality of the night when Elizabeth felt Jed's fingers fasten on the hem of her nightgown and begin to tug the sodden material upward. His fingers brushed against her leg, her hip, her waist, and there was a thrill of awareness, a breath-robbing, mind-stilling alertness, even through the dark warning of shock. The humid night air touched her skin, and her senses, her reason seemed frozen as he gently tugged the wet material over her head and discarded it.

It happened quickly, on the breath of something that was moving too fast for her to follow or control, much less fight. Dimly she was aware of crossing some invisible barrier from which there would be no turning back, and there was fear, confusion, deep and conflicting demands and imperatives. She was naked beneath the eyes of a man, beneath the touch of a man, and it was wrong and she was frightened . . . but it was Jed. Jed, who had gone through death with her, to whom she owed her very existence. And when his warm weight descended to cover her again, she could do nothing but raise her arms to welcome him and let his kisses draw her again into that sweet and helpless rush of mindless pleasure.

She felt his hands strong against her bare back, lifting her to him, gathering her close. She felt the heat of his chest through his damp clothing, abrading her swollen breasts. His taste was drugging, potent, and his hands, touching her naked skin, were tracing her curves and knowing her flesh in ways no man had ever known before.

She was trembling all over, her heart was pounding so violently that she thought it would come through her chest, and she couldn't get her breath. Later, much later, she would look back upon those few swift, whirling moments and wonder how it could be that such a thing could come upon her so suddenly, so completely, and so inexorably, without her having been in the least prepared. But, lost in the depth of sensation and newness, the thrill of life and mindless embrace of freedom, no such remnants of reason intruded. What happened between them was swift and urgent and unpreventable, and she had no way of knowing that it would leave her destiny forever altered.

Jed felt her flesh molding into his fingers, the curve of her hip, the ridges of her spine, the slender indentation of her waist, and each touch was a blow to his senses, an explosion of need that consumed his reason and plowed through his defenses.

Never had he wanted a woman like this. It was madness, it was weakness, it was wrong. But it was Elizabeth, and he knew nothing but the burning need to be with her, to bury himself deep within her and become a part of her, to blend with her and never let her go. "Elizabeth," he whispered thickly, and he felt her small fingers on his face, in his hair; he tasted her skin and the texture of her neck. And all he could do was whisper again, "Elizabeth . . ."

He felt her nakedness beneath him, smooth, white limbs and gentle, feminine flesh. He kissed her and she lifted herself to him, the softness of her abdomen pressing into his aching hardness. He knew he should stop, and he knew he could not. His clumsy fingers fumbled with the catch of his breeches, and with his knee he urged her legs apart. He saw the fear streak across her face then, and she resisted, but his heart was pounding and his vision was a blurred and heated wash of sensations; there was no thought of turning back. If she struggled, he did not know it. If she cried out, he did not hear. He knew only what was natural, the compulsion that could not be refused, the urgent, blinding demand of his body, and the joining that was inevitable.

He poised himself against her and felt the resistance of her tender flesh, saw the terror flash in her eyes. He wanted to comfort her, to soothe her, to wipe away her fear with tenderness and care. But it was too late for any of those concerns, too late for regret or retreat. The known world spun away into a mere pinpoint of urgent, consuming need, a primal intensity that would not be refused or ignored. With a muffled cry he crushed her against him and drove deep inside.

Instinctively Elizabeth struggled against the invasion of pain and the shock to her senses, sobbing as she fought to escape these unexpected and alien sensations. But his arms stilled her, and the swift, brushing touches of his lips across her face and her neck soothed her. The stinging of her torn flesh began to subside as he held her, and the strange fullness inside her was uncomfortable but not entirely unwelcome. The realization that this was Jed, that this dark, secret part of him was now a part of her, brought a deep wonder to her for the meaning of it all. Jed was so close to her, a physical part of her. She had never imagined it was possible for two people to be bonded in such a deep and personal way, but it seemed only right, only natural, for it was Jed, and it was Elizabeth, and she had been right all along. They belonged together.

He began to move himself inside her, and she cried out, alarmed, expecting him to hurt her again. But the discomfort was eclipsed by a new onslaught of alien intensity as once again the world began to whirl out of her control.

Her body forgot to resist his insistent, demanding invasion, her reason focused down into only a pinpoint of escalating, assaulting sensation. She gasped for breath and clung to him as his driving thrusts grew more forceful, and she knew nothing except Jed and herself, and what was happening to them that was unlike anything experience had ever taught her before. It was powerful, it was all-encompassing, it was strange, and it was terrifying, but it was right because it was Jed. And when at last he collapsed atop her with a final, shuddering thrust, Elizabeth was left dazed and clinging to him, buffeted by the tides of unfamiliar emotions and unknown sensations that swept her.

For a long time afterward she lay against him, her head pillowed upon his chest, her body weak and her mind numb and wondering. She could hear the sound of his harsh, unsteady breathing, feel the jerky pulse of his heartbeat beneath her palm. How strange it felt to be lying with him like this. In all her daydreams and fantasies about Jed this was something she had never imagined. She had never known that men and women could do things like this, and it was an awe-inspiring concept, an entirely new dimension to closeness, a bond of unity that simply could not have been conceived of before she had experienced it.

A week ago—even a day ago—the thought of lying naked with a man, the pain and the humiliation of the act they had just shared, would have horrified her. But after what they had been through tonight, this final and complete joining seemed only natural and right. What had begun with a soul-searing battle against death had culminated in this, the most absolute confirmation of life, and how could it have been otherwise?

After this night she did not think she would ever think about life, or herself, or womanhood, in the same terms again.

Jed lay very still beside her. His heart was beating with a slow and heavy dread, and all he could think was, *What have I done?* Elizabeth, so lovely, so fragile, lying on a scrap of canvas, naked and soiled. He had hurt her, and the last thing in the world he had wanted to do was bring her to harm. Once she had said she loved him, but now . . . now she would only hate him. And her scorn was all he deserved. Elizabeth . . .

His lust had made a mockery of his rescue. He had saved her life only to use her . . . and ruin her. Only the most despicable of men would take advantage of a terrified, distraught woman to satisfy his own passion. He had intended only to protect her, but he had violated her in the most unredeemable and unforgivable fashion.

He closed his eyes slowly, blocking from sight, but not

from mind, the figure she made, curled up like that against him. A deep and empty agony rose up within him, and if he could have, with the power of his will, erased the events of the past half hour from all time, he would have done so. But Jed knew only the strength of his hands, the force of determination, and he knew the limits of both. He could not rewind time, he could not undo wrongs. He could only somehow find a way to live with them.

He felt the light touch of her fingers on his face, and he knew he should turn to her, hold her, say something to her. . . . But he didn't know what to say. That he was sorry, that he had never meant to hurt her, that he wanted the best for her . . . but none of that would matter now. And the words would not come.

Jed got heavily to his feet, and perhaps in a dim corner of his consciousness he heard the movements, or caught a flash of warning, long before he acted upon them. But his reflexes were slow, his mind numb and aching, and it took a moment for the approaching disaster to register.

But when it did, he moved quickly. He saw the glimmer of a torch through the cracked boards; he heard the murmur of voices. He found Elizabeth's nightgown and instinctively wrapped it around her shoulders, all the while knowing it was too late.

Just when they thought the worst was over, it had only begun. For when Jed turned, straightening quickly, the murmuring and the movements outside ceased abruptly. There at the opening of the shack, silhouetted against the rising sun, were Captain Chapman, William Bledsoe, and Miss Nancy Lea.

CHAPTER
Ten
---

*T*he hotel parlor was small, rudely furnished, and hardly could be considered a parlor at all. There were no carpets on the floor, and the thin muslin curtains that were pulled back from the window were stained with dust and tobacco spittle. But it was the only private room where a lady might receive a gentleman in all of Galveston, and Miss Nancy conducted herself as though it were the drawing room of Windsor Castle. She sat upon a straight, unpadded chair behind a card table that also served as a writing desk. Her face composed and her back stiff, she calmly addressed the man sitting across from her.

"I want to settle this between us, Mr. Fielding, and as soon as possible, before Mr. Bledsoe is forced to call you out."

Jed's face was immobile. His buckskins were stained with cinder holes and water marks, his shirtsleeve torn, his palms blistered, and his knuckles scraped. His face was unshaven, and shadows of exhaustion circled his eyes. But he held himself straight and still, and he met the woman's eyes evenly. "I hope he doesn't try, ma'am," Jed answered quietly. "Mr. Bledsoe's a fine man, and I'd hate to have to kill him."

Miss Nancy blanched. His statement was so matter-of-fact, his expression so reserved, that she realized, for perhaps the first time, the kind of man with whom she was dealing. She had no doubt he could kill William, in a duel of honor or otherwise, and perhaps he had killed before. What, after all, did she know about this man except that he was a ruffian and a lecher? Oh, how could this have happened to her dear, innocent Elizabeth?

Quickly regaining her composure, Miss Nancy tightened her clasped fingers atop the desk and returned coolly, "I'm afraid, sir, you have little choice in the matter."

"No, ma'am, that's where you're wrong. I always have a choice."

Anger flared in Miss Nancy's eyes and shook her voice as she declared, "You have ruined a lady of quality, sir! This is not one of your barroom sluts! This is Miss Elizabeth Coleman of Larchmont Plantation—a blameless, innocent young girl who at this moment lies helpless in her sickbed—"

"I am neither helpless nor abed, Miss Nancy."

Elizabeth stood at the door, her head high, her face composed. She wore a plain calico dress loaned to her by the proprietress of the hotel; it was too large for her about the bodice and waist, and the hem dragged the floor by several inches. Her face was pale with the strain of the past twenty-four hours, and her eyes were dark with fatigue. But there was determination in the set of her lips, dignity in the lift of her chin and, as always, pride in every move she made. She lifted her skirts and crossed the room with the same regal grace with which she had moved through the garden of Spring Hill, and she said quietly, "This does not concern you, Miss Nancy. It is between Mr. Fielding and myself."

Jed got to his feet, seeing no reason for Elizabeth to undergo further humiliation on his behalf. But before he could intervene, Miss Nancy spoke up, indignation sharpening her tone.

"It most certainly is not! I have been entrusted with your care, and I will see it to a satisfactory conclusion, though for myself I'd prefer to see the blackguard horsewhipped and jailed!"

The flare of incredulity in Elizabeth's eyes was immediate and unexpected. "Why?" she demanded. "He has committed no crime."

For a moment Miss Nancy was so taken aback, she could not gather a reply. And then, with quiet force, she said distinctly, "He has ruined you."

Jed, impatient and weary of it all, started to speak, but a glance at Elizabeth's face stopped him. She was staring at the other woman as though she had never seen her before, and she said slowly, "He saved my life! Would you rather I had died?"

Miss Nancy's lips grew taut, an angry color painting her cheeks. She said, with great dignity, "Some ladies would have preferred it."

Elizabeth stared at her, and all she could think was how farcical it was, Miss Nancy prattling on about reputation and ladyhood as though such things really mattered. A scant sunrise ago Elizabeth had felt her very life slip from her hands, then it had been miraculously restored to her by no mechanizations of her own. How could anyone ever look at life again in the same way after having so nearly experienced its loss? *It doesn't matter*, she thought, and the thought filled her with wonder at the simple realization of its truth. None of those things Miss Nancy has always believed important matter in this time, in this place...perhaps they never did.

Elizabeth lifted her chin, saying with simple, clear dignity, "I, madame, am not one of those who would have preferred to die."

Miss Nancy's horror was as tangible as a gasp. "Elizabeth, you cannot mean that! You are beside yourself—"

"I am perfectly myself," Elizabeth said coolly. "And I would appreciate your leaving this matter to be handled by the two people it concerns."

Miss Nancy's eyes showed her struggle between outrage and despair. Her lips went tight with anger, and she rose abruptly. "Very well, Elizabeth. I never thought I would see this day. I wash my hands of you." She swept past Elizabeth, and at the door she turned back. "And you, Mr. Fielding," she promised icily, "will consider your duty or answer to Mr. Bledsoe."

Elizabeth watched her go with a throb of sorrow and confusion that made her momentarily helpless. Nothing would ever be the same between herself and Miss Nancy again. She had loved the other woman like a mother, had taken all she knew from her, had clung to her as the only perfect thing in an imperfect world. But now...now Miss Nancy was no longer perfect. Nothing was the same.

Perhaps because Elizabeth, herself, would never be the same.

She looked cautiously at Jed, waiting for the shame and the horror that Miss Nancy would have expected her to feel to come. All she saw was the weariness on his face, the strong jaw bristled by the golden beard, the hands raw with burns.... All she could remember was his strong arms lifting her, carrying her into the night air, his voice whispering,

"I'll be with you, I promise. . . ." He had given her life at the risk of his own, and later they had shared the most intense intimacy of life itself. There was no shame in that.

Elizabeth knew that the young girl who had left Mobile scarcely a week ago would have, along with Miss Nancy, preferred death to what had happened afterward, and the trauma of being discovered like that with a man. Elizabeth thought now, with some small wonder, that, given it all to live over again, she would not have done anything differently.

Never for a moment did she stop to think that Jed had no way of knowing it had all filled her with joy, not horror.

Jed's eyes were sober as he looked at her, and she could not imagine what he was thinking. She only knew how she felt.

He said simply, quietly, "I can get a preacher for this afternoon if you'll be ready."

Elizabeth caught her breath, searching his face cautiously. "Is that . . . what you want?" she said softly.

Jed's tone was flat, his face expressionless. "It's what must be done."

Something chilling began to seep into Elizabeth's chest. She tried to smile but couldn't quite. His eyes were so blank. "You make it sound like a jail sentence."

A flicker of apology softened Jed's eyes but in a moment was overcome by a measure of gentle frustration. He stood apart from her, at a distance of four feet, and she thought for a moment that he would move closer, to touch her. But he did not. He said, with difficulty, "This is not what I wanted for you."

Elizabeth's heart began to beat rapidly. She thought it was with hope, but it might have been dread. Something was wrong. This was not how she had imagined receiving her first marriage proposal. This was not how she had expected Jed to behave on first seeing her again. . . .

She searched his eyes anxiously, desperately looking for some shred of affection or tenderness. "But . . ." she began, and her throat felt tight. "After what happened between us—"

All vestiges of emotion were completely wiped from Jed's eyes, and his face went as blank as a clay sculpture. He said flatly, "What happened between us was a big mistake."

She felt the blow of his statement in her chest like a fist. Suddenly she had difficulty getting her breath. She couldn't take her eyes off his face. So hard and so remote. "How . . . can you say that? We love—"

Jed's eyes moved away restlessly, impatiently, and his tone was harsh. "You've got a lot to learn about men and women, Miss Coleman. And what happened between us has got nothing to do with love."

Out of the corner of his eyes Jed saw her hand flutter to her throat, and every muscle in his body tensed in furious self-derision, but there was nothing he could do to take back the sting of his words. Nothing he could do to take back the truth.

From the moment he had met her he had wanted her. The beautiful lady in her fancy riding habit on the thoroughbred horse who had so unexpectedly invaded his world, a symbol of all he never could have. He had lusted after her obsessively, unflaggingly, just as once he had lusted after the grace and beauty of Spring Hill. And just as he had known the refined life of the Southern aristocracy was not really what he wanted at all, so he had known that Miss Elizabeth Coleman was not for him. But she was the unobtainable, the dream every man has to hold on to, and he had not been able to stop wanting her. He had known it was wrong, but he hadn't stopped.

This was the price he paid for taking what he wanted. He

had ruined a fine lady, made her believe in fairy-tale endings and impossible ever-afters. Now she was looking at him with stricken, hurting eyes, and there was nothing he could do to make it right.

He hated himself for what he had done, and looking at her only reminded him of it. Suddenly she had come to represent nothing but the worst side of himself. He found it difficult even to be in her presence, so great was his self-disgust.

For a long time they stood silent, the room hot and dusty, the distant street sounds all they heard. Finally Elizabeth managed to say stiffly, "I will not force you into marriage, sir."

Jed turned, and he couldn't prevent the bitter smile that twisted his lips. He was weary of pretending or searching for gentleness that wouldn't come. All he knew was his own misery, and what he had inflicted on her, and his helplessness to alleviate either. The helplessness made him angry—at himself, at fate, and even at Elizabeth. He said, more harshly than he should have, "Grow up, Miss Coleman. Who do you think will marry you if I don't? Do you think you can just sail back to Alabama and find a husband?"

Elizabeth's head was reeling, her chest aching with such deep, unquenchable pain that even her stomach muscles tightened against it. What happened between them had changed nothing! For a brief moment he had been her hero again, but now he was nothing more than a cold and pragmatic man who did not want her. How many times must she suffer the shattering of her illusions to learn that there was no truth in romance, no place for a man like Jed Fielding in her fantasies?

She struggled to hold on to what little dignity she had left. Her head jerked up, and she returned sharply, "And who do I have to thank for that? I trusted you, I believed you, and you used me for... the satisfactions of your animal passions, just as you would use a common street girl!''

She saw a flush stain his cheeks, but there was no comfort in seeing how effectively her words had wounded him. She was wounded, too, more deeply and more painfully than he could imagine, and all she knew was to strike back. He had taken something beautiful between them and turned it into an ugly, animal impulse, and did he now expect her simply to forget it?

She swallowed hard, grasping for composure, and her fists clenched at her sides. She said as firmly as she could manage, ''However, you needn't concern yourself for my sake. If this is what marriage means, I shall never marry.''

Her innocence, and his own guilt, hammered down upon him like pelting stones. She was so naive, so unsuspecting of life and its harshest realities, that he wanted to shake her, to take out his frustration and his self-disgust in a plain and physical way... but of course he couldn't. He could only stand there, a victim of the hurt and the contempt in her eyes, and hate himself with all the intensity in his soul.

Jed said cruelly, ''What if you have a baby?''

Elizabeth went white with shock, and she could only stare at him. That a man should refer to such a thing... Not even husbands and wives discussed matters of such delicacy between themselves. How could he stand there so crudely and call up the consequences of their union?

Her voice was choked as she whispered, ''You were right. You are not a gentleman.''

He said nothing.

Abruptly the last veil fell away from Elizabeth's eyes. There was nothing beautiful or romantic about this. It was no tragic opera or heart-wrenching poem. It was vulgar words and stark consequences and a light of reality that could not be avoided. It was a moment of thoughtless passion in a deserted beach shack that left her reputation in shatters and her honor forever torn; a man with unshaven face and tired, impatient eyes setting forth the consequences of her future.

As she stood immobile and staring, Jed took a breath and quickly released it. He walked over to pick up his hat. "This marriage is not what you want or what I want," he said simply. There was no expression in his tone at all. "But it will take place. I'll do what has to be done."

Without another word he walked out the door.

Elizabeth stood alone in the shabby little room for a long time, and a great and empty weariness settled upon her. She felt stripped, battered, and so numb that she had not even the strength to cry.

For he was right, of course. This was the real world, and her awakening to it had been brutal, but she had to face the truth now. There was no choice.

So often she had dreamed of this, yearned for it...marriage to a strong and handsome hero in a romantic faraway land, adventure, excitement, passion. This was what all her foolish fantasies had brought her to. Not a great romantic love but a matter of honor and a forced marriage; not her bold and dashing hero but a harsh man with cold eyes who did what had to be done.

Elizabeth wandered over to the window and rested her cheek against the frame, looking out unseeingly. A faint, sad smile traced the corners of her lips, and then faded into bleakness. So often Miss Nancy had cautioned her to be careful what she wished for.

And now she knew why.

CHAPTER
Eleven

*E*lizabeth was married that afternoon in a dove-gray cotton dress hastily purchased at the dry-goods store. The ceremony was performed in the shabby parlor of the house where the Presbyterian minister and his wife lived. The wife was thin and flushed with the heat and rather disgruntled, and the minister was large and scrubby, dressed in a dusty white shirt with deep perspiration stains under the arms. There was no organ music, no flowers, no beaming friends and relatives to wish Elizabeth well on her journey into marital bliss. There was not even a wedding ring. The vows were simply said, and it was done.

William finally broke the awkward silence that lingered after the ceremony, moving forward with a blustering smile to take both of Elizabeth's hands and place a light kiss upon her cold cheek. "Well, now. Congratulations to the both of you."

He turned from Elizabeth to shake Jed's hand, and his determined attempts to regard this as a happy occasion were both pathetic and embarrassing. But William was a gentleman, and he knew no other way to deal with unpleasantness except to ignore it; those were the standards of the world from which he came. "May I suggest we return to the inn for a glass of wine? We must toast the future."

They had taken rooms at the Planters Hotel on the strand, a short walk across broken boards and mire from the minister's house. At another time, perhaps, Elizabeth would have been enthralled by all the sights and sounds that assaulted her, for Galveston was a booming town of rapidly expanding entrepreneurship. The sounds of construction were endless, and the movement of freight wagons and buggies through the muddy street kept traffic in a tangle.

During the brief walk to the hotel they circled no less than three piles of lumber being rapidly thrown up for shops and saloons, skirted a furious altercation between a mule driver and a Mexican vaquero with a quirt, and barely missed being spat upon no less than half a dozen times by disreputable-looking men who lounged outside the building chewing tobacco and using bowie knives to pick their teeth or trim their nails. The filthy stench of rotting oysters permeated the air, and shouts and curses from the saloons competed with the sound of hammers and the rattle of wheels. Galveston was a wild and uncivilized place, a little frightening but teeming with life. In contrast, the shabby little parlor of the Planters Hotel, with its plank furniture and stained floor, seemed almost elegant.

William poured four glasses of inferior sherry procured from the proprietress at great cost. He hesitated, obviously uncertain as to an appropriate toast. A green fly buzzed around the open bottle, and the breeze brought in the scent of decay and mud from the open window. At last he smiled, said, "To prosperity," and drank quickly. Elizabeth found her throat too tight even to swallow and did not lift her own glass. Jed did not look at her.

Elizabeth wandered over to a deacon's bench and sat down, and a meaningful look passed from Miss Nancy to William. The good lady had done her Christian duty; she had seen Elizabeth married. From now on the matter was in William's hands.

William cleared his throat under the weight of the awkward responsibility and lifted his arm as though to rest a companionable hand on Jed's shoulder. The gesture fell short, however, and the silence was strained until William cleared his throat again.

"Well, sir," he began, and the effort to keep conviviality in his voice was audible. "While I do understand your reluctance to return to Mobile for the ceremony, under the circumstances . . ." He flushed furiously at the near faux pas but forged determinedly on. "However, I trust that now you will reconsider. Mrs. Lea and I will be returning on the next steamship—we can hardly continue our journey as planned, having lost our trunks and our—er—confidence in our guide. After Lord Hartley's display at the poker game I've come to see he is not a gentleman and certainly will not endorse him further, you understand. . . ." His voice lowered somewhat at the last, for Lord Hartley's behavior, however detestable, did not begin to compare with Jed's, and at any rate it was not a subject to be discussed in front of ladies.

"Naturally," William continued, picking up the point of the conversation with a bit more gusto than was strictly necessary, "we hope you and Elizabeth will be accompanying us. Mr. Coleman will be expecting you to live at Larchmont, and speaking as a fellow planter, I know he will welcome your assistance in running the plantation. However, if that does not suit, I would be glad to—"

Jed said quietly, "I'm not a farmer." His eyes were on Elizabeth. She sat straight and still on the hard wooden bench, her face pale and composed, her head high, and her eyes focused calmly on the open window. He turned back to Mr. Bledsoe. "I have a ranch," he said, "and people waiting for me to return. I've been away too long already. I'll be leaving for home today."

William had not been completely unprepared for this. He knew Jed Fielding as a stubborn man, and up until the very vows were pronounced, he had lived in fear that he would be forced to call him out. Fielding was no gentleman, as he had proven well, but he held a peculiar code of ethics that both surprised and disoriented William. He was never quite certain how to deal with him and knew only that he would be happiest not dealing with him at all.

William's expression grew troubled, and he touched Jed's arm lightly to turn him away from the ladies. He cleared his throat again and added quietly, trying not to be overheard, "Have you considered, sir, the wisdom of taking a young lady like Elizabeth to the frontier? She has been most delicately brought up, accustomed to a way of life quite different from your own. You will be taking her away from not only the comfort of her family and friends but also from all that is familiar to her. I fear it would be a most unhappy state of affairs."

Jed looked at him soberly. "That's why," he answered, "she will be going back with you."

A cautious measure of relief crossed William's face. He did not know how Miss Nancy would welcome this solution, but to him it was the only sensible way. Sometimes these things were best decided by men, who could think clearly and logically without the encumbrance of emotion.

"I'm glad you agree, sir," William murmured, and took

another sip of his sherry, relaxing. Jed's eyes wandered again to Elizabeth.

He knew it was the only thing to do. She, doubtless, would be glad of it too. But he could not leave her thinking he was discarding her like a scrap of soiled clothing. He had to speak to her before he left.

Jed excused himself and walked over to Elizabeth. He hesitated a moment and then sat down beside her, his hands linked awkwardly between his knees. He turned to look at her and tried to think what to say. How could this have happened? It never should have been like this for her. . . .

"Elizabeth . . ." he began, and then he couldn't go on. Elizabeth. He must have uttered her name in the depths of his passion, but this was the first time he had addressed her formally without the polite title of Miss. But that was who she was: Elizabeth Fielding, his wife.

The realization shook him profoundly, and he had to drop his eyes. What man would not fight to the death to keep a wife such as she? Beautiful, regal, all that represented grace and civility and quiet dignity . . . Everything a man could possibly want. All the things a man spent a lifetime dreaming of . . .

At last he made himself lift his eyes again and look at her. She met his gaze briefly, and then her eyes skated away. He did not blame her, and the sorrow twisted at him like the turn of a knife. He wished he could make it different. He wanted to tell her he was sorry, but sorry would do no good now. He had never intended this for her.

He said at last, quietly, "Elizabeth . . ." and once again was at a loss as to how to proceed. He stared at his hands and knew no other way than to be out with it. "Bledsoe and Mrs. Lea are taking the next ship back. You should go with them. You're my wife, and it will be known. There's no shame in it. And if there's a child . . . you'll never want for anything I can provide.'' A foolish promise. She had everything and he had nothing. The only thing he could do for her was to let her go.

He felt his muscles tighten with determination, and he forged on. But he still couldn't look at her. ''You'll be better off with your own folks, in your own house. . . . I've told you what it's like here; you've seen some of it for yourself.'' His eyes wandered briefly to the window, and then back to his hands. They were large, brown, and strong, but helpless to prevent the pain she was experiencing. Helpless to do anything for her at all.

He looked back toward the window and spoke to it. ''This is a land for men to try to get along in the best way they can, and they want their womenfolk safe at home, back East. Folks know that. We are married, and nothing will change that. But you belong in Mobile with your father. And my life is here.''

How simple it sounded when he said it. Elizabeth's heart began to pound, slowly and heavily, first with the mere sound of his voice, then with the implication of his words.

Desperately she wanted her father, the cool, spacious rooms of Larchmont, the soothing sound of Negro voices. . . . There she would have the peace and solidity of a well-ordered world, a world where nothing ever changed and nothing ever threatened. But would that world ever be the same for her?

She looked at Jed, and this time her gaze did not waver. She said quietly, ''You will never come back to Alabama.''

Jed said nothing.

Elizabeth gathered her courage, lifting her chin a fraction. A brawl broke out in the street outside; glass crashed, a man shouted, and a horse whinnied angrily. What lay before her was frightening and unknown, yet behind her was nothing but her abandoned childhood. She said softly but firmly, "You are my husband. I will go where you go."

Jed did not know what he had expected from her, but that was not it. He objected gruffly, "Elizabeth—"

"You can send me back," she continued quietly, "and I will return. You can leave me behind and I will follow. I am married to you and I belong by your side."

Jed's face went dark, and he said flatly, "No. I won't allow it. You don't have any idea what kind of life you'd have if you went with me—"

"But I know what kind of life I would be going back to," Elizabeth said coolly. "To send me back would be the simplest solution for you, but for me there would be nothing. I would be a wife without a husband, neither widowed nor married nor unattached. I would be returning to scandal and gossip, without a home of my own and without prospects, my girlhood gone and nothing before me but a lonely old age. And that, sir," she announced with a lift of her chin, "*I* will not allow."

Jed was taken aback once again by her unexpected display of spirit. What could he say to that? She was right. He had been thinking only of the easiest way out of a messy situation, and he felt a rush of shame for it. She was his wife, and there was no choice. He had to take full responsibility for her.

Jed looked at her for just another moment, and then he got to his feet quickly, before she could change her mind— or before he could. He returned to Bledsoe. "My wife refuses to be left behind," he stated, amazed at the sense of wonder that simple phrase inspired within him. *My wife*. For better or for worse, and for the rest of their lives. He had never expected it to happen like this.

He saw quick objection form on Bledsoe's face, and Miss Nancy moved forward with an alarmed sound, but Jed turned smoothly back to Elizabeth. "Will you be ready to leave in a couple of hours? I'd like to get some traveling done before dark."

Elizabeth rose. She did not look at William Bledsoe or at Miss Nancy, only at Jed. There was tranquillity in her eyes, the mark of an unwavering decision. "Yes," she answered. "I have only to . . . write some letters home and I'll be ready."

There was nothing more to say. He nodded, turned, and left the room.

Jed crossed the street to the mercantile and spent his time replacing the supplies he had lost in the fire. But only half his attention was upon the routine of his purchases. Most of it was absorbed in memories of the woman he had just departed.

Whenever possible, Jed tried to think a situation through, to reach a calm and calculated decision by examining all the facts he knew. Sometimes that ability for cool and rational thought was the only weapon a man had, and Jed knew its value. What he had done today was neither calm nor rational, and he knew he would live to regret it. But he did not seem to be able to find any other solution.

Bledsoe and Mrs. Lea would try to talk Elizabeth out of going with him, and part of him hoped they would succeed. The other part of him didn't know what he thought—he only knew how he felt. The events of the past days had been intense, explosive, and highly emotional. Jed could deal with danger, real or imagined; with threats and adversity of any kind. But he did not know how to deal with his own emotions. He had never had to learn.

All he wanted was the best for Elizabeth. He had made a mistake, an unforgivable and unredeemable mistake, in that night of highly charged emotion on the beach. But it was done now, and regrets and recriminations would not take it back.

Remembering the quiet strength in her tone, the stubborn lift of her chin, he felt a brief and unexpected surge of possessive pride—even admiration—and in the process of examining a bridle, he almost smiled. She was his wife, and she refused to be left behind. Though he knew it was wrong, there was still a part of him—the selfish and needing part—that was glad.

He purchased a wagon and team for the trip to the steamboat, which would take them up the Brazos, and made arrangements to have his supplies loaded onto it. It occurred to him that if not for the money won from Hartley that night, he would not have been able to so easily recoup his losses from the accident. But he did not give the matter much thought. If he had not won the money, he would have earned it, for a man did what he must to get by. There was no point in trying to second-guess fate.

It was therefore with little surprise that the first person he saw when he walked into the saloon was Lord Hartley. He was sitting alone at a table, and he was drinking brandy—not an easy commodity to come by in these parts. His face was still deformed with bruises and cuts, but he was perfectly groomed and had wasted no time in having a new suit made. Whether this was his first drink of the day or one of many, Jed could not tell. He suspected that on a man like Hartley it would make no difference.

Though it was early in the afternoon, the saloon was not empty. In a place like Galveston, with ships constantly coming and going, there was always plenty of business. There were a couple of serape-clad Mexicans leaning against the bar, a table of card players, and some folks all dressed in store-bought clothes who had "tenderfoot" written all over them. A farmer was shoveling down a breakfast of beans and pork, and two trail-weary range riders glanced up when Jed entered, took his measure, and then returned to their silent drinking. Hartley noticed him immediately and called him over with a wave of the hand. "Well, well, if it isn't the happy bridegroom. Come, do me the honor of toasting your health."

Jed's lips dryly turned down at one corner. He really did not want to deal with Hartley today. "Somehow, Hartley, I think my health is the last thing you want to drink to."

Hartley returned a mirthless smile, which blended into the swollen side of his face and looked like a grimace. "How right you are, my friend. But join me, anyway."

Jed walked over and pulled out a chair, keeping his hands free and his back to the sun. Because of the wedding, he was wearing no gun, and that made him uneasy. "Did you ever get that fancy knife of yours back?" he asked casually.

Hartley chuckled and gestured briefly to the bartender. "So I did. But you needn't worry. I've thought better of public assassinations."

"Can't tell you how relieved I am to hear that."

The bartender brought a bottle and glass, poured, and left both on the table. Here, as anywhere else he went, Hartley's authority was absolute and unspoken. He was born to command, and he commanded what he could.

"So." Hartley took up his glass and leaned back in his chair, watching Jed narrowly through one swollen eye. "You must be quite pleased with yourself. In a very short time you have become richer by one hundred and eighty-five thousand acres, several hundred dollars, a wealthy bride, and an aristocratic name. I must say, I am impressed." He lifted his glass. "To a man who knows how to work the odds."

Jed did not drink. Whatever satisfaction he had ever felt for his victory over Hartley was gone now. Too much had happened, and in retrospect the entire card game and the fight that followed seemed childish. At any rate, that, too, was over and done with, and Jed saw no point in rehashing old business.

"I doubt my good friend Coleman will be pleased to hear about this hasty wedding," murmured Hartley. "I rather think he had more ambitious plans for his daughter. I shouldn't wonder but that he brings you to an accounting for this."

Jed sipped his own drink but kept his eyes on Hartley. The disfigurement of his face made the coldness in Hartley's eyes look even more ugly than usual. "I reckon that's between me and him."

Hartley chuckled suddenly. "No wonder you weren't interested in my proposition, back at Spring Hill. You had much bigger things in mind."

"Not as big as you did." Jed lifted his glass again and drank. He added mildly, "I reckon you'll be heading on back to the States now. Not too much left for you here."

Hartley poured another casual measure of brandy into his glass. "Not a chance in the world, my friend. I've still got several thousand acres in coupons to register."

"I'd do that, was I you," commented Jed, "before I lost them."

Hartley cast him a sharp look, but Jed's expression was implacable. Hartley's fingers tightened imperceptibly on the glass, but he deliberately smoothed out his face. "You've registered yours, of course."

"All legal and proper-like. I tacked those acres right on to the ones I already had, and now I own the prettiest corner in east Texas, all to myself." Jed was a methodical man who knew the importance of details. Though those land coupons had been last on his list of priorities, he had taken them to the land office the first chance he got, just to be rid of them.

Though they meant little to him, to Hartley they were worth killing for. And Jed had responsibilities now.

Hartley was watching him with the same flat, cold patience with which a snake watches a bird. What was going through his mind was deep and unreadable, but Jed could guess. "I was wrong about you," he murmured at last. "I rarely make that kind of mistake. I knew you were a rough man, but I had heard you were fair. That you played by the rules."

Jed finished off his drink and did not desire another one. "Out here," he told Hartley simply, "we make our own rules."

Hartley's expression did not waver. Jed had seen that look on the face of a battlefield commander as he weighed the odds, on the face of the enemy as he sighted down the barrel. Jed had worn that look many times himself.

Hartley said simply, quietly, "I'll remember that."

Jed pushed up from the table. "Thanks for the drink, Hartley. My best to the folks back East."

He circled around toward the door so that he could keep Hartley in the edge of his vision, and he did not completely turn his back until he was outside. He knew it was not over with Hartley, but he was not one to borrow trouble from the future. Next time he would not be caught unarmed.

He glanced at the position of the sun and knew they had better be starting out. Galveston, for all its rough and rowdy ways, was still a town, and like all towns it made him feel stifled. He couldn't wait to get home.

And then it struck him. He was going home, only this time he wouldn't be going alone. He never would be alone again. The concept was too big, too alien and unplanned-for, for him to completely accept. Perhaps he never would.

There was a drummer on the street corner selling goods from the back of his wagon. Jed stopped by and looked over his merchandise idly. Most of what he needed he had already purchased, but he picked up a couple of packages of needles and paid a penny for them, and then he saw the books.

"Ah, a reading man," exclaimed the drummer, noticing his interest. "What is your pleasure, sir? Philosophy, law, poetry . . . I'm sure you'll find something that interests you."

There were six or eight of them, all tied together with a leather strap. "How much?" Jed asked.

The drummer hesitated. "Well, now, which one did you have in mind?"

"I don't want to read them," Jed answered, "just buy them."

They dickered for a while, and Jed bought the whole stack for three dollars, not even glancing at the titles. Elizabeth set a great store by books, he knew, and it would get lonely for her out on the trail.

CHAPTER
Twelve

*A*t sunset on Elizabeth's wedding day they reached the landing on the Brazos and boarded the steamship for the voyage upriver. During the long journey up the Brazos, Elizabeth saw very little of her new husband, for the conditions on the tiny riverboat were very much similar to those while crossing from Mobile to Galveston. Elizabeth shared the only available cabin with a widow woman who was going to live with her son in Houston, and Jed slept on deck with the other men. Most of the time Elizabeth spent sewing to replenish her lost wardrobe, but there was no lack of excitement along the way.

From Jed's previous description of it Elizabeth had expected Texas to be a wild, windswept land, beautiful in vista but untamed and unpopulated. All along the Brazos, Elizabeth saw scenes not unlike what she had left behind in Mobile—cotton plantations, rows and rows of the white gold nodding in the sun, slaves loading bales of it into waiting wagons, warehouses full of it, barges loaded with it. She heard voices lifted in familiar spirituals and saw gentlemen mounted on fine horses. Once she even saw a carriage drawn up at the landing with a well-dressed lady and her two children waving as the steamboat passed.

Elizabeth's disappointment was mixed with relief, for although this was not quite the adventure she had imagined, there was comfort in the familiar. No matter how remote Jed's ranch or what the life-style he had chosen, this was a planting society, and she would be at home here.

As they traveled farther upstream the ship would sometimes lodge against the sandy shoals, and the male passengers would work alongside the crew with ropes and pulleys, hip-deep in sandy water, to dislodge it. Occasionally they passed a stretch of desolate land, the tangled riverbanks draped in Spanish moss and climbing vines. Now and again she caught a glimpse of a ramshackle building that looked as though it had been constructed from parts of crates. These, the captain informed her with amusement in his tone, were the inns or trading posts where travelers might pass the night. The characters who hung around the waterfront near those buildings were dirty, mean-eyed, and unshaven, and Elizabeth was glad she did not have to pass the night there.

Jed was remote and distant and seemed to go out of his way to avoid her. Though he made every effort to see to her comfort, nothing of a personal nature ever passed between them. He passed his days with the other male passengers, and after supper he walked Elizabeth to her cabin and said good night. They were never alone.

Sometimes Elizabeth would catch a glimpse of him, standing in conversation, perhaps, with another passenger. She would notice the glint of the sun on his hair, the narrow, weathered lines radiating from his eyes toward his bronzed temple, the movement of his hand—and something would catch in her chest, a fluttering or an aching, and she remembered her golden-haired hero in the wood. She remembered, and it seemed like another lifetime. Was this what marriage was, then? A polite agreement between strangers? Was this what he wanted from her . . . silence, obedience, distance? How could she know? She knew nothing of marriage or men . . . or Jed.

They disembarked at a landing called Yellowood, a riverfront town consisting of a long log building filled with merchandise of every description, a corral, a saloon the size of a packing crate, and a circular area of muddy, churned-up ground around the whole, which passed for a street. They arrived at dawn, and it took Jed less than an hour to purchase a wagon and team and load their supplies onto it. Barely five hundred yards from the riverfront all signs of civilization—paltry as they had been—disappeared, and only wilderness lay before them. For the first time Elizabeth began to realize what Jed meant when he had used the word *frontier*.

"Have we very far to go?" Elizabeth asked after perhaps an hour or so on the jolting, rutted wagon trail.

Jed kept his eyes on the yoke, the reins held loosely between his fingers, his broad-brimmed hat pulled down to shade his face. "Two days' ride," he answered briefly.

The silence stretched long and heavy between them. It was a silence that had begun the day of her wedding and promised to go on indefinitely. How much longer could he pretend to ignore her? What had happened to the man who had enthralled her with his stories, taken her breath away with the poetry of his words? How much more of this distant, unbreachable silence could she take?

Her tone was a bit acid as she pointed out, "Two days is a long time to share a wagon without speaking."

Jed looked at her. How lovely she looked sitting beside him in the crisp green traveling suit she had bought in Galveston, with her starched white collar and spotless gloves. Her bonnet had a flower on it and was tied with a big white bow that shadowed her cheek and caressed her chin. The tips of her little shoes were polished kid. Not even the complete loss of her wardrobe would daunt the impeccable style of Miss Elizabeth Coleman; she looked as regal and composed as if she were traveling in a velvet-curtained carriage with a team of matched bays, instead of a broken-down wagon and two drays.

On the boat, still among the vestiges of civilization, he had been able to push aside the truth of it somewhat, to avoid the inevitable reality. But here, alone in the wilderness with her, the full impact of what he had done struck him. He could no longer avoid it. She was here, as out of place and unsuited for the world into which he had brought her as a china doll in a bullring. She was here, and he was responsible for her for the rest of his life. All he could feel was a smoldering helplessness, a nagging frustration, and a resentment he couldn't control. He had done this. He had brought her here. What was he to do with her now?

He jerked his eyes back to the team and answered, rather gruffly, "What do you want to talk about?"

Elizabeth looked at him with a flash of impatience and then at all that surrounded her. She waved a hand. "This!" she declared. "I want to know where we are, where we are going, what I'm seeing—why, there are a thousand topics for conversation with every step we take!"

Jed turned the reins slightly to guide the team around a spill of rocks. "It's just country."

Elizabeth tried not to scowl. "Perhaps to you, sir, but it's quite unlike anything I've ever seen before."

"But then, you haven't seen much." His drawl was flat and disinterested, his eyes on the trail ahead. "Wait another hour—you won't be too interested in asking questions. The country gets rough and then gets rougher. By the end of the day your pretty white gloves will be dirty, your dress muddy, your ribbons sagging. You'll be covered with dust and sweat, and the only thing you'll care about is getting out of this wagon. It won't seem so fascinating to you then."

Elizabeth looked at him with a mixture of dismay and frustration. "Why must you persist in being so crude and so . . . so *disparaging* of everything?"

"It's only the truth, Elizabeth," he replied curtly, "and time you faced it. This is not one of your little jaunts from Spring Hill to Larchmont. You've got a long, hard trip ahead of you, and no point in you thinking it's going to be a Sunday school picnic."

"So far," Elizabeth retorted, "the only thing about this trip I've found unpleasant is my traveling companion."

"Not too much you can do about that, now is there?" Jed responded, and slapped the reins lightly.

Elizabeth had no answer for that. Simmering with indignation, she jerked her eyes away and focused on the passing landscape. The wagon moved on in creaking silence.

She had never seen countryside that looked so abandoned and unused, and the farther they traveled, the more she became certain that they would soon come upon a house, a farm, even a small hovel of a town like they had just left . . . but they never did.

At places the trail grew so narrow, it was impassable, and Jed had to leave the wagon to clear out brush or shove aside a fallen tree or a tumble of rocks. Elizabeth clung to her seat as he pulled the horses over shallow streams, and once, when he got out to urge the balky team up a particularly steep incline, Elizabeth volunteered nervously, "Shall I help?"

Jed looked at her as though the very notion were absurd and returned curtly, "No, of course not."

"But my weight—"

Jed slapped the flanks of the lead horse, and the wagon lurched upward with a force that almost flung her to the floor. Elizabeth—hot, dusty, and battered from the rough seat of the wagon—felt an unfamiliar flare of temper. When Jed climbed back onto the seat beside her, she said, with great restraint, "I do know how to drive a team. I'm not completely helpless."

Jed glanced at her, but his expression was unreadable. He clucked to the team and slapped the reins. "I didn't say you were. But I reckon the high-stepping buggy horses you're used to are a mite different from these, and this is rough country."

"I can walk," she insisted, "when it's necessary."

His voice held a peculiar edge as he replied, "It's not necessary."

Elizabeth said nothing but she could sense his anger, and she was struggling with a low thread of anger herself.

"There is no need to treat me like an incompetent," she blurted out when she couldn't stand it a moment longer.

Jed remained silent, but his eyes reflected a repressed retort.

Correctly interpreting the look, Elizabeth's temper flared. "I'll have you know I've been riding since I was six and driving my own buggy since I was twelve. I have managed a household, complete with slaves and records, since my mother first took ill four years ago, and I've done it quite well too! I can read Latin and speak French and cipher numbers. In fact, sir,'' she finished on a note of smoldering triumph, ''I think you will find there is not too much I can't do!''

She saw Jed's hands tighten on the reins and then forcibly loosen, but he gave no other visible sign of emotion. His voice was flat, and he did not look at her as he answered, ''Well, that's all mighty fine, I'm sure. And back East I guess it's a real important thing, for a woman to speak French and order slaves around and sit pretty at her husband's dinner table and impress all the folks he wants to impress. But out here a man needs a wife who can do more than set a table. It's not just cooking she has to do but bringing in the meat, skinning it, curing it, and fighting off the animals that try to take it from her.''

She stiffened with insult, but he did not notice. He fought back the tightness that came into his muscles, the anger that wanted to creep into his tone. For there was more. Out here a man needed a woman who could step into his place when he fell, who not only could take care of her but also of him, too, when need be, for oftentimes when a man took a wife into the wilderness, the only thing that stood between himself and death was the woman who rode by his side. But how could he tell her that?

''The work will be hard, and there's no end to it,'' he said roughly, not looking at her. ''If the heat and the storms and the silence don't drive you out of your mind, the loneliness will. And when your birthing time comes, there won't be no doctor, no midwife, no womenfolk to ease it for you. You'll go through it alone and likely bear a stillborn child, and then the grief and bitterness will make you old before you're twenty.''

He looked at her, and the churning challenge in his eyes could not be disguised. It was low and ugly, and instinctively Elizabeth shrank from it. ''So tell me,'' he demanded of her tightly, "how all your fancy reading and ciphering is going to help you with the kind of life you'll be living now."

Elizabeth was shocked by his crudity and furious with his cruelty. Her cheeks went hot, and her eyes blazed as she flung back, "I am sick to death of hearing what a burden I'm going to be to you!"

Jed looked at her for a moment, and she saw a rolling frustration and anger in his eyes that matched her own. But he turned back to the road, and all he said was, "You're the one that wanted to talk."

Elizabeth bit back bitter words and jerked her eyes away from him, her hands curling into impotent balls in her lap. But she could say nothing. He was impossible.

After a moment Jed ventured a glance at her, sitting stiff-lipped and flushed beside him, and a measure of helplessness rolled through him that swallowed up his anger and left him feeling only frustrated and bleak. She didn't understand. She didn't understand at all.

She could *die*. Or he could die from worrying about her when he had best be concentrating on other things. The West was a savage land that played no favorites, and any man, or woman, who sought to tame it had best be aware of the odds. Jed, like all Western men, lived with the knowledge of his own mortality so closely that he hardly even recognized it anymore, and death did not frighten him. But dying and leaving a woman behind, alone and unprotected, did.

A woman needed a man to protect her, and a man needed a woman to protect. He might, if luck were with him, be able to protect Elizabeth from death. But how could he shield her from the life that lay ahead?

Silently he cursed, then slapped the reins. He had never asked for this responsibility, and he did not welcome it. But what was done was done, and there was no way out now.

*   *   *

At noon they stopped under a stand of cottonwood, and Jed made a quick meal of beans, coffee, and some biscuits he had bought from the cook at the trading post that morning. Once again Elizabeth felt extraneous and in the way. A woman, she knew, should cook for her husband, but she did not know where anything was, nor how to build a fire quickly, nor, if it came to that, even how to make coffee over a trail fire. What Jed had said was true, and she resented having the fact proven so graphically.

Besides, she was exhausted, her face and hands felt dirty, and she wanted a nap. Her back hurt terribly, but when she pressed her hands against her spine to relieve some of the tension, Jed caught the movement with a sharp look, and she immediately straightened up and painted an indifferent expression on her face. She wanted to give him no further cause for smugness.

The beans were tasteless, the biscuits dry, and the coffee far too strong for Elizabeth's taste. Jed ate quickly and glanced at Elizabeth's barely touched plate with evident disapproval.

His voice was gruff as he commented, "I know it's not up to your usual standards, but you're not likely to get much better for some time to come. Better eat up."

Elizabeth rose, leaving her plate on the ground. "I find I'm not hungry," she said coolly, and walked back to the wagon. As she passed, she saw the beginning of a flush stain Jed's collar line, and his dark brows drew together briefly with a scowl. But whether his irritation was with her this time or with himself, she could not tell. At that point it did not make much difference.

Elizabeth passed the remainder of the afternoon in a staunch silence, her spine held straight against the rocking and swaying of the wagon, setting her teeth against the torture of the board seat. The trail took them through dank, wooded undergrowth; across open fields; through brush that scratched at her clothing and plucked at her bonnet; and into streams that splattered her skirts with mud. Not once, not even in the farthest distance, did Elizabeth catch a glimpse of anything that could remotely indicate human occupancy. She saw not a curl of chimney smoke, not a signpost, not even a stage stop.

Late in the afternoon big puffy clouds began to gather against the horizon, and the air grew hot and still. Lazy black flies buzzed around the horses, and Elizabeth waved them away from her face with a handkerchief. They were traveling across relatively open land now, the long, rippling grass broken occasionally by a stand of pecans or cotton-wood. She could see what Jed meant by the *bigness* of Texas. The land was so vast and so empty that it stunned the senses and made Elizabeth feel very, very small. And alone.

Occasionally she cast a covert glance at Jed, just for the reassurance of his strong and solid presence. He wore a gun in a holster he had bought in Galveston, belted low on his hips. Elizabeth had never seen him wear one before. It was a big, brutal-looking thing. The mere sight of it was awe-inspiring, revealing yet another part of this man she did not know.

The clouds in the horizon were darkening, and a faint wind was puffing up. Elizabeth was glad for the relief from the heat and the flies. The heaviness in the air was ominous, but it at least filled the emptiness. She wondered if Jed had made plans for where they would pass the night, or if they were to sleep outside. She did not relish that idea at all, but no matter what her distaste or fear, she would not let Jed know. And then she wondered if he would come to her tonight. . . .

The thought was sudden and unexpected, and it sent a

swift heat to her cheeks and an uncomfortable pounding to her chest that was distressingly difficult to hide.

She glanced at him and was struck again by the strength of him, the unvarnished beauty that seemed so perfectly at home in this environment. Just the sight made her chest tighten. She stared at his dark wrists, sprinkled with golden hair and glinting with perspiration, which controlled the team so effortlessly. Her gaze moved up to his muscled arm, shaped by the buckskin, and the curve of his neck and the fringe of hair that curled damply against his collar. His elbows were resting on his knees as he held the reins, and Elizabeth's eyes, as though by compulsion, followed the shape of his knee, the strong, muscled thigh above. . . .

The heat began then, the stinging prickle of embarrassment and remembrance, and quickly she moved her eyes back to his hands, but that was even worse. Too well she remembered those hands on her tingling, unclothed flesh, and with the memory came a tightening inside her stomach, a heat inside her veins, and it was more than embarrassment. Jed was the same man who had lain with her that night and changed her life forever, yet . . . he was different, in ways she couldn't define. She was married to this man, subject to him in every way. She must make his home and bear his children and do what he expected of her in the very best way she knew how. She was no longer a romantic girl; she was a wife.

Tonight they would be alone together for the first time since their marriage. Of course he would come to her.

She averted her face quickly so that he would not notice her sudden color, nor guess the direction of her thoughts. So intent was she upon her study of a patch of ground at the side of the wagon that it took her a moment to notice that he had stopped, and another moment to realize that he was staring with arrested attention toward something half hidden in a thin wooded area not twenty yards ahead. Elizabeth followed the direction of his gaze, and all the breath left her body.

A monster—there was no other description for it—lifted its ugly head and fixed its eyes directly on Elizabeth. Perhaps she registered a dim resemblance to a cow, but it was unlike any cow Elizabeth had ever seen. It was huge, rugged, rangy, and fierce-looking. It was longer than a horse, and Elizabeth could have stood on tiptoe and not reached its neck. Atop its head were a pair of twisted, pointed horns that looked to her as if they could have spanned the breadth of the wagon. They were sharpened to ferocious points that could have, with no effort at all, gored both horses and lifted the wagon off its wheels.

That was not the worst of it. The animal who stood snorting and staring at Elizabeth was not alone. Scattered throughout the wood, small trees and bushes crushed by their passing, were others of his type. Their mottled hides were muddy and scarred, and their horns churned up the earth as they sought fresh graze. They were the biggest, most hideously deformed animals Elizabeth had ever seen, and they were much, much too close.

Her fingers were gripping Jed's arm without her having knowledge of moving toward him. She whispered hoarsely, "What . . . what are they?"

"Wild cattle," Jed answered. His tone was maddeningly unconcerned. "Spanish."

Her fingers tightened. The horses were as nervous as she was, and Jed had to tighten the reins to keep them from bolting. The beast before her shook his head, those huge horns tearing at the leaves above him, and she started, moving closer to Jed.

"Will . . . they attack?" she managed. She could not take her eyes off the animal.

Jed glanced at her, but she looked so terrified, he knew he could not go into it with her now. He replied only, "They're just cows. They're not going to bother you."

"They're so . . . big!"

He chuckled. "The bigger the steer, the bigger the steak . . . and the higher the price."

She could only stare at him.

He nodded toward the monsters and commented, "Right now they're headed for some place to bed down for the storm. I reckon we'd better do the same."

He lifted the reins, and that was when Elizabeth noticed how ferociously she had been gripping his arm. A little stiffly she uncurled her fingers and moved back to her side of the wagon. The last thing she wanted to do was give him cause to think she was more foolish than he already believed.

Jed carefully skirted the path the herd had cut through the ground until the big brindle who had been eyeing them lost interest, and Jed then picked up the trail again. The path was crisscrossed with random tracks made by the wandering herd, and Jed made a mental note of the location. They had probably staked out a good graze nearby and would make an easy catch.

The storm was picking up speed more quickly than he had expected. He knew it would be foolish to try to reach the campsite he had picked for the night. By the time he pulled the wagon up under the shelter of an oak, the wind was gusting in cold, electric bursts, rattling the trees and turning up the pale underside of their leaves, and the sky was a threatening violet. Thunderstorms in open country like this were enough to concern any man of common sense, and it would be foolish to push farther on.

Jed leapt down from the wagon and went to unharness the team. "I'm going to take the horses down for water," he called back to Elizabeth. A burst of wind billowed his jacket and tugged back the brim of his hat. "You stay here with the wagon."

Elizabeth drew her shawl more tightly around her shoulders and looked anxiously at the sky and the whipping leaves overhead. "What if it starts to rain?" she called back, and realized immediately how silly that sounded—as though she literally did not have sense enough to get out of the rain.

But Jed was busy with the harness and did not even spare her a disparaging look. "Get under the canvas," he returned. He grabbed his rifle from the wagon seat and tugged on the lead rope as he turned. "I won't be gone long. I'm just going to tie up the team."

The sky was darkening rapidly, and Jed had gone only a few steps down the small incline before he was swallowed up by an artificial dusk. Nervously Elizabeth looked around, from sky to swaying landscape, and then thought, in dismay, Rain. As if the day hadn't been trying enough, they were now caught out in the open in the middle of a rainstorm...and from the looks of it, it was a vicious one as well.

She remembered again, briefly, the young girl who had longed for adventure. But, as with so many fantasies, hers had conveniently overlooked such discomforts as dust and fatigue and monotony and soaking storms. There was nothing exciting about being caught without shelter in a storm. It was cold and muddy and wet and distinctly unglamorous, and for a moment—just a moment only—she felt a prickle of resentment toward Jed for allowing it to happen. Couldn't he at least have found a farmhouse in which they could stay the night?

She felt a single drop of rain splatter heavily on her bonnet rim, and in the next moment a blast of wind threatened to snatch the hat from her head. A clap of thunder echoed, and she peered anxiously through the gloom for Jed. The leaves on the tree above her were standing straight up, their white undersides flashing a beacon to the storm.

Elizabeth was getting anxious, but she tried not to acknowledge it. Jed knew what he was doing. He was only a few yards away, and he would be back in a moment.

Another drop of rain splattered, and she peered anxiously at the sky. It was deep purple now, almost black, and a flash of silent lightning backlit the shape of a thunderhead. The entire landscape had taken on a surreal, violet-yellow color, and grass and bushes were bending helplessly to the wind. Elizabeth knelt on the seat and turned to unfasten the canvas that covered the supplies. The wind caught the edge of her skirt and whipped it over her head, rustling her petticoats for all the world to see. Straightening quickly and grabbing at her skirt, another gust of wind almost knocked her off the seat, and then she realized it hardly mattered, for there *was* no one to see. . . .

Jed. Where was Jed?

She could not unloose the tie that held the canvas in place, and it was just as well because the wind was pounding so ferociously at the canvas that a single loose tie could have caused the whole to fly off. She dug her hands under the canvas, careless of her petticoats now, and came out with a rolled blanket. Fighting to hold on to it against the wind, she wrapped it around her shoulders.

The rain was still limited to a sporadic, heavy splash now and again. But the next explosion of thunder, followed immediately by a jagged streak of lightning that actually popped as it hit the air, caused Elizabeth to start and grip the sides of the wagon for support. Her eyes desperately searched the landscape for signs of Jed's return, but it was too dark and too hazy. Where could he have gone?

She clambered down and stood beside the wheel, hugging

the blanket around her shoulders, looking for Jed. The wind tossed her skirt up to her knees and snatched at her petticoats again. Elizabeth shivered, but not from cold. What if something had happened to Jed? What if he were hurt or lost or trapped by an animal or—or an Indian? Her heart pounding in her throat, her breath coming in a shallow stream through her lips, she looked around.

She had no idea where they were, nor what kind of dangers lurked in the forest. She thought of Jed, injured and alone, with no one to depend on for help but herself.

And then she thought of herself and what would happen if Jed didn't come back. It struck her with an impact that went through her entire body like a stab of cold steel. For the first time she realized, truly realized, what she had done by coming here. Jed could die, and she would be *all alone*. There was no one for miles around, there were animals and treacherous forests and empty fields and Indians and nothing else. She was alone and helpless, and Jed . . .

Jed was out there, somewhere, needing her.

Thunder rent the air, followed by an explosion of lightning so close that the entire landscape flashed in the blue-white glow and she could taste the dusty sparks of electricity in the air. Elizabeth did not hesitate.

She cried out, "Jed!" and lifted her skirts, fighting the wind as she hurried in the direction in which she had seen him go.

Jed was examining the tracks of the cattle, marking out their direction, when he heard her cry, so faint and far away, it might have been a trick of the wind. He had left the horses tied near a small cave he knew about, and it had taken him longer than he had expected to get them calmed down enough to leave them. Then he had come upon these tracks and they had worried him a little, for they were fresh.

Elizabeth was safe enough back at the wagon, and he would get her to the cave before the serious rain started. But then he heard her voice, and he couldn't believe it.

He stood up, every sense alert, and he heard the voice again. It was not coming from the wagon.

A bolt of panic went through him, and it took every ounce of will at his command to stand still, to search the darkening wood for signs of her passing, to listen again for the direction of her voice. Elizabeth, wandering alone out here with a band of wild cattle spooked by the storm and ready to stampede... Elizabeth, lost and defenseless... The moisture left his throat, and his heart stopped beating and he listened, listened. . . .

He heard it again, and in a blind fury of desperation, he took off at a run in the direction of her voice.

Rain had started to pelt the leaves overhead furiously when he saw her shadowy shape in the wood. The roar of the creek and the rush of the wind combined to snatch the word from his mouth when he called her name. In two furious strides he broke through the undergrowth and grabbed her arm, whirling her around.

Desperate relief lit her face as Elizabeth cried, "Jed! I was worried about you! I thought you were hurt or—"

But rage and fear had twisted his face and tightened his fingers on her arm, and he shouted, "What the hell are you doing? I told you to stay with the wagon!"

Elizabeth jerked back, her own fear and worry combining with the shock of his treatment and leaping with sparks of anger to her eyes. "Don't shout at me! I—"

"I'll damn well shout at you if I please! Are you out of your mind?"

Elizabeth pulled her arm away furiously, her eyes blazing. "How dare you! You have no call to use that tone with me! You left me alone, you—"

"I told you to stay put!" Even above the wind and the rain Jed's voice roared. They stood in a paralysis of crackling emotion and furious words, while the rain beat on the canopy of leaves above and slashed across their faces. Jed wanted to shake her. Didn't she have any idea what she had done? Wandering through unfamiliar woods was bad enough. She had seen the herd for herself and she knew . . .

How could she have known? He had told her there was no danger.

He saw her face, flushed with temper and scarred by rain, and her eyes, sparking and defiant. His lips compressed grimly against a renewed surge of impotent fury, but this time his anger was with himself. He flung an arm around her shoulders wordlessly and, ducking to avoid low branches, began to half drag, half lead her toward shelter.

The rough scramble through thorny bushes and rain-slicked ground did nothing to improve Elizabeth's temper. Wet branches slapped at her face, and the wind cut through her skirts as briers snatched at her ankles. She tripped over fallen logs and hidden holes, and Jed dragged her ruthlessly onward. By the time he pushed her into a small, mossy-smelling cave, she was gasping for breath, her side hurt, and tears of rage stung her eyes.

It was gloomy inside the cave, the opening screened by a tangle of blackberry bushes that blocked the heavy splashes of rain. The cave was not over six feet deep, and its roof was just high enough for Elizabeth to stand in comfort. Jed had to bend considerably, and once he pushed her inside, he turned away, kneeling on the ground to gather bits of dried bark and straw for a fire.

Elizabeth turned on him. Displays of temper were unladylike and undesirable, and never before had anyone had such power to infuriate her past the point of ladylike behavior. But she was hurt, she was angry, she was tired, and she was afraid. Her nerves were drawn to the breaking point, and the fact that she had screamed at him like a banshee in the woods only compounded her own frustration and misery. He had had no *right* to yell at her. No one had ever yelled at her like that in her life. She had done nothing to deserve his treatment of her all day, and she could not—she simply could *not*—let it go unreproached.

The blanket slid to the ground as she clenched her fists at her sides. Her eyes were glittering, and as much as she tried to control it, her voice was sharp and furious as she said, "I will *not* be treated like an intractable child, sir. I will not be shouted at, or—or cursed at, and I will not tolerate being jerked about like a puppy on a leash! How dare you abuse me so! What have I done to deserve your anger?"

Jed's muscles were tight as he struck a match and guarded the small flame at the entrance of the cave to a gentle fire. When he looked up at her, her face taut and her eyes sparking with justifiable outrage, he was overcome with a wave of frustration and self-reproach. Didn't she know how frightened he had been? Didn't she know how he had felt when he knew, in that moment, that after all they had been through, all they had survived, he might lose her not fifty miles from his own ranch? The very fears and desperate concerns that had been gnawing at him all day had, in those few moments of wild searching in the wood, almost become manifest. Didn't she realize what that had done to him?

He had lied to her about the danger of the wild cattle and the storm, thinking he was protecting her. That was his first mistake. How many others would he make?

Jed turned, and he looked at her for a long time. Even in the flickering light provided by the fire his expression was unreadable. But something about it took the edge of anger away from Elizabeth and replaced it with confusion. He surprised her by reaching up and taking her hand, then drawing her down beside him before the fire.

He did not hold on to her hand but remained close. He began to feed sticks into the fire as he said, simply, "There were tracks of wild cattle all over these woods, Elizabeth. They're vicious animals under the best of circumstances, and when spooked—well, there's no stopping them. They'll attack a wolf or a grizzly or a mountain lion just because the notion strikes. They'll gore a horse and chase the man who was riding it until they get him too. That's why I wanted you to stay with the wagon. I didn't know where the steers were or what mood they were in."

Elizabeth swallowed a great lump of retrospective fear and dry shock, and the lingering traces of anger were completely wiped away. For a time all she could do was stare at him.

She managed, at last, to say, "You should have told me."

Jed did not look up, but in the orange glow of the fire she thought she saw the lines around his mouth tighten a bit. He said only, "I know."

Elizabeth shivered, and Jed reached behind her to drape the fallen blanket over her shoulders. With that simple gesture the last of their anger drained away, as though the storm itself had dissipated the savage energy that had propelled them. Elizabeth looked only tired, and Jed was thinking of nothing except what had to be done.

Because of the speed of the storm and the protection of the leaves, their clothes were merely water-splotched, not really wet. But it wasn't from dampness or cold that Elizabeth shivered. It was from thinking about this place and about all that she did not know. Jed had been frightened for her. But he could have been hurt as easily as she. . . .

Jed said, looking around for more sticks to add to the fire, "The storm won't last long, but I think we'll bring our grub down and camp here for the night. It's used a lot by travelers, and whoever uses it last always leaves tinder for the next fire.''

He was talking just for the sound of his voice, which was not something he was accustomed to doing. But she was looking at him with those wide and staring eyes, and talking gently seemed to be the only way he knew to take back the taste of those harsh words he had shouted at her before.

Elizabeth said tightly, ''Don't . . . didn't you say that you . . . rounded up those cows, to sell?''

Jed glanced at her. ''Some. Most of the cattle we run are mixed-breed—the wild cattle that the Spanish left have crossed with some of the domestic American stock, and they have a little better temper. Easier to drive.''

''But . . . isn't it dangerous?''

Jed glanced at her and was tempted once again to minimize the situation. But he had learned his lesson. ''It can be,'' he admitted. ''I've seen men get gored or trampled or lose a finger or two if they rope too quick. But you don't go into this line of work if you don't know what you're doing.''

''But why?'' she insisted, and dismay tinged her tone and was reflected in the firelight that shadowed her eyes.

Jed smiled a little, trying to relax. ''That's the way I make my living.''

She said nothing, just looked at him with confusion and interest in her eyes.

He explained, ''There are hundreds of thousands of head in Texas. We drive them to pasture, let them fatten up through the summer and graze where they will, then gather them all together and brand them—''

''What's that?'' Elizabeth asked with a small frown of confusion.

How good it felt to talk to her again, to look at her and feel easy with her and forget, for a while, all the things he had to feel bad about and worry about. He said, "It's a design, burned into the hide of the cow with a hot iron, to let folks know who they belong to." The moment he said it, he knew that a lady of her sensibilities would be appalled, but a quick glance at her revealed nothing but alert interest on her face. Encouraged, he picked up a stick and traced a pattern in the dirt floor, a clover with the number three inside. "That's my brand. The Clover Three. The three comes from the name of the ranch—Three Hills."

"Three Hills?"

"The house site and corral are surrounded by three hills, a kind of natural fort. I can see anybody approach from any side, and the high ground around cuts back on the wind and the worst of the weather. It's a pretty spot. Real pretty."

A warm glow seemed to grow within Elizabeth at the animation in his voice and the pleasure on his face. He was talking to her, just as he once had, sharing things that were important to him, bringing his world alive for her. The isolation, the awkwardness, even the fear that had plagued her since the wedding was miraculously gone, and from nothing more than the sound of his voice. The rain drummed outside, and in the distance was the muffled roar of thunder, but inside this cozy place the fire flickered and crackled, and Jed was with her, talking to her.

"Tell me about your ranch," she said. She shifted her position a little, gathering her feet beneath her and leaning back so that she could rest her head and shoulder against the wall of the cave and look at Jed more comfortably. "Is it very large?"

"Size don't mean much to a stockman. The cattle are free to whoever can brand them, and all you need is a place to hold them while you do." He glanced at her, looking so alert and interested, yet relaxed and wonderfully feminine, leaning against the wall in the glow of the fire. Then he looked away, and he had to add honestly, "It's bigger now than I planned on, though. I won some acres from Lord Hartley in that card game."

He hadn't planned on telling her about that; he hadn't, in fact, given it much thought at all. Almost before the words were out, he regretted them. Hartley was a friend of her father's, and he came from her class, her world. She wouldn't understand. Women weren't supposed to understand what went on between men, and he had no reason for telling her.

Elizabeth said, her eyes brightening a little with quick understanding, "So that's why you were fighting that night. I wondered at the time."

Jed should have let it go at that. He gazed back at the fire and admitted, "No. Not exactly. He was cheating."

Her eyes went wide, and she sat up a little. "Lord Hartley? But . . . he's such a gentleman! He never would do such a thing. It's quite beyond belief."

Jed said curtly, "He pulled a knife on me. I disarmed him. And he wouldn't leave it at that."

Elizabeth's head was reeling, both from the impact of the statement and from the secret drama it recalled. "But . . . why?"

Jed did not look at her. He had gone too far to stop. And something within him—some twisted sense of morality, perhaps—dictated that she should know the truth about him now, before it went on too far. Just like she should have known the truth about the wild cattle.

"I cheated too," he said flatly. "And beat him at it. He'd taken some of the boys for money they couldn't afford to lose, and I thought it was only fair they get it back. Then I took Hartley for what he couldn't afford to lose, and he isn't a very forgiving kind of man."

She was silent, and he knew he had gone too far. She

would be appalled, indignant, quick to rise to the defense of her own kind. She would hate him. Thinking about it, he could feel his muscles go tight, and he despised himself for a fool. He should have left well enough alone. He never should have told her.

"Do you know," she murmured, deep in thought, "I never liked him, not really. He was always very courteous, of course, and it was never anything I could actually object to, but he made me uneasy. I think that Papa sometimes felt the same way. But I never would have guessed," she added, a small frown shadowing her brow, "that he could be so unscrupulous. He was always such a perfect gentleman."

"There's gentlemen and there's gentlemen," Jed pointed out, and surprised relief weighed in his voice. "You can't always judge by what you see."

"No," she agreed softly. "I suppose not." Yet another illusion had evaporated before her eyes. Was nothing she knew of life or civilized behavior true? Couldn't she trust even her own judgment?

He moved next to her, resting his back against the wall and planting his feet flat to prop up his knees. It seemed the most natural thing in the world to slip his arm around her and offer her his shoulder to rest her head on. She came easily, automatically, and snuggled her head into the hollow of his shoulder. Jed's heart began to beat faster, just for a moment, with the surprise of her nearness.

For a time there was nothing but the plop of rain on the leaves outside and the crackle of the fire. Elizabeth felt comfortable with Jed's arm around her, secure and at ease. He smelled of dampness and buckskin, familiar scents that belonged exclusively to him. She could see those strong brown fingers draped lightly over her lower arm, and his nearness, his warmth and scent, caused that peculiar tingling to gather in her stomach again. It was a pleasant feeling, not alarming at all. It felt right, having him near and holding her. It was almost like it used to be.

Jed glanced down at her. "Are you hungry?"

She shook her head lazily against his shoulder. "A little tired." In actual fact, only now, wrapped in the security of Jed's protection, was the full toll of her exhaustion beginning to make itself known. The aching of her back had subsided somewhat, but her muscles were heavy and her head fuzzy with fatigue. She wanted only to sit like this with him and rest.

Jed glanced down at her and smiled. How good it felt to have her curled up against him like this. How long since he had known the softness and comfort of a feminine body, relaxed and inert, against his own.

Dancing shadows of firelight played over her face, illuminating a curl that had escaped from her bonnet and lay against her cheek. He could feel the soft rise and fall of her breasts against his ribs, and the slender curve of her arm beneath his fingers. He wanted to turn her to him and kiss her, and thinking about it made his blood quicken. He wanted to lift his hand and touch her face, and he wanted to see her eyes grow bright and alive with welcome. He wanted to kiss her gently, and then more deeply, and then he wanted to spread the blanket on the ground and lay her down. . . .

Since the night of the fire he had buried those thoughts, those needs, deep inside his mind, and allowing them to surface now was a painful process. He had hurt her; he had shamed her. Now she lay against him as soft and trusting as a child, but if he touched her, if he let her know his want for her, would those eyes fill with disgust and reproach? Could he expect her to welcome him now, after all that had passed between them?

No matter what difficulties or hostilities had brought them

to this marriage, no matter what his turmoil or his conflicting emotions, he still wanted her with a deep, obsessive need that gave him no rest. Neither logic nor common sense could fend off this growing desire, neither anger nor guilt nor tenderness. . . . Would there ever be an end to it? He knew that making love to her would not solve anything. But that did not stop him from wanting her.

He held her, and he listened to the sound of her breathing, and nothing could prevent the tightness that settled in his loins. The heat from the fire was minimal, but he felt flushed and anxious, and he couldn't control the slow thudding of his heart no matter how he tried. He wanted to be near her. He wanted to hold her and feel her and discover her . . . and he didn't want her to hate him. He looked at her, but her face was shadowed against his chest and he couldn't see her expression. *Elizabeth*, he thought. *Just let me kiss you.* . . .

He lifted his hand to touch her face, and then let it fall silently away. Her eyes were closed, and she was deeply asleep.

After a moment he untied her bonnet strings and removed it gently. Carefully he lowered her to the ground and covered her with the blanket, cushioning her head with the folded bonnet.

Then he walked to the mouth of the cave and stood looking out for a long time. After a while the rain stopped, and he walked back to the wagon to get his own bedroll.

His wife slept, undisturbed, throughout the night.

CHAPTER
Thirteen

Near sunset the next day, Jed halted the team.

"This is it," he said. A quiet, peaceful look of satisfaction came over his face as he looked around. "This is the smallest of the three hills. The house," he said, gesturing toward the sloping valley where a thin trail of smoke could be discerned filtering through the tops of oaks and sweeping evergreen, "is over there."

It was a gentle summer afternoon, and the spot was indeed beautiful. Down toward the smoke the valley rippled with shades of greens, from the deepest olives to the softest blue, a breathtaking sight from any point of view. Surrounding them atop the hill was a field of yellow daisies, and the scent of honeysuckle teased the air. Directly opposite was another majestic hill, with a sweeping path of bluebells at its base. To the right the third hill completed the circle, a long, narrow rise that joined the other hills in a dip of evergreen, enclosing the valley in a clover-shaped wash of sweeping greens and pale, tawny grasses.

Elizabeth turned this way and that, filling her eyes eagerly with all of it. She saw the glint of a silvery stream far below in the distance, and a graceful doe munching on some berries not twenty feet away along the trail that wandered into the wood beside them. The sun slanted through the pines and danced off a small pool hidden in a glen. The air tasted of woodsy herbs and mellow hay, and the clear, rich blue of the sky was a sharp and brilliant contrast to the shades of green and gold that slept below it.

She had seen some striking countryside in the past two days of travel, but nothing as lovely as this. Jed had not exaggerated. If Elizabeth had traveled the world over, this, too, is the place she would have chosen to build her home.

Home. Four walls around her, a bath, a bed, and a meal cooked on a stove. She was so weary of traveling, so anxious for the small comforts of everyday life, that the simple knowledge of journey's end was like a heady potion to her. They were home, and all the hardships they had passed through to get here seemed insignificant.

"Oh, Jed, it's beautiful!" she exclaimed, and her glowing eyes reflected the truth of it.

Jed stood up in the wagon, holding the reins loosely in one hand, and shouted, "Hello!"

His voice echoed in the clear air, tossed back by the hills. Just as it died, there came a faint, answering, "Hallo!"

Jed had mentioned others who lived at the ranch, but he had never spoken of them personally. Elizabeth felt reassured by the proof of someone waiting for them.

Jed half smiled at her and sat back down, though it seemed a cautious, rather stiff, expression. "That's so they won't shoot at us," he explained, and started the wagon down the hill.

They approached the house from the side and back, the wagon bouncing over rough terrain and down into the valley. The meadow gave way to a cleared area where the grass had been worn away by trampling hooves to leave a bare dirt yard surrounding a rough log corral that held several head of mixed-breed horses and a small, squat building with a leaning roof and a crooked stone chimney. Before the building a black pot was hung on a tripod over a camp fire, and around the fire lounged three of the most disreputable characters Elizabeth had ever seen.

The three men cautiously got to their feet as the wagon approached, staring with unabashed surprise at Elizabeth. Elizabeth could feel the tension in Jed, which completely subdued the elation she had felt upon his first announcement that they were home. Her own happy anticipation faded into a confused uneasiness mingled with equal parts of anxiety and dread.

The men stared at her as though they had never seen a woman before. Elizabeth felt herself growing hot and nervous under their unrelenting gazes. They were unshaven, dirty, and hard-eyed, each one of them wearing a gun low on his hip just like Jed, each one of them looking as though they would as soon use it on her as not.

There was a huge, greasy-haired man in a stained and faded undershirt with at least a week's bristle on his jowls, whose bushy-eyed scowl made Elizabeth want to shrink behind Jed for protection. Next to him stood a skinny blond man with a bowie knife stuck in his boot. Last was a swarthy Mexican of about Jed's age, who wore a faded blue calico shirt and whose narrowed dark eyes caused Elizabeth to repress a shiver. All of them wore dirty, napkin-sized handkerchiefs of dark prints around their throats, and all of them held themselves with the alert, animallike wariness that spoke of danger waiting to happen.

Elizabeth could feel the stiffness in the muscles of Jed's arms as he helped her down from the wagon. He did not touch her again as he turned to the waiting men. "Elizabeth," he said, "this is Rio"—the Mexican nodded to her—"and Dusty . . ."

The blond man muttered, "Ma'am," and quickly evaded her eyes. To her surprise Elizabeth saw that he was, in fact, a boy, surely no older than she. But the only place his youth showed was in the delicate fuzz on his sunburned cheeks—everything else about him was as hard and untamed as a rugged mountain peak.

"And over here is Skunk."

Elizabeth blushed at the vulgarity of the name. The large, jowly man spat a stream of tobacco that landed perilously close to her skirts. He never took his hard, squinting gaze off her.

"Boys," Jed said flatly, "this is my wife."

If they were surprised by the announcement, they did not show it, and none of them commented. After a moment the boy called Dusty went to unhitch the team, and the other two moved to unload the wagon. Jed went to help them, and Elizabeth, finding herself alone and at a complete loss, ventured hesitantly into the shack.

It was a hastily thrown together, one-room shelter of unbarked logs built flat upon the ground. There were no windows, and the only light came from the open door, but Elizabeth could see enough of the interior to make her feel ill.

There was a dirt-and-stick fireplace against the opposite wall, a crude table and two chairs. The bedstead was held in place between the logs of the wall on one side and rested on two log legs on the other. It consisted of what looked like a piece of cowhide stretched between the corners of the frame and a dusty blanket crumpled at the foot. The dirt floor was littered with kegs and half-empty sacks, and the walls were hung with coiled rope and strings of rawhide. Cooking utensils and tools were scattered wherever they happened to fall.

Gingerly Elizabeth touched the edge of the table, and her gloved finger came away encrusted with grime and dust. She swallowed hard and looked around again, trying to fight back her despair. Jed had mentioned a log cabin, but Elizabeth had never seen one—it was 1839, after all—and she had never imagined anything like this. Even the slaves lived better than this.

The men began to carry in crates and kegs, and Elizabeth moved quickly out of the way. She needn't have bothered, however, for these men were not the kind to take any extra steps. They dumped their loads just inside the doorway, barely leaving a path to cross the cabin. Not one of them let his eyes wander her way, and she may as well have been invisible. Elizabeth did not know whether she was glad for that or resentful.

When Jed came in, carrying a fifty-pound sack of flour over his shoulder, she said quickly and somewhat timidly, "Shall I—shall I help put things away?"

He just stared at her, and Elizabeth immediately realized her own foolishness. Where was there to put anything, except on the floor?

Jed dropped the sack and said, somewhat gruffly, "No. You just sit down out of the sun. We'll take care of it."

Elizabeth took off her bonnet and gloves and looked for someplace to put them where they would not get more soiled than they already were. The only place she could find was the contraption that passed for a bed.

As the men unloaded the wagon she heard their voices, punctuated with grunts of effort, floating through the open door.

"I thought you was just goin' East for canvas and flour. Didn't know you was shoppin' a filly." From the big, heavy sound of his voice, Elizabeth identified the speaker as the one they called Skunk.

Jed only said, "I didn't know it, either."

"Kinda puny-looking." That must have been Dusty. "But purty. Real purty."

Rio chuckled. "Me, I like a señorita with more to hold on to, eh? A man needs something to keep him warm at night, like a good feather mattress."

Skunk spat on the ground. "And when was the last time you slept with a feather mattress, Mex? Or anything else besides the fleas?"

Elizabeth was blushing furiously, busily trying to find something to distract herself from eavesdropping. Then she heard Jed's voice. It was grim and harsh and all too clear. "I'm married to her, and there's not a thing talking can do about it now. Let's get this stuff inside."

Elizabeth turned away as they came in, pretending to check the wick in a lantern so that no one would see the hurt on her face. But it didn't matter, for no one glanced in her direction. Not even Jed.

She could hear the scuffling of feet outside, the clink of utensils, and in a moment Rio appeared at the doorway, a tin plate filled with some sort of stew in one hand, a battered cup in another. He grinned at her and ducked his head in what was the first gesture of friendliness Elizabeth had seen since she had arrived. "Some food, señora. It is not much but good."

With a quick, though stiff, smile of gratitude Elizabeth came forward and took the plate and cup from him. "Thank you."

Rio went quickly and joined the others at the fire.

The men sat on the ground, dipping out plates of stew

and talking among themselves. Jed was sitting on a stump, hunched over his plate, and did not even look up to notice her. For a moment Elizabeth stood awkwardly in the doorway, wondering whether to join them. But no one issued an invitation, and she did not want to intrude. She had never felt so cut off, so isolated and out-of-place, in her entire life. Her husband seemed to have forgotten her completely.

Why should it be otherwise? This was his world, his home, and he had been away for a long time. He had more important things to deal with than a timid and overwhelmed wife who could not find a place for herself.

She hovered in the doorway, listening to their conversation.

Skunk said around a mouthful of food, "We lost a heifer yesterday. The little red one."

Jed did not glance up. "Wolves?"

"Mountain lion. Tore her throat out and left her for the buzzards."

"Finally put a loop on that brindle, though," commented Dusty. "Damn near gored me too. But we got him into the bunch."

"Good." Jed scooped up a spoonful of stew. "He's a leader. Make the drive a lot easier. How many selling stock do we have?"

"Maybe a couple hundred head. Twice that in yearlings."

Elizabeth dipped her wooden spoon into the concoction on her plate and tasted it gingerly. It was some kind of beef in a heavy broth, seasoned with onions and potatoes and herbs she couldn't define. She was surprised to find it quite good, and had not her appetite been so dulled by the events of the past half hour, she would have enjoyed it thoroughly.

"We can double that before fall," Jed said. "Fatten them up and drive them to New Orleans. They're giving twenty-five a head for five-year-olds now."

"Si," agreed Rio with a grin. "Pretty ladies, they like pretty things. You will need the money now."

Elizabeth turned and went inside.

Skunk's voice, grumbling, followed her. "We'll have to work sunup to sundown to make that kind of gather."

"We've done it before. Where've you got the herd bunched?"

"Over in that arroyo by Rock Springs. Plenty of graze and water. They're happy as can be."

"We'll have to bring them out before the muddy season. Move them over to Crooked Rock. We can do the branding there."

Elizabeth set her plate on the table and took a deep breath, fighting back despair. It was worse, far worse than she had expected. But it wasn't as though Jed hadn't warned her . . . only that she had chosen not to listen. She had been so certain she could handle anything.

But she was never meant to live like this.

And Jed . . . he had brought her here, deposited her like a piece of luggage, and promptly forgotten her. The closeness that had reappeared so briefly between them in the cave the night before was completely gone, and now Elizabeth wondered if it had ever been. Maybe that had been a fantasy too. She had thought for a moment that she had seen tenderness in Jed's eyes, heard affection in his tone. But he must have only felt sorry for her. Now she had to live not only with his resentment but his pity as well.

After a while the conversation from outside became more sporadic, and she heard shuffling and moving around as the men dispersed. It was barely sunset, but it was dark inside the cabin. Elizabeth, with another breath of determination, looked around for a match. She did not even know where to begin.

She moved toward the crates and barrels that had been

unloaded from the wagon, and her eyes fell upon something she had not seen before—a stack of books tied with a leather strap. Kneeling on the dirt floor, she picked them up, concentrating to make out the titles in the uncertain light. There was a volume of Shakespeare; a collection of verse; philosophy by John Locke and Rousseau; and *Stories of Adventure and Daring* by someone of whom she had never heard. There were also two of her favorites, *Pilgrim's Progress* and *Pride and Prejudice,* and with each cover she touched, her heart grew lighter, her despondency less. The familiarity of crisp pages and cloth bindings in such an alien and hostile place was a connection with home, a comfort to her battered spirit, and for a moment everything seemed brighter.

"I thought you might like them." Jed stood above her. "I know how it pleasures you to read."

Elizabeth turned, surprise and gratitude lighting her face. But her delight faded into awkwardness as she got to her feet. She had not forgotten what he had said to the other men about his marriage. She could not look at him without remembering. "Yes," she answered, her voice subdued, her eyes moving away from his uncertainly. "It does. I'm sure I shall enjoy them very much."

Jed crossed over to the lantern on the table and struck a match. The wick flared briefly, then lowered to a dim yellowish glow. The chimney needed polishing badly.

Elizabeth could smell the smoke of the dying fire outside and hear the occasional murmur of voices. A bucket clanked as it was hit by a boot, and a horse blew gently. Jed stood by the table, the planes of his face showing in the lantern light, his hair rumpled and disarranged by his recently removed hat, and he looked at her. Elizabeth met his gaze, and she knew what would happen next. Her heart began to beat slowly with the knowledge.

This was her husband. They were home, there was a door to be closed, a light to be extinguished, and they would be alone. He would take her hand and lead her to the squalid bed. This was the first night of her marriage, and the inevitable was before her.

The frantic coupling on the beach seemed far away and unreal, like someone else's memory. Then it had been sudden and unexpected, overwhelming and out of control. And because of it she was in this awful place, married to this stranger. . . .

But she was his wife, and she knew what was expected of her.

Jed looked at her, and he waited for the resurgence of desire he had felt for her last night. But all he could see was the way she stood, looking so lost and out of place in the midst of the filth and clutter of the little room, her shoulders squared staunchly, her face lined with exhaustion, and her eyes filled with dread and resignation. All he could feel as he looked at her was guilt and regret.

He came toward her, and her heart tightened against her ribs. He paused a few feet before her, and his eyes moved away, briefly, over the filthy, cluttered room. When he looked back at her, there might have been the briefest trace of sorrow, of apology, and a kind of struggle she did not understand. He said, as though with difficulty, "Elizabeth..." And then he didn't seem to be able to finish what he was going to say. He half lifted his hand as though to touch her, and then let it drop.

He said only, "I'll sleep outside tonight."

He picked up his bedroll and left her, closing the door behind him.

For a long time after he was gone, Elizabeth remained standing, swallowing slowly to clear her throat of stickiness, focusing her eyes beyond the repeated floods of moisture that blurred them. Faintly the memory of a twilight garden glimmered before her; she grasped for it and faltered as it slipped away. How had she come from that place to this? How could it all have gone so wrong?

Yet she had no right to ask that question. From the beginning she had thrown herself at Jed; she had pursued him to Texas. Now he was married to her and did not want to be. Yesterday, for a brief time as they sat together sheltered from the storm, things between them had been almost as they were at the beginning. He had been only Jed, smiling at her, touching her, talking to her as though there were nothing he could not say. She had drifted to sleep in his arms with the rain pattering outside their snug enclosure, and the world had seemed once again as lovely as a fairy tale. Today he was only a stranger with rough clothing and distant eyes, and she was reminded once again of the bleakness of circumstances that had brought her here. This was no fairy tale, and there was nothing beautiful or romantic about this marriage at all.

After a time she crossed the room and began to undress slowly. Outside, the crickets began to chirp, and she could hear the men shaking out their bedrolls. She changed into her nightgown and took the lantern with her as she crossed the room. She lay down gingerly on the stiff cowhide that served as a bed, pulling the dusty blanket over her, and turned down the lantern. Only then, curled up on her side and staring into the darkness, did she let the sluggish tears fall.

CHAPTER
Fourteen

*I*n her dream Elizabeth could hear the snap of the flames; she could see the tendrils lapping at the door, crawling across the floor. Her lungs were choked with smoke, and panic was crushing her chest. She tried to breathe but gasped in only mouthfuls of acrid, scorching air. She couldn't move. She couldn't fight, she was dying. She struggled, but it was useless. She tried to run, but her legs were paralyzed. It was too late. The flames were creeping closer, everywhere she looked there was fire, and there was no one to help her, she was going to die. . . .

Elizabeth sat bolt upright in bed, her eyes wild and staring, dragging in a gasp of smoke-tinged air. Panic was shaking through her limbs and thundering in her chest, and in her mind's eye she could still see the flames, she could still smell the smoke. Frantically she tried to move, she tried to scream. . . .

And then she realized that the walls surrounding her were rough logs and not on fire, and the smoke she smelled was coming from outside and was only the smoke of a cook fire. She was not on the boat and she was not dying. She was here, in the wilderness, in Jed's cabin.

With one more shaky breath she lay back down, heavily, and let her eyes adjust to her surroundings. Pinpricks of bright morning light forced their way through the chinks in the mud that cemented the logs together, creating a crisscross pattern through the dimness. The air smelled rank and old, like something unwashed and on the verge of decay. A large wood spider was complacently building its home in the corner above Elizabeth's head. She watched it, letting the bleakness and despair creep into her very pores.

Last night she had been in such a state of shock, she had hardly been able to absorb the full impact of her surroundings. But now she looked around from her position on the rough bed and was filled with such disgust that she was hard put to restrain a shudder.

Even her nightdress was soiled with a dusty gray film from sleeping in this room. The odor of uncleanliness would cling to her skin and clothes. This was more like a storehouse than a home . . . no, it did not even rate that dignity. The stables at Larchmont were kept cleaner than this place, and every sensibility Elizabeth possessed was offended. Humans were not meant to live like this. Miss Elizabeth Coleman most certainly could not.

But here she was and here she must stay. It was too late to look back, too late for second thoughts. The only thing to do was . . . to do what she could.

Gingerly she caught the corner of the moth-eaten blanket and tossed it back, hardly daring to wonder what kinds of creatures had shared her bed last night. She swung her feet to the floor and jerked back with a muffled cry as a lizard scurried toward the corner and disappeared into a crack in the logs. With a determined breath she got out of bed and hurried to dress.

Rio was squatting beside the fire when she came out, lazily chewing on a piece of grass. He got to his feet with a grin when he saw her. *"Buenas días, señora."*

Elizabeth forced a cheerful smile and smoothed her hands on her skirt. There had not been even a basin in which to wash her hands and face this morning. "Good morning, Rio."

"I have coffee and breakfast." He began to scoop up a concoction from the pot over the fire. Elizabeth tried to hide her distaste when she saw it was the leftover stew from last night.

She accepted the plate with a weakening smile. "Thank you." She looked around the bare and scrubby yard. "Where is my husband this morning?"

"Today they go to cut trees. Tomorrow we start to build a bunkhouse. The next day, or maybe the next, we catch cows again." He poured a measure of thick black coffee into a cup and handed it to her with a lazy shrug. "There is much to do, but there is also much time." He grinned again, slowly. "Me, I like to take time. And today I stay with the señora, to watch over her, *si*? So much better than cutting trees or catching cows."

Elizabeth smiled again, uncertainly, and realized that she had taken the men's sleeping quarters last night. Because of her presence, they would spend time building a bunkhouse that they usually would have spent with the cattle. She knew she should have felt guilty for that but could not quite manage it.

She walked over to the stump where Jed had sat last night and, carefully arranging her skirts, sat down. Rio squatted down again and began to poke sticks into the fire, but she could feel him watching her through the corner of his eye. She took a sip of the coffee and tried not to grimace. It was hideous. Discreetly she placed her cup on the ground and began to push around the food on her plate.

"Have you known my husband long?" she asked pleasantly.

"*Sí*, long." Rio, at least, did not seem to have the problem with communication the other two men did and, in fact, seemed most pleased to have someone to talk to. "Before the war I worked for a fine don and his lovely señora. He was a powerful man, and his rancho one of the largest in all Mexico. And the señora . . ." His face softened a bit. "She was beautiful." He glanced at Elizabeth shyly. "Much like you."

He shrugged, as though embarrassed, and continued. "Then came the war, and I think I will make a better soldier than vaquero. Then I am captured by a big colonel with yellow hair and I think I am dead. But Señor Fielding, he thinks I am too good a fighting man to die, so I am his prisoner. Now war is over and I am his friend."

Elizabeth was fascinated by the story. What kind of man was Jed, that he could so easily turn an enemy into a loyal friend? But was it such a surprise to her, considering what she knew of the man who was her husband . . . and all she did not know?

Rio had turned back to the fire, and Elizabeth steeled herself to taste her breakfast, not wishing to offend. She lifted the spoon and took a small bite. The stew was as tasty as it had been the night before, and she was really quite hungry, but the thought of such a concoction for breakfast was almost more than she could bear.

Rio cast an anxious glance at her, and she smiled, swallowing. "This is quite good, Rio. Do you do all the cooking?"

"*Si*. I am the only one who can, so . . ." He shrugged again. "I do."

Elizabeth looked around. "Where is your garden?"

He looked puzzled, then answered. "No garden, señora."

"But . . ." She took up another small spoonful of stew. "How do you season your cooking? Where do you get the vegetables?"

"We take what we can find from the woods—onions and wild cabbage and good plants. Sometimes we find potatoes that the Indians grow."

Elizabeth's eyes went to him in quick alarm. "Indians?"

But he was unconcerned. He leaned back on his haunches and plucked up another blade of scrub grass. "*Si*. They do not mind."

Elizabeth swallowed hard but decided not to pursue the conversation. What more surprises awaited her?

They foraged the woods like animals. They had leftover stew for breakfast. They lived in a hovel unfit for a hunting hound, and how right, how horribly right, Jed had been all along.

Elizabeth had been bred for a much different life than this. She knew how things were supposed to be done, but she had never had to do them herself. She could give orders; she could not perform tasks. She knew recipes but she did not know how to cook; she knew how to embroider but not to mend; she could paint landscapes but she had never scrubbed floors. . . .

But there was no time like the present to learn. It did not appear that she had much choice.

She put her plate aside and looked at Rio with a faint, resigned smile. "Rio," she said simply, "I must tell you the truth. I want to be a good wife to Jed, but I'm not sure I know how. I can't cook as well as you, and I don't know anything about gathering herbs from the woods or digging potatoes or''—she spread her hands helplessly—''anything that I should know to make a home for him. Will you help me?''

Rio looked at her, and slowly his dark face lightened with a pleased grin. She did not know it, and it had not been her intention to coerce, but with her unabashed desire to please his good friend the Señor, and by her display of wisdom in coming to the right man for advice, she had earned Rio's unwavering respect and loyalty. *''Si, señora,''* he replied simply. ''I will help. You have but to ask.''

Elizabeth smiled, relieved. ''Thank you. Perhaps I can watch you, when you cook, and learn from you. And tomorrow . . .'' She glanced at her plate on the ground and suggested, ''Tomorrow, perhaps we could make eggs for breakfast?''

Rio stared at her. ''But we have no chicken.''

Elizabeth hesitated. ''Well . . . then I think we must get one. Wouldn't you like to have eggs for breakfast?''

Rio chuckled, certain she was joking. The nearest chicken he knew of was in New Orleans. *''Si, señora.* That would be good.''

''And ham,'' she added, and Rio's chuckles faded.

He looked at her cautiously. ''No pigs in Texas, *señora.''*

''But that can't be true,'' she protested. ''I distinctly recall the captain of the steamboat telling us that East Texas abounded with hogs.''

Rio said nothing, growing uneasy. The hogs with which East Texas abounded were more commonly known as wild boar. They would kill a horse and chase a mountain lion, and more than one good man had spent the night up a tree while a wild boar snuffled and dug at its roots. As far as Rio knew, no one had ever tried to eat one.

Elizabeth, taking his silence for agreement, got briskly to her feet. ''Well, we will worry about menus later. Now we have other things to do.'' She unbuttoned her cuffs and cast a single bracing look toward the house. ''I will need plenty of hot water,'' she announced, rolling up her sleeves, ''and some strong lye soap and fresh broom straw. We haven't a moment to waste.''

Rio stared after her as she squared her shoulders, picked up her skirts, and marched determinedly into the cabin. Then he hurried to fill her request.

The two men approached each other in the wood, one from the east and one from the west. The one rode a sturdy unshod pony bareback. He wore a red-blanket coat and a turban wrapped around his head and carried a rifle decorated with foxtails. The other, wearing a broad-brimmed hat pushed away from his forehead, sat tall in the saddle and held the reins delicately in his fingers as he brought his horse to a stop. The two men faced each other about five feet apart, each countenance dark and strong, each pair of eyes observant and unreadable.

Finally Chief Red Wolf said, ''You have been away a long time.''

Jed reached into his saddlebag and withdrew a pouch of tobacco. ''For the great chief.'' The Cherokee accepted the gift wordlessly. Jed presented him with a package of needles. ''And for his wife.''

The chief put both gifts inside his coat, and his eyes did not stray from Jed.

''I have brought back a woman,'' Jed said.

Red Wolf inclined his head in the most imperceptible manner. ''It is good. A man should not die without sons.''

''She is a town woman.''

''She will learn.''

The horses lowered their heads to crop the grass, and the two men sat easily. Nothing was said for a long time, but for the Indian there was no time, and little need, for words. After the turmoil of the past weeks this, to Jed, was the most comforting thing about being home.

"What news of the river villages?" Red Wolf asked presently.

"The Raven travels to council with the friends of the Cherokee. He will return before the leaves change." Sam Houston, known as the Raven to the Cherokee who had adopted him, had left Alabama for Tennessee, where he would meet with Andrew Jackson and others to try to gain support for the annexation of Texas. The Indian problem was always a major concern in such meetings.

"Troubled times come for the Cherokee," said Red Wolf. "The new chief, Lamar, would take from our people the land given by the Raven. In Nacogdoches the tribe grows uneasy."

Jed was no politician and he had no desire to be one; he was happiest in ignorance of the affairs of state. But he was a Texian, and like all the other men and women, Indian and white alike, who had shed their blood and built their homes on this soil, he was an integral part of the destiny of the nation. He could not ignore the men who shaped it.

President Lamar had risen to power on Sam Houston's coattails and now seemed determined to destroy all that Sam had built. While Sam was diligently fighting for American annexation, Lamar was raising an army and a navy to support Texas's claim to independence. While Sam invited strong foreign dollars into Texas, Lamar printed worthless Texas currency. All the promises that Sam had made to his Cherokee friends, Lamar was diligently setting about to break, one by one.

The prospects, Jed knew, looked grim. Texas had its share of trouble with the Comanche to the west, so they need not invite mistrust and discontent from the Cherokee.

Jed said, "Red Wolf is a strong fighting man with many braves."

Red Wolf's face was carved with the lines of too many battles unfought, and his eyes were old with the changes he had seen in his lifetime. His was a culture older than that of Europe, a philosophy rich in the security of his place in the world. His people had forsaken the nomadic ways long ago and had lived in peace with the land as farmers for centuries before the coming of the white man. But they had not forgotten war. The sorrow for what was to come was deep in his eyes.

"We will talk," he stated. "Then we will fight, and many will die. It is the way of our people to seek peace and meet war."

War—a word seldom used by the Cherokee, and Jed knew Red Wolf did not utter it lightly. Since the Cherokee had been forced to come West, the white man had been at peace with them in East Texas. But now . . . now, when Jed had a woman depending upon him, another life to be responsible for, things seemed certain to change.

Jed was known among the Cherokee, and he did not fear personal danger. But a war was no place for a woman.

His gaze traveled uneasily toward the direction of the cabin, and Red Wolf knew his thoughts. "You are my brother," the Indian said abruptly. "When the fighting comes, whose sword will you carry?"

Jed met his gaze without wavering. The Indian respected bravery, demanded loyalty, abhorred a lie. But above all else he knew survival. And so did Jed.

"You are my brother," he answered, "but my gun is my own. I will do what is mine to do."

For a moment the harsh lines of the other man's face seemed to soften, the briefest gesture of approval. "You have learned well the ways of life, Yellow Hawk,'' he said. His eyes were steady. "And so will your woman."

Red Wolf turned his horse to go. "When the time comes, we will move. I will not bring blood to the doorstep of a friend."

Jed watched him go and sat his saddle for a long time, listening to the retreating steps of the other horse. Finally he jerked his reins and turned to leave, but his movements were slow and heavy and his mind was not on the work that lay ahead.

The three men returned at dusk, tired, grimy, and not in the best of spirits. The life of a range rider was not by any means an easy one, but to those accustomed to living their days on horseback, any kind of work that could not be accomplished with a rope and saddle was far too strenuous for their liking. They had spent the day felling and dragging trees, splitting logs, and stacking timber, backbreaking work whose only reward was that it was done. Tomorrow they had nothing to look forward to but dragging the logs into camp and building the bunkhouse, a prospect that held no excitement for any of them.

They unsaddled their horses in a mostly disgruntled silence and rubbed down their mounts with handfuls of hay. Rio came out to help, and to Jed's terse inquiry about his wife Rio replied only, "*Si, señor,* she is a fine lady." No one noticed the secretive grin that accompanied his words.

They started toward the cabin at a weary pace, prompted by the inviting smells of supper. A few feet before the door they met a sight that brought them up short.

Elizabeth Fielding stood in the doorway, as fresh as a spring morning in a crisp blue calico dress, a white apron at her waist, and a wooden serving spoon in her hand. Not a hair was out of place, and her smile alone was enough to make any man stop and stare. "You'll find a washbasin and towel by the watering trough, gentlemen," she said pleasantly. "I'm just getting supper on the table."

She turned with a soft rustle of skirts and petticoats to go back inside. It took a grinning nudge from Rio to get the look of stupefaction off Dusty's face.

Jed went quickly to splash water on his face and hands, but on second thought, he stripped off his shirt and used soap on his chest and arms. He left the other men looking warily at each other and the washbasin, and he went inside.

He had to stop and look around for a long moment. It was not the same place.

Shelves had been built of packing crates on the walls, and all their supplies had been neatly arranged upon them. The few items of cookware hung from nails over the fireplace, dishes and utensils polished and gleaming on the shelf nearby. The table had been bleached with sand and lye soap until it was almost white, and the peeling bark scraped from the log walls. The hard-packed dirt floor had been swept so thoroughly that not even a trace of dust stirred when he walked, and the lantern chimneys polished to such an extent that light bounced into every corner. She had made a mattress for the bed of white muslin stuffed with clean dry grass, and folded at its foot was a length of navy wool Miss Nancy had insisted Elizabeth purchase for a winter coat.

The aroma of fried steaks and tortillas filled the air, and Elizabeth bent over the stove to lift a pot of greens onto the table—a rarity in their diet, for Rio said they were too hard to gather. Apparently, Jed noted, he did not think anything was too hard when Miss Elizabeth asked him to do it.

Before Jed could say anything, or even think of what it was he should say, the other men appeared at the door behind him. Their astonishment was as complete as his own, and they stood looking around uncertainly. They hadn't eaten inside since the ice storm the winter before, and they had no idea what the new mistress of the household had in mind for them.

Elizabeth set a platter of tortillas on the table and stepped back, removing her apron. "Shall we be seated?" she invited with a smile.

Quickly Dusty whipped off his hat; Skunk followed at a slower pace. Jed had cause to be glad of his recent brush with civilization, or he would have no doubt forgotten too. Elizabeth took the chair at one end of the table, and Jed took the other one. The men shuffled in awkwardly and found seats on the kegs she had pulled up to the table for each of them.

The table was set with tin plates and cups, and somehow she had managed to find a knife and a fork for each of them. Skunk immediately took up his knife and speared the top two steaks on the platter but froze in the movement as Elizabeth said gently, "Jed, would you please lead us in grace?"

Jed had not said grace since he had last sat at his mother's table over ten years before, but when all eyes turned toward him, he knew he had to give it a try. Skunk's arm fell abruptly away from the platter, and everyone was waiting. Jed lowered his eyes, and somehow he bumbled through.

There was just another moment of awkward silence after Elizabeth's voice echoed sweetly, "Amen." No one seemed to know what to do. Once again it was Skunk who reached for the steak platter, and once again Elizabeth stopped him with a soft clearing of her throat. Skunk shot her a glowering look.

Beside each plate was a folded square of calico, and Elizabeth lifted hers, opened it, and placed it deliberately in her lap. Quickly the other men followed suit—except Skunk, who snatched his up and started to tuck it into his collar. A sharp nudge in the ribs from Dusty changed his mind, however, and still scowling darkly, he placed the small scrap of cloth over his big thigh. Then, almost as though afraid to make another move, he watched Elizabeth.

Rio seemed to have the edge on them all. He politely removed Skunk's knife from the steak platter and returned it to him, then passed the platter to Elizabeth. She thanked him with a smile and served herself, then passed to the left.

Many times over the following years Jed would look back upon that meal, and each time the memory would inspire new chuckles of wonder and admiration—the night civilization came to Three Hills. Each one of the men sitting at that table had fought and killed and would do it again on a moment's notice. They were accustomed to sharing their canteens with their horses and their bedrolls with whatever crawled out of the ground; their meals usually consisted of whatever they had just killed and tossed into the coals. But all it took was the presence of a woman to remind them of who they were and where they had come from—or perhaps even what they could be. Each one of them, in their separate fashions, was remembering another woman—wife, mother, sister—and times that once had been better than these.

Later Jed would realize all this and be amused. Even as he sat there with Elizabeth across from him looking as lovely and composed as though she were presiding over the finest banquet table at Larchmont Plantation, he felt a stir of gratitude and wonder. But on that first night he was mostly just struck by how alien her presence was. In some indefinable way he saw her as threatening, and that made him feel very, very helpless and angry.

The meal was a quick and silent affair, for despite their newfound manners, eating was a serious business among hungry, hardworking men. Elizabeth realized this and made no attempt at polite conversation. She took dainty bites of her meal, used her napkin frequently, and pretended not to notice the quick glances shot at her by men who couldn't believe how quickly they had forgotten all the things a woman brings to life. Nor how much they had missed them.

They gulped their coffee, then pushed away their plates, one by one. It was Dusty who stood first, clutching his hat. He cleared his throat. "Mighty fine supper, ma'am."

Elizabeth smiled at him. "Thank you, Dusty. But it was Rio who did the cooking, you know."

Dusty blushed to the tip of his blond fringe. "Yes'm. But it was mighty fine, all the same."

Skunk stood up, started to clap on his hat, then hesitated. He shot a glance at Elizabeth from beneath lowered brows. "Good to sit down at a table again, ma'am," he muttered gruffly, and turned and strode toward the door.

Rio paused beside Elizabeth's chair. "*Buenas noches, señora*. Tonight..." His face softened with the hint of a fond smile. "Tonight I remember old times, in the fine hacienda of the don and his lovely señora. It has been too many years," he said simply. He bowed to her with quiet dignity and closed the door softly behind him as he left.

Jed lingered at the table, his fingers hooked around his coffee cup. His eyes moved across the room in what he hoped was a casual fashion, but all the while he kept Elizabeth within his peripheral vision. The lamplight glinted off her unswept hair and painted shadows into the graceful folds and creases of her dress. She sat in that perfectly composed drawing-room manner, sipping chicory coffee from her battered tin cup as though it were imported tea from the finest porcelain. Her face looked like all that was tranquil and beautiful about the world, and just a glimpse of her, here in this place and so close to him, caused a wrench of yearning in his heart that was so intense, it actually hurt.

He did not want this woman in his world. He had never wanted her; everything about her was inappropriate, out of place, and worrisome. But she sat across the table from him sipping coffee, and all he could think about was how much he wanted her.

What kind of man was he, to resent a woman and desire her at the same time?

She sat gazing at him with that lovely serenity in her eyes, as though this were the way she was accustomed to spending her evenings and could not desire anything more, as though she had been here forever. He was moved by a compulsion to touch her, to feel the softness of material against his hand, the warmth of flesh, to assure himself that she was real. For nothing had seemed less real to him in his entire life than she did at that moment, in this place.

He tried to imagine her scrubbing walls and sweeping floors and moving boxes and emptying kegs . . . performing tasks that even her house slaves, back in Alabama, would disdain. Elizabeth Coleman, who was not even accustomed to doing up her own buttons without two maids in attendance, had worked today like a field hand—and for what? For a bunch of men who were more used to the company of cows than the company of women? What did she hope to accomplish? Lines on her face and blisters on her hands, an ache in her bones and bitterness in her eyes, that was all her efforts at reforming this place would bring her. Didn't she see that?

He said abruptly, gesturing around the room, "You didn't have to do this."

His voice sounded gruffer than he had intended, and she registered the fact first with surprise, then with coolness, in her eyes. She lowered her cup slowly. "I didn't do it for you. I did it because I personally don't care to live like an animal, even if I am forced to live *with* one."

The moment the words were out, she went cold with shock, and she could not believe she had said them. But she was tired and anxious, and the tasks she had performed today had taken as much out of her mentally as physically. She had been knee-deep in filth, she had seen and done things that a month ago she would have swooned at the mere prospect of doing, and none of it had been easy.

She did not expect praise, and she felt no particular smugness for her accomplishment; she had merely seen what had to be done and she had set to it. But neither did she expect the anger in Jed's tone, nor the brooding in his expression. When he spoke to her in that manner, something inside her seemed to snap. She refused to be chastised when she had done no wrong. She had learned too much about her own strength today to sit still for it.

She saw the quick flash of shock in Jed's eyes that reflected her own, but almost immediately it was replaced by blankness again, a swift, protective distance. She was just gathering herself to apologize when he pushed up from the table and turned toward the door. "I've got to be up with the sun tomorrow," he said.

"No." Her voice was firm and her eyes ablaze as she stood. "No, sir, you will *not* leave without talking to me. You will not treat me as though I don't exist. We are married, and though I know the fact is not of your choosing—"

Jed turned, his face cold and dark. "No," he said flatly. "It's not."

That was too much. Rage broke inside her, tightening her cheeks as she shot back, "Do you think this is the way I imagined marital bliss?" Her hands gripped the edge of the table, and her voice shook with a note of wildness as she demanded, "Do you think this is the way I would have chosen to spend the rest of my life? This is hardly a palace by the sea, and you, sir, are no Prince Charming!"

"You might as well get those ideas out of your head right now, woman," Jed returned harshly. The emotion that flared in his eyes was as potent as balled lightning, dancing through the air. "Take a good look around you. You left your fairy tales back in Alabama, and this is what you've got."

"I am perfectly aware of that!"

"You had your chance to go back!"

"Maybe I should have!"

"It's not too late." He stood before her, both hands clenched into fists at his sides. "I'll take you back tomorrow—hell, tonight! You can be having breakfast in bed and crying on your daddy's shoulder before the sun sets on another Sunday!"

Elizabeth went stiff with shock; she drew herself up. "Is that what you want?"

Their eyes met and dueled, and the seconds ticked off.

Jed looked away first, lifting a tense hand and dragging it through his hair. "I don't know what I want," he said curtly. His voice was heavy with defeat as he moved his eyes to a point across the room and said, "I just know it's not this."

Swiftly Elizabeth moved around the table. Her heart was pounding in her throat, her chest was flooded with anxiety and helplessness. This was not what she wanted, either. Not this anger, not this coldness, not this defeat . . .

"Why are you so angry with me all the time?" she demanded. "I've done nothing to deserve such treatment! What do you want from me?"

Jed looked at her, and the confusion that flooded him left him weak. He had never known a woman like her, so honest, so completely without guile, so unafraid to face her own feelings and to put them into words. Everything she did, everything she said, was a challenge to him, for he understood nothing about women, and even less about emotions . . . especially his own.

What did he want? He wanted her to be away from here, back in her own safe world where she belonged. He wanted to be free of guilt, of worry, of helplessness. . . .

He did not want her anger, or his own. He did not want to hurt her. And he did not know how to tell her any of this.

He released a breath, and he half turned away. "I'm not angry with you, Elizabeth. I never have been. I'm angry with myself."

She only looked at him, and her confusion made him frustrated.

"Damn it, Elizabeth, don't you understand?" Tensely he paced the few steps to the fireplace. "This is my fault, all of it! You shouldn't be here, you shouldn't be married to me, you shouldn't have to live like this. I traded both our lives for one moment of blind passion, and I never intended—"

Elizabeth colored quickly with the memory his words brought back, and the shock that he would refer to it. But before she could stop herself, she was objecting, indignant, "*Your* fault! You were hardly alone!"

He whirled on her. "You are a child." His voice was bitter. "I knew better, and I—"

"I am not a child!" She drew herself up to her full height, her eyes smoldering again. "And I refuse to be treated like one! Haven't I proven today that I am capable of anything you demand of me? What more must I do?"

Jed looked at her, and there were a hundred things he wanted to say, wanted to make her see, wanted to try to explain. But in the face of the indignation in her eyes he did not even know where to begin. "Elizabeth," he said, and then stopped, shaking his head with a short breath. His eyes moved slowly around the room, then back to her. "You haven't changed the world you live in," he explained curtly, "just the way it looks."

Elizabeth met his eyes unwaveringly. "I have to start somewhere."

Jed drew another breath, but arguing with her was pointless. Standing before him, her cheeks flushing and her eyes snapping with determination, she looked more beautiful than he had ever seen her. He felt a twinge of admiration and, yes, a strong pull of desire, but most of all he felt completely at a loss. She was the most stubborn, intractable woman he had ever known. There was no way he could control her, conjole her, or reason with her. What was he to do with a woman like this?

She stood only a few feet before him, her face upturned, her eyes alight with the stubbornness of a foolish vision, and a surge of helpless despair exploded within him. "Damn it, Elizabeth, this is not one of your afternoon tea socials! You can't organize this and rearrange that and expect everything to be all right. You're still walking around with blinders on, expecting everything to be pink frills and sunsets just because you say so. Will you for God's sake wake up?"

Frustration and impotency battled inside him, making him shout when he didn't want to, making him angry without his knowing why. He took her by the shoulders, and he wanted to shake her, to make her understand, to startle her out of her complacent little world and see the truth . . . but her eyes were snapping up at him, her lips were parted for a defensive retort, and he didn't shake her at all. He drew her hard against him and kissed her.

That was when he knew why he was angry. That was when he knew the source of the frustration that churned inside him, the helplessness and anxiety that gnawed at him and prodded him and wouldn't let him go. He felt her breasts crushed against his chest, her soft mouth was caught on a cry of surprise, and all he wanted was to possess her, to keep her still, to somehow infuse himself into her and make her see. He wanted to claim her, to subdue her own reckless spirit and heedless optimism and thereby keep her safe.

Those emotions were so savage and so wrong that they frightened him. She wanted a husband, a home, civility, and security, and he could give her none of them. He wanted nothing but her, and in a moment he would take her on the floor like the animal she had accused him of being.

He tore his mouth from hers and pushed her away abruptly, breathing hard, his color high. She stood looking at him in stunned bewilderment, her lips swollen from the force of his, her breasts rising and falling rapidly. He released her arms and brought his hands deliberately to his sides, his fingers closing slowly into fists of impotence.

He said tightly, "Now do you see? You can clean up the house, you can make the cowhands eat from a plate instead of a pot, and you can dress yourself up and pretend you're back in Daddy's big fine house . . . but you can't change me, any more than you can change those hills out there or the lions and the bears that live in them.

"This is it, Elizabeth," he said flatly. "This is what you have for a husband, for a home. It's not what you wanted, not what you expected, not what you dreamed it would be. It's not what I wanted, either, but it's just the way it is."

There was a courage in the lift of her chin that denied the slight waver in her voice, the slight hurt in her eyes. "We are going to be married forever," she said with dignity. "I can only do the best I can, and I am sorry if it is not enough. But it's more than you're doing. At least I am trying to build an agreeable marriage and be a good wife."

He wanted to be her husband. He wanted her to be his wife, in every sense of the word. The need was still clawing at him, the pumping demand of energy, the thirst unsatisfied, and all that was still unsettled between them hung in the air like a half-finished question. But how could he subject her to more demands after the harshness that had just passed between them? How could he expect her to share intimacies when everything that had happened tonight had only pushed them farther apart?

And how could he leave her with the echo of hateful words in his ears and the memory of the hurt in her eyes?

He wanted to show her tenderness. He wanted to erase all the ugliness. He wanted, with all his might, for things to be different. The last thing he wanted was to turn for the door.

But that was what he did.

Elizabeth watched him go, battling frustration and defeat, not knowing what else to say, not even certain what had happened. Her fingers went to her lips, still bruised and throbbing from the force of his kiss. She wanted to call him back, but she did not know what she wanted him for. She did not want him to leave, but she did not know why.

His hand fell upon the latch, and then he stopped. He did not want to leave her like this. He could at least try. . . .

He turned slowly. His eyes met hers and held for a long time. This marriage was forever, and neither of them could change the past. But perhaps, together, they could begin to change the future. Or at least they could try.

He said quietly, "I don't want to sleep outside tonight, Elizabeth."

CHAPTER
Fifteen

*H*e crossed the room back toward her, and she could feel her breathing escalate, the muscles of her stomach tighten with anticipation. Where once there had been hot and tangled emotions in his eyes, now there was a controlled certainty that she found more alarming than his temper had been. This was Jed . . . but a Jed she had never seen before.

All she thought she had learned about passion from those few moments of frantic coupling on the beach dissolved around her in tatters as she realized that that, too, had been only an illusion. There had been high, desperate emotion propelling her from a brush with death to the only natural expression of life; there had been no fear, no shame.

Now she was married to a man she did not know, and when she tried to recapture the wonder, the satisfaction, and the thrill of being held in a lover's arms, all she could

212

remember was pain, confusion, and the embarrassing nature of the actual act. For the first time she had to ask herself whether she welcomed her husband's intimacy, and the answer was that she didn't know.

Jed stopped a few steps before her. He lifted his hands to rest lightly upon her elbows, and he said quietly, "There is more to being a wife than keeping a man's house, Elizabeth."

She met his gaze evenly, but he could feel the increased pace of her breathing and see the consternation in her eyes. "I know my duty, sir," she responded steadily.

Was that what he wanted from her—duty? This was Elizabeth, as much a fantasy to him as she had ever been, and yet so real, so present and alive that it was unnerving. A lady such as she would never welcome the baser side of marriage, and he was a cad for forcing it on her. But she was his wife, and this, too, was a part of life she could not change.

But he had never wanted her to look at him with such staunch resignation in her eyes and accept his attentions as no more than her duty.

He lowered his eyes briefly, and Elizabeth, watching the shadows formed upon his taut cheekbones by that dark fringe of lashes, felt a new, surprised speeding to her pulse. There was something endearing about the way he looked just then, reminding her poignantly of the first time she had looked at him and known how striking he was to the eye. She wondered what those lashes would feel like to the touch, whether they would be as silky as they looked, or coarse and bristly, as male as the rest of him.

Jed looked back at her, and there seemed to be a hint of sadness in his eyes, almost of apology. His fingers were light upon her elbows, barely penetrating her sleeves with warmth, not hard and forceful like they had been when he had grabbed her a moment before. Both sides of him—as he had been then and as he was now—were fascinating, confusing, and equally alarming.

"Elizabeth," he said, his voice edged with just a touch of hoarseness as his eyes moved over her face. She saw a muscle in his jaw tighten, as though in determination. "I'm not a gentle man. I know that a woman like you expects to be courted, crooned to, and romanced. I don't know any of the pretty words you'd like to hear, and I don't have any of the manners you're used to. I'm crude and blunt, and sometimes I'm going to hurt you, and the best I can say is that I'm sorry. You wanted to make me into your Prince Charming, and I know you're disappointed. Maybe that's the real thing that makes me angry—with myself and with you. Because I don't know what to do about it."

Elizabeth felt her dread slip away into tenderness, even surprise. For though the words were uttered gruffly, they were backed with care, and she knew they were hard for him to say. The best times of her life were those shared with Jed, in easy, unconstrained conversation, when he talked of himself and told her things that were important to him— secret things, things she knew instinctively he had never shared with anyone else. He had never told her anything this important before.

She did not know how to respond, except to say, somewhat timidly, "I don't *always* find you disappointing, you know." She managed a shy, uncertain smile. "Only when you act like a beast."

She saw the faintest hint of a smile begin in his eyes, and an immeasurable amount of tension and uncertainty drained from her own muscles as he admitted, "And I guess that's more often than not."

"More often than necessary," she agreed, but she was smiling at him now and looking at the face she had loved instinctively from the moment she had first seen it . . . and beginning to remember why.

His soft, golden hair, drifting back from his temples and curling forward a little against his neck as he bent his head to look at her, those dark strong planes of his face, the heavy fringe of lashes . . . she noticed his mouth, and she could not recall ever paying particular attention to it before. It was strongly shaped and masculine, yet with a slight fullness of the underlip that added gentleness to his face and reminded her of how soft his lips could be . . . sometimes. There was a coarseness to the texture of his skin above his lip and over his lower face, the shadow of his beard. Yet his face looked smooth, sun-baked and polished, not rough at all. Had she ever touched his face? She could not remember.

"You are very handsome," she said, and she did not know where the words had come from. She had not intended to say it out loud, but like so many other truths, it just somehow became spoken.

Jed looked startled, as though the thought had never crossed his mind before. Certainly he had never expected to hear her say it. "I'm what?"

Elizabeth felt laughter bubble in her throat, partly from nervousness, partly from delight. She did not feel awkward with him anymore, and that awful uneasiness in the pit of her stomach had faded away. She forgot he was a stranger. "Has no one ever told you that before?" With a teasing boldness that surprised even herself, she pursued, "You must hear it quite often from your lady friends."

Jed flushed a little. In truth, no one had ever told him that before, and he thought very little about the way he looked. He knew that in a crowd the eye of a roving girl would usually pick him out. But who would have thought a lady like Elizabeth would care anything about a man's looks?

She thought he was handsome. He never would have believed how good that could make him feel.

He told her honestly, "I don't have any lady friends."

Elizabeth said, "You have me." And then, slowly, a little bit hesitantly, she lifted her hand and lightly touched his cheek.

Her eyes were dark and thoughtful, and she seemed fascinated by the texture of his skin. Jed could feel his blood begin to pulse with the surprise of her touch, the tiny spark that set off a rapidly building flame within him. What a wonder this woman was, what a constant puzzle, what a powerful, consuming demand. She made him angry, she racked him with confusion, she plunged him into despair. She made him want her, and she made him ashamed of wanting her; she made him afraid to touch her, and then she touched him and made him weak. She incited him to passion and she pained him with gentleness, and she made all he ever thought he knew about himself, and about her, and about what he expected from both of them, seem irrelevant and untrue.

The light pressure of her fingertips upon his skin tingled in nerve endings he had never even known he had. Her eyes were soft with concentration, and he could see twin images of himself reflected in them. Her palm went flat against his face in a gentle, feathering stroke, and then drifted down to his shoulder. He bent his face to hers.

He touched her lips with his own—lightly, for he wanted to be so gentle—in the barest brush of shared, uncertain breaths, then again, tasting. Then his hand slipped around her waist and he drew her against him. He pressed his mouth to hers fully, she molded herself against him, and he lost his very breath in her.

She was sweet and was melting against him. Heat and sparks darted through his head liked misfired heartbeats.

Elizabeth. She was magic and she was mystery, and she had a control over him he could not fight.

He felt her fingertips against the bare flesh of his neck, shyly, timidly exploring. Her touch sent a surge of weakness to his muscles and a thick rush of blood to his loins that was like a painful surprise—too quick, too sudden. The way her arm was stretched over her head caused her breast to press into the side of his ribs, an insistent thrust of soft, rounded flesh he could not ignore.

He wanted her; he had known that for days, for weeks. He had come back into this room because he intended to have her. He had not known until this moment how badly he wanted her, nor how much power that desire had over him.

His hands moved from her waist upward along her back, and her ribs, feeling the tight contours of stays, which was both a frustrating barrier and a maddening allure of femininity. Then he felt softness against his palm, the brushing pressure of the fullness of her breast, and his heart began to thud with such force that he had to take his mouth from hers to breathe. His hands went to her hair, his fingers thrusting into the full, heavy mass, tilting her head back so his lips could taste her throat. Hairpins fell, and thick, gleaming locks tumbled into his hands. He turned his face to the texture and fragrance of her hair, holding her and breathing deeply of the heady, mind-stripping sensations. Roses. Even out here she still smelled like wild roses.

Elizabeth clung to him, feverish and weak, for she had forgotten—so easily had she forgotten—what his kisses could do to her. Like a greedy, thwarted child, she wanted his kiss again, wanted the swift, throbbing weakness it pulsed through her. Single-mindedly she wanted the pleasure his embrace could induce, the adventure into dizziness and heat and simple, mindless discovery. There was no thought in his arms, no worry or anxiety. There was no anger, no dread, no shame. Just Jed, and she wanted him to kiss her.

On a shameless, needing instinct she turned her face toward his again, and his parted lips captured hers, briefly, breathlessly, and electrically, once, and twice, and then lingering a bit longer with a swift and urgent message she did not fully comprehend. Then he drew away, steadying his hands on her waist, and he looked at her. He was breathing hard, and his face was flushed and damp. His eyes . . . she had never noticed how large his pupils were before, how dark and urgent they made his eyes seem, nor how brightly they reflected the light.

His eyes touched her skin like little flickers of fire. He said huskily, "Elizabeth, let's go to bed."

He saw the moment of uncertain alarm in her eyes and the swift rush of new color to her cheeks. He was moved by tenderness and a twinge of pity and wished he could make it easy for her. The thickening inside his breeches was insistent and far too obvious, and her ignorance of it only reminded him again of her painful lack of experience. She looked at him as though she did not know what to do next, and he cursed himself for not being able to tell her without embarrassment.

If she were in her own home, she would be able to retreat modestly to a dressing room and emerge swathed in layers of silk. She could climb into her huge four-poster bed and await her husband's return from his own dressing room, decently clad in nightshirt and robe. It would all be simple, modest, and civilized.

But in this time, in this place, there was no way to avoid the awkwardness of moving from the heat of passion to the narrow, uncomfortable cot they would share. There were no allowances to be made for her embarrassment or need for privacy, and things like that were important to a lady.

He would not take her in careless, thoughtless passion as he had done before—upon the ground, her clothing pushed aside, her womanhood used and her feelings ignored. She was a wife, and she deserved the dignity of a bed—rude though it was—and a husband who came to her with care and patience. He could give her little else, but he could allow her that.

Jed let his eyes flicker away from her, and he said, "I'll . . . lower the lamps."

She nodded, her cheeks brilliant with color. She turned away from him and discreetly began to unbutton her cuffs.

Jed extinguished one lamp and lowered the wick on the other to the faintest glow, bathing the room in grainy sepia shadows. He kept his back to her, as he was sure she kept hers to him, but secrecy and anticipation choked through his veins with dark, weaving fingers of excitement he could not control, no matter how hard he tried. Jed's ears, long attuned to wilderness living, picked up sounds of movement and read their sign. He could hear the soft whisper of clothing, a turn, a step, the rustling fall of a petticoat, and then another. His heart began to thud. He sat upon a chair to remove his boots, and his fingers felt hot and swollen. It took him twice as long to get them off as it should have. On the range he traded his moccasins for tight, high-heeled boots of sturdy leather, and they made a dull, heavy thud as they hit the hard dirt floor. Even that sound, one he had heard hundreds of times before, was strangely erotic, charged with expectancy.

He stood to unfasten his pants, and he could hear the scraping whisper of whalebone and satin, a corset being removed. He listened for the soft sound of a nightdress being pulled over her head, and fumbling movements beneath the material as she slipped the chemise off her shoulders and over her hips. A stepping, the faintest brush of soft cotton, and pantalets came off. A cotton stocking, and another, and her bare feet were upon the floor. A creaking of the rawhide thongs that supported the bed frame, the crackle of the newly fashioned mattress. Then he heard nothing but the distant, muted sound of crickets chirping and the pounding of his own heart.

Jed stepped out of his pants but left his shirt on, the power of his sex tenting against its folds. He turned and walked over to her.

She was sitting upon the edge of the bed, her hands folded in her lap, her eyes diligently avoiding looking at any part of him. Her nightdress was white, voluminous, and fastened with a drawstring high upon her throat. But he could see the shadow of her naked thighs, the curve of her buttocks enfolded by the soft, grass-stuffed mattress, and three bare toes on each foot. What tiny, femininely shaped feet she had. He imagined how they would feel, caressing his naked calves, and the imagining sent a new leap of startled heat to the tight muscles of his abdomen.

She sat stiffly, her knees and her ankles pressed as tightly together as they could possibly be, her shoulders square, her back straight. When from the vantage point of her lowered eyes she caught a glimpse of his unclothed legs and bare feet, she jerked her eyes away quickly, and he saw a new wave of color swim to her face. He sat beside her on the bed, and for a moment he was hesitant even to touch her.

"Elizabeth . . ." His voice sounded strained, and he swallowed. She looked at him with an obvious effort, and her eyes were wide and green. He would have given a good part of his life to know what she was thinking then.

He lifted his arm in what seemed to him a clumsy gesture and touched her shoulder. Her hair was tumbled down just as he had left it, a magnificent cascade of waves and dark lights, and against his knuckles it felt like silk. Better than silk.

He had to look away, and all he wanted to do was to get that look of consternation and fear—was it fear?—off her face. His eyes fell upon the mattress and he said, rather foolishly, "This is nice. The mattress. I've been meaning to do it for a while but never found the time."

Elizabeth wasn't sure her voice would work, her throat was so tight. "It . . . must have been uncomfortable for you, sleeping without it."

"Most of the time I sleep outside. On the ground."

He could see her trying to keep her breathing regular. The muscles of her small shoulder felt as hard as steel beneath his hand. He wished he knew how to make this easier for her. He already had hurt her so much and in so many ways. Why should this have to be a part of it?

At last he did not know what else to do except to kiss her, lightly, trying not to fuel his own passion, trying not to let that insistent part of his body brush against her and frighten her further. Her lips were soft but her body stiff, and he ended the kiss too soon.

He cupped her small face in his hand and kept it steady, looking at her solemnly, searching for what to do, what to say, desperately wishing he were imbued with some mystical power to get inside her head and know her feelings. . . .

He had never wanted that with a woman before. It had never mattered.

"Elizabeth," he said with painful difficulty. "I won't force you. If . . . you ask me to, I'll leave you now." He hadn't intended to say that. He couldn't believe he meant it, but the strange thing was, he did. For her. Because he didn't want her to hate him.

Elizabeth looked at him with wide and stricken eyes. He

watched her color grow more intense by degrees. She said, in a small voice, "I don't know what you want me to do."

How could she know? All she knew about this part of life, about this strange communication between men and women, was what he had taught her in a few brutal moments in a deserted shack on the beach. He searched his mind frantically for some remembrance of what it must have been like for her then and found, to his disgust, that he could remember little, if anything, about that night.

It was a night that had changed his life, and all he could remember was the guilt.

He must have hurt her. He had been heedless of her virginity, and he knew that was a painful, even traumatizing, experience for a woman. Jed, himself, had no experience with the untried, but he had some notion that it should have been done with tenderness and consideration. As even now it should be. For Elizabeth there should be more than a quick and violent coupling in the dark, a release of needs. But he had never known it any other way.

Jed had never imagined he would one day have to teach a woman how to make love. He had never thought he, himself, would want to learn.

He took a breath; he released it unsteadily. With a deliberate effort he relaxed his fingers on her face and stroked her cheek lightly. He said, "Most women think men know all there is to know about . . . this. Loving and bedding. They kind of expect us to, I guess. But we don't. Most times we just do what we want. I think there should be more to it than that."

He lowered his eyes briefly, to the tightly clasped hands in her lap. It was hard, looking at her again, talking about such things to her. "Maybe I don't even exactly know how it's supposed to be done—in the marriage bed, I mean, tender like, and sweet. It should mean something between married folks.''

Elizabeth's eyes were dark and interested, and some of the tightness had gone out of her muscles. The sound of Jed's voice did that. "And it doesn't . . . other times? When you're not married?''

He was embarrassed, talking to her like this. But she wasn't looking at him with such dread anymore. "Well,'' he admitted, "there's pleasure in it, for the man.''

"But not for the woman?''

He answered her honestly. "I don't know.''

His figure was grainy in the dim light, shrouded and rather intimate. She could see his face and every expression on it. But the rest of him was shadowed from her, and she found comfort as well as mystery in that, for she could not help remembering that he was wearing nothing but a shirt and that his legs, bare and sprinkled with light hair, were very close to hers. She had never seen a man's legs before. She thought she should be ashamed of even being curious about them.

She said, hesitantly, "What we did before . . . was a sin, wasn't it?'' She colored deeply.

His expression was sober. His hand had drifted down to her shoulder and was massaging it with an absent, soothing motion. "I reckon it was. But we're married now.''

Elizabeth did not understand how it could be a sin once but not the second time. The worst part was that she did not feel as though it had been a sin the first time.

She said, very softly, staring at her hands, "I want to be a good wife.'' But what did she know about making love . . . or even loving? Everything was so different now.

"I know you do.'' His breath was soft and almost steady as it fluttered across her cheek. He wanted to be a good husband. He had never realized how badly he wanted that until this moment.

His hand felt the soft skin of her neck, just beneath her hair. One finger slipped inside the tight ruffle of her nightgown, high on her neck, and the movement seemed to startle her. Her skin was very heated there, and the secret exploration of what he could feel, but not see, was intensely exciting.

He said huskily, "I've never had quiet time like this, with a woman. I'm not used to it, and maybe I don't know the right things to say, or do . . . but I want to try, Elizabeth. I don't want you to hate this part of being married. A man needs a woman he can come to, and he doesn't want to think she wishes he wouldn't."

His finger, stroking the flesh of her neck just beneath the barrier of her clothes, seemed insinuating and innocent. It made her skin tingle, and not just where he touched. She wondered if he would take her nightgown off, or make her do it, and that thought made her hot all over. She wondered if he would take off his shirt.

He had known her naked before. But that had been different.

She looked up at him, and it seemed like one of the hardest things she had ever had to do, thinking the thoughts she was thinking. She could see a sprinkling of light blond hair caught in the faintness of light, just below his collar. She wondered if he had hair all over his body, and then her throat went so tight that she couldn't even speak. Not if her life had depended upon it.

He lifted his hand, and his fingers went deeply, slowly, into her hair. He brought his face forward until she could see the small pores in his skin and feel his breath. His nose touched hers. And then his mouth on her parted lips. Lightly. Breathlessly. With a heated shock. Her heart thudded against her ribs, and a quick suspension of breath made her dizzy. His lips barely touched her throat, and his breath flooded her skin, causing a strange tickling sensation deep within her stomach. His hand cradled her neck, and she clung to his upper arms as he guided her to lie down.

He leaned over her, still sitting but close. She could feel his knee against her thigh. His heat filtered over her. His eyes were intense, so aware of her. His fingertips caressed her throat, and his voice was thick. "Your skin is so soft."

Then his fingers tugged at the bow that held her night-gown together. She made herself lie very still, every muscle suspended, as he loosed the material and pushed it down, over her shoulders, exposing her breasts to the heat of his gaze. She tried not to squirm, resisted the impulse to cover herself. The quickening she saw in his eyes, the slight, almost imperceptible catch of his breath made her feel strange . . . nervous and excited.

His warm, heavy hands cupped her breasts and she gasped. He murmured, "So lovely. Your womanhood. I just want to touch you." She felt the soft, caressing pressure as his hands closed, lifting her breasts, enfolding them with the rough texture of his palms. Floods of sensation poured from his touch, and she had to close her eyes, fighting the strangeness of it.

His fingertip brushed the center of her breast and she felt a hardening, a rush of tingling, maddening heat that seemed to be connected in some strange fashion from the place he touched to a secret, aching part of her deep inside. He took her nipples then, lightly between the thumb and forefingers of each hand, and stroked, worshiped, caressed, and she had to compress her lips to keep from crying out. It was maddening, her head was spinning, and there was this tingling trail of fire sparking out to every nerve path in her body . . . and she did not know whether she wanted to beg him to stop or to continue. Her fingers clenched, then moved, and she was touching the part of his thigh covered by his shirt. With a deeply drawn breath he covered her mouth with his.

As he kissed her his hands went down her arms, tugging at her sleeves, pulling them from her wrists. The caress of his hands against her skin was wonderful, dizzying; his mouth infused her with a heat that swirled with rising intensity and a thousand, thousand sensations she could not begin to describe. She felt his hands on her bare waist but hardly knew that he was pushing her nightgown down until he left her mouth to slip the material beneath her hips and over her feet. By then her head was whirling, her breath was shallow, and a multitude of tremors had afflicted every fine muscle of her body; and she knew nothing until his mouth found hers again. And then she knew that he, too, was naked.

It was a shock. His chest, warm and firm, against her breasts, the blending of skin, sent an electric jolt of sensation through her. She knew nothing but gentle, abrasive swirls of hair against her tender skin, dampness and heat, and the scent of maleness. His mouth covered hers, caressing her, lightly touching her face and her throat and then her chest . . . and then her breast.

The sensation was unlike anything she had ever known or imagined. She thought she had learned of passion that night on the beach, but she knew nothing, nothing at all. . . . This was moisture, heat, pressure, and tight-winding, anxious wires of pleasure twisting through the core of her. Awareness flashed, intense and brilliant, as reason receded into a dim and helpless thing. She was feverish, aching, and there was a flood of warmth between her legs that embarrassed her. It went on and on, the cup of his hand, his kissing her there, the heat of his mouth, until she thought she surely would cry out from the maddening, frightening pleasure of it.

He lifted himself, and she felt the heated dampness of his face against hers, the rush of his breath, the touch of his lips. His full, naked weight was upon her, his arms embracing her, his lips claiming hers. His thighs, hard and muscled, his chest, his abdomen firm against hers, and the heated, engorged strength of his manhood pressed against her thigh. Elizabeth's entire world was throbbing with sensation, familiar and unfamiliar, welcome and terrifying. His kisses drugged her, and his heat, his strength—it felt so right, covering her. She wanted him against her.

She lifted her arms and felt the heavy silken texture of his hair falling between her fingers. Then she explored, cautiously, headily, the lean, strong muscles of his back. She had never felt a man's skin before, his sheathed muscles and reined power. How smooth it was, and hard, and how dizzying to explore. Kissing him, feeling him, holding him . . . it was all so new and intoxicating and wonderful. She trembled from the force of it, and her stomach ached and her pulses and her breath whirled in a wild untutored dance toward a powerful, abandoned crescendo. She was weak and lost in him. Her lips were bruised and her skin aflame, and she couldn't get enough of him holding her and kissing her.

His weight lessened, and he lifted his face slightly, touching her with dizzying kisses of rapid breath. His hand moved between their bodies, soothing over her breast, tracing her ribs, sliding over that awful ache in her abdomen, tracing the point of her hipbone . . . and slipping around her thigh.

A bolt of panic slammed into her chest, and she resisted, suddenly infused with a sharp awareness and a runaway thunder of pulses that threatened to cut off her very breath. Faintly she heard him whisper, "It's all right, Elizabeth, I'll try not to hurt. Tell me if I hurt."

Her eyes fastened on his, and she saw the blur of brightness in his eyes, the intense, suspended anxiety in his face. Damp curls of hair feathered his temple and shadowed his forehead, and his eyelids seemed heavy, slumberous. His skin was flushed and dark, and his lips were parted with the flutter of breath that touched her cheek. He moved her thighs apart.

She felt him hard against her, that large and heated male part of him ready to invade her soft and tender feminine flesh. She tried to make herself still, but she was trembling helplessly and her heart was pounding ruthlessly against her ribs. She steeled herself against the pain.

Jed slipped his arms beneath her back, embracing her, and instinctively she wrapped her arms around him, clinging to him. He kissed her gently, soothingly, and then more deeply. She felt the low, sliding pressure of his entry, his width, his heat pushing inside her, filling her.

There was no pain. All Elizabeth could feel was his smooth ironlike length, deep inside of her, and deeper still, and the sensation tore a gasp from her. Herself, a deep and unknown part of herself, wrapped around him, muscles closing to welcome him. This part of him, so large and alien inside her yet feeling as though it should always have been there, as though she had never been complete without him there.

He lifted his face and eased his weight onto his elbows. His hair brushed her cheek, and his breath touched her lips. "Elizabeth." His voice was thick and husky, so that he sounded as dazed as she felt. And that was all he said. "Elizabeth . . ."

His movements were gentle and mesmerizing, stroking sources of sensation she had never imagined existed before. When her body began to move instinctively with his, it seemed only right, and beyond her control. She was caught up in a place and a time where nothing existed except Jed and the blending of their bodies and the sharing of wonder.

Nothing could have prepared Elizabeth for this—the abandon

that raked her senses and bombarded her mind, the intensity that blinded her, that snatched at her breath, that flooded her body and consumed her soul. She heard her own helpless cries muffled against his bare shoulder; she felt her fingers digging into his slippery flesh; she heard his ragged gasps of breath as his movements became faster, deeper, more demanding. She fought for control but couldn't grasp it, and with each one of his forceful thrusts she lost more of herself to him until in a single, paralyzing moment he drove deep into her and held himself there, pushing against the very core of her womb. She lifted herself to him, clung to him, lost her breath. And she knew the flood of joy that transported her into a world of flashing dark and light, a world without time, without care, a world where there existed nothing but Jed and herself and the destiny that decreed they should be forever joined together.

They had both found the peak of pleasure in it. But there was more than pleasure, more than corporeal delights. What they had shared was beyond human knowledge, as though God, in His infinite wisdom, had separated them only so that they might be one day joined together like this. In doing this they had touched and exchanged a portion of each other's souls so that they would never be completely separate again.

She curled into the curve of his arm, weak and drained and still pulsating with the intensity of what she had just discovered, yet infused with such a strange and helpless exhilaration that her thoughts would not be still and her heart seemed to swell with every breath. This was why they called it making love. She had never known before.

Her arm was thrown loosely over Jed's bare chest, and she could not stop touching him. She felt the lean, defined muscles of his upper arm, relaxed now but still strong, alien, and fascinating. Beneath her fingers she felt slickness and warmth and a slight unevenness in the texture of his skin—a scar? She wanted to see him, to touch him, to know every part of him. Deliberately she made herself be still.

Would he be shocked if she told him of the pleasure she had experienced? Her eager response, abandoned movements, and soft cries had been shameless and wanton, but perhaps he had not noticed. Women were not supposed to enjoy it. She wanted to tell him. She wanted to say a dozen things, a hundred, she wanted to share with him every nuance of everything she had thought and felt and experienced . . . but hesitation, uncertainty, and the simple overwhelming newness of it all held her captive, and for once the truth that demanded to be spoken fell helplessly silent on Elizabeth's lips. She could only lie against him, wrapped in silence and warmth, and feel more than she had ever felt in her life.

She loved him. She had loved him from the secure fantasy of her silver-tinged world in Mobile; she had loved him as the hero who risked his life for her own; she loved him now as just a man—stark, simple, and unadorned.

But he had never said he loved her. She wished, more than anything in the world at that moment, that he would say it, just once.

But that, perhaps, was asking too much.

Jed moved to draw the wool blanket over them both, then settled back again. His lips brushed her hair, lightly, lingeringly, and he relaxed, his arms sheltering her. She felt the deep, regular sound of his breathing.

She thought he was asleep, and it occurred to her how strange it would be to sleep like this, naked in her husband's arms, throughout the night. Strange yet wonderful. A smile touched her lips, and she closed her eyes. This was the beginning of her married life.

CHAPTER
Sixteen

By the time Elizabeth awoke the next morning, the men had already breakfasted, departed, and returned with the first load of logs for the bunkhouse—and the rosy glow of sunrise had barely left the sky. Jed had left her side without disturbing her. Even though she could hear his voice in the yard as the wood was lifted and stacked, by the time she was dressed, he had already left again.

Perhaps it was best. She could not think about the night that had passed between them without going hot all over, and to find herself awakening naked... She did not know how she would be able to keep those memories from her eyes whenever she looked at Jed. And she did not know how he would look at her now.

As it happened, the morning was too busy to allow much time for reflection on anything, and Elizabeth was grateful for that. She was appalled to have overslept—although back home at Larchmont the slaves would have barely had the fires lit by this hour—and determined to make up for lost time. Jed and his crew were not the only ones who had plenty to do.

She set a kettle to boil over the outside fire and dissolved a measure of soap in it for laundry. She mixed up bread dough and left it to rise, hoping her many years of watching Cook had not failed her. She used the last of the muslin she had intended to turn into petticoats and made a set of sheets for the bed—the wool blanket had been scratchy against her skin and too hot for this time of year.

She found a length of rope and stretched it between the two trees for a clothesline, and all the while she was aware of curious, interested eyes darting toward her every move. When she started toward the spring for more water, Dusty was quickly at her side, hat in hand, volunteering to do it for her. When she started to lift a heavy pot of beans that Rio had left soaking onto the cook fire, Skunk was beside her with more speed than she would have thought him capable of, muttering something about scrawny little girls and putting the pot in place for her. Rio made more trips than necessary to check the progress of the midday meal.

Once, as she was hanging damp laundry on the line with bent hairpins, she felt a gaze of such intensity upon her back that she had to turn around. Jed was there, but he was turning quickly to mount his horse, and she must have imagined that he was looking at her. Still, the sight of him made her heart beat faster.

The noon meal was a casual and hurried affair, each man stopping by the fire to scoop a measure of beans onto his plate and eating while he stood, then hurrying off to work again. Elizabeth did not push for a more civilized atmosphere, feeling she had made enough progress for one twenty-four-hour period. Besides, she was almost too busy to eat herself, and if Jed stopped by the fire for food, she had not seen him.

Rio showed her how to place her bread in the coals of the fire and cover it with stones to bake, and how to mix wild onions and chopped beef with beans and broth for the evening meal. The building of the bunkhouse began with much clattering of hammers and muted, bitten-back oaths—each one accompanied by a guilty look toward the cabin. The men took turns hammering and going for more logs, and each time they passed the clothesline, fluttering with feminine stockings and petticoats, they flushed and averted their eyes. Elizabeth was embarrassed, too, but decided it was something they were all going to have to live with. She began to wonder how she could tactfully persuade the men that their own clothing would benefit greatly from a bout with the laundry tub every now and again.

She had brought a chair outside and was hemming napkins by the light of the sun when a shadow fell over her. She looked up, and Dusty stood before her, shifting uncomfortably on his feet, a big bouquet of black-centered daisies in his hand.

"Thought you might like these, ma'am," he said, thrusting them abruptly toward her. He wouldn't look at her. "To spruce up your table."

Elizabeth gave an exclamation of delight and got to her feet, bringing the daisies to her face. "Why, Dusty, they're lovely!"

"My ma used to like flowers on the table," he offered, and looked around uncomfortably.

Elizabeth smiled at him. "She must have been a gentle woman."

Now he looked at her. "Yes'm, she was. A lot like you."

Elizabeth was deeply touched, for though she was hardly old enough to be his mother or even remind him of her, she knew Dusty meant it as the highest compliment he could give. "Where is your family now, Dusty? Don't they worry about you?"

"No'm." His eyes squinted toward the distant sun. "We was headed west to homestead and Comanche attacked. I was out gathering firewood, came back to find the wagon burned, folks scalped. Never even heard nothing. Guess they didn't have time to yell."

Elizabeth stared at him, an awful horror clutching at the pit of her stomach. "How . . . how awful for you." She could barely get the words out. "Was it . . . recent?"

" 'Bout eight years ago."

"But . . . you were just a child!"

He shrugged. "You grow up fast out here."

Elizabeth tried to imagine that. A boy—he couldn't have been more than ten—discovering his parents' mutilated bodies, everything he had in the world gone, left alone in the wilderness. How had he survived? What must it have been like? How could such things happen in this day and age?

She had heard stories, of course. But until now they had been only stories.

She lowered her eyes to the flowers, and Dusty shifted his feet nervously. "Well, I'd better be getting back, ma'am."

"Thank you for the flowers, Dusty."

Elizabeth smiled at him gently. The very sight of that smile made Dusty flush, but it was hard to look away. He tipped his hat with a jerky movement. "No trouble."

He started to go, but she stopped him with a sudden inspiration. "Might I ask . . . where you found them?"

He hesitated, then gestured. "Just over yonder a piece. 'Bout midway up the low hill, near the willow branch."

Elizabeth remembered glimpsing a patch of daisies when she and Jed had come in from that direction the first day. She glanced over her shoulder, into the cabin. There was nothing that demanded her immediate attention. All day she had been wondering what she could do to make the place look less shabby, a bit more like home. Now she knew, and there was nothing stopping her from beginning right away.

She said, "I'd like to ride up there."

Dusty hesitated. "You want me to go with you?"

Elizabeth gave him a grateful smile. "Thank you, but you've got your own work to do. I was wondering, though, if there might be a saddle around that I could use?"

"Mought be."

The voice came from behind her before Dusty could answer, and Skunk stood leaning one shoulder against the side of the cabin, his cheek deformed by a wad of tobacco, his eyes squinting at her. He said in that same flat, mountain drawl, "What you fixin' to do with a saddle?"

Elizabeth flashed a smile at him. "Put it on a horse, I think. Do you know where there's one I might use?"

He moved his eyes lazily toward the corral. "Which horse?"

Elizabeth looked over the selection. Jed did have a fine collection of horseflesh; none of them were thoroughbreds but all of them were sturdy, healthy, and well cared for. "The roan, I think."

"You take the bay." Skunk spat on the ground. "The boss say it's all right fer you to have a horse?"

She looked back at him kindly. "I'm sure he won't mind. I must have a horse if I'm to get around, mustn't I?"

He seemed to consider this, then slowly pushed his great, hulking frame away from the wall. He said to Dusty, "You get on back t'work, boy. You been loafin' long enough."

He hitched up his sagging gun belt, pushed back the brim of his hat, and lumbered over to the corral. In a moment Elizabeth saw him lead out the bay.

She went inside to put on her gloves and bonnet and despaired over the fact that while she was in Galveston she had not thought to buy riding gloves or a habit—or even boots. But until she had another opportunity to go to town, she would simply have to make do.

When she came out, Skunk was holding the bay, neatly saddled and ready. Elizabeth tried to hide her dismay. "Oh . . . is that your saddle?"

He spat on the ground. " 'Tis now." The man to whom the saddle had belonged lay buried in a rock grave somewhere south of the Sierra Madres, but Skunk didn't think the lady needed to know that. He also didn't think she needed to know who had put the man in that grave. "Climb on. I'll hold 'im."

Elizabeth cleared her throat delicately. "I think you misunderstood. I need a sidesaddle."

He squinted at her. "Ain't but one kind of saddle, miss. This here's it."

"No," she tried to explain. "A sidesaddle is for ladies. It enables them to sit atop the horse as if they were in a chair, you see, instead of astride, as a man rides."

Skunk stared at her as though he were trying to determine whether or not she was making a joke. At last he turned his head, spat decisively, and announced flatly, "That's the biggest bunch of damn foolishness I ever did hear. You gonna ride or not?"

Elizabeth said gently, "Mr . . ." She paused. "Do you have another name? I can't seem to quite make myself call you Skunk."

Skunk blinked at her. It had been so long since anyone had called him anything else, he had almost forgotten his real name. "It's Jessup," he answered gruffly, after a time. "Hugh Jessup."

"Mr. Jessup," Elizabeth said with pleasure. "Didn't you ever have a sister or a wife?"

His eyes shifted away. "Had me a missus once, back in Tennessee. Fine gal. Died of the cholera."

Elizabeth could see, even in this rough, unkempt man, a tenderness for the memory, and she paused in a moment of silent sympathy. Then she inquired, her voice gentle, "Did your wife ever ride a horse?"

He looked back at her, then at the ground. "Hel—" He stopped, catching himself, and finished, "We never had nothin' but an old mule. Used him fer haulin' and totin'."

Elizabeth nodded, understanding. "I see." She looked back to the big Western saddle that adorned the bay. "Well, never mind, then. I think this will do, after all. Could you find me a box to stand on?"

He looked at her for a long time, as though he weren't sure he had heard her properly. Then, reluctantly, he went to do as he was bid.

He held the bridle as she stepped onto the box and gathered the reins neatly in her gloved hand. Dusty stopped work and stood quietly out of the way, fascinated by the proceedings. Both men watched as she slipped one foot into the stirrup, grasped the pommel with both hands, and, swinging her body around, lifted herself to a neat sitting position with one leg hooked gracefully over the pommel, as pretty as if she were perched in a rocking chair.

Skunk stared up at her. "That ain't never gonna work, Miz Fielding," he said flatly. "You climb on down before you kill yourself."

Elizabeth laughed and adjusted the reins between her fingers. "It will be fine, Mr. Jessup. Although next time I would appreciate it if you would shorten the right stirrup a bit. The horse might be nervous when he feels it hanging loose like this."

"How's that horse gonna know what you want him to do?" demanded Skunk as he adjusted the stirrup.

"Why, I'll guide him with the reins," answered Elizabeth, surprised. "How do you control your horse?"

"The only way there is," returned Skunk adamantly. "With my—" He broke off. He might say *damn,* and even an occasional *hell* in her presence, but he would never say a word like *leg* to a lady like Miss Elizabeth Fielding.

Elizabeth smiled brilliantly and lifted the reins. "Thank you for your help, Mr. Jessup, and for the saddle. I'm just going to go up to the hill, to the willow branch. I'll be back shortly."

She turned the horse prettily and started off at a brisk walk, her skirts fluttering in the breeze.

Dusty came over to Skunk, removed his hat, and wiped the inside. Both men watched until she disappeared over the rise.

"Makes a lot of sense," commented Dusty at last, and replaced his hat.

Skunk peered at him suspiciously.

"You think about it," advised Dusty sagely. "Would you want to marry a woman who sat a horse any other way?"

He walked off, and Skunk stood for a moment, scratching his head, a ruminating look upon his face. Then he shook his head a little, slowly, and replaced his hat. He was still thinking about it as he went back to work.

Jed lashed the last log into place on the platform, affixed the rope harness to the two drays, and mounted his own horse, wrapping the lead around his pommel. Given his choice, he, too, had rather be riding the range, but he had been raised on hard work, and when it was his to do, he was fit for it. But he was glad this was the last load.

He had managed to slip out of bed that morning without disturbing Elizabeth, dressed silently in the dark, and was gone before she even knew it. Outside, the men were already up and around, and there wasn't a doubt in his mind they knew every detail of what had gone on in the cabin the night before. He avoided their knowing looks but caught a grin or two behind his back, and it was damned embarrassing.

Sleeping close to the door as they did, they hadn't missed a sound. That was another reason Jed would be glad to get this bunkhouse built. Elizabeth would not survive the knowledge if she ever guessed how little privacy she really had.

Even in broad daylight, even with sweat running down his back and muscles stinging from hard work, he couldn't stop thinking about her and seeing her in his mind's eye and feeling her and smelling her. . . . He made extra trips to the house just so he could look at her, then left quickly before she could see him. He didn't know what would be in her eyes when she looked at him after the night before.

As soon as this bunkhouse was finished, he was going to build a partition in the cabin, screening off the bed so that she would have some place private to dress and do the things women had to do. After that they would have to build an outhouse. With four men around there had never been any need for one—they were never much at the cabin, anyway—but with a woman . . . with a woman living there, a lot would have to change.

He was beginning to think for the first time it might not be such a bad thing.

He had never slept with a woman before. He had never taken off his clothes for a woman before and felt every part of her skin against his. He had never known anything like what he had experienced last night with Elizabeth.

Never had he been so deeply moved, so profoundly touched, by what was, after all, a simple act of nature. He had never known it could be like that, and the discovery left him more uncertain of himself, and her, than he had ever thought it was possible to be.

He worried that he had been too rough. He was large and stronger than he realized, and she was so small, so easily damaged. Yet she had not wept when it was over, as he had heard it was customary for ladies of quality to do. She had not cried, he remembered slowly, the first time, either. All of it only again reminded him of how little he knew about women.

Next time he would be gentler, he promised himself. Or at least he would try.

Thinking about the next time made a new sweat break out on his forehead, even beneath the shade of his broad hat. His horse picked up his tension and stepped up its pace, and Jed had to jerk his attention back to his work, calming the dray team that pulled the heavy load behind him.

How was it possible that a woman could twine herself so completely, so inextricably inside a man's head, his senses, his very soul? What had happened to him the previous night, lost in the depths of her, that had never happened to him before?

Other times it had just felt good, something a man needed to do, and when it was over, it was forgotten. With Elizabeth it was never over. It left him racked with uncertainty and tight with anticipation and plunged into turmoil for all he didn't understand and wished he did. Every minute that passed was filled with waiting to see her again.

Jed rode into the yard, and he didn't see her.

He unhooked the team, looked around, then thought she might be in the cabin. He caught a glimpse of her petticoats, fluttering on the line behind the cabin, and he felt a heat go up the back of his neck and a tightness begin inside his pants.

He asked casually, "Where's Elizabeth?"

Dusty put down the hammer. "She rode off."

Jed stared at him.

"Damnedest thing I ever did see," muttered Skunk, pounding a nail.

Jed demanded curtly, "Where?"

Dusty jerked his head to the east. "Over to the willow branch. Said she wouldn't be gone long."

Jed swore and swung into the saddle. Dust sprang up behind him as he wheeled the horse and took off.

CHAPTER
Seventeen

There was something so exhilarating about the Texas air. It was a warm June, and the sun spread out in brilliant golden rays, but the cloying humidity Elizabeth was used to in Alabama was missing. Everything was bright, clear, and oven-warm, beautifully still. There were no barking dogs, no rattling wheels, no distant voices. Just the rustle of water and the still whisper of meadow sounds.

A stream branched off into a trickle of clear, sun-splattered water at the edge of the hill. Elizabeth tied her horse to one of the willow trees that lined the bank. The daisy field was just where she remembered, a brilliant splash of yellow and black beyond a small slope about fifty feet away. She left her bonnet and gloves on the grass by the branch and found a small, sharp stick with which to dig. She tore up several clumps of moist moss for wrapping the roots and crossed over to the daisy patch.

She might have, with her subconscious hearing, noticed the approach of the horse, but she was too absorbed in the sun-warmed peace of the day, the delightful and alien feel of soil beneath her fingers, to pay it much mind. She hadn't played in the dirt since she was six years old, and she had forgotten the cool feel of the layers of earth, the woodsy scent of growing things. All of it—the air, the sky, the earth, the sun—reminded her of Jed.

She did not hear the footsteps at all until a rough hand grabbed her upper arm and jerked her to her feet. Even then she was so delighted and surprised, she did not notice the anger in his face.

"Jed!" she exclaimed. "I was just—"

"What the hell do you think you're doing?" he roared at her.

She recoiled, pulling her arm away, but she replied calmly, "I'm transplanting flowers."

"Are you out of your mind? Who gave you permission to go gallivanting around—"

She lifted her eyebrows. "I was not aware I needed permission."

"You do!" he snapped back at her. "What's the matter with you? Don't you know better than to go riding off alone—"

"Oh, for heaven's sake, Jed, I know how to ride!"

"You got lost within half a mile of the Mobile road. You don't even know this country—"

"I knew where I was going. I can practically see the cabin from here!"

"You don't have any idea of the kind of things that could happen to you—"

She gave a small sound of exasperation and turned away from him with a flounce of her skirts. "If I hear one more word about mountain lions and wolves and bears," she declared adamantly, "I shall scream!" She knelt on the ground again and picked up her digging stick, prying at the delicate roots of a clump of daisies with a vehemence that left them little chance for survival.

Jed stood above her, glowering, for just a moment longer. He said curtly, "Let's go home."

"No."

"Damn it, Elizabeth, I don't have time—"

"Then pray, do not allow me to waste it." Her voice was calm, but the set of her shoulders was stubborn. She determinedly fought against allowing Jed's foul mood to spoil the loveliness of her day or the beautiful thoughts of him that still lingered from last night. "You go back to the cabin if you wish. I have work to do here."

Jed remained, not about to leave her, his brows drawn together fiercely, fighting back useless fury. His stomach still hurt from the fear that had punched it when he first realized she was gone, the panic that mounted when he saw her horse abandoned and her gloves and bonnet on the ground... and the weakness that assailed him, followed quickly by rage, when he saw her picking daisies in the sunshine.

No one had ever been able to drive him to fits of temper like this woman. Anger was a wasteful emotion; it clouded the head and deprived the senses, and a smart man could not afford to be victimized by it. But Elizabeth contrived to make him forget every clear-minded rule of survival he had ever known and left him helpless beneath the onslaught of emotions he couldn't control.

She did not even glance up at him. The sunlight glinted in her hair and flushed her face with a delicate pink translucence, casting a pale and perfect shadow of her over the ground. He watched the movements of her small shoulders as she worked the earth, the material of her dress tightening and loosening, shaping and caressing. Everything about her was innocent and maddening. He wanted to snatch her up bodily and fling her onto her horse. He wanted to tumble her to the ground and push up her skirts. It was with very great self-control that he refrained from doing either.

"What do you think you're going to do with those weeds when you get them out of the ground?" he grumbled.

"I'm going to plant them around the house," she replied complacently.

"They'll only get tromped on."

She lifted another clump of flowers out of the ground and carefully wrapped the roots in moss. "The first boot heel that makes contact with even one of these daisies will answer to me."

Grudgingly, very much against his will, Jed felt a smile tug at the corner of his lips. He muttered, "Yeah, I guess it would." With her, anger had a way of disappearing as quickly as it came, no matter how hard he wanted to hold on to it.

Elizabeth slid a glance in his direction, but all she could see were booted feet, planted far apart, and tight calves molded by buckskin. Had his legs always looked so long and lean and strong? she wondered. Or was it only now that she remembered they were covered with a furring of golden hair, and that when they brushed against hers, they were all sinew and heat and hard bone?

He demanded, "How much longer are you going to be?"

Elizabeth concentrated on the ground, on the now aimless motions her fingers were making in the soil. It was an effort to keep her voice casual. "I don't know. I may stay awhile. It's pleasant out here."

It was pleasant. The sun was still, the colors were vivid, and the sky went on forever. It was all that Jed loved about Texas wrapped into one gentle summer afternoon, and now

Elizabeth was sitting in the midst of it. There was nothing in the world he would rather do than stay out here with her for a while. But Jed had more to do than he could possibly accomplish in a day three times this long, and he had never shirked his share of the work before.

That would be only one of many firsts.

After a moment Jed turned and walked over to a willow tree that was not too far away and methodically began to strip off the branches. Elizabeth looked after him. "What are you doing?"

"Willow branches." He did not look around. "They're good for weaving into baskets and suchlike. And the tea is good for fever."

Elizabeth remembered the tea he had made for her that first day. What a miracle he had seemed to her then, a fictional character so much larger than life. Everything about him—his strong, vibrant looks; his low drawl; the incredible stories he told—all seemed alien and half made-up. Now she looked at him—his magnificent hair covered by a big hat; his torso enclosed in a sleeveless vest, his shirtsleeves rolled up above the elbow; his moccasins exchanged for pointy-toed leather boots; and one strong thigh decorated by the huge, ugly gun belt—and it struck her suddenly. This was the man who had tamed and loved a wolf. This was the man who had been nursed to health by Indians, who had crossed the mountains and walked the plains where few had gone before him. He was real, present, and very much alive. He was her husband. And he was more thrilling to her than he had ever been when he was only a fantasy.

She was not aware that she had sat back on her heels and was gazing at him with wondrous absorption until he turned and began coming toward her, his arms filled with willow branches. She turned with what she hoped was a negligent motion back to her work, although she had long since lost interest in the daisies.

She said, glancing at him, "Why do you wear that?"

He dropped the branches onto the ground and sat down beside her in the grass. "What?"

"That big gun, in the belt like that."

"You have to carry a pistol out here." He took one of the longest branches and wound it around the others, forming a bundle.

"Why?" She looked at him with curiosity and some amount of foreboding. "You carry a rifle on your saddle."

"And if I get thrown, I lose my rifle," he explained to her patiently.

"So?"

"So, a lot of things. And one of them is if your foot gets caught in the stirrup, you could be dragged to death by your own horse if you don't have a gun to shoot him."

Elizabeth let her hands fall still, looking at him. He had drawn out a slender willow twig and was methodically peeling back the bark, completely unaware of the image that simple, matter-of-fact statement had evoked. There were implications there, somber-tinged reminders of the dangers he walked hand in hand with every day, that Elizabeth did not want to examine.

She turned abruptly back to her digging. "You're not on a horse now."

"That's right."

"Would you . . ." She glanced at him a little hesitantly. "Would you mind . . . not wearing it when you're with me?"

He looked at her, puzzlement clear on his face. "Why?"

"It makes me nervous."

Jed hesitated, then gave something resembling a half-formed shrug and unbuckled his belt. Elizabeth caught the movement of his fingers, low on his abdomen, unfastening the catch, tugging the leather taut and then releasing it. Color tingled her cheeks, speeding her pulses, and she did not know why. Or perhaps she did.

He lay the gun belt on the ground, close beside him, and picked up the willow twig again. There was something about being free of the weight of the belt—essentially removing a part of his clothing—here in the open with Elizabeth sitting so close that started his thoughts wandering down an inevitable path. And not thoughts, exactly, but feelings—good, warm, almost lazy feelings. Today—if he could have her today—it would be like that. Long and slow and easy, and it would last forever.

Elizabeth took up the clump of daisies, packed them in moss, and sat back. She did not want to work anymore. She looked at her hands, which were stained with black soil, but instead of horrifying her, the sight amused her. Miss Nancy would have been horrified. But Miss Nancy had no part of this world.

She leaned her weight on her palms behind her and looked out with tranquil satisfaction over the vista that stretched before them. Rich rolling hills and deep lusty colors, a panorama of life that went on forever. "This is beautiful," she said softly.

Jed glanced at her. He couldn't help noticing how the way she sat, with her arms stretched out behind her, pushed her breasts forward tautly against the bodice of her dress. He moved his eyes away. "It is that," he agreed.

"You told me, but I couldn't imagine it." Her voice was lazy. "It's perfect cotton land."

"I guess."

She looked at him curiously. "Why don't you grow cotton, Jed? Everyone else does."

"Not everyone."

She turned toward him, her eyes alight with an eager certainty, and she insisted, "You could make a fortune if you grew cotton here. Look at all this rich bottomland" —she swept a hand down the hill—"and all the water. Why, it would practically leap right out of the ground overnight!"

He glanced at her in some astonishment. Did the woman have an opinion about everything? But that had been one of the first things that fascinated him . . . the way she talked, so easy and natural-like, as though she had never known a secret nor had a reason for keeping anything she thought to herself. It still amazed him, the way she talked. Before Elizabeth, he had never imagined that a woman could have anything to say that he would be interested in hearing.

He turned back to the willow strips he was plaiting absently. "I'm not a farmer."

"You used to be."

"Maybe that's why I'm not anymore. Too much hard work."

Her eyes grew wide with disbelief and reproach. "Harder than chasing those hideous cows?"

He chuckled. It was amazing, how good she could make him feel without even trying. Not ten minutes ago he had been angry enough to strangle her. "It's different." He shrugged. "It takes money to grow cotton . . . and slaves. I'm not interested in anything I can't do with my own two hands, and I'll not be beholden to any man."

He paused, his fingers falling idle for a moment, his brow knitting faintly as he tried to put it into words for her. Only Elizabeth could make him want to talk about himself like that, to explain things to her he didn't even understand himself. "On horseback," he began, "out there alone—it's hard work, but it's moving, and it's staying busy, and you're always seeing something. Not just the way the steer trampled the brush when he went by but the tracks the ground squirrel left when he came later, and the way the wind turned the brush during the last storm, and the stone somebody who came before you used as a marker . . . and everything you see tells a story. You're always learning something, seeing something new.

"Out there, all alone, you're depending on nobody but yourself, and if you've got anything to show at the end of the day, it's because you were able to do it. I reckon I like that feeling. Working cattle," he said simply, picking up the willow strips again, "it don't much matter if you don't make a gather, because at the end of the day you've got something to show for it, even if it's nothing more than being a little smarter than you were the day before. Farming's not like that."

It was beautiful when he said it, and Elizabeth almost thought she understood. Sitting beside him, watching those big fingers weave strips of wood into a delicate pattern and listening to the sound of his voice, reminded her intensely of the day they had first met. Only he was even more beautiful now.

But she had to pursue the subject. "It could still be like that. The land wouldn't change just because you raised cotton on it, and you wouldn't change. And just think of it, Jed." Her eyes grew bright again with possibilities. "Why, with all the land you've got, it could be the biggest plantation in Texas . . . in the whole South! You'd be a rich man in no time at all. A veritable baron!"

He cast her a sharp glance. Something about the way she said that reminded him of Hartley and his empire, and the recognition brought a sharp twinge to the muscles of his chest. And why not? She and Hartley came from the same world; they thought in the same ways.

He lowered his lashes to shade his eyes. "That's important to you? Riches?"

Elizabeth hesitated, aware that she was treading on very tenuous ground. "Of course I like nice things, Jed," she admitted. "Everyone does. But that's not what I meant. I just..." She moved her eyes to the ground with its splattering of daisies, and then, cautiously, back to him. "I don't like to think of you fighting those big cattle and...having to carry that awful gun on your belt in case your horse throws you when life could be so much easier, and there's no reason it shouldn't be."

What a strange feeling that was: a woman worrying about him. It took Jed a few moments to come to grips with it, and then he decided he rather liked it. But he looked at her, and all he could tell her was, simply, "That's my life, Elizabeth."

She said tentatively, "You don't want to be rich?"

Jed laughed. He didn't know why except that, coming from Elizabeth, who had not yet completely gotten used to being anything other than rich, it struck him as funny. "Of course I do. And who knows, I may be yet."

"From cattle?" She looked dubious.

"Why not?"

She did not have an answer to that. It had only recently begun to occur to her that it was perhaps not quite proper for a wife to be discussing her husband's business in this manner and offering such intense and forward opinions.

Jed put down the braided strip of willow bark and looked at her. His eyes were so clear that she could see the little golden flecks in them that outlined the irises. He explained, just as though it mattered to him what she thought, "Those folks that are growing cotton think they're getting away with a fortune out of Texas. And maybe they are, but it's window dressing compared to what they could have. Not even a third of Texas is fit for growing cotton, but you can run cattle anywhere. And when you think about how big Texas is, that's a hell of a lot of beefsteak.''

He shrugged, tipped back his hat, and leaned on one elbow in a semireclining position. The movement drew his pants taut across one thigh and stretched the material of his shirt over his muscled upper arm. "So, if a man is smart, he gathers him a herd, sells it, goes back and gathers more. And he keeps on doing that until he's got his own little fortune. One thing for sure: Texas is not going to run out of cattle, or land to run them.''

It made sense, in a basic, down-to-earth way. Elizabeth would still rather have seen these hills covered with cotton than with those ugly, horned cattle, and it still frightened her to think of Jed working with them. But she was a woman, and she had no right to interfere. She had come perilously close to overstepping her bounds already.

He sat up suddenly. "Look," he said.

She followed the sweep of his hand down into the valley, beyond a stand of rolling pines to the exact center of the three converging hills. "That's where I'm going to build my house when I do get rich. Right next to that stand of cottonwood. The prettiest piece of land on the whole place.''

"Oh, yes," Elizabeth agreed eagerly. "A great big house with windows all along the front and big Corinthian columns.''

Jed shot her an amused, skeptical look. "Columns out here?''

Elizabeth nodded enthusiastically. Gazing at the future site of their home before her, she could almost see the house materialize out of the ground. "And French windows, Jed. You know the kind you open and step through? And a big veranda that goes all around the house, where we can sit on summer evenings or dance when we have guests.''

We. Maybe that was the word that did it. Jed had never

shared his dream of a home with anyone before. But when she spoke of it, Elizabeth suddenly became part of it. It would be her house too. Everything about the future would have her in it, from this moment on.

He said warily, "Sounds like that house would fit better on a cotton plantation than on a cattle ranch."

"What does it matter?" she declared blithely. "We will build it the way we want to. A man of stature should have a grand house to reflect his importance."

He glanced at her, and her face was aglow with innocent, unwavering certainty for what she had determined would be. His house was only a daydream, a half-formed fantasy that he used to entertain himself when the days were long and the nights were lonely. He had never intended to make her believe that it was really possible, and he knew he should relieve her of that impression immediately. She had married a poor man, and all he could promise her was what she had already seen. It was a dangerous thing to start believing in things that weren't likely to be.

But looking at her, so lively and lovely in the gentle afternoon sunshine, he couldn't quite bring himself to crush her fantasy once again. Besides, looking at her and listening to her, he half believed it himself.

So he only muttered derisively, "Columns," and picked up the braid again. But a smile had turned down the corner of his lips, and the word came out a trifle less gruffly than he had intended.

When he had stretched out, his leg had come forward, without his realizing it, to rest atop the long flow of her skirts. Now that he was sitting again, she found herself partially trapped by his presence, his bent knee almost in contact with her hip, her skirts weighted down, and his shoulders and chest filling up her line of vision.

His lashes were lowered in concentration on his work, his

face relaxed and young, denying the lines that sun and weather had etched onto it. She remembered the way his face had felt beneath her fingertips, how surprisingly soft his skin had been. And his hair . . . she wondered what he would do if she removed his hat now and drew her fingers once again through the heavy fall of his hair.

She inquired aimlessly, "Do you have a scar on your arm, near the top?"

He shot her a surprised look, accompanied by the faintest hint of color creeping from his collar. "I have a lot of scars. Why?"

Elizabeth's own color rose horribly. She did not know what had possessed her to say that, except that she had been thinking . . . He must know perfectly well what she was thinking. She murmured, avoiding his eyes, "I thought I noticed it . . . last night."

Jed swallowed hard and quickly focused his attention back on his weaving. Who would have expected her to bring up a thing like that?

He said uncomfortably, "It's from a Comanche arrow. Just a nick, but it tore off a hunk of skin." He wasn't thinking about Comanche. He was thinking about her fingers flowing over his bare skin and how she had smelled when he buried his face in her neck—with the wildness of musk and the sweetness of roses. He was thinking about her body beneath him and how it felt, deep inside her.

He was thinking other things too. How her voice sounded when she was animated about what she was saying and how good it made him feel when she talked to him. How her shoulders squared with stubbornness and how her eyes snapped when he raised his voice to her. How her face had lit up when she talked about his house. He was thinking that these past moments with her, here on the hillside, had been some of the best of his life. And he wanted her more than he had ever thought it was possible to want anyone or anything.

But the last thing he had expected to do was talk about it.

"Elizabeth." He wanted to tell her how she made him feel, how he had never known it was possible for a woman to move him, and touch him, as she had done last night. He wanted to tell her beautiful, adoring, poetic things; instead he found himself almost apologizing. He kept his eyes on his work. "Last night . . . I didn't mean to be so rough. I don't want you to think that I think bedding is all there is in being married."

Her cheeks went hot again, and she looked at him hesitantly. "But perhaps . . . one of the best parts?"

He couldn't hide the shock in his eyes. "What?"

"I like being married to you, Jed," she said softly. She glanced at him beneath shyly lowered lashes. "And I like . . . making love with you."

Astonishment battled with wonder, and a slow-growing pleasure grew inside him. Would she never stop surprising him?

"You said it was different with married people," she said, looking a little anxious. Her color was brilliant with embarrassment and uncertainty, and her eyes the deepest green he had ever seen. "Don't . . . all wives feel this way?"

"No." His voice sounded hoarse and strained. He had to look at her, had to drink in the sight of her. "I don't think so."

A smile tugged at his lips as he moved his eyes back to his work. "If they did, I don't guess there'd be so many unhappy husbands."

Elizabeth released her breath in a small stream of relief. For a moment she had thought he was upset with her. She smiled at him hesitantly. "Do I make you happy, Jed?"

He looked at her, and he felt so humble that he could hardly even make his voice work. He brought his hand lightly to the side of her face, caressing it. He said simply, "Yes."

And then, with absolutely no warning, he reached for her hand, pulling it forward between his strong, warm fingers. He slipped upon her third finger the ring he had made of braided willow strips.

"There," he said, and emotion made his voice gruff. "Now you look like a married woman."

Elizabeth caught her breath and stared through suddenly brimming eyes at her hand, small and white, caught between his big dark one, and at the gift he had made her. The design was intricate and tight, the hue of the bark as smooth as silver, and she thought she had never seen anything more beautiful in her life. He had done it for her.

Jed saw the sparkle of a tear wet her lashes, and he quickly moved closer, awkwardly placing his hand alongside her face. He hadn't meant to make her cry. He said, trying to coax a teasing smile, "Someday it'll be gold. When I get rich."

Her eyes flew to him in fierce, protective objection, and he had never seen such brilliance, such beauty, as now flamed in those emerald eyes. "No! I don't want a gold one." Her hand closed as though preventing him from snatching the ring away and, in the process, clasped his own fingers tightly. "I just want this one. Always."

Her face was alight with a deep, almost ethereal joy that spread like a fountain over him and left him cleansed and renewed. And then, before he even felt her movement, she was against him, one arm around his neck in a tight embrace, the hand that wore the ring clasped tightly around his.

What flooded through him then was deep and swift, the

kind of pure white joy that can paralyze and blind. He wrapped his arm around her, bent his head into her neck, and he had to part his lips to drag in breath. He held her, aching with the wonder and the beauty of her, for a long, long time. That was when he knew he was already a rich man. He could ask for nothing more.

"I love you, Jed," she whispered.

He took her face in his hand and looked into those deep, brilliant green eyes. He ached for her and with more than wanting her. He couldn't even speak. He kissed her gently, and the experience was like spring rain falling on a thirsty blossom. He lowered her slowly to the ground.

His hair was like spun gold around his face, his eyes alive with promise and dark with wanting. Her fingers explored the texture of his hair tentatively, and then, as his lips covered hers again, more boldly. He tasted of sunshine, and he filled her with joy so rich and soaring that she hardly could contain it.

Her heart pounded and the daisy-bright day whirled around her as he moved his lips to her throat, and then lower, to the material that covered her breast. What sensations he could evoke within her with only the touch of his lips! What wonder, what urgency, what need.

She closed her arms around him, feeling the warm texture of his neck beneath his hair, the swell of shoulders against his shirt. His lower body pressed against hers, and already her thighs were loosening for him, welcoming him. She felt his fingers working the tiny buttons on her bodice, and then her breasts were open to the sunshine and his caress. She closed her eyes, a breath of wonder escaping her, and gave herself to the joy of loving and being loved. How wonderful was this state of marriage! All her life she had lived in darkness, never knowing what an empty shell her existence was. Being here with Jed, sharing this special communion, she felt as though she had never lived before this moment.

She felt the quickening of his breath as she bared his chest to her caresses, as she tasted the texture of his throat and neck. Her own pulses began to cascade when his hand slipped beneath her skirts and his fingers, warm and rough and intimate, stroked her thigh.

As in a gracefully choreographed dance their clothing was pushed aside and they came together beneath the Texas sky, washed in sunshine. It was beautiful, natural, the most divine of destinies, and Elizabeth clung to him in rapture and wonder as the intensity of pleasure built to bursting. *My husband*, she thought. *My love. Jed*. The beauty of it brought tears to her eyes.

For there was more to intimacy than pleasure. The true wonder of it was in the sharing, in knowing that for this single, exquisite moment out of time they were joined as one, without shame and without hesitation. Today she learned to give pleasure as she received it, and there was a heady thrill in knowing that he delighted in her as she delighted in him. The rhythms they created were of two souls moving as one, instinctual and primal, yet as sacred as life itself. When the world burst around them in dizziness and joy, they were forged together on the edge of eternity, no longer two but one. For Elizabeth it was like being born again.

She lay curled in the circle of his arms, feeling her heart beating in rhythm with his, her breath synchronized to his. Peace surrounded her like a beneficent aura; joy and contentment throbbed through her veins. *Wife*. Surely there was no more beautiful word in the English language. Unless it was *lover*.

She looked at him, his strong, gentle face flushed with sunshine and dampened with exertion, his eyes tender and hazed with the same wondrous happiness she, herself, was feeling. Lightly she touched his chin and his jaw, delighting in the texture of his skin, the shape of his bones. She whispered, ''Oh, Jed. I do love you so.''

He smiled, and his dark lashes lowered slumberously. He kissed her cheek once, lingeringly, tenderly. And then he said huskily, stroking her face, ''We'd better be getting back.''

That was when Elizabeth realized that he had not said the words to her. Not once.

The lovely glow within her began to fade, and though she grasped for it, the moments before were already slipping through her fingers. She tried to tell herself it didn't matter, but it did. It mattered more than anything else in the world. She loved him, but already he was turning away from her.

Jed rearranged his clothing and stood. She, too, dressed quickly, and then he extended his hand to her. He smiled at her, and she made herself return his smile as she placed her hand in his. But her heart was heavy as she rode beside him back to the cabin, and the day seemed much less bright than it had before.

CHAPTER
Eighteen

The steer had trapped himself between a rockfall and a tangle of brush, and the only way he could possibly go was the way Jed wanted him to go. With a grin of satisfaction Jed circled his horse around, shaking out a loop just in case the animal made an unexpected move.

He gave a whoop, and the startled steer crashed through the thicket, scrambling up the hilly incline. Jed guided him expertly, his mustang responding more to his thoughts than the movement of his body, swinging around to cut off the steer's sudden lurch to the right, dropping back when the animal caught scent of his own kind and made a straight track to join the rest of the herd.

They had gathered about thirty of the remaining hundred head that had been grazing in the Rock Spring pasture that morning, and it had been easy work. The animals were fat and lazy from their summer grazing and needed little persuasion. All told, they had branded about five hundred head this season, calves included, and all that remained was to move this bunch out of the creek bottom before the autumn rains set in. They would make a good drive to New Orleans come September, perhaps as many as seven hundred head.

Dusty was bringing in a heifer at the end of a rope while Rio whipped his hat after a maverick that had taken off into the brush again. At the top of the incline Skunk kept the herd bunched, circling around with an eye for strays while the cattle lowed and cropped at the grass lazily. Jed made his way toward the herd at an easy pace.

It was a bright August day, heralding the end of summer with a trumpet of heat and a splash of color. The sun baked Jed's shoulders, and the heat from the saddle rose up between his thighs, reminding him too poignantly of the night just passed in Elizabeth's arms. But then, everything reminded him of Elizabeth lately.

It was a collection of little things, really, that had woven themselves into the tapestry of his life and made the whole of it almost unrecognizable from what it had been before. Watching her do up the buttons on her blouse in the mornings, she so comfortable with him that she was hardly aware he was watching. Listening to the sounds she made moving around the cabin, mixing bread or sweeping or doing any one of the thousand homey, comforting-sounding things she did. Sitting across the lamplight from her at night, her head bent over a piece of sewing or a book while he braided a riata or mended a saddle, not talking, just listening to the night and feeling better than he had ever thought it was possible to feel. Sometimes she would read out loud to him, and the sound of those words, which had always given him so much difficulty, sounded like pure magic from her lips.

And the nights. Making love to her in silence, making

love to her with words. Sometimes not making love at all but just lying with her small, warm form curled into him, holding her and thinking nothing at all, just feeling how good it was. There was nothing better in the world than having a wife, and most times he couldn't even remember why he had resisted the idea for so long.

She still made him anxious. She was still careless and foolish and exasperated him to the point of temper more often than he would have liked. But now their arguments flared briefly and ended in laughter or passion, and sometimes he thought he provoked her just to see her emerald eyes flash. There could be no other reason; worrying about her was just as futile as it had ever been. And there was very little to argue about, at any rate; the last two months had been so idyllic that even he could find little to complain about. It was as though Elizabeth, with her everlasting optimism and unflagging determination, had transformed life on the frontier into the very daydream she had always imagined it would be, through nothing more than the sheer force of her will.

Thinking about her now, Jed could feel impatience gather in the pit of his stomach, anxiety and anticipation thickening his loins even as he rode. It happened like that, unexpectedly and without cause, at any time of the day or night, whenever the memory of her scent or her shape or a little unconscious movement she made would cross his mind. Then he would not be able to think of anything else. Surely there was something unnatural about that, that a man should feel such a constant, obsessive desire for his wife.

There were days when he couldn't concentrate at all for yearning for her, remembering her, wondering about her. It made him short of temper, irritable with himself, and about as good with a rope or a horse as a green girl. He took teasing from the men with ill grace, and nothing would calm his feverish spirit until he was home, early like as not, and looking at Elizabeth's welcoming smile again.

Frowning a little, he nudged his horse into a canter and joined Skunk at the head of the herd. "How many more?"

Skunk nodded down the incline. "Dusty's gone after a couple hid up the crick. Rio's got a rope on a bull. Take the rest of the day to get 'em all out."

Jed squinted over the herd thoughtfully, shifting restlessly in the saddle. "What do you say we take this bunch out, brand them, and be home for supper?"

Skunk grinned and spat on the ground. "Sounds like one hell of an idea to me, boss. No point in letting Miss Elizabeth's corn pone get cold."

Jed grinned back, saying, "Yeah." He pushed back his hat and went to help Rio with the bull.

Elizabeth's presence had made itself felt in more ways than one over the summer, and none of the men were anxious to be away from the cabin longer than necessary anymore.

The ground around the cabin was now lined with at least six different varieties of wildflowers, blooming lustily from daily watering by one or more of the men. Skunk, who hated any labor that could not be done from a horse almost as much as he hated bathing, had spent one entire afternoon splitting logs and building chairs to go at Miss Elizabeth's table. He also made it a point to bathe in the creek with soap at least once a week, and sometimes he even shaved.

Dusty had come up with a laying hen—no one dared ask him how—who was now stabled in a weasel-proof coop and producing fresh eggs twice a week. No one would ever forget the day that Rio had ridden in dragging a wild shoat from the end of his rope. The mean-tempered little hog had broken down his corral twice, terrorized the horses, and bitten his keeper on the arm, but come winter they would have plenty of fresh bacon and pork chops—if Rio didn't shoot the hog out of spite first.

The cabin was no longer a place to squat over the camp fire and stir beans into stew when there was nothing better to do; it was more than a winter's camp or a shelter from bad storms. Now it was a home where a woman was, with smells of baking bread and the swish of skirts. It was a place none of them were anxious to leave and all were eager to come back to. That was the difference she had made.

Jed and Rio herded the recalcitrant steer up the incline just as Dusty was coming around. "Let's head 'em on in!" Jed shouted, standing in his stirrups. Dusty and Skunk responded with a wave of their hats.

They spread out, Jed on the left flank, and Rio, whose turn it was, riding drag, to move the herd across the fields to the branding corral. The day was only half over, but what waited at the end of it was worth it.

Jed sat back, easy in the saddle with the feel of the sun and the shuffle of the cattle, and thought with satisfaction over the summer's work. At twenty-five dollars apiece, seven hundred head would make a nice little gather. He would buy something for Elizabeth—a glass pane, maybe, for the window she was always complaining she didn't have. Maybe he would get yard goods, and books. She had read the ones he had bought her in Galveston over and over again, and he had a mind that he might try reading a bit himself, on the long winter nights ahead.

The shot whizzed past him and cut a branch over his head so unexpectedly that Jed did not even identify it for what it was until it was all over. But his instincts were still intact, and he swung around, grabbing for his rifle in the same motion he used to bend his horse into flight for cover. The explosions tore the air, the fire coming from all directions.

The cattle took off across the hill with screams of panic and tearing hooves.

Jed never saw what became of the other men. He swung off his horse and behind a cottonwood for cover, firing into the hillside from which the first shot had come. The cattle were stampeding in four directions, gouging up turf in wild-eyed fear, breaking through brush, leaping the creek. Jed heard return fire and knew that at least one of his men was alive—for now.

He reloaded with quick, mechanical precision, his eyes scanning the furor of stampeding cattle and dust-fogged countryside, his ears deafened by the thunder of hooves and the bellow of animal screams, trying to make out the direction from which the hostile fire was coming. Another shot whizzed by his head and made a screeching ricochet off the rock behind him before he got his rifle reloaded. When he looked up again, a steer was pounding toward him, its eyes rolling, foam flying from its muzzle. Jed leveled the rifle and squeezed off a shot. The animal fell with a spray of blood between its eyes not five feet before him.

Jed didn't think. He didn't have to think. All he knew was that they had somehow walked into an ambush and Elizabeth was alone at the cabin. He grabbed the reins of his horse and led him into the cover of the brush, returning fire as he mounted. Keeping low and covering himself as best he could, he circled around through the woods toward the cabin.

Under normal circumstances he never would have led the enemy into his home camp. Under normal circumstances his prime duty would have been to track and eliminate the attackers, to stay and meet the fight. But his herd was gone, his men might well be dead or dying, and there was Elizabeth, alone. He had no choice but to break every rule of survival he had ever known.

He came upon the cabin from the back, and he had had no chance to cover his trail. He made himself stop and look down, stilling his heartbeat so that he could hear, clearing the panic that blurred his vision so that he could see what awaited him.

Below, all was still. A faint thread of smoke came from the chimney. The door was open. He didn't hear a sound, and furiously he strained his ears. They could be in there now, holding her captive. She could be bound and gagged. They could be raping her. She could be unconscious. She could be dead already. Or they could be holding her at gunpoint, waiting for him to ride up. . . .

He tied his horse behind a cover of pines and began to move down the hill, rifle in hand, as silently and as quickly as he could. Every few moments he stopped, looked, and listened. And then he knew.

His horse gave a faint, alarmed whinny from far behind him, signaling the approach of an unfamiliar horse. They had followed him.

Half crawling, half sliding down the hill, he circled around, approaching from the corral. At that moment Elizabeth came out.

She had a washbasin in her hand and moved to toss the water over her flower garden. Jed glanced behind him and saw the glint of sun on metal—a rifle being raised. He had no choice. He dashed across the yard, grabbed Elizabeth's arm, and flung her inside just as a bullet slammed into the doorjamb above their heads.

Elizabeth's gasp of alarm turned into a cry of terror as she hit the dirt floor and the bullet whined against wood. Jed rolled over on the floor, out of the path of the open door, and shouted, "Stay down!"

Elizabeth cried, "Jed, what—" and started to get to her

feet. Another bullet hit the outside of the house and she screamed.

"Stay on the floor, goddammit!" he shouted at her, casting a frantic glance over his shoulder. She was on her knees, her hands pressed over her ears, her face white and twisted with terror and confusion. "Get your goddamn head down!"

She didn't move.

Jed used a poker to push out mud chinking and sighted his rifle through the hole. He aimed in the direction from which he had seen the flash of a gun barrel and fired. Another bullet ricocheted against the roof; a closer one tore a chunk out of the doorjamb. There was more than one man firing from the hills at the cabin, and they were moving closer. Elizabeth was screaming.

"Damn you, Elizabeth, *get down!*"

He tossed down his rifle and drew his pistol, sighting as best he could. The pistol was a futile weapon against rifle fire at that distance, but he didn't have time to reload the rifle. He guessed three, maybe four, men were firing now, and that was more than enough to surround the cabin anytime they chose. He fired the last random shot from the pistol and began to thumb in cartridges from his belt. A shot hit the dirt floor in front of the door, and another slammed into the mantelpiece, spraying dust and wood chips everywhere. He looked over his shoulder, at the three extra rifles stacked by the fireplace. He was separated from them by the door, but Elizabeth . . .

"Elizabeth," he said roughly, pushing the barrel of his pistol through the hole in the wall and squeezing off another shot. "Pass me those rifles, one by one—don't get up, just push them across the floor. Now!"

Elizabeth was huddled in the corner, her fists doubled against her white cheeks, her eyes streaming with silent tears. He fired again and tossed a frantic, impatient glance toward her. *"Elizabeth!"*

She started to move, then shrank back as another bullet cut a river in the dirt between them. "Don't!" she screamed, and she was screaming at him. "Stop it, Jed! Don't, please—"

Furiously he tossed down his pistol and grabbed the rifle again. While he was reloading, two rifle shots slammed into the room, one of them shattering a lamp on the table. Either they had damn good eyesight out there, or they were moving closer. He squeezed off a shot from the rifle, then picked up his pistol to reload. Sweat was streaming from his face, and in his hurry he dropped a cartridge. "Damn it, Elizabeth, pass me those rifles!"

"No! Jed, stop it, please!"

She started to get up, as though to run to him, and he had no choice. He had only gotten three shots into the pistol, but he ran across the open door, firing as he went. He felt something sting his ribs, and he slammed into Elizabeth, not even hearing her cry as he pushed her hard across the room and onto the floor. On the dirt himself, he grabbed the rifles and belly-crawled toward the door, getting to one knee, the door frame as his only cover. Taking a quick glance out, he saw a spot of blue against the green brush in the distance and fired.

A bullet whizzed past his ear and scattered bark from the doorjamb. Then there was crossfire, splitting the dirt in the yard, tearing the air. His own men, one or more of them, had returned, and the odds were closer to being even.

The firing was intense for several minutes, and then suddenly it was over. There was a last round of sporadic gunfire, then the sound of hoofbeats. Jed waited, his heart ticking off minutes to the sound of Elizabeth's dry hiccoughs behind him, his hand aching to squeeze the trigger on anything that moved. Nothing, and he released his breath; he laid down his rifle.

A moment, no more, to register relief. He was alive. She was alive. Then panic, fury, and sheer, uncontrollable wild energy rushed through him, obscuring his vision with a red haze, and he pushed to his feet. She could have died. Damn it, she could have *died*.

Elizabeth was pressed against the wall, her face streaked with dirt and tears, her eyes wild and unseeing. Tiny childlike sounds of dry sobs came from her throat, and when he pulled her to her feet, she didn't even respond. He wanted to slap her, though whether the impulse was motivated by her state of hysteria or his own blind rage and terror for what might have been he did not know. He grabbed her shoulders and shook her furiously until her hair tumbled down and her head lolled weakly and that blind shock in her eyes was replaced by a stark and conscious fear.

"Damn it, Elizabeth, when I tell you to do something, you *do it!*" he roared at her. "I could have been killed! Is that what you want? God damn you, you're supposed to be my *wife!*"

Hysteria whirled like a wild and visible thing between them. Her own guilt and helplessness was fueled by the backlash of anger and fear he had misdirected at her. He was right. She had failed him. He had needed her, and she had been paralyzed, impotent, terrified. . . .

That same terror still blocked out all reason, all feeling except the mad need to strike out at something, someone. She screamed back at him completely without logic or rationality, "You were shooting at them! Why were you shooting? You should have stopped, you should have—"

She was pushing at his shoulders, trying to disentangle

herself, and he let her go, shouting back, "Are you out of your mind? What the hell did you expect me to do?"

She fell back against the wall with his abrupt release of her shoulders and braced herself with her hands. Her face was still chalky, and tendrils of hair caught in the tears on her cheeks, but her eyes were dark with turmoil and blazing in self-defense. He stepped back from her, dragging in a breath, and went to reload the rifles.

It took a moment, only a moment, a swift look around, and a breath for Elizabeth to register—or begin to register—what had happened. Someone had been *shooting* at them. Mindless, unprovoked violence had invaded her home, her marriage, her very *life*.

Glass and oil from the broken lamp littered the floor. A scar had been torn in one of the chairs that Skunk had worked so hard on. Bullets had gouged holes in the log mantelpiece and the walls. Cartridges littered the floor from Jed's guns, and the acrid smell of gunpowder still tainted the air, the echoes of explosion ringing in her ears.

This was her *home*, her fortress, and it had been raped, viciously assaulted by something she couldn't control. All she could do was cry helplessly, "Why? Jed, why did this happen? Why did they do this?" The tears started again, and she fought them back with the last of her courage, looking around the torn and littered room. Terror still trembled through her, and it was hard to get her breath. "What did you do to them? Why—"

She saw Jed's lips tighten grimly as he shoved the final shot into his pistol and holstered it. "Rustlers," he said briefly. "They stampeded the herd. I don't know who they were."

Her mind was whirling. She took a half step toward him. "You should have sent for the sheriff! You have to report this, you have to—"

The look he gave her was tinged with pity. "There's no law out here, Elizabeth," he said flatly. "We take care of ourselves."

It dawned on her slowly, then hit her with a force that made her reel. No law. This was not even a state, barely a country; the trappings of civilization did not apply here. The truth of what she had just experienced struck her forcefully and without compromise.

She had been so proud of her little accomplishments, so determined that she could make a place for herself in this alien land. She had made a home of a shack, a garden of a wilderness; she had built for herself a little oasis in the middle of nowhere, and she had thought that was important. But the things that were really important—the life-and-death struggle she had just witnessed, the violence that could only be fought with violence, the incomprehensible upheavals of all the rules of civilization—of these she knew nothing. When Jed had needed her to fight by his side, she had been frozen with fear, helpless and incompetent. Jed had told her all along. She did not belong here.

Here men took care of themselves, here criminals could roam free, here everyone carried a gun and used it at random—hurting, maiming, killing—and there was nothing anyone could do about it. Elizabeth Coleman Fielding, with all her grand ideas and castles in the air, was as helpless as a kitten in a cage and about as useless.

Jed picked up a rifle and started toward the door. She lurched toward him. "You're not going out there? You're not going after them?"

"Have to."

He grabbed up a handful of ammunition and stuffed it into his vest pocket, and his hand came away sticky with blood. Jed uttered a short, foul word under his breath, and Elizabeth felt consciousness recede in a cold wave.

She gripped the table, willing strength, fighting nausea. Her vision cleared, but all she could see was the blood on Jed's hand, the dark, spreading stain on his shirt as he pulled back his vest.

"You're hurt," she said hoarsely, and her head swam again. Jed had been shot, Jed could have been killed, and she hadn't moved, she hadn't done anything to help!

He said curtly, "It's nothing."

Suddenly his muscles tightened, and he swung behind the cover of the door, his pistol going into his hand in the same instant.

From outside they heard a shout: "Hello, the cabin! Hold your fire!"

It was Skunk's voice.

Jed dropped his gun back into the holster and released a breath. Elizabeth moved quickly toward the washbasin on the table. "Sit down," she commanded.

Jed pulled out a chair and sat, but she knew it was not because she had requested it. He kept his rifle close by and waited for Skunk.

Elizabeth dipped a cloth in water and squeezed out the excess moisture, moving because she didn't know what else to do. "You can't go after them. Please don't go after them. I can't stand any more...."

Jed looked at her, his expression tired. "Elizabeth, you don't understand."

Those words seemed like the worst he had ever spoken to her. She didn't understand. He had asked for her help and she hadn't moved. He could have been killed. There was blood on his shirt and pain in his face, and she *didn't* understand, she never wanted to understand a place where something like this could happen. Why couldn't *he* understand?

She dropped to her knees beside him. Her hands were

shaking so badly, she could hardly hold the cloth. "Take off your shirt."

He pulled his shirt gingerly out of his pants, and she saw him wince as the material scraped over the wound. His side was smeared with blood from rib cage to waist, and she went weak again.

She heard the horses come into the yard. She tightened her muscles with the greatest of efforts and made her hand move to wipe away the blood. "You're right," she said tightly. "I don't understand. I'll never understand why you want to live like this—it's barbaric, it's inhuman, people were never meant to live like this. We don't have to live like this, there's no reason for it—and if you go after them, it's only going to make it worse. They'll come back and there'll be more shooting and it will never stop—"

"Damn it, Elizabeth, we were attacked!" His explosion was harsh, and his eyes were dark as he turned on her. "You make it sound like I'm the goddamn criminal! We've got to protect ourselves! Who the hell do you think is going to do it if we don't?"

"I don't know! I don't care!" The bloodstained cloth dropped from her shaking fingers, and she got quickly to her feet, whirling to find another. "I want nothing to do with this! I didn't ask those people to shoot at me. I didn't bring them here! All I want to do is live in peace and make a home. You're the one who has to solve everything with your fists or a gun—"

"That's the only way some things can be solved." His voice was low, but his eyes were blazing.

"That's not true! That's insane! Nobody wears a gun back home. People don't go around shooting each other like wild animals in Alabama—"

He turned on her. "Then maybe that's where you need to be," he returned harshly.

She lost her breath in a gasp. "That's what you want, isn't it? That's what you've always wanted!"

Weariness lined his face, and he shook his head slowly. She could see the effort he exerted to remain calm, but it was lost on the hysteria that raged within her. "No, Elizabeth, it's not what I want. It's just that there are some things a man has to do that a woman can't understand, and this is one of them."

"What about me?" Her face was wild and her voice high. "If you get yourself killed, what is going to happen to me? Don't you care?"

He looked as though she had struck him, and his own pain went through her like a knife. She wanted to take back the bitter, accusing words, but it was too late. Their eyes locked in shock and hurt, and a wall went up between them at that moment that no words could breach... perhaps nothing ever could.

In an instant each of them saw how fragile was the world of false security and contentment they had built for themselves, based on nothing but wishes and illusion. This day had torn the foundation from that world, and there was nothing either of them could do to repair it. A chasm of disillusionment and unmet needs gaped between them, and neither could breach it, no matter how hard they tried.

Skunk came in, followed closely by Dusty and Rio. In the confusion of their stamping feet and muttered curses, Elizabeth turned quickly to scramble through her scrap bag for bandages.

"Did you see them?"

"No. Tracked 'em for a while, figured you might need us here in case they doubled back."

"Caught some blood on the grass. Think we got one of them."

"They were headed back toward the spring—lost their tracks in the stampede. You hit bad?"

"Just a scrape."

Elizabeth tore a scrap from a petticoat she had intended to mend and came back to Jed. He had covered the wound with his dirty shirt, and she pushed his hand away, swallowing hard as she dabbed away the blood that stained his skin. She couldn't be sure, but she thought it was bleeding less.

"Them steers is scattered from here to hell. We'll never get a clear sign in all that mess. Do you want us to scout around?" Dusty asked.

Jed swore as Elizabeth touched the area close to the wound, and she jerked back. She could see it now, a neat cut in the flesh over his ribs, oozing blood, surrounded by angry blue swelling. Her heart began to pound with a sick, runaway rhythm, and she had to struggle for a deep breath. Was it only last night that her hands had played so lovingly over this very flesh? Beautiful and perfect and strong . . . now torn and violated by a stranger's bullet, marred and ugly and seeping blood.

Jed answered Dusty's question tersely. "No. I want you all here, at the cabin. I know where to go."

"No!" Elizabeth cried out. She looked up at him with swimming, pleading eyes. "You can't go after them! Let them go, they won't come back, promise me you won't go after them . . . please, Jed! Promise me. . . ." The last was a broken whisper, and she folded her hand on his thigh helplessly, looking up at him with nothing but fear and pleading in her eyes.

The men shifted and glanced at her in sympathy and embarrassment, and Jed turned his eyes upon her. His expression was hard, but far back in his eyes she saw a trace of pity. He said quietly, "I'm not making any such promise, Elizabeth."

She choked back a sob, trying with all her might to lift her hand to the wound again. But all she could see was that ugly, oozing tear; all she could feel was the terror and the weakness that washed over her in cold waves; and she couldn't help him, she couldn't stop him, she couldn't even stay . . .

She got to her feet and stumbled outside, pushing blindly past the awkward group of men at the door. She made it to the side of the cabin before she collapsed on the ground and was violently sick.

Dusty found her a few moments later, sitting on the grass, her head leaning weakly against the side of the cabin. He knelt beside her awkwardly and offered her a cup of water. "Come on now, Miss Elizabeth," he said gently. "Let's get back inside. It's not safe here."

It wasn't safe anywhere. How could she ever feel safe again in a place where things like this could happen? They had attacked her husband and drawn blood, they had invaded her home with the scream and tear of bullets, and she felt exposed, violated, vulnerable, and afraid in a way that went right to her soul.

She couldn't forget the anger and accusation in Jed's eyes. He had asked for her help, and she had been helpless. But how could he have expected her to do otherwise? She knew nothing of violence, of guns, of killing; she had no part of the ways that ruled this world. She didn't understand; she didn't want to understand. . . .

She took the cup from Dusty's hand, but her own fingers were shaking too badly to bring it to her lips. She was tired, a heavy, bone-stripping weariness that left her numb. She wanted to crawl away and hide, to put the moment when a nightmare had ripped through her life far behind her, and pretend it had never happened. . . . Jed. Where was Jed? Why wasn't he here, comforting her, holding her, making it all go away?

She heard footsteps leaving the cabin, and she saw Jed's form moving toward the corral. She struggled to get up, clutching Dusty's arm. "You've got to stop him. Dusty, he can't—"

"He's all right, ma'am," Dusty said soothingly, "just a scratch. Skunk fixed him up fine."

Elizabeth looked up at him with frustration and desperation backing her voice. "Dusty, don't let him go! Please stop him!"

Dusty looked at her as though she had uttered a blasphemy. "I can't do that, ma'am."

"But he could be killed!"

"I reckon he knows that." Then, quickly realizing he wasn't being much comfort, he added, "Miss Elizabeth, your man can take care of himself. He's a dead shot and a damn good tracker—beggin' pardon—and he ain't about to walk into nothing where he can get hisself killed. You rest easy."

Jed walked the horse back to the cabin, his hand on his holster. Skunk came out to help him switch saddles, and Elizabeth heard the two men talking. Her knees were weak and she couldn't stand up. All the water in her cup had spilled to the ground.

"He won't go alone, will he?" she pleaded, panic tightening her voice. "You won't let him go alone?"

Dusty looked back thoughtfully at Jed, but nothing was visible of him except his shadow and the silhouette of his booted leg. "I reckon he will," he answered. "Was it me, that's the way I'd want it. Safer that way, you see. You don't have to worry about nobody but yourself, and a man alone can sneak in and out of places a bunch of men couldn't. Don't you worry, he knows what he's doing."

Elizabeth looked up at him in despair. She had thought she knew them, all of them; she had thought she understood their strengths and their tenderness and their reasons and their wants. She did not understand this. She did not understand the life she had vowed to share. It was as alien and incomprehensible to her as the vicious criminals who had attacked them without provocation.

She said brokenly, "Dusty, how can you do it? How can you live like this?"

Dusty, who had survived an Indian massacre and buried his family in unmarked graves on the plains, who had lived thirty hard years in a mere eighteen and had spent most of them fighting, looked at her blankly. He said simply, "Because that's just the way it is, ma'am."

Jed mounted the horse and circled the cabin, moving away from her without even looking back. She heard the hoofbeats disappearing into the brush.

Dusty reached down and took her arm. "Come on inside now, Miss Elizabeth, and don't you worry. Everything's gonna be all right."

Elizabeth got to her feet and let him lead her inside. But everything was not all right. And she did not think it would ever be again.

CHAPTER
Nineteen

J ed opened the door of the lodge and walked inside. Red Wolf sat at a crudely built table in the center of the dim and smoky room. His wife moved silently from the fireplace to the table and back, her eyes averted. Jed sat at the table opposite Red Wolf.

"Five men," said Red Wolf at length. "Four ride today. One large, with a scar on his face. One rides a spotted pony. One wears three guns in his belt, and all carry two rifles. Another is small, with silver on his hat. The war chief, who does not ride, has yellow hair and town clothes. He carries a big knife with a black handle and ivory stones. He waits, safe in a canvas lodge, for others to return."

A muscle in Jed's jaw tightened grimly, but he said nothing.

Red Wolf leaned forward and began to trace a map in the dirt. "Here," he said, pointing to a mark between two creek beds. "There they camp, three suns. They do not hunt, leave no tracks. They wait."

They waited until Jed and his men came to them. They were assassins, hired gunmen, and they knew their business.

Jed got to his feet. "I must be away from my lodge with my men much of the time. My woman will be alone."

"Your woman will come to no harm as long as my braves ride these hills. You go. We will watch."

Jed nodded and pushed open the door. Dimness and dust settled in behind him.

The place Red Wolf had indicated was less than ten miles cross-country from the Indian village. Less than an hour after Jed had left Three Hills, he was on his way again. And this time he knew what he was riding into.

It was dusk when Jed approached the camp. There was a large canvas tent before the camp fire, on which bacon sizzled in a skillet. The horses were picketed close by, and saddles had been drawn up in a semicircle. There was no sign of life, but from the surrounding woods Jed heard a rifle cocked, and then another. He rode straight up to the fire.

Lord Hartley pushed aside the flap of the tent and came out, buttoning an embroidered waistcoat over his white shirt. "Well, well," he said, smiling. "If it isn't our good neighbor, Mr. Fielding. Come on out, gentlemen, and say hello."

One by one they stepped out of the woods. The one with the scar on his face Jed knew. He had shot three men out of the saddle on the road to Nacogdoches; no one knew why. The young one with three guns and four cartridge belts strapped at angles across his body was called Kid Baker. The other two were strangers, but Jed knew their type. One of them had a bloody bandage wrapped around his upper arm. All of them had rifles leveled at his chest, forming a loose circle around him. Jed rested his hands on his pommel, in plain sight.

Hartley moved toward the fire, his gait relaxed. "Can we offer you a cup of coffee? It's rustic fare tonight, I'm afraid; we didn't expect you so soon." He lifted a cup, but Jed said nothing, didn't move. Hartley shrugged and filled a cup for himself.

"What the hell are you doing here, Hartley?" Jed said softly at last.

Hartley lifted an eyebrow of mock surprise, straightening. "Why, that's right. You don't know." He sipped his coffee and made a slight grimace. "Foul-tasting brew, this. You were wise to refuse."

He leaned back on his heels, meeting Jed's gaze. "You do recall the matter of my remaining land coupons? I have registered them, and wonder of wonders, my land parcel seems to connect with yours, just beyond that stream there. As a matter of fact, my friend, you are trespassing at this moment."

Jed was silent, and Hartley took another sip of coffee. "Those cattle, as well, that you attempted to take off my property this afternoon belong to me. I believe you Texians have a rather nasty name for it—rustling? A hanging offense, I believe."

Jed said quietly, "This here is open range."

Hartley's glance was sharp, but his voice unperturbed. "Not anymore, it isn't. You see, Mr. Fielding"—his lips twisted into a cool semblance of a smile—"I am learning to play by Texas rules. One takes what one wants out here, and I intend to take only what is mine."

"You've got nothing here, Hartley."

"Indeed? We shall see." He looked at Jed. "You were an easy target this afternoon, I understand. I hope you realize that it is only through my grace that we were allowed to meet again. I owe you a certain debt, I believe, from one night aboard a flaming ship, and this was your warning—a display of strength, if you will. From now on I brook no mercy. I told you once that I would destroy you, and now I can pick my time and place. It is a matter of honor, don't you see, and I do not forget debts of honor."

Jed's horse blew gently in the night. The two men's eyes met and held for a long time. Jed's face was harsh and immobile; Hartley's implacable in the dancing shadows of the fire.

Jed said quietly, "You do what you have to do."

He lifted the reins, and his eyes were cold, his voice as deadly as steel. "But you keep this between you and me. Because if you come near my wife again, if you cause her the slightest harm or the first worry, I swear before God I'll kill you."

He turned and rode away.

Rio was on watch when Jed rode in. The two men nodded, but Rio did not take his eyes off the night landscape; his questions would wait until tomorrow. Jed unsaddled his horse, rubbed him down briefly, and went wearily into the house.

Skunk was sitting before the fireplace, whittling a piece of pine, and Dusty was by the door. Both had rifles across their knees, and both had freed their hands for firing when they heard Jed's footsteps. They relaxed when he closed the door.

Jed glanced toward the blanket wall that partitioned the bed from the rest of the room. "She's asleep?"

"Doubt it," Dusty answered. They kept their voices low. "She's pretty worked up."

Jed went to the fireplace and picked up the coffeepot that

rested on the coals, pouring half a cup. Skunk said, "You find anything?"

Jed stared into his cup. "Kid Baker, Newt Johnson, a couple of others."

Skunk whistled. "Shee-it. What's that bunch doin' out here?"

Jed tasted the coffee. "They came with an old friend of mine."

Dusty stared at him. "You could use some learnin' on how to pick your friends."

Skunk scowled. "Kid Baker coulda picked the hair off our hides from an apple tree in Maine. What was going on out there—a turkey shoot?"

Jed glanced at him briefly. "Something like it. My guess is it'll be quiet for a while, but we're not taking any chances. We watch our backtrails from now on."

Skunk got to his feet. "Well, hell, I'm up fer it. Ain't been no excitement around here for ever so long."

"Newt Johnson," muttered Dusty. " 'Bout time somebody put him outta business. I'd like to be the one to do it."

But he looked uneasy, and Jed didn't blame him. No man in his right mind would tackle that bunch voluntarily.

"We're not starting anything," Jed warned. "We've got a herd to get to market, and that's just what we're going to do." He set the coffee cup down. "I need to stretch out for a few hours. My side's paining me some. I'll take third watch."

Dusty nodded and followed Skunk to the door. "We'll all be sleeping out tonight. That bunkhouse was getting a little cramped, anyway. Wake you about moonset."

They closed the door behind them, and Jed lowered the lantern. He pulled off his boots and his vest, then his blood-stiffened shirt, but he was too tired to undress further. His wound was stinging something fierce.

He pulled aside the curtain that separated him from Elizabeth and stepped over to the bed.

She hadn't undressed, either, but lay curled up on the narrow cot with her clothes in a tangle, her hair trailing down, as though she had fallen asleep without intending to. Even as he watched, she moved restlessly, a small, stifled sound coming from her throat. Jed was torn by a wrench of pity and helplessness that twisted through him like a knife. She shouldn't have had to live through what she had seen today. Her world should always be sunshine and roses, gentle laughter, and soft summer evenings. . . . But it wasn't. And there wasn't a thing in hell he could do about it.

He bent down to draw the sheet over her, for as badly as he needed to lie down, he couldn't disturb her. And then he turned and walked outside.

Elizabeth opened her eyes but didn't move. She lay silently in the dark and let the desolation come. Until today, perhaps until this very moment, she had not realized how much she depended on her husband, how much she needed him. But when she needed him most, he wasn't there.

There was not a more horrible feeling in the world for a woman.

He had brought violence to her doorstep over nothing more than a few head of ugly cattle. People had shot at her, bullets had torn through her home, her security and her happiness had been utterly destroyed, and Jed had been able to do nothing to prevent it. She never had had cause to doubt her husband before, nor even imagined a reason for doing so. But now her trust in him had been shaken, and she was left alone and frightened and more helpless than she had ever been in her life.

She had begged him to stay; she had pleaded with him not to risk his life. He had had a clear choice: either to run off killing and maiming or to stay and protect his own. He had chosen to leave her. He had set his own course, and it was a course she could not understand, nor even be expected to. But how was she supposed to feel now? What was going to happen to her and to her marriage? How could she forget what had happened, and almost happened, today?

Hugging herself tightly against the chill of loneliness and the tears that wouldn't fall, Elizabeth closed her eyes and tried, determinedly, to convince herself that everything was going to be all right.

But that night she dreamed once again of fire. When she awoke, gasping and sobbing, there was no one there to hold her.

CHAPTER
Twenty

Two days later Dusty rode in with the report that Hartley had struck his camp. The trail led southeast for as far as he could follow it, and it looked as though the group was gone for good.

"I ain't right sure I like it," Skunk muttered, lifting his hat to scratch his head. "First they stampede our herd, then move out so's we can gather it again. Take potshots and don't hit nothin'. Don't make no sense."

"The man we're dealing with doesn't have to make sense," Jed answered. But he didn't like it, either.

Rio grinned confidently. "Could be they got a taste of what is too hot for their tongues, eh? Wise men turn and go."

No one believed that. But it was by mutual consent that they pretended to.

Borrowing trouble from the future was not the quickest

285

way to stay alive, so none of them spent a lot of time pondering the consequences of their enemy's sudden retreat.

It might have been that they had caught sign of the Indians who were watching the house. It might have been, like Rio said, that they hadn't counted on tackling four riflemen and had regrouped to improve the odds. Perhaps Hartley even had a conscience about Elizabeth, for she was a family friend and he had no grudge against her. But Jed didn't think so. He was certain, with the rest of them, that Hartley had merely moved his camp farther out, hidden his trail, and was waiting for the next chance to strike.

They went about their work, roping and branding, with slightly more confidence, knowing that the enemy was not in their backyard. Red Wolf's braves watched the cabin every day, silent and unseen, and that was the only thing that allowed Jed to feel safe in leaving Elizabeth alone. Still, they never worked far from the house, and all the men were back at the cabin to stay before dusk. They kept a guard throughout the night and rode with their rifles in hand during the day.

Jed did not tell Elizabeth that it was Hartley who had terrorized the house that day. He thought she had enough to worry about without putting a face to the nameless threat.

During the following week life took on a semblance of normalcy that was only a disguise for the deep chasms of unrest beneath the surface, like a shiny polished apple that was worm-eaten and decayed on the inside. Elizabeth went about the house with her usual brisk efficiency, smiling at automatic times, performing her tasks with her accustomed tireless energy. Her relief was genuine when Dusty told her that the intruders had been chased away, and for a time it seemed as though everything would be the way it once had been.

But Jed, harried by night patrol, came to her bed at odd times or not at all, always when she was exhausted or he was. They didn't make love; but worse, they didn't talk, not even to argue. They said words, polite words, mundane words, routine words, but words that had no meaning. Elizabeth never referred to that day when her tenuous hold on the world she had built for herself had begun to slip, and Jed did not want to bring it up. Deep scars that both pretended to ignore ran through their lives, and they hoped, perhaps, that the passage of time would heal them. That blissful day on the hillside when life had seemed so certain and so beautiful dimmed and began to fade, but there was little either could do to bring it back. They could only go on, day by day, and continue to pretend everything was all right. Perhaps after a while it would be.

They were sitting down to supper eight days after the attack on the cabin. Elizabeth had just put a pot of stew on the table and was turning to scoop up patties of fried corn bread.

Dusty commented, "Smells mighty good, ma'am."

Rio grinned. "She learns well, does she not? Soon you will no longer need a trail cook."

Skunk guffawed. "Since when did we ever have a trail cook? 'Lessen you call that slop you fling together cooking."

Jed stretched his long legs under the table and watched Elizabeth bending over the fire. The heat of the coals brought an artificial color to her cheeks, and the tendrils of hair that brushed her face were becomingly feminine, but was it his imagination or had she lost weight? What was it about her that looked less healthy than he remembered? He frowned a little, convinced he was imagining things.

"We should be able to finish up the branding this week," Jed said. "I figure by the time we cut the young stuff, we should have—"

They all heard the hoofbeats at the same time. Jed was the first on his feet, gun in hand, pressing himself against the shadow of the open door. Elizabeth whirled, her face going white and stiff with terror, and the platter she had been carrying clattered to the floor. Skunk, Dusty, and Rio moved as one, Skunk placing himself in front of her, Dusty and Rio flanking her, all with pistols drawn.

Then from outside came a lazy call. "Put that fowling piece down, you old mountain goat, before you shoot something. Can't a man pay a friendly visit without getting his head blown off?"

Jed reholstered his pistol, a relaxed grin spreading over his face, and sauntered outside.

"Sam Houston, you son of a mangy cur. What're you doing in this neck of the woods? They run you out of the States?"

"Worse. My fellow Texians elected me to office."

Sam was swinging down from his horse by the time Elizabeth ran to the door, her face alight and her heart skipping with incredulous delight. The great general was dressed in a beaded doeskin shirt, wide hat, and riding boots, and he, too, wore a pistol around his hip. But other than his dress, he was no different from when Elizabeth had last seen him. He was a face from home.

"General Houston!" Elizabeth exclaimed, coming forward to meet him. "What a wonderful surprise!"

Sam had tossed his reins over the hitching post when he heard her voice, and in the moment he turned, he could not hide his shock. At first Elizabeth thought it was because he had not expected to see her, but then she knew exactly what it was. He had not expected to see her like *this*.

The Elizabeth Coleman he had met in Alabama had been a blooming young belle in silk and hoops, perfectly coiffed, immaculately groomed, as delicate as an apple blossom. The woman he saw now bore scant resemblance to the young girl he had left behind.

Her hair was escaping from its tight bun and straggling

down her neck in strands and tendrils, damp from the heat. Her nose was freckled from too much outdoor work without her bonnet, and the hand she extended to him was rough and chapped. The weight of seven petticoats had quickly grown too much in the Texas heat, so that, in addition to the fact that they were impossible to keep clean, Elizabeth had long since discarded the crinolines for a single muslin undergarment. As a result, her skirts hung lankly on her too-thin body and dragged the ground. The apron she had wrapped around her waist was stained, and perspiration had darkened the material under her arms. There were mauve circles under her eyes, and her face had lost its plump and creamy color. No wonder the good man was shocked.

But he hid it admirably as he bent over her hand and declared, "Miss Elizabeth, how lovely you look. And how delightful to see you again. Your gracious presence has made the trip worthwhile."

Elizabeth smiled uneasily at the blatant lie as he straightened, and her hand went nervously to her untidy hair. Sam beamed warmly at her. "My belated congratulations, Mrs. Fielding, on your wedding. And you, sir"—he turned to Jed—"are the luckiest man I know. Well," he corrected, "perhaps the second luckiest." He turned back to Elizabeth. "It is my greatest pleasure to announce that I have asked Miss Margaret to become my wife, and she has done me the honor of accepting. We plan to be married in the spring."

Elizabeth lost her own discomfiture in a surge of excitement for her friend. "Oh, General Houston, I'm so happy for you both!" She clasped both his hands impulsively, her eyes sparkling. "I must hear every detail! Oh, but what am I doing, making you stand in the yard like a field hand. Come inside, please. We were just sitting down to supper." She glanced at him shyly. "It isn't much but—"

Sam laughed, putting her immediately at ease. "If it's anything other than jerked beef, it will be most welcome."

From that moment on there was a flurry of confusion as the men came out to greet the general and tend to his horse, each of them as anxious for news as Elizabeth was. She realized for the first time what a rarity visitors were, how starved they all were for a new face, how much more precious than gold was talk from the outside world. She had grown so used to living this isolated existence that she had hardly missed what she did not have, but Sam's presence was like a window flung open to sunshine and fresh air, sweeping reminders of another life into the stale, dank corners of her world.

Sam was a perfect gentleman and a good guest, and by the time they sat down to supper, he had steered the conversation away from the matters of men and toward the things Elizabeth most wanted to hear. He brought greetings from her father and news from home; he told of the latest fashions and who had given what party and who was in attendance. He reported on births and marriages and betrothals, and which debutante had made the most conquests that season.

Elizabeth listened with rapt and eager attention, barely touching her meal, deriving sustenance from something more filling than food. Several times during the course of the meal Elizabeth caught Jed looking at her with a peculiar thoughtfulness, but she hardly noticed. For the first time in recent memory her husband was not the center of her life.

Elizabeth had made a pie of wild berries Dusty had brought her and was glad to add this note of festivity to the supper table in honor of their guest. When she got up to serve it, Jed asked Sam, "You never did tell me what brings you out this way."

Sam chuckled, still trying to keep the conversation light for Elizabeth's sake. "Well, while I was off gallivantin' around in Tennessee, the good people of Texas elected me to their House of Representatives. I'm on my way to Austin.''

"Takin' the roundabout way, ain't you, Gen'ral?" Skunk asked.

The men gathered around the table, attentive and alert. Sam Houston was not an unfamiliar figure on the ranch, but he was not a man to make social calls. They all knew his visit this time was prompted by more than an impulse to pay respects to the newlyweds, and they waited for the news. The way Sam's face sobered with Skunk's words suggested that it was not good.

"I thought you'd want to know," Houston said quietly. "There's been trouble in Nacogdoches."

Elizabeth set a plate of pie before her husband, but he barely glanced at her. "Lamar?" he inquired of Sam.

"Thank you, Miss Elizabeth. It looks mighty good." Sam picked up his fork but did not touch the pie Elizabeth set before him. When she turned to cut another piece, he put his fork on the table again.

"That madman." Sam's voice was low and vicious, and it made Elizabeth look back at him, startled. "He's going to destroy it all, Jed, everything we've worked for, fought for. . . ."

Jed said, "What's he done now?"

Elizabeth returned with two more slices of pie for Dusty and Skunk, and Sam kept his eyes on his plate. "He decided the Nacogdoches reservation was free for the taking. He wanted the land for himself and his friends, so he drove the Cherokee off. Chief Bowl tried to negotiate, of course"—he lifted one shoulder in what was meant to be a negligent manner, but his tone was far from careless—"but in the end Lamar sent out an army. It was a massacre. Women, children, old men . . ." He let the sentence trail off, and the silence was thick and heavy. No one at the table moved.

Jed said quietly, "I am so sorry, Sam."

Sam Houston's hand tightened into a fist atop the table. His face was tight with pain, though he kept his voice steady. "Chief Bowl died," he said simply, "with my sword in his hand. His murderers had to pry it from his fingers."

The other men were silent, but the emotion that flowed between Sam and Jed was as palpable as a cry. Elizabeth knew that both General Houston and her husband had friends among the Cherokee, but what they were feeling now she could not completely understand. Once again Elizabeth felt like a stranger in her own home. After the lighthearted atmosphere of the supper table the recognition of her inadequacy, her inability to comprehend the workings of these men's minds and the events that shaped their lives, was especially painful.

Dusty broke the silence matter-of-factly. "They're on the warpath?"

Elizabeth felt a lurch in her chest as she returned to the table with the last two pieces of pie. She placed one before Rio and the other at her own place and sat down, her eyes on General Houston. *Warpath.* She had read the word in newspapers back home, heard it bandied about when men talked about the Western territories, but it had never had much meaning to her. It had never been a viable thing, with the power to make her heart skip a beat. . . . She wasn't back home anymore. She was in Texas. And here everything was real and threatening.

Houston replied, "Most of them have been driven across the Red River, but they're not going to take it lying down, you can be sure of that." His face tightened grimly. "The Cherokee are a proud nation who've tried their best to live in peace. But they have a long history as fighting men, and their braves haven't forgotten how to defend themselves. Already there've been reports of skirmishes, a few raids on settlers—"

Elizabeth couldn't keep silent any longer, and alarm quickened her voice. "Where?"

Sam glanced at her and swiftly saw his mistake. He cut his eyes to Jed apologetically and hastened to assure her, "It's nothing for you to worry about, Miss Elizabeth. I didn't mean to upset you. You're perfectly safe here, you must know that."

Elizabeth knew nothing except that once again her home, her way of life, her very existence was being threatened by something she didn't understand. She had not been safe here before . . . how could she possibly be now?

She looked at Dusty, and all she could think of was how he had found his family murdered and mutilated. The other men had turned to their pie with enthusiasm, but Elizabeth's throat was dry and her stomach in a turmoil. She looked across the table to her husband. "You told me the Cherokee were civilized," she said, and she couldn't keep the note of accusation out of her voice.

Jed put down his fork. His eyes were quiet. "Any man will fight back when he's pushed too far, Elizabeth" was all he said. "Even the most civilized one."

That was hardly the reassurance she had sought from him, and he must have known it, for an awkward silence fell. Sam finally broke it, with an enthusiasm in his voice that sounded too loud. "Well, where are my manners? This is not a fit topic for the supper table, and I take full blame. And not only my manners but where is my mind as well!" He pushed his chair back a little and reached into his pocket with a wide smile. "Miss Elizabeth, I do declare, your beauty and your good cooking is enough to rattle any man's brain, and I nearly forgot. I've brought you letters—from your father and my betrothed."

Elizabeth sprang upon them with the eagerness of a starved child, leaving her seat in her excitement. Sam's distraction had had exactly the effect he intended, and for the moment all thoughts of Indians and fear were wiped from her mind. The folded papers with their wax seals and blotted ink were like a treasure chest to her; her face lit up and her eyes grew bright the moment she held them in her hands.

She breathed, "Oh, General Houston, thank you! It's been so long. . . ." Her fingers burned to tear them open and scan the lines, but she knew that would be rude. Besides, she wanted to savor every word, to read each one over and over again, at length and in private, until they were committed to memory. Reluctantly she sank back to her chair.

Dusty scraped his plate and pushed back his chair. "Best pie I ever had, Miss Elizabeth," he told her.

She smiled at him with a brightness that was generated only by her anticipation of the letters that rested in her skirt pocket. "Thank you, Dusty. I'll make another as soon as you bring me more berries."

"That's a bargain, ma'am." He picked up his rifle as he started toward the door. He had the first watch, and the sun was setting. "Lookin' forward to talking to you more, General. I want to hear more about them pretty little gals back in the mountains. 'Course, being a spoke-for man, I doubt you'd know much about that."

There was a burst of masculine laughter that made Elizabeth blush, but the tension that had permeated the room with the first mention of Indian troubles was quickly fading away. Skunk and Rio went out to tend the horses, and Elizabeth quickly cleared up and did the dishes while Sam and Jed lingered at the table, sipping coffee and talking about political things that did not interest her. All she could think about were those letters.

At last, wiping her hands on the apron she had just removed, she turned back to them. "Gentlemen, could you possibly excuse me a few moments?'' Her cheeks were still flushed with eagerness. ''I don't wish to be rude, but . . .''

''But you want to read your letters, of course,'' supplied Sam graciously, getting to his feet. ''I was just about to invite your husband outside for a cigar.''

Elizabeth gave him a grateful smile, and Jed stood. ''It's been a long time since I had a real cigar, Sam. You didn't roll it yourself, did you?''

The two men went out the door, laughing, and Elizabeth hesitated only a moment before hurrying behind the partition, closing the blanket door behind her, and sinking to the bed to read.

The first lines brought a blur of unexpected tears to her eyes. ''My dearest daughter . . .''

She had to stop and focus on the moth-eaten blanket that closed off her little corner of the room before she could go on. *Papa,* she thought, and the ache that swelled up inside her was sharp and intense and all the more paralyzing for the fact that it was so unexpected. *I miss you so much. . . .*

But quickly, impatient with herself, she blinked back the tears and returned to the lines.

> It is the most painful destiny of a man to lose his daughter to another, and the fact that I cannot be with you at this time only makes it doubly so. However, I will not waste precious sentiment with reproaches or recriminations when there is so much I wish to say to you, and knowing that even as I write, it will be weeks, perhaps months, before my lines reach you.
>
> The letter you wrote me on your marriage day is like a talisman to my heart, for having read it, I am left with no doubt that it is only the greatest of loves that persuades you to turn your back on

the only life you have ever known, and strengthens
you to follow your husband into the wilderness.
It was such a love that I had for your mother, and
she for me, and if it brings you half the joy that
we had in our life together, you are richly blessed.

I feel my failing as a father in not having known
Mr. Fielding, but I have corresponded at length
with Mr. Houston and others as to his character
and am greatly reassured. I confess to a heaviness
in my heart as to the life you will be leading on
the frontier but hope to persuade your husband,
in time, to allow me to assist in improving matters.
In the meanwhile I ask only that he cherish you
as you deserve, and that in due course he will allow
you to visit me or accept my presence in your home.

You have the wisdom of your mother, my dear,
and the strength of your father, and I know that
you will be a good and proud wife to this man. I
miss your loving presence more than words can
tell, but I wish only your happiness. You are always
my most beloved, and I remain as ever,

Your adoring father

She couldn't stop the tears as she folded the paper, and
they splashed down onto the pressed linen like sluggish
raindrops, blurring the ink. She wanted her father. She
wanted the smell of magnolia and water cypress and the
sound of Negro spirituals floating on the breeze of a summer
evening. She wanted the gracious dining room at Larchmont,
the wide table lit by a dozen candles and groaning with the
weight of overfilled platters. She wanted the smell of
beeswax and the gleam of silver. She wanted the sound
of the pianoforte and her father's fond, affectionate smile of
approval as she played. Would she ever see her home again?

"Only the greatest of loves," he had said, "would have persuaded you to turn your back on the only life you have ever known...."

But was that enough?

With a swift, determined breath Elizabeth wiped her tears with the back of her hand and opened Margaret's letter. Sam Houston's visit, and all he had brought with him, had been a gift from heaven, and she was not going to spoil it all with self-pity.

She heard Sam and Jed returning to the house, their boots crunching on the dry dirt yard, their voices carrying on the evening air as they lingered outside. She hurried to read Margaret's letter, and the first lines brought a rather wistful smile to her face.

> Elizabeth, you are the most fortunate girl in the world! Imagine, running off into the wilderness with your true love—I always suspected you capable of such but never, ever dreamed you would actually do it! Mother has been most tight-lipped, let me assure you...

Elizabeth skipped that part. She could well imagine what Miss Nancy's attitude had been when she returned home and did not want to dwell on it.

Elizabeth, distracted, divided her attention between the men's voices and Margaret's letter. She could smell the aroma of cigars drifting through the open door; the men were standing just outside and talking about Alabama. Margaret wrote with girlish enthusiasm of her plans for her wedding.

> ...It will be at Spring Hill, of course, and oh, Beth, if only you would stand up with me, I would be the happiest girl in the world! I am sending to

Paris for fabric of the most exquisite shade of oyster rose for my attendants...

Margaret went on to describe her own wedding gown, the important names that would be included on the guest list, the extensive preparations that were already in effect for the event, and Elizabeth felt a lump of envy form in her throat. It would be a beautiful affair, the kind of wedding she had always yearned for... and would never have. All her life she had dreamed of her own nuptials, herself descending the wide oak staircase at Larchmont decked in lace and pearls, candlelight flickering over the faces of grandly clad guests—

Her reverie was interrupted by Jed's voice, which came to her clearly through the doorway. "I can't believe you're serious, Sam. Bringing a woman like Miss Margaret Lea out here—you must be out of your mind."

"I wouldn't have thought it of you, either, with Miss Elizabeth."

A pause. "I had no choice."

Sam's voice was discreet but implicit. "I thought it was like that. My future mother-in-law was a staunch defender, but there was gossip nonetheless."

Elizabeth's face was burning. Obviously the men did not know how easily their voices carried, and she knew she should make her presence known. But she couldn't. She had completely lost interest in Margaret's letter, and she listened helplessly to the voices outside.

Sam went on, "Her father was pretty upset, let me tell you. But I assured him you were a good man and that you'd take care of his daughter. I'm counting on you not to make a liar out of me."

"You know me better than that, Sam." Jed's voice was terse. "She's my responsibility now. I'll do my best by her."

"Well, it doesn't seem to be working any great hardship on you, if I do say so." Sam was trying to ease the tension that Elizabeth could feel, even through the protection of her blanket door. "I always did say all you needed was a good woman to straighten you out."

"Taking care of a woman out here is a big responsibility, Sam, and not the easiest thing in the world to do."

Sam's voice was sly. "I'm betting your bride could take care of herself if you'd give her half a chance."

Jed snorted, but his voice sounded uncomfortable, almost uneasy. "You're crazy, Sam. I always did say you knew less about women than any man I know, and as for a fine lady like Miss Margaret Lea . . . she won't survive out here, not for a month. You know what life is like and what it's going to be like, same as I do. It's not something you want to offer a lady like Miss Margaret."

Sam's chuckle was relaxed. "There's one thing you've got to understand about Southern women, my boy. They're stronger than they look. They are, in fact, the strongest women in the world. Hasn't your own bride proven that?"

Elizabeth did not want to hear Jed's answer. She had heard far too much already. There was an empty, aching feeling in the pit of her stomach, and her thoughts were in turmoil, but not for her life would she let the men know she had overheard—nor how it had affected her.

She got up and walked outside, emerging with a bright smile. To both men's startled, rather guilty looks, she declared, "Margaret writes the most charming letter, General, but she only leaves me famished for details! Please, if it won't trouble you too much, tell me all about your plans for the wedding."

CHAPTER
Twenty-one

The evening had gone on interminably, for as glad as Jed was to see Sam, he wished his visit had come at any other time. Or perhaps no time was good for Elizabeth to be reminded of what she had left behind.

At first Jed had thought this unexpected lift in their routine was exactly what Elizabeth needed. He had watched her eyes sparkle and her face grow animated again over the supper table. Even though it had plucked at his heart to see, so sharply and unexpectedly, how desperate she was for the things of home, some of the tension that had grown into a constant knot in the back of his neck over the past week relaxed, because she was happy.

She wasn't happy anymore. He had seen the changes she had gone through in the evening as clearly as if they had been drawn with charcoal, each moment a separate picture. First envy, then restlessness, then homesickness, and then despair. It was only natural, he supposed. But it couldn't have come at a worse time.

They had talked well into the night. Skunk had taken the second watch, and Rio and Dusty had gone to the bunkhouse to catch a few hours' sleep. Elizabeth had left the cabin a few moments ago, presumably to attend to her bedtime needs, and Sam got up shortly after. He and Jed stood outside the cabin, quiet beneath the stars, smoking a last cigar.

Sam said quietly, "I heard about your trouble."

Jed's eyes wandered toward the corral where he could see Elizabeth leaning against the rails, absently stroking the muzzle of the roan. She looked small and forlorn, standing there alone.

He answered, "It's nothing I can't handle."

Sam glanced at him. "I didn't know it was going to turn out like this," he said soberly. "Can't help but feel it's my fault for bringing you to Hartley."

Jed shrugged and tasted the cigar. "Trouble has a way of finding a man sometimes. Can't say it's anybody's fault."

"Do you want me to try to see what I can do?"

"No, it's gone too far for that. And I've dealt with worse."

Sam followed the direction of Jed's gaze and picked out Elizabeth's form among the shadows. "Does she know?"

"No. She's got enough on her mind."

Sam glanced at him. "She might surprise you."

Jed said nothing.

Sam dropped his smoldering cigar on the ground and stepped forward to crush it, his boot making soft grinding sounds in the dirt. He said easily, "We've been through hell and high water together, Jed. I like to think I've taught you a thing or two, and God knows you've shown me some. But

I've got to tell you, the man standing beside me now is the biggest fool that ever wore pants.''

Jed met his gaze with eyes narrowed against the smoke of the cigar, but he said nothing.

Sam looked back toward Elizabeth. "You're in love with your own wife," he said simply, "and you don't even know it."

There was a brief, sharp silence. "You're a romantic old fool, Sam Houston."

"That's right," Sam agreed mildly. "I'm also a very happy man." He stepped away from the cabin. "I'll sleep out tonight. It won't hurt to have an extra man with a rifle, just in case."

He had gone about three steps before Jed's voice came behind him. "It don't matter."

Sam turned.

Jed was staring at the tip of his cigar, and he moved his eyes slowly to Sam. "Loving's not important when you look at the rest of life. It don't matter."

Sam smiled. "No," he said quietly, "that's where you're wrong. It's the only thing that does matter."

Jed stood there until he could no longer hear Sam's footsteps. Then he tossed the cigar away and crossed the yard, toward his wife.

The roan tossed his head and pranced away, and Elizabeth folded her arms on the fence post, resting her cheek against them. The sky was brilliant with stars, their combined light filtering through the darkness like a thousand tiny rips in the fabric of the night. Absently she searched for her lone star but couldn't find it. How clear it had been that night, a lifetime ago, as she stood on the deck of a ship waiting for the man she loved. How clear everything had been then.

She had been a child filled with girlish romance and

mystic certainty. Where had all her dreams gone? How had she ended up in this place, alone and unsure and at odds with the world that surrounded her? She couldn't even remember anymore.

Home seemed so far away, as distant and untouchable as the innocent girl she had been when she'd left. Margaret, her father, Miss Nancy Lea . . . for a time Sam Houston's presence had brought them all back so clearly, she felt as if she could almost touch them. But even now the memory of their faces was slipping away like ghosts dissolving in a dream. She doubted if any of them would know her now. Even her own father would not recognize the haggard, careworn woman his little girl had become.

In the distance a coyote howled, and she shivered. The sound seemed to echo forever over these clear, empty hills. Even if she went home today, she would never forget that sound, the empty, pained wail of an animal alone.

She felt something touch her shoulder, and she whirled with a soft, frightened gasp. Jed, moving as silently as an Indian across the soft earth, stood beside her. He said, dropping his hand, "I didn't mean to startle you."

He was barely a shadow in the night, his hair a gentle aura that shaped but did not define. He brought with him on the night air the faint tinge of cigar smoke and the smooth bourbon Sam had brought. Elizabeth's father had drunk bourbon.

She smiled faintly. "I guess I'm a little jumpy."

What she wanted to do was to lean her head against his chest and let his arms go around her, let him hold her and soothe away the empty, aching feelings inside her. It had been so long since he had held her. She wanted his warmth and strong muscles, the feel of his chest rising and falling against her cheek, the sound of his heartbeat. But he seemed so remote, a shadow without substance in the darkness, a hint of something remembered but not quite real, and she could not make herself go to him. Everything seemed different between them now. Or perhaps she was just seeing things differently.

She turned again and leaned against the rail.

Jed said, "It was good to see Sam again."

Her voice was soft. "Yes."

Jed wanted to touch her but couldn't quite bring himself to do it. He felt awkward with her, searching for something to make her feel better, having no idea what she needed. He said, "We could try to go back for the wedding if you like."

She didn't even turn around. "That would be nice." She didn't believe it. Her voice sounded barren.

He moved toward her, leaning his hip on the rail beside her. She looked chilled and stiff, though the night was warm. He wanted to put his arm around her shoulders, to offer her warmth or protection. . . . He didn't know what he wanted to offer her. Perhaps it was something he didn't even have.

He said, looking out toward the shadowed hills, "I hope you're not going to worry about what Sam said, about the Indians. There's no reason—"

"No," she said a little too quickly. "I'm not worried."

But she was. He knew she was. Why wouldn't she tell him that? She had never been afraid to talk to him before. He didn't know what to do for her.

He looked at her hand, lying quietly atop the rail. Small and fragile, adorned only by the wedding ring of willow bark. He remembered the day he had given it to her, and it seemed an eon ago. How tenuous a thing happiness was, after all; how difficult to hold on to. He wondered what she would do now, how she would feel, if he took her hand in his and pulled her slowly against him. It had been so long, too long, since he had held her in the natural warmth of affection that had flowed so easily between them for too brief a time. Barely a week in actual days, but a scar of truth and violence separated the fantasy of summer days from this still night at the edge of autumn. He did not know how to bring the sunshine back.

He said, "When Sam brings back his bride, you can visit with her. We'll make the trip to Austin, or she can come here. It'll be good for you to see another woman once in a while."

"Yes." A single syllable, automatic and emotionless.

He had never seen her so dispirited and withdrawn. Almost beaten. Where was his Elizabeth of the fiery eyes and unfailing optimism? He wanted her anger, her laughter, her sassy retorts, and her quick, enthusiastic words. She was slipping away from him, inch by inch, moment by moment, and he did not know how to bring her back.

Would it matter, Elizabeth, if I loved you? Would it?

He slipped his hand beneath hers, turning up his palm and closing his fingers around hers. He felt the smooth texture of the willow ring, the coolness of her skin. And he heard a little catch in her breath when he touched her. Had it been that long, then?

He said softly, "Your hand is cold."

"I'm all right." But her voice sounded a little breathless, almost anxious.

So much lay unsettled between them. Jed had hurt her, in ways he knew and ways he didn't know, and he wanted to tell her he was sorry. He wanted to make everything right between them again.

He wanted to be inside her, holding her, soothing her, giving her a part of himself, and he wanted it with a deep and powerful intensity that seemed to strain at his very soul. And not for himself but for her. Because she needed something from him, and that was the only thing he knew how to give her. He was desperately afraid it would not be enough.

He tightened his fingers around hers, stepping away from the rail, bringing her with him with a gentle tug. She looked up at him with eyes that were questioning and hesitant. His heart was pounding. It had been too long. Were they such strangers? How could a few days make such a difference in their lives? It felt like the first time. He was afraid she wouldn't want him.

He looked at her soberly in the starlight. He said huskily, "Elizabeth . . . come inside with me. For a little while."

She lowered her lashes so he could not see her expression. But she laid her cheek against his shoulder, and his heartbeat swelled. He slipped his arm around her, and they walked slowly to the house.

Jed closed the door behind them, and Elizabeth could not look at him as she crossed the room, slipping behind the blanket partition. Her heart was beating rapidly, and she was nervous. She wasn't sure this was what she wanted. She hadn't expected Jed to want her tonight. She had never refused her husband before, never even thought of doing it, never wanted to. But now . . .

Now she didn't know what she wanted. She was afraid it wouldn't be the same. Something had happened between them that day over a week ago; she had failed him or he had failed her. Now he was a stranger who looked at her as though he did not know her, either. Everything had changed and she was anxious, uncertain, deep in the pit of her stomach. Her fingers fumbled with the hooks on her bodice, and it seemed wrong somehow. It was her husband who would be coming to her, not a stranger. She wanted so badly for everything to be right between them. But she was desperately afraid it would not be.

Jed pushed aside the curtain and stepped inside, and she whirled, startled. He had not turned down the lanterns, and he was fully dressed, except for his bare feet. His face was very sober, and his eyes were quiet. He came over to her and laid his hands lightly upon her shoulders. He said softly, "Tell me if this is not what you want, Elizabeth."

She looked at him, her eyes reflecting the torn and helpless feelings that pulled at her inside. She didn't know the truth herself until she spoke it.

"Yes," she whispered. "I—I want to be with you." She wanted his arms around her, his strength protecting her; she wanted everything to be as it once had been between them, and she wanted it to be like that forever. Only she didn't know if that was possible. . . .

She saw his soft inhalation of breath, the gentle lowering of his lashes, which obscured whatever emotion her words had caused. His hands lifted to her hair, fingers threading through it, freeing it of pins. His smile was faint and reassuring, as though he, too, had been anxious. His eyes were rich with deep, unreadable colors, like moss and earth on the darkest part of the riverbank. Slowly he brought his face to hers, and his lips rested lightly, tenderly, on her forehead.

"I only want to make the bad things go away for you, Elizabeth," he said. His voice was husky with an emotion she had never heard before. "That's all I ever want."

She lifted her arms and encircled his neck, and he pressed her against him, slowly, gently, and then more tightly, fitting her shape to every line and plane of his hard body. She let his presence flow through her and sink into every pore, squeezing her eyes closed, inhaling of him. It was Jed, the man she loved, and nothing had changed. His power still strengthened her, his touch still weakened her. Jed and the unfamiliar scents of bourbon and cigars; but Jed in the familiar, warm texture of his neck, his thick and silky hair, his ropy muscles tightening for her. It was the same but not the same. She needed him more desperately than ever.

He did not kiss her, he did not move. He simply held her, firmly and possessively, for the longest time. Finally he lifted his face, moving just a fraction away from her. He caught her hair lightly in both hands and brought it to drape over her shoulders, his fingers arranging and caressing the strands. A smile softened his face and gentled his eyes as he did that, and Elizabeth felt beautiful.

He said simply, "I've missed you."

She had missed him too. But at that moment her throat was too tight to tell him so.

Her heart leapt into sudden startled motion as his fingers left her hair and moved to the fastening of her bodice. Without a word, his eyes never leaving hers, he began to undo the hooks.

He had never undressed her before, not completely, not like this. Elizabeth had the vague idea that this was not something that husbands did for wives. She had never thought that he would want to do it, or that she would want him to. It seemed so personal, so intimate, his large fingers moving one by one over the tiny hooks of her gown, freeing them, exposing to his dark gaze the white skin of her shoulders, the thin fabric of her undergarment. Yet that was precisely what made it so new and strangely exciting. That was why she did not stop him, though she knew she should demur to privacy and finish herself. She could only stand entranced with expectation and let him perform for her this most intimate of tasks.

The shirtwaist fell open, and he tugged it from her arms, letting the garment fall to the floor. He found the catch upon her skirt, and then the tapes on her petticoat. She stood protected from his rich, dark gaze by nothing more than chemise and pantalets, her shape outlined by the lamplight through the thin material. Nervousness, perhaps even shyness, quivered in the muscles of her abdomen as she stepped out of the skirts and petticoat that bound her ankles and pushed them away with her foot.

Jed said softly, "Elizabeth, you are beautiful."

She had to lower her eyes. "I'm not. My hands are ugly and I'm too thin and I haven't taken good care of my skin. I—" She glanced at him quickly, her anxiety undisguised. "You must have been embarrassed for your friend General Houston to see me like this."

Something swift and painful crossed Jed's face that Elizabeth couldn't understand. He took both her hands and held them lightly in his. When Elizabeth tried to curl them into fists, ashamed of their rough texture and chapped appearance, the scars and blisters of abuse, Jed deliberately held them open with his thumbs.

"No," he said softly. "I wasn't embarrassed."

He brought her hands to his lips, one by one, and kissed first the palms, then the backs. And he placed her hands on his waist.

His arms slipped around her, and his eyes held hers, quiet with a passion she had never seen before. She felt his hands slip down her back, below her waist, until they firmly cupped the curve of her bottom. Slowly, deliberately, he brought her against him until her thighs fitted into his, and his manhood, hard and heated, pressed into her stomach. He held her there, with his eyes and his hands, until her heart raced and her cheeks flamed, for he had never done that before. Not so purposefully, so meaningfully, through the press of their clothes and in the light of the lamp.

With that single, very masculine gesture he was reminding her of all they had shared, all they knew but did not know, all the secrets that could no longer be secret between them.

It spoke of all the conventions that did not bind them, the words that should not separate them, and the closeness which, for tonight if only for tonight alone, would be theirs. It made Elizabeth tremble with its power, and anxious for its promise.

She lifted her hand, placing it lightly above his heart. She could feel the forceful, powerful beating. Boldly she slipped her hand inside his shirt, fingers moving over bare flesh and heat, brushing threads of masculine hair, her palm forming the swell of a strong breast muscle. She could feel the quickening of his breath, and her own heart was racing.

His hands moved upward over the fragility of her ribs, cupping her breasts through the material. She felt dizzy from his touch, from his bare skin against her fingers. He inhaled deeply, his fingers tightening, his palms flattening and pressing with a primal, untutored need that sent a roar of swift and blinding sensation through her. She went weak against him, her hand moving upward to circle his neck, drawing his mouth to hers.

She needed him. She had never known how much until this moment.

He covered her mouth with his, engulfing it with desire that was bold and urgent and unashamed. His hand went between their bodies, tugging at his shirt, freeing buttons, and then she felt the press of his bare chest against her breasts, heat penetrating the thin fabric of her chemise. With his mouth still fastened to hers, he took her hands and brought them down until they rested against his chest. The sensation of smooth muscles and unclothed flesh against her fingers caused her breath to catch in her throat, caused her to go weak again all over.

He lifted his face from hers and, with his hands, tilted her head back to look at him. His eyes were obscured with color, burning with a deep light, and filled with her. She saw the constriction of his throat as her hands drifted down to his waist, the darkening of his pupils as her palms caressed the soft material that covered his hips. He stood very still, his hands beneath her hair, holding her, letting her see what her touch did to him. He wanted her to touch him, to know him, to explore him. It had never been like this between them before, and Elizabeth was filled with the thrill of discovery, a pure wonder that went far beyond the physical. He was telling her he belonged to her.

He moved his hands down to the straps of her chemise, pulling the material off her shoulders, down to her waist. He released the tabs of her pantalets, and she felt the caress of warm air and strong fingers as she stood, suspended even in breath, and let him strip away the fabric until she was naked before his gaze. Each brush of his eyes was like a whisper of fire, making her tremble, searing her skin.

With his arm he encircled her shoulders, not drawing her closer, just sheltering her. His fingers lightly stroked the cords of her neck. She could feel his breath laboring to remain soft and see the flush that hazed his cheeks. And then she saw only the slightest hint of hesitation and questioning in his eyes as he took her hand and guided it to the top button of his pants.

At first her fingers clenched instinctively, and she did not know if she could do what he was suggesting, what she wanted so badly to do. What was hers to do. But his face above her was so tender and quiet, so dear and familiar, and he was her husband. He belonged to her tonight as he never had before.

She released the buttons with shaking and clumsy fingers, feeling the power of his private flesh burn against her hands. She tugged the material from his hips and let it drop to the floor; he stepped free of his clothing and dropped his hands to her waist, and he let her look at him.

She had never gazed upon that part of her husband before, not intentionally, not in full light. What she thought she knew so well had never been familiar to her until now, and she felt the tingle of shame and the power of fascination. Other sensations filled her—insidious, secretive, urgent sensations that made her heart thud and her legs weak and a tingling anxiety form in her lower regions, just from looking at him.

She drew in her breath in a long gulp as he brought her against him, his hands covering her bare hips, his breath upon her neck, all parts of his body—strong and smooth, insistent and probing, heated and moist—molding against hers. He held her like that for a long time, until she could feel the strong, rapid rhythm of her heart overpowered and synchronized by the beat of his own, until her very skin felt as though it were a part of him, until her muscles were weak with wanting and even her breath did not seem her own anymore.

She hardly knew when he bent to lift her into his arms, carrying her the few steps to the bed. His face was a blur of gold and bronze above her, his eyes reflecting all the colors of the universe. She reached for him, but he caught her hands.

"No," he said softly. "Let me do this for you. Let me give to you, tonight . . ."

Wordlessly, with the gentleness of a whispering breeze, he began to caress her. Over and over his soothing strokes played upon her body, from head to foot, each plane and curve gentled, adored. It was mesmerizing, it was wondrous; she lost herself in his soothing touch, her muscles melting, her skin alive, until nothing seemed to exist except Jed, who in this strange and beautiful way was making her a part of him. The tension of anticipation, even the ache of eagerness, floated away into mindless pleasure, and when his hands moved between her thighs, they separated for him without thought or volition, welcoming him home.

She kept her eyes open and through a gauzy veil of rapture she saw his face above her, meeting his gaze as she felt his sweet, low, sliding entry. She saw his eyes, the brightness, the slumberous pleasure, the darkening and the deepening of intensity. She felt him inside of her, a part of her. She thought, Yes . . . this is the way it was meant to be. It hasn't changed. . . .

She lifted her hands, pushing them into his hair. His face softened with a hazy smile. She luxuriated in him; she adored him with a sweet and abiding power that took her beyond herself, into the deepest part of him. *Surely,* she thought, *nothing bad can happen to us when we have this to share. . . .*

His movements were slow and deep and long, sustaining the wonder. The crescendo built and swelled and held them poised, trembling, at its peak. Pleasure spiraled downward in the same slow waves of intensity with which it had grown, and even when passion was past, they clung together, formed together; they could not let go.

Jed kissed away the dampness from her face, smoothed her hair. "I wish," he whispered, "it could be like this forever."

She wished it, too, with all her might. That they might never be separated, that they could hold their world together as they held each other, safe and secure. But even as she tightened her arms around him he was moving away, slipping from her, becoming a whole and separate being again. Nothing she could do could stop him.

The sounds of the night began to intrude, the shuffling of horses, the trilling of a tree frog. In the yard outside or from the bunkhouse someone coughed. Elizabeth wound her arm around his shoulders and pressed her cheek against the beating of his heart. She couldn't stop it. The world was coming back. And he was slipping away.

She whispered brokenly, "Oh, Jed, sometimes I'm so frightened."

His lips touched her hair. "Of what?"

"I don't know." Her fist closed against his chest, fighting helplessness and her own inadequacy to tell him what it was she really feared. Not the Indians, not the bullets, not growing old and ugly in this barren place ... She feared things worse than that, deeper than that, emptier than that. Things she couldn't even define to herself.

He said, "Elizabeth, I'll take care of you, I promise. You know I won't let anything happen to you." She could feel the tension in his muscles, the strain in his voice.

But that was not what she wanted to hear. She wanted to watch her husband ride away in the mornings without wondering whether he would ever come back. She wanted to be able to lie like this with him and believe, if only for a while, that it could last forever. She wanted to laugh again, to dream again, to be free again. She wanted to stop being afraid.

She moved her head to look up at him, and her voice was soft but urgent. "Jed, it doesn't have to be like this. We don't have to be afraid all the time. No one could steal your cotton. You wouldn't have to shoot anybody over cotton. Papa wants to help. He wrote that he would. Please, if you would only think about it, if you would talk to him ..."

But even before the words were out she could feel his withdrawal. His body stiffened against hers, and the tenderness faded from his face. The magic that had blossomed so grandly between them was gone in a moment, and once again they were two people alone, straining for each other but not quite reaching, not even understanding what it was they were reaching for anymore.

He said tiredly, "Elizabeth, try to understand—"

"I don't want to understand!" The exclamation was soft and tight, and her fingers unconsciously dug into his upper arm. "I want it to be different." Her voice was thick with tears she refused to let flow. She buried her face in his chest again. "I want you safe and with me, and I want us to be happy . . . that's all I ever wanted, Jed, was to be happy with you."

"I know." His whisper was soft and helpless, filled with pity and defeat.

Elizabeth was swamped with a flood of guilt and confusion, for she knew she was being unfair; she knew she was hurting him. She wanted to take back the words, erase the selfishness that had caused such a breach between them, and bring back the wonder they had shared only moments before. Tonight he had given her something precious. Tonight they had been close in a way they had never been before, in a way that few others would ever know. But so soon, too soon, it was slipping away, and nothing had changed, not really.

He sat up and she clutched at him. "Jed, I'm sorry," she whispered. Her eyes were bright and anxious. "Don't go."

He looked at her, and she could see the lines of weariness on his face, the sorrow in his eyes. He leaned forward and kissed her hair lightly. It was an ending, not a beginning.

He said quietly, "I have to, Elizabeth. I have the next watch."

A heaviness drained through her, and she lowered her eyes. The world was back. They had held it at bay for a few moments, but nothing could keep it away. She had never felt so tired in her life.

She nodded and said nothing. There was nothing she could say.

Jed dressed silently, not knowing what else to do. He

wished it could be different, all of it. She could not know
how badly he wanted things to be different. But there was
nothing he could do.

She was lying down when he turned back to her, her eyes
closed. She was not asleep. He bent and kissed her lightly
on the cheek and tasted a tear. Leaving her like that felt like
tearing out a part of his soul.

He had given her all he could, but he had been right from
the beginning. It was not enough.

CHAPTER
Twenty-two

Sam Houston left the next morning, and his departure was at least as traumatic as his arrival had been. Jed thought he had never seen anything braver than Elizabeth standing in the yard, quietly waving good-bye to the last remnants of the life she had lost.

For Jed it was just another workday, and the days were growing too short to waste. But he lingered, fussing with his horse, making excuses about a worn rope, checking and rechecking his pistol. He did not want to leave Elizabeth today. How could he leave her with so much still unsettled between them?

Since he had awakened, he had been troubled by an ill-defined sense of anxiety, something he couldn't shake no matter how hard he tried. It had to do with last night, he knew, with Sam's meteoric appearance and disappearance in their lives, with the memory of Elizabeth's stricken eyes as she had begged him not to leave her the night before. He knew it was only guilt and regret. But it felt like more. He hadn't been this jumpy, this afflicted by that nebulous, almost precognizant prickle of uneasiness, since the day he had met her.

The day he had met her. Recalling it, he couldn't prevent a dim sense of amazement. How much had happened to him since then. Elizabeth, bursting into the stillness of an Alabama afternoon, destined to change his life forever. Who could have predicted, five months ago, the events that would bring him to this day? On that quiet spring morning he had awakened disturbed, anticipatory, wary, much as he was feeling now. By the time that day was over, his world had changed forever.

The men were getting restless, and Jed couldn't delay any longer. The sun was already two hours into the sky. He led his horse up, tossed the reins over the hitching post, and met Elizabeth as she was coming back from the chicken coop, a small basket of eggs in her hand.

She smiled faintly as she paused before him. "Are you ready to leave?"

He nodded. His eyes wandered uneasily, without knowing exactly why, to the distant landscape. The sky was clear and cloudless, which somehow did not seem right. The way he was feeling, a major storm should have been brewing.

He looked back to her. "Elizabeth," he offered, "if you're feeling nervous about staying alone, I could leave one of the men behind."

Elizabeth's forced smile faltered. A guard was not what she wanted. Didn't he understand that? She wanted her husband, and even after last night he still didn't see what her heart was crying out for. . . .

But he was trying. She could tell he was trying, and that surely was something, wasn't it? Bravely she replaced her smile. "No, I'm not nervous. Besides, you all have work to do."

Jed nodded, not in the least reassured. She had never looked more fragile than she did that morning, standing before him with her eyes narrowed slightly against the sun, trying to smile at him. She was thinner. He had discovered that fact for himself last night, when her ribs had seemed delicate enough to crack between his fingers and her waist had disappeared easily between his two linked hands.

He said, "We'll be home early." He couldn't take his eyes off her, as though, if he looked at her long enough, he would find something in her face to make the dread inside him go away.

But all he saw was a faint and gentle puzzlement as she tried to discern the reason for his scrutiny or perhaps for his awkward behavior. She said, "Good. I'm going to slice up some of that ham Sam brought. It will be nice to have something other than beef for a change, won't it?"

Jed made himself smile, and returned easily, "Yeah, it will."

Skunk called, "Sun's climbing, boss!"

Jed heard the jingle of harnesses and the creak of leather as the men mounted up, joking and talking among themselves. He turned to go.

Elizabeth, he thought, *I don't want to leave you.*

He had a swift and unexpected certainty that if he walked away from her now, he might never see her again.

The thought sent a chill through him that halted him in mid-step. It took almost a full second for him to recover, shaking his head slightly, squaring his shoulders. That was stupid. It was only because of last night, and he was getting as sentimental as a woman.

As a woman. It came to him, suddenly, clearly, and without much preparation whatsoever, the way the important things of life so often have a way of doing. This was the way Elizabeth felt every time she watched him ride away. This was the anxiety that haunted her eyes, the fear that clouded her face, the sadness that weighted her down day after day as he rode away with so much unsaid between them. He knew how she felt.

It was a simple thing, a plain thing, but the knowledge was stunning. How many times had he yearned to know her, to understand her, to share what was going on inside her head? Now he did. Now, without his even becoming aware of it, he was a part of her. The things that separated male and female were no longer important. They did not even exist. A dozen things, a hundred, he had never understood before, suddenly became clear. It was an amazing thing, a wondrous thing.

He turned around and walked slowly back to her. She stood where he had left her, the puzzlement beginning once again in her eyes as he returned. He couldn't keep the quiet glow of wonder off his face. There was so much he wanted to tell her. There weren't enough words to begin to tell her.

He stopped before her and she looked at him, questioning, waiting. He dropped his eyes, suddenly overwhelmed by the task before him.

He took her hand, lightly running his fingers over the texture of her willow ring. He heard the soft catch of her breath. He loved that little sound she made whenever he touched her. He looked at her searchingly. He said softly, "Elizabeth . . . I'm glad I married you."

Her eyes widened, and he realized with a jolt that he had never told her that before. Perhaps because he had never known it until now. But it was true—that and so much more. He saw the cautious expansion of questioning and joy on her face, and he was weak with all he felt, all he needed to say.

He took her chin lightly between his thumb and forefinger, and all he could do was smile at her, looking at her, hoping she could read in his eyes what was swelling and aching and thrilling inside of him. "It's going to be all right, Elizabeth," he said huskily. "I promise."

He bent forward and kissed her lightly on the lips, the men grinning and the horses shuffling behind him. The kiss would have lingered and deepened, but he knew if it did, he would never walk away. So he lifted his face and stood looking at her, holding her chin with his fingers. How beautiful she looked. She was stunned and flushed and just kissed, and he did not want to leave.

Skunk drawled laconically, "Say, boss, if this is gonna take a while, we can ride on ahead."

Jed smiled. "I have to go."

She nodded, her eyes still bright, her lips still parted.

He stroked her face and made himself leave her.

But even when he was mounted, he had to look back, reluctant to lift the reins, imprinting his mind with the memory of her. *Tonight,* he promised himself. *Tonight will be ours*. They would talk, as they had in the beginning, but even more. They would laugh, they might even argue, they would say the words that were important and the ones that weren't so important. He would see the sparkle in her eyes again. He would tell her of the wonder growing in him. He would say things he had never envisioned himself saying to a woman, things that couldn't wait another day to be said.

Tonight someone else would take his watch. Tonight he had more important things to attend to than his duty. Tonight was for Elizabeth and himself and all that had waited for them for too long.

I love you, Elizabeth.

Sam had said it. That was the only thing in the world that did matter.

He tipped his hat to her and smiled. He made himself lift the reins.

He nudged his mount into action, but he had to stop twice and look back, just to reassure himself that she was still there.

Elizabeth went through her morning routine in something of a daze. She did not know what she had expected to feel in the aftermath of emotions stirred up by Sam Houston's visit, but she was certain it was not this.

That morning, as she had waved good-bye to General Houston, she had been aware of a small, treacherous relief that he was not returning to Alabama immediately. If he had been, she would have been tempted to beg him to take her with him.

Now Alabama was farther away than it ever had been before, and what confused her was . . . she wasn't sorry.

What had been in Jed's eyes this morning that she had never seen before? She found herself going about her chores in a flustered, half-distracted way, and all she could remember was the way it had been between them the night before. Afterward there had been the familiar sadness and frustration, but for a few moments they had shared something unbelievably precious. How could she have thought, even in the dimmest corner of her despair, that hope could be gone when they still shared that?

At last, restlessly, she took out her letters and settled down to reread them, but today all the words held a different meaning. Margaret, whose perfect romance she had always envied, seemed childish and distant, out of place. Sam Houston loved her, and it was a wonderful thing. But Margaret had no idea what it was like to live with a real man, to know the pain and struggle that turned girlish infatuation into something solid and abiding . . . frightening, sometimes, and even hurtful. But real.

It still ached within her, the homesickness, her lost innocence. She still yearned for the peaceful lawns of Larchmont, the elegant fetes of Spring Hill. She still wished she had it all to live over again . . . only now she was certain she would not have done anything differently.

This was her home. None of them would recognize her now, it was true. Margaret would be appalled by her dress, her appearance. Her father would be amazed by the changes in her. She could cook. She could mend a buckskin shirt with rawhide and make lye soap from bear fat. She knew the herbs and the grasses that could be used for medicine, the wild vegetables that were edible. She was no longer a star-struck young girl; she was a grown woman who was making a home for herself in the wilderness, and that was a good thing. A proud thing.

She folded her letters and put them away again inside the text of *Pride and Prejudice*. She was smiling distantly and a little wistfully. She would read them over and over again, and each time they would make her sad but a little happy too. She was not sorry. How could she be sorry when, from the first moment of seeing Jed and loving him, she had had no choice?

Perhaps no one else would understand that. But no one else had to.

Smoothing her hands on her skirt with a determined breath, she went to stir up the fire for baking. Jed had said they would be home early, and she had a lot to do.

The cabin had barely disappeared from sight before Jed was seized by an urgent need to go back. It was not like other times on the range when the swell of desire plagued his blood and the loneliness for Elizabeth clouded his head. This was something different—worrisome, insistent, and nagging. He didn't know how to deal with it.

He couldn't concentrate. Once, as he was throwing a steer for branding, the animal lashed out and only a last-minute reflex saved him from a broken leg. As it was, he got a bruise that would swell and ache for days, and he cursed himself for his stupidity and carelessness. Rio grinned and pointed out lazily that in Jed's present state certain body parts were more important than others, and he had been fortunate to lose only the use of a leg. Jed swore at him and hobbled back to work, and his irritation with himself only darkened his mood. Range accidents happened, but only a greenhorn would make a mistake like the one he had just made, and it had been a long time since he had been the butt of anybody's joke.

Half an hour later, just as he was getting used to the saddle again, he saw the tracks. Once again he battled back an irrational sense of alarm. He saw marks of Indian ponies, a lot of them, and moccasins. What were they doing this far east?

He got down off his horse and scouted around, uneasiness growing by the minute. The tracks were a day old, maybe less. But the herd and his own horses had blotted out most of them, and he couldn't get a direction or much sign at all. There were women along, and children, and travois. It wasn't a hunting party.

He stood up, favoring his stiff leg, and took off his hat. Absently he wiped the sweatband, staring off in the direction of the Cherokee camp. He could be there in half an hour.

It was probably nothing. He might have misread the signs; it could have been a hunting party, or an expedition of some sort. It could have been dozens of perfectly innocent things.

But he couldn't shake that cold feeling deep down inside his gut.

He needed to see Red Wolf, anyway, to tell him about Nacogdoches, if he hadn't already heard. He had planned to postpone it, dreading it, knowing what it would mean. Maybe Sam had already told him on his way in yesterday or passing by this morning. Jed should have asked.

Half an hour, just to reassure himself. It was for damn sure he wasn't doing much good around here.

He slapped his hat back on his head and mounted. "Rio!" he called out. "I'm riding over the hill. I'll be back before noon."

Rio waved him on, and Jed slapped his horse with a sudden feverish urgency, hoping to God he wasn't going to find what he thought he was.

Close to midday, Elizabeth took the big wooden bucket and started toward the spring for water. The day was half over and she was tired, but that wasn't unusual lately. The heat was not making things any easier, and she had not slept the night before.

She thought suddenly that if she was home, she wouldn't be lugging a bucket to and from the faraway spring, its weight when filled with water almost as much as her own. If she was home, she would be sitting on the veranda in a cool summer dress, sipping iced tea and nibbling sugar cookies while two slaves moved the big palmetto-leaf fan over her head. She would be chatting in a lazy fashion with her girlfriends over the next scheduled ball or perhaps listening quietly while the young Reverend Ashbury read aloud from the Greek poets. Later she would go upstairs to her shady, high-ceilinged bedchamber with its flowered wallpaper, strip to her chemise, and lie down on cool linen sheets. Her maid would bring lemon-scented cloths for her temples and wrists, and she would close her eyes and drift into a rose-tinted sleep as the heat of the afternoon passed over her head. She would rise, bathe in a porcelain tub of tepid water, and dress for dinner. . . .

Home. It was all as far away as the nearest star.

At the grove of cottonwood that separated the spring from the house, she had to pause and look back. What she saw brought a new and tenuous lift to her spirits. Poppies and wild marigolds bloomed in a riotous profusion of color around the cabin. The shoat was snuffling and snorting in its pen, the horses munched lazily at grass through the bars of the corral. A tendril of pale smoke from the chimney signaled home, and the chicken coop, that inviolate symbol of civilization, stood stalwart in the shade. She remembered how this place had looked when first she had arrived, and she had to smile.

Perhaps it wasn't much, but it was better than what they had started with. This fall, perhaps they could get some seeds from someone, and by next summer a vegetable garden would be ripe for harvest. She could persuade Jed to bring back a milk cow and some more chickens, and they would have a beginning on a real home. Progress was slow, but it *was* progress. And it was hers.

But oh, it would be so wonderful to have a real bath, to feel crisp linen against her skin again. . . .

Determinedly she squared her shoulders and moved on to the spring, tugging her skirts away from the tangled brush that persisted in crowding the path. She would have her bath, in cool spring water. She would be fresh and lovely for Jed when he returned tonight; she would show him she was not afraid and tell him she was sorry for the hurtful things she had said. She would prove she was willing to begin again.

She set the bucket down and sat on the grass at the edge of the creek, smiling to herself as she pulled off her shoes and stripped down her stockings. The water was a cold shock against her bare toes but delightful. In a moment she would return to the house and get soap and a towel, and then she would immerse her whole body. But for now she just wanted to sit and dangle her feet over the edge and think about tonight.

She was still homesick. Perhaps she always would be. But she could go to visit, and her father would come to see her, and soon Margaret would be in Texas. She wouldn't be alone forever. Who knew, perhaps by next year . . . Dreamily she ran her hand over her flat stomach, imagining it beginning to swell and round with Jed's child. By next year anything was possible.

Everything was going to be all right. Jed had promised.

Willing herself to believe in a future more promising than the past, she pulled her feet out of the water and picked up the bucket, bending to fill it.

That was when she heard the hoofbeats.

The village was deserted. The houses were abandoned, possessions absent, horses gone, ashes cold. Not even a breath of air stirred the eerie silence, and the cold fear that had gathered in Jed's stomach clawed its way up to his throat.

Red Wolf's words came back to him: "I will not bring blood to the doorstep of a friend." They knew of Nacogdoches. They had taken their battle elsewhere.

Red Wolf, his women, his children, his braves—they were all gone. And Elizabeth was alone.

Jed knew, as certainly as though a black curtain had been drawn across the panorama of the day. There was no more denying it, no more ignoring it. He didn't pause to investigate, he didn't stop to ponder. He simply knew.

He wheeled his horse around with such force that it screamed, and he used his lariat to spur the animal into a furious gallop. The wind tore at his shirt and stung his eyes, and his heart was pounding with the beat of the hooves that churned up turf behind him. He thought a dozen things, a hundred, all of them beating at him, accusing him.

He shouldn't have left her alone. He had known this morning, damn it, he had *known*. She couldn't even shoot a gun. Why hadn't he taught her? He should have made her learn; a dozen opportunities and he had ignored them all. What if she had gone off, riding alone, as he had warned her so often not to do? She never listened to him, but he should have *made* her listen. She didn't even know. He had promised to keep her safe, but had never told her of the danger. . . . So many mistakes, so many things he should have done and hadn't, things he hadn't thought of, things he hadn't bothered with. They all came back to haunt him.

He bent low over his mount, sweat drying on his face, his teeth gritted against pain and certainty. He whipped the horse into faster and longer strides, and still he wasn't moving fast enough. He would never get to her in time. He squeezed his eyes shut.

God, don't let this happen, not now, not like this. . . . Don't let me see what I know I'm going to see. . . .

And then he smelled the smoke.

Elizabeth dropped the bucket; some instinct borne of she knew not what propelled her toward the house, not away from it. She had made it back to the grove of cottonwood before hell opened up and all its demons poured out.

They came, a dozen of them, a hundred, she did not know. They were screaming, shooting, their horses frothing and pawing the air; half naked and vicious, their faces were scarred with war paint, feathers streaming from their hair. The earth shook with the sound of their hooves, the day was streaked with the explosion of rifle fire in the air. They circled the cabin, they leapt the fences, they trampled the flowers. They were everywhere, a blur of sound and color and horror that was never-ending. . . .

Elizabeth fell to her knees, screams convulsing in her throat and dying silent there. She wanted to run, she wanted to hide. . . .

She couldn't hide. She had to stop them. It was madness, it was a nightmare, there was *nothing she could do*.

She heard the splitting of corral boards, Jed's panicked horses flailing toward freedom as the savages whipped them on. The hog squealed, and there was the continuous, rending screech of the chicken in terror. One of the demons rode his horse through the door of the cabin, and she could hear breaking, crashing, and savage, blood-curdling yelps of victory.

Do something! a voice screamed inside her. *Run, hide, stop them...fight them...you can't let this happen....dear God, don't let this happen!*

A horse flew by not ten feet from her, flinging soil and lather. But the rider did not see Elizabeth, crouched and immobile behind the trunk of a tree. His face was a blur to her, his figure a nightmare from hell, and then he was gone.

A flaming log from the cook fire sailed across the yard and caught the roof of the bunkhouse. Smoke was already billowing from its door. Flames lapped at the logs of the cabin as the Indian on the horse galloped out. Fire was everywhere, smoke was filling her lungs, she was trapped, and there was no escape....

It wasn't real. It wasn't happening. It was her nightmare again, and she wasn't going to die. Jed would come and he would save her....

It was no nightmare. It was real. And nothing Jed could do would stop it now.

She tried to scream. She tried to run. She could do nothing but bring her fists to her face and huddle, paralyzed and rigid, and watch as in those few swift, savage moments her world came to an end.

The bunkhouse was still flaming, but all that remained of the cabin was a few smoldering logs and the rock chimney. The corral had been broken down and the horses were gone.

Blood and feathers from the chicken coop were scattered over the yard; the shoat was gone, escaped into the wilderness from which he had come. The heavy pall of smoke and dust obscured Jed's vision; terror mingled with the crackling and creaking of the burning bunkhouse to impair his hearing. He couldn't see her.

He brought his horse up so hard that its back legs skidded and it almost went down, but Jed was out of the saddle before the motion was even completed. A scream was tearing out of him, but he couldn't form the word. And then he saw her.

She was kneeling in the churned-up dirt near the smoky remnants of the cabin. A small and huddled figure in a gray gown, her hair wild and tumbled over her shoulders, her head was bowed over something in her hands. In swift, heartleaping steps he was beside her. He caught her shoulders and pulled her to her feet, terror blazing on his face and hoarsening his voice. "Elizabeth, my God—what . . . dear God."

For a moment he could say nothing else. She was alive. The knowledge made him dizzy. Alive but. . . . He couldn't even strengthen his muscles to draw her close. Behind him the roof of the bunkhouse fell in with a crash, and acrid sparks danced into the bright sky.

She opened her hand. "Look," she said simply. Her voice was quiet, calm. "Look what they've done."

In her hand she held a clump of soil and a crushed poppy leaf. Panic threaded through him again with pincerlike tongues of flame, and he searched her face. It was white, streaked with soot and tears, and old, too old. Her dress was dotted with cinder burns and torn at the hem. He could barely make his voice come out in a whisper. "What did they do to you? Did they—did they touch you? Did they hurt you?"

She shook her head. There was nothing in her face except

exhaustion and an awful, awful emptiness that tore at his soul. "They didn't see me. I hid from them."

He went weak.

"Indians," she added tiredly. She looked around slowly. "They burned everything."

Jed heard the approaching horses, and his gun was in his hand before the thought was completed. Dusty dismounted a horse that was still running, Skunk and Rio not far behind. "We saw the smoke," he said, striding over to them. "Miss Elizabeth, are you all right?"

Dusty went to her and Skunk and Rio crowded around. There was swearing and confusion. Rio said, "I will look for sign."

Skunk met Jed's eyes quietly. "Shod horses."

Jed's face went black. He shoved his pistol back into his holster. He had taken two strides toward his worn and beaten horse before Skunk was down from the saddle, catching Jed's shoulder.

"Get out of my way, you son of a bitch." Jed's voice was quiet, but his eyes were dark with murder. "I'm going to kill him."

"Not now you ain't."

Jed flung up his hand and would have knocked Skunk to the ground if the larger man hadn't caught his wrist.

Jed ground out, "I said get out of my goddamn way or I swear to God I'll shoot you first."

Skunk's eyes were narrowed on him. "Damn right you got killin' to do, and if you don't do it, I will. But right now you got somethin' else to take care of."

Skunk's eyes went over Jed's shoulder, and there was Elizabeth. Dusty was with her, touching her arm awkwardly, trying to talk to her. She just stood there.

Fury, swift and hot and hating, filled Jed, choked him, cut off his breath. He wanted to be moving, acting; he wanted to chase down justice and execute it at the point of a gun, and that was all he wanted. Any other time, any other place, it would have been his. But there was Elizabeth.

Elizabeth, who had been terrorized, who had seen her home go up in flames, who had hidden and watched while violence destroyed all that she had. Elizabeth, who was so fragile and so afraid.

She looked at him. He had to go to her.

She said quietly, "You told me there was no danger from the Indians. You told me they wouldn't come here."

He reached for her. "Elizabeth, it wasn't Indians, it was—"

"No!" She drew back from him as though she had been slapped, and her eyes went wild. She screamed at him, "No, I don't want to hear any more of your lies! You told me I was safe, you told me not to be afraid! You told me you would take care of me, and this—" She flung her arm out wide. "This is what happened! Look at it, Jed! Look at what they've done! There's nothing left. Nothing! You promised you wouldn't let anything happen, but you lied, didn't you? *You lied.*"

Jed's face twisted with the effort to subdue his pain.

She took a shaky breath; she unclenched her hand slowly and let the earth and crushed flowers fall to the ground. She held her head up high, and those eyes that he loved so well were brilliant with anger and pain. "You've won, Jed," she said. Her voice was shaky, but she kept it coherent. "You told me—dear God in heaven knows you told me—and you were right."

He looked at her, so small and broken, and every second that passed tore another piece from his soul. He lifted his hands and took her shoulders lightly. Dusty, who had been hovering protectively, walked away. "Elizabeth, they're gone. I'm here now." He tried to keep his voice calm, though something inside him was threatening to break it in two. "I know what this has done to you, but it's over now. We can—"

"No." The single word was firm. "No, it's never over. It goes on and on, and there's no stop to it. It's in the air, it's in the soil, it breeds like a disease, and there's no stopping it, not ever. I can't live like this. I was never meant to live like this. I'm going home."

A blade went through his heart. He tried to pull her closer. "Elizabeth, you are home—"

She tried to twist away from him, her face wild again, her voice high. "This is not my home," she flung at him. "It never was! I hate it here, I've always hated it here. I tried, but there's nothing left! Jed, don't you see, there's *nothing left*. I can try and try until I'm dead from trying, and it won't make any difference because you were right, all along you were right!" She wrenched her arm away and stumbled backward, and he could see her hysteria mounting. "I'm going home, do you hear me? I'm going home and you can't stop me!"

He caught her, and she fought him, striking at him with her fists, screaming at him. "Let me go! You did this to me, it's your fault, you promised, and I won't believe you anymore! Let me go!" All he knew to do was to subdue her with his arms, to hold her tight, to bring her against his chest and keep her there while she rained small, ineffectual blows against him, sobbing and struggling.

"Please, don't..." He bent his head into her hair, holding her, aching for her. "Elizabeth, stop..."

The smoke lay still and heavy while burning logs fell in the background. Dusty and Skunk were silent. Jed held her, and gradually her struggles faded into exhaustion, her wild sobs into weak hiccoughs, and she clung to him, trembling. All he could do was hold her and die a little inside with each passing moment.

So close, he thought, and the horror that ignited inside him with the realization swelled into something big and cold, blotting out the sun. *How close we came.* . . . It could have happened at any time. It lurked hidden in shadowed corners or it sprang, full-grown and terrible, into the light, but always it was waiting to snatch her away. They could have killed her.

Uncounted times the shadow had hovered and then faded: on the ship at Galveston; beneath the hooves of wild cattle in a storm; from a bullet meant for him.

She was right. It never ended; it only got worse. So far they had been lucky. But how many more chances could he afford to take?

Her shoulders shuddered with dying sobs, her fingers wound into the material of his shirt, twisting it. She whispered brokenly, "Take me home, Jed. I want my papa. I want to go home. I'm so tired and scared and I can't stay here anymore . . . please, take me home. Please . . ."

He closed his eyes, struggling for a deep breath he couldn't find.

But in the end there was nothing he could do. He held and soothed her, and then promised her the last thing that was his to give. "Hush," he murmured. "Of course I'll take you home. It's over now, don't cry. You'll have your papa; you'll go home. I promise, I'll take you home."

CHAPTER
Twenty-three

A long plume of dust wound across the country-side hazing the dull greens and early-autumn yellows of East Texas with a gritty film. Almost seven hundred head of cattle were plodding south and east, headed toward the Sabine. Disinterested, desultory creatures, the cattle traveled in a loose bunch, following the lead steer. Four trained cowhands fanned out around the herd, keeping it moving, cutting off strays, collecting the weak and the lame from the drag position. Men and animals were an enormous, well-oiled machine as they cut a path across the land.

The morning was slow and easy, the cattle sluggish, their keepers familiar with the routine. Dusty used his hat to wave back a straying steer and then worked his way slowly up the herd, falling into pace at last beside Skunk.

Skunk glanced at him. "Any sign yet?"

Dusty wiped his hand across his face, leaving a streak of

dust and sweat. His eyes were narrowed to the sun. "Nope. Not a one."

Skunk broke off a square of tobacco and stuffed it between his gums. "Cain't believe they're gonna let us git all the way to the Sabine."

He offered the tobacco to his partner, and Dusty helped himself. "What I can't believe is that we're driving cattle when we should be huntin' down murderin' horse thieves."

Skunk shifted the wad of tobacco to the other cheek. "Don't see we got much choice."

"Makes me damn nervous, them outlaws riding around out there somewheres, needin' killing so bad."

But Dusty's eyes had wandered across the shifting, shuffling body of the herd to the small figure on horseback opposite. He said quietly, "Do you think she's really gonna leave us?"

Skunk leaned over to spit on the ground. "Reckon so."

"Jed won't let her go."

"Ain't much a man can do about it, onct a woman's made up her mind."

Dusty frowned at him. "He's married to her, ain't he?"

"Them was mighty bitter words," Skunk ruminated absently, "even for married folk. And that little woman, she's had a hard row to hoe. Mayhap she don't even know a harder one lays awaitin' for her."

Dusty did not know what Skunk meant by that, and he wasn't sure he wanted to know. He chewed silently on his tobacco wad for a while, spat, and chewed some more. Then he ventured cautiously, "You don't reckon he wants her to go, do you?"

"Don't know. Don't care. But I sure am gonna miss her myself."

Both of their eyes moved across the swaying, dusty backs of the herd to the feminine figure opposite. It was hard to believe that only four months had passed since she had first come into their lives. So much had changed since then.

She rode sidesaddle, as elegant as a princess in her dusty gray gown and battered man's hat, her shoulders square, her spine straight, her hands dainty on the reins. As they watched, a steer broke and began to wander, and she effortlessly cantered after it, her skirts ruffling in the breeze, bringing it back into herd with a few deft movements of her pony.

Skunk chuckled softly. "Look at that little gal. Be damned if I ever seen the like. Why, I'd have her ropin' better than Rio in another six weeks."

Dusty grinned. "Yeah. I reckon there ain't much she can't do."

Skunk commented only, "Pity she don't know it, ain't it?"

He nudged his horse forward of the herd where the lead steer was beginning to veer off-course.

At first the days had been a blur for Elizabeth; she did not remember eating or sleeping or moving around. Almost before she knew it, she was riding alongside a herd of steer, heading for the cattle station on the Sabine. There an agent would buy their stock and Jed would use some of the proceeds to escort Elizabeth via steamboat back to Mobile.

Her senses had been numb, her reason a dim and shallow thing trapped far within the recesses of her mind. She dared not think or feel. She performed the routine tasks of living by rote but kept herself silent and apart from the men, caring for nothing, thinking of nothing.

But the human spirit was a remarkable thing, an entity all its own. Almost without her being aware of it—certainly without her desiring it—she began to come back to life and the process of living.

Life on the trail was hard and basic, and the sheer physical demand of it caused a gradual though not entirely painless resurgence of awareness. One by one her senses returned to her. One day—two or three days into the ride, she could not be sure—she noticed the mesmerizing beauty of pine logs burning in the camp fire, the clear, aromatic path wood smoke cut across the cleanness of the air. She became aware of the heavy taste of dust driven up by the cattle and the cool, sharp relief of fresh water on her throat.

That night she heard the low singing of the cowhands as they circled the herd, calming and reassuring them, and the answering wail of a coyote. It was a peculiarly beautiful thing, lonely and at the same time free.

As though her eyes were opening slowly and reluctantly after a long sleep, she began to see the sun again—first as though through a hazy filter of disbelief and then in all its brilliance, a clear white-gold light that etched the land in vermilions and emerald shadows and sparkled like diamonds on a clear stream. The incredible blueness of the sky, deeper and richer and more endless in color than it had ever seemed to her before, was a source of never-ending wonder to her. At night the stars, thousands of them, hung suspended in the velvet folds of the sky like countless fireflies daring capture. She closed her eyes, dazzled by starlight and soothed by distant singing, and slept deeply and dreamlessly until the first pink-gray rays of dawn caressed her cheek into wakefulness.

Gradually she began to assume duties as cook, freeing Rio for more time with the cattle. She began to listen to the talk over the camp fire and sometimes even joined in. Because she was riding alongside the herd, anyway, it was only natural that she would begin to enact some of the responsibilities of a drover.

She smiled now and leaned down to pet the neck of her

mount, rewarding him for the good job he had done in returning the stray to the herd. It had taken the men almost two days to round up the horses that had been released from the corral, but now Elizabeth understood why they had gone to so much trouble. Each and every one of the animals was a trained cow pony who knew his job so well, he hardly needed a man in the saddle to guide him. They were invaluable on a drive such as this.

Elizabeth remembered the first time her horse had gone after a runaway steer. She had been startled out of her lethargy, then frightened, then delighted as she saw the clever little pony's intentions. He had circled the steer, blocking its movements, nudging it back into the herd with his shoulder, and all without any instruction at all from Elizabeth. Amazement and pleasure broke in a smile across her face, and it felt like an alien experience, the ability to smile.

Then Jed had ridden up. For the first time since that awful day beside the burned-out ruins of her home, their eyes had met. But his face was shadowed by his hat, and his voice was casual as he instructed her on how to guide the movements of her pony more easily. She had smiled at him and, for a moment, had forgotten all that had gone before.

In some strange way, as the days passed she felt more alive than she had ever been before, each sensory impression concentrated to its full awareness of the moment. It was an intense and self-limiting world on the trail, demanding much but giving even more in return. From dawn to dusk there was movement, constant demands on her attention, new impressions to absorb and experience, and there was little time to think. Perhaps, after all, that was the only trick to living: just to keep on moving.

*   *   *

It was nearing noon and time to give the herd a rest while the drovers took a brief meal and watered the horses.

Dusty trotted up and slowed his horse to Elizabeth's pace, gesturing with his arm. "There's a stream over yonder. Rio already took the horses up."

Elizabeth nodded and turned her horse in the direction he indicated. The men would expect beans on the fire by the time they came in from settling the herd. To her surprise Dusty rode with her.

"Pretty country, ain't it?" he commented after a while.

Leaving behind the clouds of dust and black flies that hovered over the herd, she could see the sweeping panorama of pastoral, meadowlike greenery, broken at intervals by ancient oaks and elms. In the distance ground cover was beginning to turn shades of crimson and yellow, and the air was sharp with the smell of water.

Elizabeth smiled almost wistfully. Why had she never noticed before how bright colors could be, how serene and soothing the shadows? Or perhaps she had noticed and just had forgotten.

"Yes," she agreed, "it is. It seems a bit cooler today too."

"Gonna be a mild winter."

They rode in silence for a while, putting the noise and dust farther behind them. Elizabeth resisted the impulse to turn in the saddle and, from her new vantage point, scan the landscape for Jed.

He was riding point today. He alternated between point and drag, sometimes scouting ahead for water but never riding flank with her. She was grateful for that, for it still was too hard to look at him. At mealtimes, over the camp fire at night, or curled up in her blanket beneath the stars when she couldn't ignore his presence, the sound of his voice, or a glimpse of his profile—those were the hardest times. The memories would come flooding back, and the hurt and yearning sometimes formed like a whimper in the pit of her stomach. She was finding it harder and harder to slam the door on those feelings, to coldly extinguish the memories, to keep buried what would haunt her for the rest of her life.

At night she could hear the sound of his breathing, lying in his own bedroll a few feet from her. In the morning she could not resist watching surreptitiously as he stamped into his boots and combed back his hair with his fingers before putting on his hat. But when he spoke to her, thanking her for the cup of coffee she handed him or telling her briefly about the next campsite, she could never meet his eyes. She was always afraid of what she would find there or what she would remember. She didn't want to think, she didn't want to question, she didn't want to yearn.

But day by day it became harder to resist the need to look at him, to be near him, to cautiously explore the prickles of pain and confusion his presence caused—and at the same time to take comfort in it. Jed, and all he represented, was like a habit or an addiction she struggled to break. She sometimes wondered if she would ever succeed in being free of him completely. Her frightening and heart-twisting suspicion was that the answer was no.

Dusty drew up closer, distracting her from the painful course her thoughts had taken. His face was sober. "Miss Elizabeth," he said simply and very unexpectedly, "I don't want you to go."

Elizabeth stiffened in the saddle, but there was no avoiding it any longer. For days now, reality had been hovering at the edge of her consciousness, and she was no longer able to pretend this was a journey leading nowhere.

She said quietly, her eyes straight ahead, "I have to, Dusty. You should know that better than anyone." She looked at him, and she could not keep the pain and the confusion from straining her face and voice. "Oh, Dusty, after all you've lived through, how can you stand it? Aren't you ever afraid?"

He pushed back his hat a little and said thoughtfully, "I reckon I am. Not of dyin', though. No point in that. When a man's time is up, it's up, and ain't much you can do about that. Besides, dyin' ain't the point to it all, is it? It's living."

"But why do you do this to yourself?" she insisted. Her hands tightened on the reins. "After the way your family died, how can you be so calm about the Indian attack? How can you just go back and face them again?"

Dusty looked at her with the faintest shadow of puzzlement on his face, and then he said gently, "Miss Elizabeth, them wasn't Indians that attacked the cabin. It was a bunch of outlaws and no-account white men led by some fancy dude the boss calls Hartley."

Elizabeth gasped. "Lord Hartley! But . . . Dusty, are you sure?"

He nodded grimly. "It was them that stampeded our herd and shot up the cabin that time too. If we'd'a tracked 'em down and shot 'em like the varmints they are the first time," he added bitterly, "none of this would've happened and you wouldn't be going East."

Elizabeth shook her head, somewhat dazed. "But . . . I saw them. They were Indians. Their faces were painted and they had feathers and—"

Dusty shrugged. "An old trick for cowards. They knew about the Cherokee trouble, figured it'd be easy to blame it on the Indians. Maybe they just thought you'd be scareder of Indians than white men, if scarin' you was what they had in mind. I don't know." Again he shrugged, scowling. "There ain't no figuring a man like this Hartley. Give me an

Indian any day; at least you know what to expect from them. But a crazy white man . . ." He let the sentence trail off.

Elizabeth tried to absorb this, but everything within her wanted to deny it. Lord Hartley, so refined, so contained, so proper in every way—he was in so many ways the epitome of the life she was going back to.

She said, "Dusty, you don't understand. Lord Hartley . . . I know he has his faults, but surely he isn't capable of something like this. I know him. He's a gentleman, and one of the most civilized men I've ever met. I can't imagine he would be capable of the kind of violence you're accusing him of." But then she remembered the fistfight on the ship, and she knew her protests were hollow. She had been trying to convince herself more than Dusty, anyway.

Dusty wiped his sweaty forehead with his sleeve. "Sometimes civilization is just somethin' men hide behind, ma'am," he said. "It's got nothing to do with whether you're good or bad, weak or strong."

He glanced at her. "Just like you," he said. "Who would've thought a frilly little thing like you, all prim and proper, would be ridin' herd like a cowhand? That first day you rode up in the wagon—why, I thought you'd be turnin' tail inside a week. But you fooled us all, you surely did. For all your pretty ways you're the strongest woman I ever met."

That touched her like an accusing finger, causing a shock of hurt and regret to well up in her chest. She took a shaky breath, trying to push the emotions away. "I'm not strong, Dusty," she said softly. "It just took me a little longer to break than you thought."

"Miss Elizabeth, you ain't broke." Dusty's voice was flat and certain. "It maybe feels like it now, but you got more to you than that."

No, she thought, *I don't. I left my home for the wild*

frontier, I escaped death by fire and water, I married a man who didn't want me. I've lived with loneliness and fear, and I've fought for my husband's love without ever quite winning it. I've survived a madman's bullets and my own nightmares, but this is too much. I can't take any more.

She said softly, "I can't go back, Dusty. There's nothing to go back to. Everything I tried to do, everything we built and hoped and planned for . . . it's all gone. I've lost everything."

He made a soft sound that might have been a grunt of astonishment, and he shook his head slowly. "Miss Elizabeth, do you know how many times I've lost everything? Wandering across country, tryin' to stay alive, you stop, you cut trees for a cabin, you build a winter shelter, you throw up a corral. Then the Comanche come, or the lightning strikes, or the floodwaters rise, or it all goes down in a rock slide. Then you move on, you fell more trees, you put it up again, and you're glad to be able to do it.

"Me, I make my shelter in a cave or weave branches to keep the wind and rain off. I break a few mustangs, I hire on with a Mexican outfit for a month or two. It don't much matter where I am or what I'm doing, long as I can feed myself. I've been with Three Hills going on three winters now, but it never was a home until you came."

He looked at her. His eyes were pale blue and foggy but serious. "Ma'am, it's a mighty hard thing for a woman to lose the things she's proud of, and I reckon I know it. But there's always more trees to be cut, more pegs to be hammered. Store-bought yard goods and pots and pans and the like, they can be replaced. But the things you gave us when you came to live on the ranch . . . well, there just ain't no replacing them. And there won't be no bringin' them back once you're gone."

Elizabeth swallowed hard and turned her eyes back to the path ahead. She said nothing.

But Dusty's words stayed with her, playing back and forth inside her head, coming to haunt her at odd moments for the rest of the day and throughout the night. And no matter how hard she tried, she could no longer stop herself from looking back.

CHAPTER
Twenty-four

T wo more days of traveling put them forty miles closer to journey's end, and that much farther away from the three rolling hills where Elizabeth had enacted a lifetime of growing, learning, and loving in one short summer. They had camped at the edge of a piny forest where a shallow stream meandered through a rocky bed, awaiting the rains of autumn to swell it. Sunset was fiery pink and dusky violet, mingling with the glow of the camp fire to paint their faces in lazily shifting auras of color.

Rio had found some dried chile peppers in the bottom of his saddlebag and added it to the beef and wild onions Elizabeth boiled for supper to make a tasty change from their usual fare. The coffee was thick enough to float a horseshoe, and Elizabeth had found time to fry up some cornmeal batter into a thicker version of Rio's tortillas. The meal was good, and spirits were easy. This was the time of day Elizabeth liked best about life on the trail and, she suspected, the memory that would linger the longest.

Twilight grew in darkening shadows, and fireflies danced through the pine boughs. Dusty came in to eat, and Rio left to take his place with the cattle. "They're quiet tonight," he commented, filling his plate. "Everything's as peaceful as can be."

Skunk said, "They're holding up right well, ain't lost a head. How much further you think, boss?"

Jed was sitting back from the fire, avoiding the light that could endanger his night vision. He glanced at Skunk, and his eyes accidentally met Elizabeth's. An instant, nothing more, but it was enough to make his chest twist. He dropped his eyes to his cup and sipped the coffee. "A week, maybe, if the weather holds."

"How much you think you'll get?"

"Twenty a head, easy. Sam said the price has gone to thirty-five in New Orleans."

Skunk grunted. "Still better than drivin' em all the way south. Let somebody else get saddle sores. I'll take the money."

Elizabeth knew that, had it not been for her, Jed would have made the drive to New Orleans and gotten top price for his herd. She felt guilty for that. Guilt was another new and bewildering emotion she found hard to handle—just like the one that had fluttered through her so briefly when Jed's eyes slid across hers.

She said, "I still don't see why you go to so much trouble to drive the cattle south. There are plenty of cattle farms in Louisiana and Alabama, but once, when Papa came back from New York, he said there wasn't a decent beefsteak to be found in the whole town, and even then it cost as much as a night's lodging. With all the cities and people up there it's no wonder! It's up north where they need the beef—

why, I'll bet you could get fifty dollars a head in New York."

Dusty paused with his fork halfway to his mouth. "Lord-y, Miss Elizabeth, do you know how long that'd take?"

Skunk guffawed. "Them critters'd be nothing but skin and bones, and we'd be walking on our bellies for a month."

Dusty agreed, "There's been folks that tried it, Miss Elizabeth, but it just ain't worth it. Too many risks and too blasted hard. It'd take a mighty determined man to carry a drive like that through."

Even Jed was smiling, and catching a glimpse of it, Elizabeth felt a wave of something sweet and light go through her. She had to drag her attention back to Dusty.

"Well, you wouldn't have to take them all the way to New York," she insisted. "What about the railroad?"

He hooted. "Buy tickets for a bunch of cows?"

"Why not?" she insisted stubbornly. "Wouldn't it be just as cheap to put them on a railroad car as to pay an agent to take them down the river on flatboats?"

There was a moment of silence while they tried to think of an argument to that female logic. Then Jed's voice surprised her. "The nearest railhead is still quite a way up the road."

He rarely, if ever, addressed her directly, and the fact that he was doing so now startled Elizabeth—but only for a moment. It was a familiar habit to counteract his objections and his certainties, and she fell into it without thinking. "Then drive them up the road," she replied.

He looked at her patiently. "There's no trail."

"Then make one. You've got to start somewhere."

A sharp and unexpected stab of wistfulness went through Jed with those words. Elizabeth walking into a pigsty and turning it into a home. Making them all sit down at a table and eat with napkins. Elizabeth, eyes flaming, righteously defending her determination. *You've got to start somewhere.*

She hadn't changed. The woman who had transformed a cabin in the wilderness was ready to take on the entire cattle industry. The knowledge collided inside Jed with a surge of pride, amazement, and deep longing.

He did not know when it had happened, this subtle unity with her, this habit of relying upon her thoughts and her opinions, to guide his own. Elizabeth was intensely involved in everything he did; she had taken up a part of his life he had never expected to share with anyone. Elizabeth had become his partner in all things, making him need her in ways of which he was not yet even aware.

She hadn't changed. And he loved her so much, he couldn't even look at her.

Dusty, wolfing down his dinner in a few swift bites, went for a refill. "I imagine that sounds a lot easier than it'd be, Miss Elizabeth."

Elizabeth reluctantly tore her eyes away from Jed and looked back to Dusty. What had she seen in her husband's face for just those few moments? And why had it made her feel like crying and laughing at the same time?

She replied with simple certainty, "You never know until you try."

Skunk shook his head, not wanting to laugh at her. "Miss Elizabeth, you beat everything, you know that? Next you'll be telling God how to make a better sunrise."

Jed's lips twisted down in a rueful, unexpected smile. "That's my wife. She always was one to set out an opinion on everything, whether she knew anything about it or not."

There was a moment of startled silence in which everyone, perhaps, realized they might have gone too far. Then Elizabeth laughed. It was so natural, so easy; it was just like the old times. A ripple of pleasure went around the camp fire, all of them chuckling together as though they didn't have a care in the world. Elizabeth knew of all the memories she would hold dear, this would be one of the most precious. It felt so good to laugh again.

Then it came to her, as insidious as the night, what she had known all along but had chosen not to look at before now. *She would never see them again.* Skunk, with his abominable personal habits and blunt, coarse speech; Dusty, the closest thing to a friend her own age she had had since Margaret; Rio, with his quick grin and easy humor, who had taught her how to cook and had risked his life at the hands of a wild boar for her; she would never see any of them again.

Skunk should find himself a woman and settle down to build his own ranch. Dusty, who had his whole life before him, shouldn't be wasting his days with someone else's cattle. And Rio—why, the possibilities were endless for a man with his natural charm and valued skills in this brave new land. *I wish for you all,* she thought, *the best of the life that lies before you. A home, and happiness, and a woman who will love you and take care of you.*

But she would never know. She would not see them again.

And Jed . . .

The laughter had died away, and her eyes were helplessly drawn to those of the man in the shadows. There was gentleness on his face, a softening in his eyes that held a message that was too painful to read.

My wife, he had said, and the words sounded as natural as her very next breath. Long ago he had tried to send her away from him, and she had stubbornly refused to go. *We are married, Elizabeth, and nothing is going to change that.*

And nothing ever would. But she would never see him again.

She had to drop her eyes, and a tightness was cutting off her breath from stomach to lungs. She couldn't sit still anymore and look at him, so close but out of reach to her forever. She couldn't pretend that nothing was wrong, nothing had changed. Everything had changed, and she couldn't sit here anymore at all.

Quickly and without a word, she got up and left the campsite.

Ten minutes had passed, or perhaps even twenty, before she heard the soft footsteps. She was leaning against a pine, its bittersweet resin teasing her nostrils, its rough surface offering support for her head and her spine. Silently she watched the night creep out of the wood, and she did not have to look around to know who approached. It was something a wife recognized instinctively—the sound of her husband's footsteps, the beat of his heart as it lay beneath her cheek, his heavy breathing in the depth of sleep . . . parts of him as familiar to her as her own body. All the things that made her married.

It was strange, but she could not cry. The memories—the sweetness, the laughter, the anger, the hopelessness, and the yearning—flooded through her veins and twisted around her heart. She had tried so hard and lost so much. She wanted to cry, but the tears wouldn't come. It was almost as though she had known, somewhere deep down inside, from the very first moment, that destiny would bring her to this place. Just as there was a simple inevitability about Jed's standing beside her now in the silence of twilight, waiting for words that needed to be said, knowing that words would make no difference now.

Elizabeth spoke first, softly. "I never understood before. Now I know what it is about this life that calls you."

Through the parting of a pine bough overhead she could

see the contained brilliance of a single star, and she smiled a little. "It's as though . . . out here, with the stars and the night sounds and not another person for as far as you can imagine, there never was another world. Each day is like being born again, a whole new chance at life. And when you look back and see the tracks you've left across the land, it's . . . I don't know, it makes you feel large and powerful. As though you were a part of something very important."

She turned her head against the tree and looked at him. She felt quiet and calm, sad but certain inside. It wasn't hard to say these things to him. It was the last thing they could share. "I was foolish ever to think you could be a farmer. I wouldn't want it for you now."

Jed's face was planed in the shadows, looking as serene and matter-of-fact as she felt. The last time they had met alone she had been sobbing hysterically in his arms, their hearts and minds torn apart as they watched the world they had built together in ashes at their feet. On another night much like this the air had been rich with the scent of roses and the sound of distant music, and they had stepped into each other's arms and begun the pattern that would change their destinies. Another world ago and they had been different people then. But all of it, from beginning to end, had been leading up to no more than this moment.

Jed's voice was quiet and thoughtful. "I'm not sure about much, but I've always known this was the life for me. And it's about the only thing left worth fighting for."

Elizabeth turned her head, looking again through the spiky branches at the darkening canopy of the sky. That, too, she had always known but refused to understand.

Once, long ago, she had asked him what kind of men went West. Now she knew the answer was men who could not live any other way. Men compelled to try the untried, to explore the unknown, to live close to life and to make a difference, they came West. They would work, they would fight, and they would die, and when they were gone, this new frontier would be their legacy to the world.

He was her husband, but his destiny was here. And she would never see him again.

She said quietly, "Dusty told me about Lord Hartley."

The horses, picketed not far away, shuffled and nickered. In the distance was the muffled low of a steer. The movement of the stream was a sigh and a whisper. Jed said, "Hartley told me a long time ago he was going to destroy me. I guess he's a man of his word, if nothing else."

Elizabeth turned to him, confusion pulling at her brow. "But why?"

"The reasons don't matter. The point is I'm not going to let him."

His tone was quiet, inarguable, just as was the man himself. Perhaps that had always been the difference between them—Jed, who saw what had to be done and did it; and Elizabeth, who could see no further than the end of her dreams. Jed was a survivor, but Elizabeth knew when she was defeated.

She said softly, "I wish I had your courage."

"It's not a matter of courage. It's just knowing when you don't have a choice."

Elizabeth turned her head away again, leaning against the tree. Jed had to breathe deeply to ease the hurting in his chest. Even now, after a week on the trail, she looked beautiful. With nothing but the gray dress she had been wearing the day the cabin burned, her hair caught at the nape of her neck with a piece of rawhide, her hands roughened by the reins and her shoes worn almost to shreds by the stirrup, she was still as elegant and as poised as the night she had stood before him in silk and lace in the Spring Hill garden. She was still the embodiment of all he had ever dreamed of, only more. Then she had been his fantasy. Now she was his reality and the only part of his life that had ever mattered.

He said, with difficulty, "Elizabeth . . . I never would have left you alone that day. The Cherokee braves had been watching the house for me, in case anything happened. But Hartley must have been watching, too, and he knew exactly when they moved out."

Elizabeth looked at him in slow surprise. The very Indians whom she had accused of attacking her had in fact been protecting her. . . . There was irony in that, but the real irony lay in the fact that even after all she had endured, she had learned so little—about her husband, the life he loved, and the ways of the land that guided him. Someday, perhaps, she would reflect on that with wonder and sorrow, but now all she could manage to feel was emptiness.

She said, "It doesn't matter anymore."

His voice was heavy. "No. I guess it doesn't."

The silence drew out. Elizabeth linked her hands together and felt the smooth bark of her wedding ring. She looked down at it, twisting it slowly around her finger. At last she felt the sting of tears. But it still was a pain too deep to release, and the tears clung to her, filling up her chest and burning in her throat, and would not spill.

How could she stop loving him just because she could not live with him? The very world in which he thrived would eventually destroy her, but if she asked him to come back with her . . . then he would die. He would suffocate in the conventions, he would wither from the lack of challenge, he would lose all that made him the man she loved. There was no place for him in Alabama, just as there was no place for her in Texas. They had never had a chance together.

She turned her eyes to the heavens again and caught the twinkle of a single star. She said softly, "Do you remember that night on the deck of the ship? You were so cruel to me, and I though my heart was broken forever.''

Jed said quietly, ''I only wanted the best for you.''

She nodded, swallowing hard. They had come so far together. ''And then . . . when the ship crashed . . . I was so frightened. I thought it was the worst thing that could ever happen to me, to almost die . . . but it was the most wondrous, because you were there for me, even then.''

''All I ever wanted to do was to take care of you.'' The small breath he took was not quite steady. ''But in the end I couldn't, could I?''

Elizabeth spent a long time staring at the star. ''You shouldn't have to take care of me,'' she answered at last, softly. ''You were right all along. It takes a special kind of person to make it out here. And I'm not that kind.''

He touched her shoulder very lightly, and then let his hand fall away. ''But we made it for a while, didn't we?'' he said huskily. ''We were happy . . .''

''Yes.'' It was barely a breath, and she had to close her eyes.

She struggled to keep her voice even, but still the whisper came out thick with unshed tears. She could not take her eyes off the ring on her finger, which she stroked absently with a shaky fingertip. ''Jed, I am so sorry.''

His reply was gentle and puzzled. ''For what?''

''For being so wrong—about everything.''

She heard his quick intake of breath, and he stepped toward her. ''You weren't wrong, Elizabeth.''

Jed took her hand between his fingers, holding it lightly, the rough pad of his thumb gently caressing the slender shape of bones and flesh. His eyes were on their joined hands, and his face was sober. His voice was quiet, and he spoke as if it were an effort. ''Having you . . . even for a little while, was the only thing that ever happened in my life worth remembering. You're the best friend I ever had, Elizabeth," he said simply, and he raised his eyes to her. "How can that be wrong?"

He saw the surprise in her eyes, the pain and questioning, and his fingers tightened on hers. An urgency twisted in his chest, and he did not know how he would be able to speak. But the words pushed through, slow and hurting, deep and certain, words that made no difference now but words that demanded to be said. "I should be sorry. I knew—from the beginning I knew—and I never should have let it happen. I could have stopped it all, at any time from the first moment I saw you until the day we left Galveston for Three Hills . . . but I didn't."

He dropped his eyes, focusing for a long and absorbed moment on the willow ring that adorned her finger. "I should be sorry," he said, and there was a choking, swelling sensation in his throat. "But I'm not. I wouldn't have done anything differently if I had it to live over again a thousand times, because there's that much selfishness in me. . . ."

He had to stop and take a shaky breath. Slowly he lifted his eyes, and there was torment in them he could not hide. He brought his hand up and lightly touched her raven-black hair. His voice was unsteady, no matter how hard he tried to strengthen it. "Oh, Elizabeth," he whispered, "I love you. I know it doesn't matter now, but I do."

He saw her eyes in the darkness, filmed with a brilliant pool of tears, anxious and torn with helplessness. He could hear the beat of her heart in each broken syllable of her voice. "Don't you know how badly I've wanted to hear that? Why . . . why did you never tell me before?"

He almost could not answer. His throat was tight enough to break, and his heartbeat was nothing but a strangled impulse deep within the center of his chest. He said, with difficulty, "Sometimes . . . I guess you have to lose everything before you know what it was you had."

Elizabeth let her head fall back against the tree again. He saw a single tear slip down her cheek, picking up particles of light and glistening for a moment before disappearing against the corner of her mouth. Her whisper sounded tired, broken. "What a waste it's all been."

"No." His hand tightened on hers, and he moved closer to her. "Never a waste."

"I've brought you nothing but trouble and sorrow from the beginning . . . just as you knew I would." Her voice was flat and empty. Another tear, cold and futile, rolled down her cheek. "I couldn't fight for you, I couldn't agree with you, I was never there when you needed me. The things that I tried to do weren't important at all, and now that I'm gone, no one will ever know I was there. I've failed . . . you and myself and my marriage vows, and the worst part of it all is that it doesn't even matter."

Jed touched her face and made her look at him. His eyes were as deep as the night, his face gentle enough to break her heart. "You brought me," he said, "a big white house in the valley with columns and a porch you can dance on. You brought me kisses in the morning and soft words at night. You made me angry and you made me weak, and I never knew I could be either before. You made every day a surprise, and you made me know what it was to be part of something bigger than myself. I don't deserve all the things you brought me, and I never expected them, but nothing about me will ever be the same, because you were there. That's a big thing, Elizabeth. A mighty big thing. Don't ever say any of it was a waste."

The pain welled up in her, full and alive. Jed, who had taught her about loving and fighting and standing strong; Jed, who had tamed a wolf and made a Mexican prisoner into a loyal friend; Jed, with his dreams of making a fortune on wild Texas cattle, of carving a home out of the wilderness. She would never see those dreams come true. She would never live in his house between three hills. But she never would be the same, either, because he had touched her life.

Jed's fingers were unsteady as he brushed them against her cheek, catching a tear there. He wanted to tell her to come home with him. He wanted to promise things would be different. . . .

But nothing would be different. Nothing he could do would make it different, and he could never ask her to come back.

But how could he live without her?

On a single stifled breath they came together, their arms winding tightly around each other, desperate heartbeats fusing. She drew in broken breaths against his shirt, and he buried his face in her hair. When their mouths met, it was with blind hunger and the taste of tears and the desperate, desperate need to satisfy an emptiness that could not be filled.

They held each other, wrapped around each other by muscles that trembled but would not let go. His breathing was ragged against her neck. Her face was wet against his shirt. The night was throbbing and far away, and they clung to each other silently.

They held each other while the night shadows lengthened and the moon cast its first glimmering beams through the needles of the pine boughs overhead. Neither of them could bear to let go.

But in the end they had no choice.

CHAPTER
Twenty-five

*I*t was the darkest, deadliest hour of the night. The moon had just fallen below the horizon, and the dawn was an eternity away. Dew lay like a shroud upon the land, and the air was a still cold breath waiting to be drawn.

Beneath the shadow of a broken rock, five men rolled out of their bedrolls. They donned their hats and shook out their boots in silence. One went to relieve himself, and the crackling of his stream against the leaves was a fitful sound. Someone raised phlegm and spat on the ground. Someone else tore off a piece of jerky and began to chew. They went about their business in silence and sureness, seeing with the eyes of the night.

They had made a cold camp and had no coffee, nor any food that could not be eaten cold from the saddlebag. It was the price you paid when you tracked a tracker, and each of them had known worse.

Hartley mounted first. He checked the load in his pistol and rifle with cool calculation. From the height of his saddle he swept his hirelings with a gaze that was distant and laced with contempt. "A last reminder, gentlemen. Fielding is mine. And the first man that lays a hand on the woman will answer at the point of my pistol."

Newt Johnson shot him a look cold with anger and disdain. "We ain't squaw killers, Hartley. If we'd'a wanted the girl we could'a had her before now."

Hartley's lips curled upward in a cold semblance of a smile. "Nonetheless, you will keep her out of the range of your fire. She is a family friend and cannot be held accountable for her bad judgment in husbands. I'll not have her blood on my hands."

The four who stood around him were seasoned men, killers all, and each in their own fashion had traveled a hard road to get to the point where they were now. They had killed for passion, for greed, and because it was convenient. None of them had ever met a man like Hartley, who would defend a woman while murdering her husband. They had never met a man before who killed for no other reason than the fact that he believed it was right, and it was perhaps that which made them all uneasy. Perhaps it was knowing that the man they worked for was just as capable of shooting each one of them dead as he was of paying them to do it to somebody else.

They did not like him, nor trust him. But they had taken his money and they had a job to do. Each of them was glad it was almost over.

Brooks Young spoke up, his eyes narrowed with suspicion. "And the herd is ours?"

"To do with as you please. So I'd advise you keep the noise to a minimum, gentlemen, and not start a stampede."

Methodically the men checked their weapons, tightened

their cinches. They mounted silently and walked their horses into the night, one by one.

Kid Baker fell into step with the man bringing up the rear. They had ridden together before. He said quietly, "I got me a bad feelin' about this one, Jones."

The other man glanced at him. It was a simple job. They would come upon the camp as it was rising, while heads were foggy and fingers were stiff. The night watch would be coming in for breakfast. The woman would be out gathering wood for the fire. It would be simple and quick. A sure thing.

And both men had been living behind a gun for enough years to know there was no such thing as a sure thing.

Jones said after a moment, "You think a man knows when he's gonna die, Kid?"

The other man answered, slowly. "I don't know. Don't reckon it'd make much difference if he did."

"Guess not."

They said nothing else but turned their horses, winding slowly downward toward the sleeping camp. When dawn washed its first pink-and-lemon strokes over the horizon, they paused and looked at it for a long while. Then they moved on.

They had a job to do.

Elizabeth awoke earlier than usual after a restless sleep haunted by memories and half-formed yearnings. Instinctively she reached for Jed and touched only cold, dewy grass. *How long?* she wondered bleakly. *How long will it be before I stop reaching for him?*

In the grainy blue shadows of dawn she could see the sleeping figures of the other men, forming a loose circle around her—Rio, Dusty, and Skunk. Jed would be coming in soon, perhaps was on his way even now. She did not know what would be in his eyes this morning when he looked at her. She only knew what was in her heart. And it was torment.

Silently she got up, wrapping the blanket around her shoulders against the chill and walking over to the coals of the fire. It was too early to start breakfast and she didn't want to wake the men who needed their sleep so badly, but at least she could put the coffee on for them. She added sticks to the coals until they blazed and carefully arranged a few heavy branches that had been gathered the night before. Then she picked up the empty coffee pot.

The pot made a muffled clanging sound as it scraped against a stone, and Dusty was immediately alert, his hand on his rifle even before he had finished sitting up.

Elizabeth whispered, "I'm sorry. Go back to sleep."

A little foggy-eyed, Dusty peered at her. "Where're you going?"

"Just to the spring for water." She started across the camp.

"That's my job," he muttered, and reached for his hat.

"Then do it," growled Skunk, "and let the rest of us get some sleep."

"Miss Elizabeth, wait up." Dusty was pulling on his boots. "Don't you go down there in the dark by yourself."

Elizabeth paused at the edge of the clearing, knowing if she didn't, Dusty would only make more of a fuss. He tucked his pistol into his waistband, grabbed up his rifle, and strode toward her.

Their early rising had disturbed a squirrel who rustled noisily as he jumped across a branch. A winged creature fluttered softly overhead. Something crackled on the pinestraw, and then all was still again. All except . . . all except something that moved in the shadows, something that didn't belong.

Elizabeth never knew what caused her to put it all together. Perhaps the months of living on the edge of danger had sharpened her senses, fine-tuned her nerves to a level of awareness that even she had never fully recognized before. She saw the movement, she froze, and she knew.

A half second before she heard the distinctive click of a rifle bolt she screamed, *"Dusty, look out!"* And then the peaceful dawn erupted into murder.

Dusty flung himself toward her, swinging around at the same moment and firing his rifle into the woods. Fire and sound exploded behind the cover of pines. Skunk and Rio rolled behind their saddles, opening fire that was as natural as taking a breath. Elizabeth dropped the coffeepot, and Dusty staggered backward, his shirtfront flowering red.

It happened in an instant; it took forever. One moment Elizabeth was screaming, the next she was on the ground with Dusty's head cradled in her lap and gunfire whining and roaring all around her, looking into the startled, lifeless eyes of the young boy who had been her friend.

There was no drama to it, no glory. One minute he was alive, and in the space of a heartbeat, he was dead. There was no more movement, no more laughter, no more drawling voice. He was just dead, shot down with no more thought or meaning than an elk or a deer who fell beneath a hunter's bullet. But it wasn't fair, it wasn't right, it made no sense. . . .

"Noooooo!" The scream was a roar of rage that rose up from deep inside her, primal and blinding. Bullets cut the grass between herself and the camp; she saw Rio swing around beneath the impact of a projectile that tore a red hole in his shoulder. Skunk's face, dark and twisted, was yelling at her.

She tugged the pistol from Dusty's belt, and its handle was slippery with blood. Rage drove her, not fear, for what was there left to be afraid of? With both thumbs she pulled the hammer back and squeezed the trigger at the same instant. She did not even feel the recoil that jarred her shoulders and scorched her face. There was satisfaction in it, deep and wild satisfaction. *You won't do this to me,* she thought fiercely. *You won't do this anymore....*

Confused by the pistol shot coming at such close range, the men in the woods lost the fine edge of concentration that could mean the difference. It was a split second of halted fire, but it was all the advantage their enemies needed. The woods were sprayed with rifle fire.

Behind the cover of the pine trees, the dawn turned to blood. Kid Baker felt his belly split with a gush of flame and turned his eyes toward his last sunrise. Bill Jones never felt the bullet that split his skull. Newt Johnson knew a good thing gone bad when he saw it, and he fired only to cover himself as he made his escape. Brooks Young, his shattered arm hanging uselessly by his side, came to realize that no amount of money was worth dying for and wasted no further time in retreat.

Every plan has a flaw. And the flaw in this one had been the girl.

Jed was less than fifty yards from camp when he heard the first shot, but time seemed to freeze and the last few minutes of his horse's pounding hoofbeats lasted an eternity. He had been prepared for this since the moment they had left Three Hills, but nothing could have ever prepared him for it. He approached from the back just in time to see Rio reel from a blow to the shoulder, just as Elizabeth fired the shot from Dusty's pistol. He flung himself to the ground and opened blind fire into the woods, and all he could think about was how to get Elizabeth to cover.

In an instant it was too late.

The picketed horses were screaming and pawing the air. Three rifles sprayed the woods, and no one noticed the figure that darted, as swiftly as a snake, behind Elizabeth.

But Elizabeth noticed, not with her ears but with her senses. She swung around, fired the pistol at point-blank range, and she would have killed him, she would have murdered her father's friend and a peer of the realm without thinking, without being sorry, for even the most civilized person will fight back when pushed too far.

But the pistol, a single-shot percussion-lock device, clicked uselessly.

Hartley grabbed her arm, twisting it behind her, and jerked her to her feet. He shouted, "Hold your fire, Fielding!"

Silence descended like a thunderbolt.

Hartley turned her toward the campsite and pushed her forward. When her ankle brushed against Dusty's lifeless arm, she wanted to scream, but hatred choked back the sound.

She could see Rio, white-faced and semiconscious, leaning against the cover of a tree, his shoulder leaking blood. Only Skunk's hat was visible behind the cover of his saddle. But Jed was in the open, slowly getting to his feet.

Hartley's voice was very calm, his fingers like steel on Elizabeth's throbbing arm. He said, "I could pick you off one by one, you know, with my new advantage. But that wouldn't be very sporting, would it? Kindly leave your weapons, Mr. Fielding, and step out. I want you to see the face of the man who is your executioner. We will settle this between the two of us, as it should have been done from the beginning."

Jed left his rifle behind the fallen log he had been using as cover and stepped over it into the circle of Hartley's full vision. Jed's face was as hard as wood.

Hartley gestured with the rifle he held in perfect firing position at his side. "The pistol, too, if you please."

Jed removed the pistol from his belt and tossed it on the ground a few feet before him. He said quietly, "All right. Now it's just you and me. You don't need to hide behind a woman."

Hartley chuckled. "Not my first choice, I admit. I have no ill feelings for Miss Elizabeth and wish her no harm. But you see, she rather took us by surprise this morning, and now two of my men are dead, two have skulked away like the cowards they were born to be, and I have little alternative. All things considered, Mr. Fielding, I think you must realize that she is here by your choice, not mine."

This was every nightmare Jed had ever had coming true. Elizabeth was in the hands of his enemy, and he was completely powerless to save her.

If he lunged for her, he would die first, and Elizabeth would still be helpless. If Skunk tried to shoot, his bullet might strike Elizabeth. Jed could only stand and watch it happen and think with every squeezing beat of his heart, *I'm sorry, Elizabeth, I'm sorry. . . .*

Jed never took his eyes from Hartley. He said quietly, "Let her go."

"I think not." Hartley pushed her forward another step, and then another. His voice sounded mild and unconcerned, as though he were speculating upon no more than a hand of cards. "There is little chance that you will survive my rifle fire at this range, but you still have one man able to shoot. If I let the lady go, I would never have a chance to reload."

He pushed Elizabeth forward another step. "Besides, there is something fitting, I believe, in your spending your last moments worrying about what will become of her when you are gone. Perhaps, in that way, you can repent some of your error in taking what was never yours to take."

There was nothing Jed could do. For all his life he had relied upon his wit and skill, and it had been enough. He was a fighter and a good one. He had never imagined his last moments would be like this, standing quietly and waiting for death to come. But he had never imagined there would be something he cared for more than his own life.

"You don't need her, Hartley," Jed said quietly. His was the face of a man who knew he was going to die and now was fighting for something more important than his life. "You don't want her to see you do this. There's no honor in using a woman to do your killing."

"One uses what one must to win, Mr. Fielding. I think you have always known that."

Elizabeth looked at Jed, and all she could see was the strong, quiet lines of his face; the proud strength of his shoulders; the deep, unwavering stillness in his eyes. And all she knew was that he was going to die. She had always thought the only thing she had to fear was death, but it was not. She had seen death today, and it was sudden and simple and final. The rest of her life stretching before her in minutes or hours or years, without Jed, without love, without promise, was worse than dying. Far worse.

Less than six feet and the camp fire separated the two men from each other. Nothing could change the inevitable now. Only a blind man would miss at this range, and the first shot would be fatal. Skunk might fire afterward, but it would be too late. Jed would be dead.

Knowing this, Hartley was in no hurry. There was a touch of genuine regret in his voice as he said, "You should have joined me from the beginning, Mr. Fielding. I warned you, did I not, that those who are not with me eventually find themselves being pushed out of my way? And I would derive much greater satisfaction, I discover, from having you on this side of my gun, fighting by my side, than at the point of it. It seems such a waste."

"No," Jed said simply, and he looked at Elizabeth. "Not a waste."

And Elizabeth thought, *No. Not a waste.* And then, fiercely, *Not a waste.*

Jed could not die. Not yet. *We have a house to build, a fortune to make. We have sons to raise and land to clear, and you will not die yet.*

Someday death would come to both of them, and it might be quick and it might be slow, but that time was not now, the place was not here.

There's too much waiting for us, Jed, too much we haven't finished or even begun. It will not be now. You can't die now!

Hartley was about three steps away from the camp fire. He pushed Elizabeth one step closer. He lifted his cocked rifle a fraction and prepared to fire.

Elizabeth stumbled and went to her knees. Her movement jarred Hartley's rifle aside, and from the corner of her eye she saw Jed dive for the ground. Hartley jerked her up, and in the same motion Elizabeth whirled around, a burning branch in her hand. With a roar of savage rage she thrust the torch upward, into his face. She heard his scream of shock and pain, the hiss of fire against flesh, and Jed's voice shouting, "Elizabeth, get down!" And then Hartley staggered backward beneath the onslaught of Jed's bullets.

For a moment the entire world seemed still, poised on the edge of awareness, suspended in a breath of quiet disbelief. It was over. Hartley lay lifeless on the ground before them, and for the longest time nothing at all moved.

Faintly Elizabeth smelled the acrid odor of lingering smoke and dust. As from far away, she heard the horses trampling the ground, tugging at their pickets. A bluejay screeched a brief, anticlimactic message, and the dawn filtered broken golden rays through the needles of the pines.

Elizabeth, still kneeling on the ground, stared at her hands. They were red and blistered and they stung vaguely, but beyond that she felt nothing . . . nothing except relief.

Jed stood a few feet away from her, his gun held loosely at his side. He looked at nothing but Elizabeth.

At last he said quietly, "That took a lot of courage."

Elizabeth raised her eyes to him. "It wasn't courage," she answered, and the words came slowly, as from a great distance, the dawning of a quiet truth. "I simply had no choice."

Love filled her and reached for him, breaching the gap of understanding that had so long kept them apart. So much had been lost on that road to understanding, so much risked, and so much scarring them. But through it all this one truth had emerged: Here was where she belonged, by Jed's side.

And that was worth it all.

Heartbeats passed as their eyes and souls locked. She could see the aching need within him, the certain love that reached out to her just as hers did to him. A part of them touched and clasped, even as physical distance separated them.

Yet still there was hesitation in Jed's eyes, and the words come hoarsely and with difficulty. "All I ever wanted . . . was to take care of you."

Elizabeth shook her head slowly, looking at him. "No," she said softly. "We have to take care of each other."

She got to her feet; he let his gun drop. Slowly they walked into each other's arms.

Epilogue

Three Hills Ranch, 1841

In the daisy meadow beside the murmuring branch of the stream, Elizabeth and Jed sat together, looking with sun-drowsy eyes at the valley below. It was an unusual thing for either of them to be sitting in the sun in the middle of the day and doing nothing, but there was still time in their lives for surprises. A picnic on the hillside was one of them.

In a woven basket at Jed's elbow slept the infant Daniel, shaded by the fronds of a willow tree. He was a beautiful, delicate child, blond like his father, sweet-tempered like his mother, and as hardy as both of them. Jed turned to gaze upon his son, touching the soft, blushed cheek lightly with his forefinger. The baby scowled in his sleep and shifted restlessly but did not wake up. Jed chuckled and returned his eyes to the sweeping valley below.

He said, smiling, "Do you remember the day we sat here and planned all this?"

His hand turned to indicate the landscape beyond. At the center of the convergence of the three great hills was a small, neat ranch with sturdy outbuildings, a spacious barn, three split-oak corrals filled with spirited, healthy horses. And shaded on all sides by the spread of cottonwood branches was a white house with columns, and windows that reached all the way to the ground.

Elizabeth's eyes were a brilliant play of sunlight on moss-green waters as she turned to him. "You didn't believe me then. You laughed at me."

"A lot of things I didn't believe in," he reminded her, and laced his fingers through hers. "You made me see different."

The house was not completed. But with the money Jed had made from his first big cattle drive to the railhead—Elizabeth had been right; folks up north were willing to go as high as eighty dollars a head for prime Texas beef—they had begun to build. The house had only four rooms, two upstairs and two down, but it was constructed to be added on to at intervals. Elizabeth's father, when he had come to visit his first grandchild, had brought from Larchmont paintings, rugs, linens, and such that were part of her dowry. In Galveston Jed had bought a big brass bed with a feather mattress. It was home, and with each passing day it was growing into all Elizabeth had ever intended it to be.

Texas was growing fast, too, but that was the way of the frontier—and of life itself. Nothing remained stagnant for long. A year ago Rio had gone south and had returned with fifteen hundred head of mixed-breed cattle, seven vaqueros to drive them, and a lush, buxom bride named Maria. Skunk presided over a crew of ten now, and a herd that was growing so fast, no one had yet made an accurate count. Maria ruled supreme over the kitchen, adored Miss Elizabeth, and guarded the precious *niño* Daniel with her very life.

Time moved on, and changes were exciting, challenging, and demanding. But no one forgot the sacrifices of those who went before them, nor the struggle and the loss that had brought them to this place.

On a lonely hillside at the edge of a piny forest, two graves lay side by side, each marked with a simple wooden cross. Dusty, a man of the frontier, had always known he would end his days in Texas, and death had been no enemy to him. Charles Edgecomb, Lord Hartley, had come to conquer, not to be conquered, and death had been a surprise. But the wilderness had taken their blood and swallowed up their lives and, in the end, recognized little difference between them. Such were the ways of survival.

Times were easier now, but Elizabeth never let herself get too far away from the past. She did not want to forget the price with which this world had been earned, and she would not let her children forget, either. She had had to lose everything before finding the only thing that mattered—but it was worth it all. For what she found was deep down inside her, and the only thing worth fighting for, worth dying for. She had found her love—and her dreams.

Jed's thoughts, as they seemed to do more and more naturally as the years of their marriage passed, were following Elizabeth's own as he looked down over what they had built. His eyes were sun-bright but sober as he turned to her. "Elizabeth," he said softly, "I am so glad you came back here with me, home where you belong."

Elizabeth cupped his face with her hand, stroking it gently. "How could I not," she answered simply, "when you needed me so much?"

Jed gathered her into his arms with a breath that was half laughter, half wonder, and he rocked her gently against him, adoring her. "That I do," he murmured into the rich fragrance of her hair. "That I do."

He took her face in both hands and smiled into her eyes, though his voice was very serious. "And I love you," he said. "More than life itself." He never forgot to tell her that anymore. "You are now, and always will be, the best part of me."

Elizabeth leaned her head against his shoulder, closing her eyes against the warm shower of happiness that rained over her whenever he was near. "No," she said softly, "we are the best parts of each other. And that's the way it was meant to be."

They sat for a while in silence, watching until the sun bathed the sloping roof of the house with its first rays of a pink sunset. Then Jed helped Elizabeth to her feet and picked up the baby's basket. Arm in arm they walked down the hill toward home.

Author's Note

*I*t would be impossible to write a novel set in this period of Texas history without including some mention of Sam Houston. Indeed the love story of Sam Houston and Margaret Lea remains one of the most beautiful romances in fact or fiction, and for this reason we were happy to be able to include portions of it in this novel.

Sam Houston first met Margaret Lea at Spring Hill Plantation in May 1839, not knowing that Margaret had been deeply in love with him since she had first seen him, wounded and delirious on the deck of the *Flora*, where he received a hero's welcome in New Orleans after the battle of San Jacinto. They were married in 1840, and returned to Texas where they raised eight children, among whom was a daughter, Nancy Elizabeth. In 1845, Sam Houston realized his lifelong dream of the annexation of Texas to the United States, and he was elected governor for the second time in 1859.

The British influence and interest in Texas in the early years of the republic are well documented and continued to play a noteworthy part in Texas history well into the present century.

With the Civil War the great cotton kingdom upon which the fortunes of Texas were built followed the fate of the rest of the South. But by the late 1860s, a new kingdom had risen—one based on cattle. A few men of vision and foresight had anticipated the future and were ready to take advantage of it—among them Tom Ponting, who took two years to drive a herd of cattle from Texas to New York, and Joseph McCoy, who is generally accredited with opening the Chisolm Trail. By the 1870s, cattle drives to the northern railheads were common, and the great ranching empires of Texas were firmly established.

About the Author

Leigh Bristol is a pseudonym for Donna Ball and Shannon Harper, who have written some fifty novels under various pen names, including Rebecca Flanders.

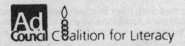